Fran Clark is a singer/songwriter and vocal coach born and raised in West London, where she currently lives and works with her musician husband and two sons.

Her desire to write had been restricted to the storytelling aspect of her song writing but she always longed to explore these stories further. The seeds of her first novel were sown in her mind about ten years before she actually put pen to paper – or finger to keyboard.

Fran is currently working towards the completion of her second album and has another work of fiction in progress.

HOLDING PARADISE

Fran Clark

Indigo Dreams Publishing

First Edition: Holding Paradise

First published in Great Britain in 2014 by:
Indigo Dreams Publishing
24 Forest Houses
Cookworthy Moor
Halwill
Beaworthy
EX21 5UU
www.indigodreams.co.uk

ISBN 978-1-909357-13-6

Designed and typeset in Minion Pro by Indigo Dreams.

Cover design by Ronnie Goodyer of Indigo Dreams Publications

Printed and bound in Great Britain by Imprint Academic, Exeter

Papers used by Indigo Dreams are recyclable products made from wood grown in sustainable forests following the guidance of the Forest Stewardship Council

Dedication

For Dad and Tuo

Acknowledgements

Because I could never have achieved this on my own I have to give thanks to a few people. For reading countless edits, unselfishly devoting time, patience and words of wisdom, I'd like to thank Anita Kelly. Thank you to Poonam Virdi and Lynne Clark for reading those early drafts. And thanks to Dawn and Ronnie for taking a chance on me.

A special thank you to my family for allowing me those times when you needed me and I was buried in dialogue and plot lines.

Pete, your belief, support and encouragement meant everything. Thank you.

HOLDING PARADISE

1

'You said you were going to call.'

'I know and I'm really sorry. It's just that something came up.'

'So what does that mean?'

'It means I won't be around for a while.'

'But Angelica, I need you.'

'I know Maddy, but I won't be gone long.'

'Are you going to tell me where you're going?'

'To see Mum.'

'What?'

'Yes, I know. I can't talk about it now Mads. I have to go.'

There's silence on the other end. I've just added my sister to the list of people I've let down. I turn and look at the kitchen. The table is still set for two. The meal, untouched.

My suitcase is packed. I pick it up and look back at the unmade bed. Memories of that night are all too vivid. The doorbell rings. I gently close the bedroom door behind me and head downstairs.

'You're doing the right thing, love. Flying off on a day like this. Not getting any better according to the forecast.'

I barely acknowledge the cab driver. I just sit in the back seat as he puts my case in the boot, slams the door and we drive off.

The plane accelerates along the runway. I close my eyes, take a deep breath and start counting backwards from ten. In ten seconds we'll be airborne, in a minute the knots in my stomach will ease, and in eight hours I'll be with Mum.

I stare out of the window. London is far behind me now. Dank, miserable London, where I felt isolated, unable to think straight. The next twenty minutes are a blur.

'Another cup of tea?' The flight attendant looks at me with pity.

I've managed to secure a window seat and I've got the row to myself, but it's hard to settle. Images of that night are still there. I remember that just before I cried myself to sleep I had a strong feeling that Mum would be the one to help me find a way forward, help me to piece my life back together, my marriage, my family, my business. Everything.

2

Josephine was the fourth child of a family of eight children. Apart from her younger sister, Eunice, the rest were boys. Josephine had a gift. Some members of her family found it frightening, others were amazed and wished they too could have such a gift. For Josephine, it could be the greatest of burdens, yet at times it made her feel special.

On several occasions, Josephine had accurately predicted the future through her dreams – vivid dreams about family, friends, local people. Every detail, each word, was fixed clearly in her mind and she would tell her mother exactly what she saw as though she'd read it in one of her school books.

Only a few of her dreams were predictions and she recognised them as such when she woke, hot, out of breath and unable to get the images out of her head. Her sister called her a witch. Josephine's mother, Rose, discouraged her from telling anyone outside the family about it for fear of what others might say.

On a cool January morning, Josephine and her family awoke one by one and left their warm beds. The younger three were loud and playful, ready to embrace each waking moment. The older children, knowing it was another school day, washed and dressed slowly, hoping to cling to as much of their freedom as possible.

Rose was unusually late that morning. She worked hard every day but would normally be the first to get up, see to the little ones and make breakfast for everyone. Today she had managed to gain an extra twenty minutes of sleep. She was surprised to discover her husband's side of the bed empty and cool to the touch when she stretched and rolled over.

Her husband stood in the kitchen – the small, low-built shack in the yard, where he had already prepared and eaten a light breakfast before his journey. He was about to travel across the island to visit his parents and to do some work on their house. They were getting older and Raphael took responsibility for helping them as often as he could.

It was five-thirty and pitch black outside. Cool and still. Most of the crickets appeared to have forsaken their chorus, only a few continuing a refrain which was about to be outdone by the morning's birdsong. Very soon, the transport to his parents' small village, an hour away, would be leaving. Raphael had to hurry.

As he left the kitchen, he hitched a small bag over his shoulder and looked up. From the top of the steps that led up to their wooden house on stilts, three sets of eyes spied him – his two youngest sons and his daughter, Josephine. He waved a quick goodbye and went on his way.

Josephine's father, Raphael, loved nothing better than to play and talk with her. His first daughter, now aged ten, was bright and intelligent and full of imagination and stories. In many ways Josephine was like her father. They shared a resemblance and similar sense of humour. They could chat endlessly, sitting as they often did on the second of the five steps to their front door, sampling fruit Raphael had picked from his garden.

'So, my Josephine. What did you learn at school today?' Raphael always made a grand gesture of presenting Josephine with the first piece of mango, melon or avocado.

'Well Daddy, Miss Brown gave us a test to see if we know our five times table.'

'And how you score?'

'Well I only get some right and a lot wrong.'

'And what that tell you?'

'It tell me I don't like times tables and I don't like Miss Brown.'

Whereas her mother would tell Josephine she should work harder, Raphael just tilted back his head, opening his wide mouth to give way to the thunderous roar of laughter which resonated in his chest. His laugh echoed around the wooden houses and told everyone that Raphael was home.

It was laughter or a cheerful whistle that would signal Raphael's arrival back from his garden. There he grew provisions like yams, plantain and green bananas both for the family and to sell at market. Packing the produce into a large sack that he carried on his head, he would walk the twenty minutes back home, whistling, his cutlass swinging idly at his side.

This morning, the children waved and called goodbye to their father but could barely make him out as he stepped carefully on his way out of their front yard and onto the dusty road. Raphael passed two houses. Outside of each, a small dog resided. From their front yards the dogs barked in unison. A little further along the road, Ma Taylor's goat bleated, as though in response to her canine neighbours. The tiny hamlet was waking up. Raphael waited only minutes beside the old Glory cedar before jumping onto the lorry full of travellers from the last two villages. By the time the villagers reached the next stop, the lorry's headlights would be switched off and the sun would be high in the sky.

The two oldest boys went into the kitchen to light the fire under the stove. Josephine lingered at the front door of the house, picturing her father finding his place on the lorry and holding tight while it accelerated along the narrow road.

Rose came out of her bedroom to make her way to the kitchen. Her arms were raised as she secured her bright red headscarf that bit tighter to her head. She caught the look on her daughter's face.

'Josephine,' she said. 'Don't look at me like that, you making me afraid.' Rose was afraid because the look on her daughter's face told her that Josephine had had a dream and that its message was not good.

It happened just like the dream.

Raphael left his parents' house in the late afternoon. He'd worked hard all morning. It had been particularly hot for that time of year, but the temperature had since dropped to a comfortable level. Amongst his jobs around the house, he had fixed a broken window latch in the bedroom. A strong breeze at night would make the window rattle and his mother, finding it difficult to sleep lately, would have one less disturbance to worry about.

He kissed both of his parents before rushing to the road to catch the transport home, stopping briefly at a water tap for a quick drink. The sun set early in the evening and his wife insisted that he travel in daylight as far as possible. The roads around the island were mainly mountainous, fairly narrow, with potholes of various sizes dotted haphazardly. The islanders complained that the Government should improve the roads – neighbouring islands were a lot more developed and this was 1936 after all.

Passengers travelling in a lorry approached by another would take a silent but sharp intake of breath. When the two vehicles passed each other safely, the passengers would give a loud cheer and shout, 'Very good driver!'

Just like the dream, people chatted and laughed during the journey. Everyone was in high spirits except for Raphael. He suddenly felt as though he'd been dealt a forceful knock to the side of his head. He dropped his bag to the floor and held one side of his face for a moment. A sense of panic gripped him as the pain grew stronger. As the lorry bumped its way along, some of the other passengers noticed his distress. Raphael appeared to be gasping for air, his eyes flitting from one passenger to the next. But he seemed not to recognise any of them.

'Stop the truck.' Raphael thought he'd said this loudly but his instruction was a breathy whisper that only Thomas, standing by his side, could hear.

'He say stop the truck, driver!' Thomas shouted on Raphael's behalf. Someone else banged on the roof of the lorry's cabin and the driver pushed firmly on his brakes until they came to a halt.

'This is not a stop,' cried the driver. 'It dangerous to stop here.'

'Is Raphael Douglas, he look sick.'

16

The lorry buzzed with comments of concern about the health of their fellow passenger. Each spoke with authority on the situation, their voices loud but their words indecipherable to Raphael. They gesticulated, pontificated and argued though Raphael felt no real sense of being part of the commotion. He soon found himself being lifted from the lorry and put to sit by the side of the road.

By now Raphael's breathing was becoming shallow. Someone was loosening his top button, someone else was fanning him with a large leaf but no one knew exactly what to do or what was about to happen.

'Pick him up. He needs the hospital,' one of the passengers shouted. Another flagged down a battered old car that was heading in the direction they'd come from. In the time it took for two men to raise him up from the ground and carry him to the battered car and its bemused driver, Raphael's life ended.

They placed his body carefully into the back seat of the old car. Thomas got into the passenger seat and looked over his shoulder at his old friend lying still, as if asleep. One woman from the crowd of onlookers wailed. The rest of the party watched in silence as the old car disappeared. The last trace of daylight was engulfed by the night sky as Raphael's body was carried along in the dark toward the island's only hospital.

When darkness fell on the Douglas house, Rose was standing in the kitchen cursing her husband for not observing her specific instructions about travelling the roads by night. She replaced the supper utensils purposefully as she cursed.

Rose finished her work in the kitchen, stopped, and looked up at the house where she saw Josephine sitting by the open door looking down at her feet, a solitary figure hunched on the top step. Rose felt a cold shiver sweep over her body. She had gone about her day not wanting to hear anything about her daughter's dream. She'd packed the oldest off to school, washed and changed into a simple dress, entertained the young ones, swept the yard, tidied the house and adjusted her favoured red headscarf several times. Even during dinner, Rose had avoided remarking on Josephine's distant stare.

Looking out of the little kitchen window toward the road, Rose saw the light of a torch and could identify the figures of a small group of people walking toward the house. Their voices were low at first, muffled. As she stepped, tentatively, into the yard, she could hear someone crying. The group of people closed in on her. Her children, now aware of the stirring of the crowd, gathered at the front door to see what was going on. Josephine rose from her seat.

Spilling from the mouths of the people surrounding Rose came a million words, some in English, some in their other language – simultaneous, jumbled. Rose struggled to find her breath when she finally and clearly heard the words, 'Ma Douglas, your husband dead.'

The children leapt down all five steps and clung tightly to their mother who stood trembling in the yard. Her right hand covered her mouth, her thin eyebrows raised and joined to form an arch as she searched each face to make sure they hadn't been mistaken. She pulled off the brightly coloured headscarf and covered her eyes with it.

Josephine stepped backwards, away from the crowd. As her family cried with the others in the small yard, she moaned in a low monotone hum. She felt sure that had she not had this *gift*, her father would be standing here now and not this uninvited party of visitors. Josephine shook, she wept uncontrollably. One woman caught hold of her and in an attempt to calm her, held her arms firmly to the sides of her body. Ma Taylor pushed through the crowd and pulled Josephine's arms free, shouting, 'Let her cry. Her father just died. Let her cry.'

When the crowd finally dispersed, the family sat in one room. Sadness filled every corner of their tiny house. The little village had lost a great man, a family had lost its backbone, and a woman had lost her most precious love.

18

The sun rose as normal the next day, dogs barked in their yards, people took their washing to one of the 365 rivers reputed to flow through the island. But those who had known Raphael spoke about the events of the night and the number of tears shed for him and claimed that river 366 had appeared that morning.

3

I flick through the laminated leaflet again: 'What to do in case of an emergency'. I had completely ignored the flight attendant's safety drill earlier. I stared at her waving her arms, putting a life jacket over her head, pretending to blow a whistle, but I had been thinking about seeing Mum. It had been a long time. Instead of listening to what to do in the event of the plane making an emergency landing, I was listening to Mum's stories in my head. A picture of my childhood was obscuring the safety measures and for a while I could forget the pain, loneliness and desperation of the last two months.

How old was I when Mum's stories started making sense? When I was a teenager, Mum's stories were a hindrance. Her words stifled me, prevented me from going to discos, parties, sleeping in on a Sunday because I was expected to go to church.

Assisted by the word of God and a lifetime of experience, Mum raised us on those stories. A story about a girl who was assaulted when she went out on her own told my older sister, Del, that she must be chaperoned if she wanted to go to a party. A story about a young man who ended up on the streets because he turned his back on his family told my older brother, Marcus, that he should not leave home at nineteen to share a flat with friends without sufficient savings.

Mum started each story with, 'I'm not an educated woman but ... '. and made the sign of the cross at the end. The sign of the cross also signified the end of discussion and there was no sense in arguing with it.

My parents had been strict, unbearably so it felt at times. I know that West London in the 1950s, when they first arrived, had been a far cry from their island in the West Indies. They had five of us to raise. I know they did their best.

My eyes feel heavy. The nights of not sleeping are taking their toll and the plane's relentless hum lulls me into a trance until my eyes close completely.

A lanky, teenage girl. Walking to school in the pristine school uniform of the Catholic School for Girls where they wear grey, knee-length socks. She's smiling, listening to stories that the other fourth year girls are telling about their weekends: boyfriends, eyeliner and would she like to come to the disco with them at the Church Hall next Saturday? It's a Rockabilly one, they're always good. They chatter on, but the teenage girl is hearing another voice.

'I'm not an educated woman but I know what happens to girls who want to go to discos. A girl I know go to a disco. They were taking drugs at this disco and she have to have her stomach pump because so much drugs she take. After that she even sneak out the house to go again. Before anyone know – she was an addict. Three times the girl already have her stomach pump. But the last time, no doctor on this earth could save her life. Her poor mother had four daughters and now she only have three. I have three daughters and I don't want to end up with two because one of them wants to go to a disco.'

I haven't made the sign of the cross in a long time, but I'm waking from a dream and doing just that. The flight attendant walks by and gives me a strange look. I wonder what else I've done in my sleep. I look at my watch. Five minutes have gone by.

I must avoid looking at the couple across the aisle. I remember them from check in: young, in love. Probably off on honeymoon. They were annoying me then, too. But being cynical isn't going to help me. I had what they had. If I think back far enough I can even remember my first love. Mum married hers. If only life could be that easy for the rest of us. Why some of us have to go through the trials and tribulations of finding that perfect match is a mystery to me. I'd give up all my past loves for one lasting one. Like Mum's.

21

They say you never forget your first love. Some of the detail gets worn away with time but the big things last. Nineteen eighty-seven saw my first heartbreak. Anil came from a Hindu family and his parents naturally expected him to marry someone of their own religion and class. As far as they were concerned, I was only ever going to be a temporary distraction. My credentials as a lapsed Catholic from a West Indian family would never be good enough.

We started dating in my late teens and by my twenties I'd started to think about marriage and children. I knew I could never have this with Anil, but it was so hard to leave him. We had broken up a couple of times before, practice runs before the real thing. It was during one of those breakups that Mum told me the story of Julie Daniels.

'Mrs Daniels' daughter, Julie, went out with an Irish for ten years and he never marry her. The last anyone heard, he went back to Ireland and marry an Irish girl and they have eight children. Now Julie have forty-eight years. She never marry, she never love again. All her young and beautiful years she waste on someone who never love her enough to marry her.'

It was the story that made my mind up. I had to end it all with Anil, for me and for Julie Daniels.

It was New Year's Eve nineteen eighty-six. We'd left the party early and gone to Anil's.

'Where do you see this all going?' I asked as I sat up in bed.

'Mm?' he replied, pretending to be sleepy and not understand what I meant. We'd been here before, and I knew he wanted to avoid a confrontation. That night of all nights.

'Look, Anil, I really can't do this anymore. Next year I'll be twenty-six and before I know it I'll be thirty and soon I'll be forty-eight like Julie Daniels.'

'*Who?*'

'Never mind. The fact is, you say you want to be with me but eventually your parents will insist you get married and eventually you'll be mature enough to want to. When you are, you'll do it their way and where does that leave me?'

'What are you talking about, Angelica? Nothing will change. We'll always be together.'

'I want to be with someone who loves me enough to want to marry me – even if his parents *don't* approve. To have children with me and not care that a bunch of people, most of them living in another country, won't accept them as part of the family. Someone who wouldn't feel as though it was a tough choice to make between marrying me and keeping his parents happy. There wouldn't be a choice because I would be all he wanted. And that's not you is it, Anil?' He closed his eyes and a tear ran down the side of his face, onto the pillow.

'No, Angelica, that's not me.'

I got up and put my clothes on. He never tried to stop me or ask if he could call. We both knew there would be no point. There is never a good time to have your heart broken – but for it to happen on New Year's Day … .

I cried in my car as I drove home. I cried in my bed that night. I cried all the next morning and through to the afternoon. When I told Mum what had happened, she said I did the right thing. I was in my twenties and men would still be looking at me – her words. The older you are the harder it is to get a man, she said, and sat on the edge of my bed as she told me at least three stories about single women she knew, now in their sixties, who wasted their lives chasing the wrong kind of men.

'I'm sorry, but do you mind if I sit in this seat for a while?' My daydream ends abruptly. 'It's just that I need to spread out a bit. Loads of paperwork for my meeting to get in order and I noticed no-one else was sitting in this row and my bosses are expecting me to come back with results. So, is it okay?'

I half-smile to acknowledge him. He's probably about my age – mid to late forties. Slightly overweight, wearing a formal shirt but no tie and smelling of aftershave and new clothes. He sits in the aisle seat and takes a laptop out of its case.

I'm slipping in and out of sleep, and daydreams. My fake smile says that I don't mind someone sitting next to me but I was better off as I was, lost in my thoughts. I'll just stare out of the window. Maybe he'll sort out his papers and go back to his seat. *Please don't talk to me. Please don't be here when they bring lunch.*

Unlike this stranger, who'd just revealed to me the reason for his trip to the Caribbean, the burden of working for a boss was something I'd left behind long ago.

I was clueless when it came to career choices after I left school but I managed to get a reasonable job. I had no idea back then that I'd end up running a business. Or who I would be running it with.

When that New Year had started I was not only heartbroken, but desperately keen to leave my job, despite my promotion to Office Manager. I felt a change was needed after two years of trying to manage a team of middle-aged women, who seemed intent on making my life a misery. Whatever their problem was with me, it was time to make my exit.

I enrolled on an evening class called 'How to Start a Small Business'. On the first evening I met a friend from school that I'd completely lost touch with.

'Angelica?' I felt a tap on my shoulder as the class of about fifteen people waited patiently for the tutor, who was off trying to find the key to the classroom door. I turned around.

'My God! Jasmin! How are you? It's been like, forever.' I hugged her. I was surprised and happy to see her.

'Yeah, I'm good thanks. Angelica, you haven't changed in all this time, you look amazing.' Jasmin still had that wide, gleaming smile of hers, that head of beautifully thick black curls and she was as stunningly attractive as ever.

'This is unreal. You're back in London.' We hugged each other again and giggled as though we were back at school. 'How is married life treating you? Any children yet?' I asked.

'Well the marriage ended a few years back. Didn't really get started.' She was still smiling about what I thought to be bad news. 'To tell the truth … ' She moved in closer. ' … he turned out to be a real bastard and no, we never had any children.'

'Oh I see. I'm sorry.'

'The only thing to be sorry about is that I'm back home with the folks.' She gripped her throat and stuck out her tongue. I could see the noose, I knew it well.

Jasmin had an English mother and a West African father who was stricter than both of my parents put together. We were nineteen when she'd announced that she was getting married and moving to Canada. It had been a shock, but I'd suspected back then that she was trying to escape her father. She wrote to me a few times once she'd settled in Canada and I replied each time. But then her letters stopped.

'What about you?' She asked. 'Married? Kids? String of divorces?'

'No, no and no. Just trying to get my act together. Wasted too much time on someone.'

'Mm, I know the feeling.'

We were slowly filing into the classroom. It was hard to sit next to Jasmin and not talk. We had years of catching up to do. We'd become best friends in the Sixth Form. I suppose we were drawn to each other because, amongst the other girls, we stuck out like a sore thumb. Those girls in the Common Room with their fashionable shoes and coats, their constant talk of boyfriends and clubs. We wished we could be like them but that was only ever a dream when we were seventeen.

The man in the aisle seat is smiling at me. I thought my closed eyes would serve as a conversation deterrent, but I was wrong.

'I've just found this picture on my laptop,' he says. 'This is my daughter Phoebe. An absolute darling.'

I smile back.

'Any children yourself?' He's still beaming as he asks.

'One. But she's all grown up now.' My voice is croaky. This is the most I've said to anyone since I got in the taxi at six am this morning. *Please see that I don't want to talk.*

'A grown up daughter? You don't look old enough.' He grins at me. Nice face. Ordinarily I would chat but I can't fake it. I rub the side of my head as though it hurts and rest my head on my hand so that my face is turned away. It's rude but what can I do?

By the second week of the course Jasmin and I had already decided to rent a place together. It was that simple. We started renting a flat a short distance from Mum and Dad's. Dad had said that I should really think about buying a house rather than renting so that I would have security. My parents were planning to go back home, so they wanted me settled.

Jasmin and I had a frenzied first month of playing music loud, shopping and clubbing. It was the most fun I'd had in a while. I was getting over Anil.

The man in the aisle seat clears his throat. 'Sorry. I think I've dumped my case on your headphones. There you go.' He smiles at me as he hands them over. They must have slipped onto the floor without me noticing. I don't want these. I'm not interested in seeing a film, listening to the radio or seeing how far we'd flown. I take the headphones, still in their plastic wrapper, and fiddle with them.

'Decided on a film?' He tries to maintain a conversation. 'I like to bring my own entertainment. Or just chat. You meet a lot of interesting people when you're travelling. I travel a lot. How about you?'

'Not a lot, not really. First time in a while.'

Duty Free is approaching. I'm not interested but he's looking keen. I plan my escape. I'll just grab the in-flight magazine and bury my face in it, look engrossed. He'll take the hint. Good looking people on the beach. I remember Michael.

I never saw Michael on a beach but he had an amazing body. We

26

met at a health club and I'd spent more than a sneaky half hour eyeing him up from the treadmill whilst he lifted weights: dark brown skin that would contrast well with my mid-brown, tight muscles, cheeky smile. I wouldn't say he was handsome but I certainly didn't refuse when he asked me out that day. Anil wasn't quite out of my system but I felt Michael would help that along quite nicely.

I'd bumped into Michael one morning in the health club café, where he was drinking a fruit juice and I'd just ordered hot chocolate and a chocolate covered flapjack. I didn't notice him at first until I was paying for my snack and heard a voice from behind a newspaper saying, 'I guess you've earned that.' And there was Michael, with his cheeky smile, making me a little uncomfortable about my food choice.

'I think so. That was a tough workout today,' I took a seat at the table next to his.

'I see they're having another of their social events.' He nodded to a poster by the door advertising a cocktail party. 'Do you ever go to them?' He sipped his juice while I sat, too embarrassed to unwrap my flapjack.

'No, I've never been. I don't think it's my kind of thing anyway.'

'What is your kind of thing?'

'Well, you know, restaurants, theatre, cinema.'

'So how about a film tonight?'

The plastic wrapper and headphones slip off my lap. I bend to pick them up.

'I think I'll watch a film after all.' My travel companion tries again. 'Should be able to fit one in before lunch. If I drop off before they serve, will you give me a prod?' I think I'll do more than prod him if he doesn't shut up. He's got me thinking about food now. I realise I'm starving. I know I'll complain about it when it comes. Always do. Food is my business. I know food.

'Do you know something?' I said to Jasmin. 'I think we've gone off the beaten track. We're letting men take over our lives.'

It was Sunday morning. Jasmin had just come out of the bathroom and I was drinking a smoothie. She looked puzzled.

'Well since you started going out with Nigel and I started seeing Michael, we haven't once mentioned starting our own business. How many brainstorming sessions have we had? How many lists have we drawn up?'

Whenever Jasmin and I planned anything, we made a list. Lists help you focus and keep you on track. The number of lists we'd made was piling up and all focus was lost.

'Tell you what,' said Jasmin. 'One thing we've never done since we've been here.'

'What's that?'

'Have a house-warming party.'

'Jasmin. What's a house-warming party got to do with starting a business?'

'Nothing at all. But they're fun.'

The craziest thing about that conversation was that it was the house-warming party that led to our business starting up. About thirty people crammed into our little flat, dancing, chatting and eating the never-ending supply of food we'd made. Jasmin and I had gone a bit far and I could see us eating albondigas and spring rolls well into the next month.

I was doing some clearing away in the kitchen when Michael's sister Karen walked in.

'Who did the catering for this party?' she asked.

'Oh that was me and Jasmin, we've been cooking since yesterday.'

'The food is fantastic. I've asked my secretary to sort out the catering for a do I'm having for clients. If you two are free on the eleventh would you like the job?' She was perfectly matter of fact.

'Wait a minute, Karen. You know Jasmin and I are not professional caterers don't you?'

'Well your food tastes professional. So, how about it? Just call my secretary on Monday. I'll tell her about you. We have to throw these little soirées once in a while to keep our clients sweet. Our American company does it and we have to follow suit. It's a real drag. The last thing you want to do on a Friday is to spend an evening answering questions about your clients' account. There'll be eight of them and then a couple from the firm. So, for ten people then?'

'I'm not sure we could do it. We'd need to work out the menus, hire equipment. It would take a lot of planning.'

'Well, I'll leave all that to you. Food just like tonight would be great. Call the office. Michael will let you know the number.' She poured herself another glass of wine and joined the others in the living room. I wondered if Jasmin would be keen to take on a job catering for some posh company.

'Of course we'll do it,' she said. 'As soon as we're sober we'll make a list.'

We had no idea what to quote Karen's secretary, so I'd phoned around various catering companies asking for quotes for the kind of food we would make until Jasmin and I settled on a price, taking into consideration hiring crockery, cutlery and glasses. Working out how much wine we needed was the hard part. Did everyone drink as much as Jasmin and me? We'd planned everything to a tee and only had to write five lists to make it all possible. Karen was very impressed. She said she would definitely use us again and would recommend us wherever she could. She was true to her word and we got a couple of catering jobs on the strength of that first party.

'Maybe we've finally found our calling,' I said to Jasmin after the second party. 'Maybe this will be the thing that gets us out of our nine to fives. I can see a future in it, with the right planning. What do you think?'

'I'm glad you said it because it's exactly what I've been thinking. I've got lots of ideas about marketing and that kind of thing but, oh my God, I'm so excited. When can we start?'

The flight attendant stops at our aisle. Crouches slightly with her hands on her knees.

'Are you going to have your lunch here, Sir, or will you be having it in your own seat?' She's looking at me while she asks this question. Wondering if I'm up to visitors I suppose. He's looking at me now and pulling off his headphones. Looking so much like a lost puppy – how can I turn him away? I smile and give a shrug that says 'you decide, I don't mind too much.' That's all he needs.

'Yes, I'll stay here then.' He says to the flight attendant, who gives me one last look that asks, *are you sure about this*?

'Oh and mine was the vegetarian option.'

'Yes Sir.'

When I broke the news to my family about my plans for starting a new career, it was met with the kind of enthusiasm that only my family could have.

We were all having Sunday lunch at Mum's when I told them. My parents were worried about me keeping up rent payments if I wasn't going to be paid monthly any more. I tried to assure them that we wouldn't give up our jobs until we knew it would work. My brothers and sisters, and their partners, all had an opinion.

'I always remember you complaining when Mum wanted your help in the kitchen,' Marcus said.

'But Angie,' said Del, 'do you know what it takes to run your own business? You need commitment and you need to be able to trust your partner. I don't know much about Jasmin, she's only your age and already divorced. Not that good at sticking with things is she?'

'Have you thought about all the long hours and how antisocial it can be?' Maddy, my younger sister, added to the onslaught.

With the exception of my younger brother, James, who was a writer, my other siblings and their partners all had nine-to-fives. Regular incomes. Of course it was hard for them to understand where I was coming from or to be in the least bit supportive. I knew that deep down, their concern was not that it was a bad idea but that they weren't convinced that I had it in me to see it through. I was determined to prove them wrong.

'Jasmin, this thing is do or die,' I said to her that evening. I'd had a whole afternoon of holding my tongue at Mum's. 'We've got to give this business everything we've got.'

'Ange, I'm with you. I've already got a failed marriage under my belt. My mum doesn't get it. My dad thinks I'm some kind of flake, and he's probably washed his hands of me.'

'So, we're doing it?'

'We're doing it. I think we should call ourselves Angel Catering. That way we get listed high up in Yellow Pages and people are more likely to call us before they give up and get bored looking down a long list.'

And she was right. We got lots of enquiries and many of them became jobs. Eventually we were turning business away because we were only working weekends and evenings. Winter came and we could see that Christmas was going to be busy for us. It was time to give up the day jobs.

One wine-induced evening, we composed our letters of resignation. Jasmin typed them both up at work. I remember breathing a huge sigh of relief on my last day at the office. I was free and as far as I was concerned my life would never be the same again.

4

'Josephine!'

Josephine rubbed her eyes and yawned.

'Josephine, wake up! Don't forget to take those sheets by the river to wash. Leave the boys with Ma Paul, and take Eunice with you. She can help. We going to market.'

'Yes Mama.' Josephine rolled lazily onto her back. This was no time to dream. It was Saturday morning and her day had already been planned. There was no need for her mother to remind her of her duties.

Four years had gone by since her father died. Josephine had been consumed by guilt and had put the blame on her gift. She'd sat by the river watching her mother wash clothes.

'Is something your father already had,' her mother, Rose, had said. 'In his brain. The doctor told me it could happen at any time. Your dream never cause this Josephine.'

'I don't want to dream anymore.' Josephine's tears had spilled over her face and into the cool of the soapy river to mingle with the bubbles. Rose had turned her face away and dried her eyes with the upper part of her sleeve.

That was the day Josephine decided she would look after her mother and never leave her side.

She had seen Rose draw strength from the willingness to fill their father's shoes that the three oldest boys adopted during those years. Each took it in turns to accompany her to her allotment on a Tuesday and Thursday before school: to tend the land, gather ground provisions and carry them in a sack on their head, holding steady to their father's old cutlass all the way home. And, in turn, each had left home and bid a sad farewell to the family before setting off to find their way.

Rose said that Josephine had made her proud because of her dedication to helping her. But by the age of fourteen, she had suffered with her health and had taken a lot of time off school. Having been kept back for two years, Josephine sat amongst a class of ten and eleven year olds and felt perfectly ashamed. She was embarrassed by her very womanly form and would often hide in the lunch hour while her contemporaries sat and chatted. She felt out of her depth. The more they tried to include her the more she would shy away from them.

One day, Josephine left school at lunchtime with her arms folded across her ample bosom and her books firmly shut on the desk in the classroom. She marched home, determined that things would change. Rose spotted her daughter walking toward the house with her head held high and lips creased together in a thin line.

'Why are you back so early, Josephine? School haven't finish yet.'

'I know Mama but I can't do it anymore. I'm too big for that class and I don't belong there. All the way home I been thinking and I have an idea. I'm going by Ma David. She always said she would teach me to sew and Veronique has left her now, so maybe she need someone to help her, someone new to train. I know I am good at sewing and I could make a good seamstress.'

Rose didn't have to consider this for very long. She knew how much her daughter suffered. They had discussed it several times whilst they worked around the house.

'Alright,' said Rose, 'let us go now and talk to Ma David to see if she can take you.'

At fifteen, Josephine knew everything Ma David had to teach. She had an absolute flair for designing and making dresses. Many of the women who had clothes made there would secretly wish that it was Josephine taking charge of their dresses rather than Ma David herself. Josephine could cut the fabric just right and make exact alterations and the number of satisfied customers grew so fast that jobs were coming in from villages further and further away. Ma David revelled in her new found popularity and satisfied herself that it was her ability as a good teacher that made Josephine so good at her job. All the while Josephine was saving up for her own sewing machine. She had made up her mind to set up on her own one day.

The classy young woman that Josephine was growing into did not go unnoticed by the villagers. One in particular had always been attracted to her. Like the others, James Dennis would watch as she walked like a film star along the dusty road, carrying an umbrella to keep the sun off and with a handbag and shoes which matched her dress.

'Good afternoon, Miss Douglas,' James called one day. Josephine recognised his voice but did not slow down or turn around.

'So now you are ignoring me? Well okay, you don't have to speak, but you can't stop me from walking along this road too.'

'You can do as you please, Mr Dennis.' Josephine nodded her head slightly but made no eye contact with her admirer.

James did everything he could to make progress with Josephine, but she never fell for the chat-up lines that worked so well on the other girls. Josephine had a fixed idea in her head that she would never marry and that she would remain with her mother and take care of her in her old age. She was the oldest sibling at home and she took her commitment to stay with Mama very seriously.

'You know there's a dance on Saturday?' James was not ready to give up.

'I believe I heard about it from Dora, yes.' Josephine walked a little faster now and James hastened his pace.

'Anyone ask you to go yet?'

'A few boys have asked.'

'And you going with any of them?'

'No.' Josephine turned her gaze to a passing neighbour and nodded. James took this as an opportunity to block her path and stand in front of Josephine. He smiled.

'Would you consider, would you like to … . I wonder if I can escort you?'

Josephine paused and appeared to be considering the offer.

'Well, no, I don't want to go,' she said finally. 'Maybe someone else might accept you.' Josephine turned and took the path to Ma David's house as James stood and watched her go.

'You breaking my heart Josephine. You know that?' he called to her. But she had already disappeared behind the red hibiscus bushes that hid Ma David's house from the main road.

The six remaining members of the Douglas household lived a peaceful enough existence. Josephine shared a bedroom with her sister, Eunice, and the three boys, Benjamin, Caleb and Little Raphael, slept on couches to the back of the main room, which was sectioned off by a curtain at night time. Rose slept on her own in the bedroom she had once shared with Raphael. Although she was a young and attractive woman when her husband died, she never looked at another man and she would never love or marry again.

Every Sunday the family went to church. It was there, at about age twenty, that Josephine became the object of attraction of one Milton Clarke, a twenty-eight year old police sergeant of the most serious disposition. He never approached Josephine himself, but he made it known to any eligible bachelors that he wanted to marry her.

One Saturday afternoon, with all their chores done, Rose, Josephine and Eunice sat chatting in the main room and heard the distinct sound of horse's hooves approaching from the roadside. They stopped to listen as they heard the trotting become louder and stop just outside the house.

'Ma Douglas,' a voice called. 'May I speak with you please?'

Rose knew this must be a policeman as only they were likely to be on horseback. She came to the door expecting the worst, only to see Milton Clarke in his sergeant's uniform, his cap firmly fixed onto his head. The afternoon sun beat down hard on everyone it would seem, except Milton, who remained cool and focused and without one bead of sweat visible beneath the peak of his cap. When he saw Rose, he showed his teeth.

'Good afternoon Mrs Douglas. No need to look afraid. It's only me, Sergeant Milton Clarke from Pontville. I've come to ask your permission to marry Josephine.'

'What?' From inside the house, Josephine gasped. She was taken aback and horrified by the suggestion that she would even contemplate marrying such a fool. So much so that she decided it would be best to stay put rather than to risk offending him by going outside to turn him down.

'I cannot speak for my daughter. She has never mentioned you, why you think she would want to marry you?' Rose screwed up her brow.

'I don't,' Josephine whispered under her breath. Eunice giggled and could see several faces beginning to congregate near their yard.

'I feel Josephine is at an age for marriage. I am a hardworking man and I will take good care of her. Being as she has no father ...'

'Get out! Get away from my house. You are a fool.' Rose clapped her hands and the horse rose up on its hind legs. Milton tried to steady him.

'Josephine will choose her own husband when she is ready and I'm sure it will never be you. Now go away and look for someone else.' Rose was so angry she shook as she returned to the house saying to Josephine, 'By the way, you didn't want to marry him did you?'

'No Mama, you said exactly what I would have said.'

Eunice opened the curtain and peered out at the disgruntled Milton Clarke who was muttering under his breath that this was the last time he would ever ask a countryside girl to marry him and that the girls in town had more sense.

Marriage was the last thing on Josephine's mind but now, approaching twenty-four, she would listen to the stories about

36

what her friends got up to when they were alone with their partners. Although these stories could be quite thrilling, Josephine focused on her future plans, making and selling clothes and looking after Mama. She told herself that she could live quite happily without that kind of intimacy. Even her younger sister, Eunice, teased Josephine and said to her one day, 'Do you think you are the Virgin Mary? You will marry you know, you won't stay by Mama forever.'

There was truth in Eunice's words. Although Josephine didn't want to admit it to herself, in all these years of wishing to stay a single woman, she was starting to have feelings for a particular man and what surprised her most of all was who that man was.

James Dennis had been asking Josephine to go out on a date with him for as long as anyone could remember and every time she had refused. It was no secret that he was a womaniser and according to reports, he had slept with practically every girl Josephine knew. He had even slept with her best friend, Dora, who was about to get married. Knowing full well that Josephine disapproved of his reputation, he decided to change his tactics. Instead of trying to sweet talk her, he had begun to write a series of letters. She read most of them in the beginning and did find them appealing. But she could not bring herself to accept any of his offers. At the end of each letter he would ask her to come for a walk or to meet him after church for a chat. It had come to the stage that when a letter arrived, and sure enough there would be one every week, she would simply tear it up without opening it.

'What is wrong with James that you can't give him a chance?' asked Eunice, incensed, one day. 'He is good looking, he have a job, and all the women want him, except you. What are you waiting for?'

'You have him if you want. He's just not my type.' Josephine was busy packing a case because she was on her way to stay the night at Dora's house. It was the eve of Dora's wedding day and Josephine was to be on hand to dress the bride and fix her hair.

'Well, if he looked my way, I would, but anyone can see that

37

he only have eyes for you.' Eunice was looking through the wardrobe at Josephine's clothes. Although Josephine had repeatedly told her not to touch them, Eunice couldn't help but try on Josephine's dresses. Sometimes she wore them to go out when she thought she would get away with it and very often came home with a little tear here, a spilt drink there. She would put the dress straight back into the wardrobe without saying a word. Josephine became exasperated by her younger sister's antics but always forgave her.

There was a six-year gap between them and Josephine still saw Eunice as a little girl. Eunice was always restless, a live wire, quick to put a person in their place if she thought it necessary. Her temper was as volcanic as the island they lived on.

'In fact everyone only have eyes for you, don't they?' Josephine did not answer. She was already on her way out of the door and kissing Rose on the cheek. At which point Eunice dragged out Josephine's burnt orange blouse from the wardrobe and put it on. She also kissed Rose on the cheek and left the house saying, 'Josephine told me to catch her up, she needs me to help at Dora's.'

The last thing Eunice was going to do was catch up with Josephine. She was off to meet friends to hang around outside Anton Bardouille's liquor bar. Her group of friends sat next to a big old tamarind tree, laughing at people passing by and at the people going in and out of Bardouille's. The yellow racemes of the tamarind would make the perfect backdrop for Eunice in her nice new blouse. She was bound to have everyone talking about her and the way she looked, just as they did Josephine. It was obvious to a lot of people that Eunice was envious of her sister. Josephine never saw this.

As Eunice hurried along the road she saw a familiar figure walking towards her. It was James, tall and broad shouldered, looking very handsome to her in the crisp, white shirt he wore for church. As a carpenter he would often be seen in tatty work clothes, shirtsleeves rolled up, hair in a mess. This evening he had a swagger and a warm smile for Eunice as he approached.

'Going somewhere nice?' he asked her.

'Nowhere special. How about you? Where are you going so dressed up?'

'Well as a matter of fact I was going by your place.' He smiled.

'Oh, really? Maybe I should have stayed home so I could receive you properly.' Eunice grinned back. Her eyes never left James'.

'Well, um, I wanted to talk to Josephine. Do you know if she might reply to my letters or what? What is she saying?' James felt a little uneasy because of the way Eunice stared so deeply into his eyes.

'Josephine is gone out. She gone by Dora so she can talk about her boyfriend.' Eunice looked away now, not wanting James to see how disappointed she was to have to talk about her sister.

'Josephine have a boyfriend?' He asked.

'I believe so. I heard them talking, she and Dora. If you are going to Dora's wedding you will see them together. Are you invited?'

'Yes, I … .'

'And who you taking?'

'Well I was hoping … .'

'Josephine already spoken for. I am invited but I wouldn't mind an escort.' Again she smiled and focused her gaze on James who swallowed hard, composing himself before he spoke.

'If you need an escort, I suppose I could come for you. Will ten o'clock be all right? I will come in a car. You think Josephine will mind, or your mother?'

'No no, they will be happy I'm going with someone they can trust.'

'Josephine say I'm someone she can trust?' James brightened and was about to give way to a smile.

'Well is Mama who say it, James. Josephine don't want to hear. You know she tear up all your letters? She never read a single one. I would be angry if I were you. When you pick me up you can tell

39

me all about how you planning to forget about Josephine and find yourself somebody else.' With that Eunice turned and headed along the path to Bardouille's, trying her best to walk like a sophisticated woman. She had the reputation of a naughty young girl and she hoped James did not regard her in that way.

James had supposed that his coming to the wedding with Josephine's little sister might, somehow, please Josephine. He wouldn't be turning up with some other woman and had hoped to slip away from Eunice at some point and try again to talk to Josephine about the way he felt.

On the morning of the wedding, Josephine was probably more excited than the bride. Dora would be wearing the first wedding dress she had ever made and Josephine couldn't wait to see how her friend would look, floating along in the ankle length gown with flowers in her hair. It was tradition for the bride's party to walk to church in a procession. The church bells would ring twenty minutes before the party was due to arrive at the church and then stop once it had reached the churchyard. If the party was late, and very often it was, the bells would just keep on ringing. Josephine made sure that Dora was not late getting ready.

The wedding party left the house and began the procession. Those who were not invited gathered along the roadside to catch glimpses of the well dressed, well groomed party. An occasion such as this would bring out the brightest and most colourful of outfits. Women in rich coloured dresses and hats, men in crisp suits and patterned ties. The invited guests would already be at the church, which this morning was full to the rafters, with voices at volumes louder than the bells themselves. The packed out little church very obviously included people who had not been invited but so many of them just couldn't resist a good wedding.

The bride and the morning were beautiful. The sky was now bright blue and cloudless. There was, unusually, no breeze and by late morning it became unbearably hot. The overly long ceremony ended and the wedding party gathered at the church hall for the wedding breakfast. A small band played guitars and the local chanteuse sang. Everyone laughed, drank, ate and danced.

Josephine couldn't help noticing how her younger sister followed James around. She was embarrassed by her sister's forwardness and wished Eunice could have a little more decorum at times. Rose sat with a group of older members of the party, fanning herself with a large woven straw fan, pretending to be interested in the conversation but all the time staring at Eunice who ignored everyone, her eyes fixed on James.

'I thought you said Josephine have a boyfriend, Eunice.' James said. 'I've had my eyes on her all day and she isn't with anyone. I don't see a boyfriend.'

Eunice couldn't fail to notice where James' attention had been since the ceremony. She had spent most of the day trying to keep him engaged in conversation, just so that he could look her way once in a while.

'What do you see in Josephine? She is not like any of the girls you hang around?' Eunice was hot with anger and tried desperately to appear calm.

'What I see in her is exactly what I don't see in anyone else.' James excused himself and headed to the table of drinks where Josephine stood having someone pour her a tumbler of punch.

'You look very pretty today Josephine,' he said. James positioned himself with his back to Josephine's admirer who soon knew his presence was no longer required.

'I thought you only had eyes for my sister.' Josephine sipped some punch and stared into the glass as the orange fluid danced inside it. Her hand trembled slightly.

'Eunice is a child,' said James and raised his eyes to the ceiling. 'Would you like to come outside for some air? It's such a nice afternoon and so stuffy in here. Maybe it would be better outside?'

'It's just as hot outside I think.' Josephine felt Eunice's eyes penetrating her skin and turned her head slightly to see her sister about to boil over like a sulphur spring.

41

'Alright, let's go outside.' She thought Eunice would fly at her at any moment and wanted to avoid a scene. One of Eunice's outbursts was bound to ruin Dora's day. She put down her drink and followed James, trying to avoid Eunice's glare.

The pair stepped out into the hot afternoon air and walked a short way along a nearby avenue of white cedars that lead to the neighbouring playing field. They stood under a cedar tree for shade. Neither of them spoke for a moment. James' warm smile made Josephine nervous. She felt as though the hot afternoon sun had taken up residence about two feet above the tree. James searched for the right words. He didn't want to put Josephine off him as he had often done in the past. All he managed to say was her name in a slight whisper as he gently placed a kiss on her lips. Then he held both of her hands and pulled her toward him, placing her arms around his waist and holding her trembling body next to his. They stood like this for several minutes. Neither of them noticed the people coming out of the church hall one by one, smiling at the couple who stood as if posing for a photograph.

Eunice joined the onlookers. Rose had followed close behind her and placed a firm hand on her daughter's arm. Eunice's face never revealed the flaming anger she felt. Her thoughts were on her sister.

Once again, Josephine had managed to get something she wanted. Eunice knew in her heart, though, that what Josephine had, she could always find a way to take.

5

'I can never really get used to this bit.' He looks tense.

'I'm sorry?'

'Turbulence.' He's glad to have my attention again. 'They say flying is the safest form of travel, but I can never stop wishing I had control of the levers when this happens.' I'm not sure I like where this is going. 'It's not that they don't know what they're doing. Of course they're trained. But do you ever do that thing when you sit in someone else's car, they're a bit of an erratic driver and you start pushing on imaginary brakes in the passenger side? You haven't got control but you feel you must do something. That's how I feel about turbulence. You know. Whoa, it's getting bumpy – let's put on the brakes.' He gestures 'stop' with his hands to illustrate his point. I wish I knew what point he was trying to make. There's nothing you can do about turbulence but ride it out. There are just some things we don't have any control over. You just go with the flow.

I was doing just that when the business was in its early days. Going with the flow. But at the same time, finding myself becoming more and more distant from the family. Angel's went from strength to strength: little jobs here and there, and when the big occasions came up we had to take on temporary staff, mostly in the form of Jasmin's sister and her mates. They were easy to train and didn't cost too much. We also started a sandwich delivery service. Got a load of flyers printed up and delivered them to the Business Park near the High Street. The only decent sandwich bar or café was on the High Street and a good fifteen minute walk from the Business Park. That was an opportunity right there. An outlet on the High Street. Something new and different. Jasmin and I set our sights on opening our own premises one day.

The increasing level of work didn't impress Mum too much. She complained that I never called her enough or came around as often as my sisters did.

'I'm not an educated woman but one thing I know is that a mother's love for her children never dies and too many children break their parents' hearts. You see Mrs George? Mrs George had six children, three boys and three girls, and she loved all of them. She did everything she could to care for them and raise them up to be good children. They were so good, most of them became doctors or lawyers, one of them even had a shop on the Harrow Road.

But when all of them marry, have children, make lots of money, they never have time for her again. She bake cakes for them, put ice-lollies in the freezer for the grandchildren and none of them come to visit her. When she see no one care anymore, she go and lie down in her bed without eating – and die. Her children never discover her body for *six* months.'

'Mum, that could never happen to you.' I said down the other end of the phone. 'Even though I get really busy you'll always have Del and Maddy.'

'Well is three daughters I have.' She'd hung up on me that day without saying goodbye, replacing a farewell with the sign of the cross I suspected. Another of Mum's stories and I was on a guilt trip. I didn't want Mum to think I was turning my back on her. That was far from true. My work was important. But, no matter what I did, there would always be a part of me that cared what Mum thought.

The *Please Fasten Your Seatbelts* sign flashes. He's the first to do so. Rattling the buckle so loudly, I wonder if he needs help. I'm not sure I believe his claims about being a seasoned flyer. He grips the edges of his seat.

44

'You alright there?' I have to ask.

'Oh yes, yes. Perfectly fine. Just that I hate this bit.'

'I'm sure we'll go through it soon. Must be the time of year or something. I don't know.' I look away. I can see he's gearing up to carry on the conversation. All I wanted to do was placate him.

'Shifting wind currents in the sky,' he says. 'That's what I read. In fact it doesn't do any harm to keep your seatbelt on for the whole flight. I've read a lot of reports about serious injuries in a plane when turbulence came on suddenly.' He stops to smile at me. 'But I won't frighten you with those.'

Yes, turbulence can come on suddenly. Just when you think everything is running smoothly, it hits you.

'Angelica!'

'Yes. It's me. Who were you expecting? Just thought I'd surprise you. I knew you weren't doing anything. Our party got cancelled a few hours ago so I thought I'd rustle up some treats and come and cook for you. You always complain I don't cook for you enough.' Michael hadn't moved from his spot so I pushed one of the carrier bags I was holding into his hand and brushed past him with the other in the direction of the kitchen.

'Just put the bag down, go back to your music and I'll start. Hope you like lobster.'

I hadn't noticed the expression on Michael's face but I noticed from the hatch that looked onto the living room that there was someone sitting on the sofa wearing a pair of black ski pants and patent leather stiletto heels. I couldn't see the top half from the angle I was in until I stormed into the living room. Michael followed behind me, one hand on his mouth, the other reaching to turn off the music. Miss Ski Pants rose from her seat and just stared at me. She was tall and beautiful and reminded me of Sade.

'I, I wasn't expecting you,' Michael managed to stutter.

'Evidently,' I said, looking from one to the other.

'Please tell me this is your sister.' Sade Ski Pants turned to Michael and pursed her ruby red, lipstick lips together.

'No, actually, I thought I was his girlfriend.' I interrupted before he could answer. 'What the hell is going on Michael? This is the last thing I expected of *you*.' I stopped to take a breath and no-one spoke for a second.

'My God, I don't believe this. How long have you two been … ?' I pointed my finger from one to the other.

'I've been seeing him for a few months now,' she answered. Michael was obviously having difficulty trying to speak. 'I *knew* he was up to something. Last night I answered the phone to someone who hung up suddenly. Was that you?'

'No, it wasn't me.' I looked at Michael and I still couldn't believe what he'd done. I'd brought my knife set. I might get to use it after all. 'I was working last night and he was supposed to have been visiting his mother. Do you know what Michael? I'm just going to leave you to this. Whatever *this* is.' I raised my right hand to stop him offering any kind of excuse. 'Do you know what? Forget it.'

I went to get my bags from the kitchen while Sade was getting her things from the bedroom. We both stormed out at around the same time with Michael calling 'Hey wait! I can explain everything' from the front door. She sped off in a little red sports car and I drove away in my delivery van. Speeding off at zero to seventy in six seconds would have been a much more dramatic ending than ambling out of Michael's cul de sac at fifteen miles an hour in my Ford Transit.

I watch as the flight attendants glide effortlessly down the aisles with their trolleys, delivering service with a smile in narrow quarters.

'Here you go. One chicken and one vegetarian. Enjoy your meals.'

'This looks good,' he smiles. The *Please Fasten Your Seatbelts* sign switched off ages ago but he's being safe rather than sorry by the looks of things.

'*Bon appetit.*'

It was a lot easier getting over Michael than it was Anil. I threw myself into my work. My pastry course started a month or so after we broke up. It was a two-week course at a private college. I had to get up a bit earlier to help Jasmin with the sandwich orders but she was happy to do deliveries on her own. On the first day of the pastry course I was completely mesmerised by the kitchen. It was just perfect and contained all the things I dreamed of having for myself one day. I fully intended to absorb everything. My mind was on the course and nowhere else.

The tutor was a very attractive French chef. I tried to sum him up before he'd even opened his mouth. I would have placed him in his thirties, probably married but definitely attached. His name was Jules. Good humoured as well as good looking, not too much taller than me, a kind face. As the days went by I noticed he never lost eye contact with me whenever he explained anything and stood very close when he demonstrated techniques. Of the six students on the course, I was the only woman. On the last day, we all went for a drink. I'd asked Jasmin to join us which pleased all the guys from the course. Jules was oblivious to Jasmin, though. He kept his eyes fixed on me and had talked only to me the whole time we were there. After a few rounds, Jasmin felt she just had to know what our private conversation was about and signalled for me to accompany her to the ladies.

'That guy, Jules,' she said, 'he really has the hots for you.'

'Do people actually say "the hots" anymore, Jas? This isn't a 1950s movie.' I fixed my hair and tried to act cool and collected. I was the one with the 'hots' for Jules but all I knew about him was that he was amazingly attractive. Since Jasmin had broken up with Nigel we'd been bemoaning being single. But we'd pledged to be more selective in the future so that we didn't end up being hurt again.

'Jas, you know we said that we had to stop dating undesirables?'

'Yes.' Her voice lingered on this word as she looked at me via the bathroom mirror while applying lip gloss.

'Well now the course is over, I suppose the only way I can find out more about Jules is to accept his offer of dinner.' I kept up the pretence of being nonchalant.

'He's asked you out to dinner?' she shrieked.

The door opened as a girl walked in. Through the open doorway I could see the guys at our table and wanted to get back to them as quickly as possible. I waited as Jasmin shook out her curls and wished, not for the first time, that I had them too. We made our way back to the table.

'So Jules,' said Jasmin as we sat down, 'are you married?'

'No,' he smiled, 'I am not married.'

'Girlfriend?' she asked. He looked quickly from me to her.

'No, no girlfriend either. Sad, no?' He smiled and looked back at me.

'Well that really depends on who wants to know I suppose.' She giggled like a teenager. I was so embarrassed, I wished that there was a trap door under Jasmin's seat that would open and stop her asking Jules any more of these leading questions.

'Hey Jas,' I said. 'I think it's time we were on our way. We've got that thing later.'

'What thing?'

'You know that thing I told you about that we had to do later. Well it's later and we'd better get going. It was really nice to meet you guys. Good luck with everything.' I drank the rest of my wine, about half a glass, in two seconds and began to put on my jacket. Jules immediately stood up to help me with it.

'If we are to go for a meal I must have your telephone number,' he said. I could virtually hear Jasmin squealing with delight behind the ridiculous grin she was wearing. The other men were looking disappointed that she was going and started finishing their drinks, wanting to leave. I reached into my bag and found one of our sandwich service flyers and gave it to Jules.

'You can get me on this number.' I smiled. Jasmin and I left. That last mouthful of wine had gone straight to my head and made me feel woozy. Jasmin had to link my arm and prop me up as we walked out of the pub. She understood that I had to make a sophisticated exit and not bump into a stool or a punter as I left.

'How is it?' He's been trying to attract my attention since the flight attendant put our trays down. Now he's talking to me with an unchewed lump of food inside his mouth. He smiles and waits for me to respond.

'Oh fine, thanks.' He wants more. 'And yours? How's yours?'

'Well not too bad. Yours looks a lot better. It's not that I'm actually vegetarian. My wife always insists on getting the vegetarian when she flies. Says she doesn't trust meat on planes. Doesn't believe they know how to store things properly. Won't drink the water when she's abroad either.'

'I suppose she's right in a way. Some places are a bit risky.' I wonder if it's safe to take another mouthful. Will he want to ask me something else?

Jules was passionate about food. He always insisted on cooking for me rather than the other way round. His ambition was to open his own restaurant in France one day. He finally admitted to me that the only reason he came to London was to follow the woman he had fallen in love with. She was English and working as a translator in France, and had dumped him after he told her he loved her. The fact that I was a rebound girlfriend got shifted to the back of my mind because of my growing feelings for him.

I loved how he made me feel. He laughed at my jokes even though I'm sure he didn't always understand them. He charmed both of my sisters, although my older sister, Del, advised me against going for looks and going for security instead, insisting that that's what I needed now that I was in my late twenties. I was too busy getting wrapped up in Jules to care what she said.

Jules and I had been dating for a few months and everything had been going well. We saw each other as often as we could. But a very busy time at work came up for me and two weeks had gone by since the last proper date. I'd called Jules, but a good few days had gone by and he hadn't returned my call.

I thought it strange, at first, and wasn't sure if I should just wait, call again or if I should be worried.

'Who could that be at this time of night?' The buzzer for our flat had sounded. Jasmin and I were already in our pyjamas. She looked at me and smirked.

'Must be the Latin lover, wanting a midnight rendezvous.' Jasmin hadn't noticed that I hadn't had a date with Jules for a while. She was too busy falling for her new man, Steven, a Managing Director from one of the companies we delivered sandwiches to.

'Well, he's early. It's not eleven yet.'

I sighed a weary 'hello' down the intercom and was relieved to find it was Jules.

'I'm sorry it is so late. I would like if you can come with me for a drink.'

'Everywhere will be closing.' I was angry with him but wanted to see him all the same. 'Well, just wait there a minute. I'll be down.' Jasmin winked and made rude gestures as I pulled on a sweatshirt and jeans and grabbed an old jacket.

'We can talk?' he asked. I was owed an explanation. I took him to the restaurant-bar about five minutes from our flat. They closed the curtains when it was after hours and never hassled their punters to leave.

It was a bit of a dive and the music was awful but it gave Jasmin and me a good laugh once in a while. They tried so hard to be chic but they would religiously serve stale peanuts with drinks. The owner had no front teeth and his wife's enormous bosom toppled out over her low cut, tight dresses. Jules and I missed the funny side that night.

'I will be going back to France soon,' he said. 'I've arranged for the person renting my apartment to be out by the end of the month and I've made enquiries for work. I think I have at least two possibilities. Everyone remembers me there.' He smiled briefly. My expression changed and my heart sank. I finally realised he meant that he was going to France for good. Not just a short trip as I'd first assumed.

'I'm sorry it seems so sudden but there are some things I really needed to say to you before I go.' My mouth was open but I couldn't find anything to say. He took a breath and continued.

'When I came to London it was for a purpose but I think I stayed too long. I started to get over Casey, straighten out my brain.'

'Your head.' I finally said.

'Excuse me?'

'Your head, straighten out your head. That's the proper term. Not your brain.' I never usually corrected his English but there he was, casually telling me I was dumped, what did he expect?

'Sorry, yes my head. My head has been everywhere it seems this year. First on Casey, then on my career and now on you, Angelique. You see, I'm not ready so soon to be in love again. I need time to sort out my head once and for all and when I first saw you I thought you could help me do that. But now I feel I am falling in love with you and I need to stop before I get too deep.'

'Why do you have to stop? We could fall deeply in love and sort each other's brains out.'

'Heads. You mean heads, no?' He paused, waiting for my answer but I was out of words. 'My mind is made up. It's right for me to go now. It's not fair on you with Casey still there in my head. I have to go back and start fresh to regain my sanity. Can you understand Angelique?'

I always wondered what would have been if I'd said, no I don't understand. If I'd pleaded for him to take me with him and tried to convince him that he might change his mind about me. But there was no point. I knew it then and I know it now.

'Well, Jules, I wish you luck. I hope your head gets sorted out soon. Maybe you will invite me to a meal at your restaurant one of these days and I can invite you to mine.'

The door swung shut behind me and I never looked back. I never told him I loved him. I had that at least. Although, I wish he could have known how much.

When I walked in Jasmin was all smiles, grabbing at my left hand with mock excitement. And that's when the floodgates opened.

'Tea or coffee for you?' I'm not sure how many times the flight attendant has asked the question. I'm miles away. I turn to see my new flying buddy, all teeth and pointing at his cup.

'Is it tea or coffee? I'm guessing you're a coffee person. Am I right?'

What the hell has this man got to be so damned happy about?

'Tea please.'

Jasmin was my absolute rock during the next phase of my life. She tried to take my mind off Jules and focus it on getting a business plan together. The time was right for trying to open premises. We had envisioned a sandwich bar with a decent enough kitchen to work in. All of the High Street banks turned us down for a loan. But Jasmin had a plan B to put to me. Her boyfriend Steven wanted to invest in the business and this would give us the capital the banks said we lacked. But Steven was a boyfriend and boyfriends let girlfriends down.

'But it wouldn't be a boyfriend, girlfriend thing. It's business and there would be proper drawn up contracts that are effective whether we're sleeping together or not. Steven's not an idiot. He's not doing it for love. He's seen our business plan and he knows how good this thing is. If we took his money and went back to the bank we could be in our perfect unit by next week.'

It wasn't quite as quick as a week. But before we could walk into our new premises, there was one more river to cross.

I need to stretch my legs for a bit. Splash my face. Maybe put on some lipstick. Might make me feel a bit more with it. Maybe I'll stop snarling at the guy sitting next to me.

'Excuse me.' I turn to him and force a smile. 'Just need the ladies. Thanks.' He makes an elaborate gesture of vacating his seat and standing like a doorman in the aisle whilst I make my way to the WC. He practically bows.

Peace at last. As I suspected, I look awful. My eyes have dark circles. Anyone can see I haven't been sleeping properly. I put my bag down and turn on the cold tap. The water feels great on my face. I take out my lipstick and apply two coats but I still look about the same. I might as well go back to my seat and admit defeat. But hold on, he'll still be there and might want an after lunch chat. I'll just wait another minute.

'Just one minute and we'll know for sure.' Jasmin had a furrowed brow and a smile at the same time. That was her worried, but pretending not to be look. The first test had already proved positive but Jasmin insisted she pop down to the chemist to try a different one, just in case.

'We had to wait for a blue line, right?' I came out of the bathroom holding the second pregnancy test stick.

'Yes?' Jasmin had her hands clenched together.

'Well according to this I must be expecting twins because this line is navy. What the hell am I going to do?'

'Sit down Ange. You've got options and you don't have to rush into anything you don't want to do. There's no pressure. Just relax and think, okay?'

'Yes, okay.' I sat down.

'Well. What are you going to do?'

'I don't know Jas. What the hell *should* I do? Shit. I suppose I should tell Jules? But he'll be gone soon. I guess this is up to me now.' I paused and took a deep breath. 'Jasmin?'

'What?'

'How do I tell Mum about this?'

I make my way back down the aisle of the plane. He springs to his feet to let me get back to my seat. He really is a nice guy.

'Thank you,' I say.

'Not a problem. You were gracious enough to let me sit here. I'll just get my laptop out and do some work. Shan't bother you anymore.' Have I been such an obvious bitch? He doesn't deserve to be treated that way.

'Oh you're not bothering me really. I've just been caught up in my thoughts today. Just wanted to be quiet and sort things out in my mind.'

'Oh. I see. Escaping are we? Is it problems at home or work?' I look at him sharply

'There I go again. I'm being a bother. I'm sorry. I just can't help myself sometimes.'

'No, don't apologise. It's just … .' I don't dare tell him. 'Well work is a bit all over the place right now. Just taking a break from the grind.' I'm fingering the plastic bag with headphones in it. There's still a chance I can shut him out for a while.

'What is it you do?' he asks.

'I have a catering company.'

'Oh, that sounds impressive.'

'Well it's not huge or anything but it does quite well.'

'Good. Good. You the sole owner?'

'Well, I started with a friend. It's all mine now, though.'

'Must be tough going it alone.'

Alone. That word again. I retreat into my shell once more. Open the plastic wrapper, take out the headphones and search. Film, radio. I don't mind. I don't want to be reminded about why I'm here.

6

May arrived in the way May always did. Dependably warm, sunny and dry. A feeling of calm always prevailed during this month and the islanders were entranced by the serenity that was only ever present in May. The rainy season started in June and the five to six months of stormy weather that was about to take over the island were somehow forgotten.

Josephine was in a mellow mood when May came. She had finally admitted to herself that she was falling in love with James. They saw each other often and it felt so natural to her to be walking in a wood by the river holding hands with him or sitting beneath a hibiscus with the petals falling about them. They would talk well into a Friday evening until it was dark and James would walk Josephine home by the light of a torch.

'You seem to be spending a lot of time talking to that boy,' Rose commented one Friday night. 'You used to be taking in mending and now you don't seem to have the time. Didn't you say you saving for a sewing machine?'

'I know, I haven't forgotten. I can still do mending but I haven't any customers at the moment.' There had been a light rain while Josephine was out and she shook raindrops from her cardigan onto the front steps where she stood, trying to trace the light of James' torch, which was slowly becoming fainter and which eventually disappeared.

During the last year, James and his brother Rudy had bought an old house, very close to their family home and had set about fixing it up. The house was almost as good as new, but during the time it took to undergo repairs, Rudy had made up his mind that he was going to live on another of the islands. A couple of Rudy's friends had managed to find reasonably paid work there and he was enticed away from home, hoping to emulate their success. Several islanders were talking about moving abroad, some as far as England. Jobs were scarce on the island and competition was high.

James was struggling too and had to travel into the capital most days, trying to secure contracts or find casual work. The rest of the time he spent trying to finish the house his brother had left to him, whilst contemplating the prospect of going to England, making his fortune and coming back a rich man.

Josephine got ready for bed and came back from the outside toilet to find Rose still sitting on the low sofa in the front room.

'What do you find to talk about anyway?' Rose's tone was serious. 'I don't know what get into you. You never like his ways before. His father was just the same with his dry eye, always looking at so many women.'

'Mam, I know I always said I wasn't interested in any men and that I would always stay with you … .' Josephine was almost apologetic.

'Is not that I don't want you to love, Josephine. Is who you choose I worry about. You *will* marry someday and I want you to stay happy and not have to keep wondering which woman house your husband is at.'

'Maybe he has changed. I had a dream.' Josephine's eyes found the floor and she traced the patterns in the small, worn rug. She always told Mama her dreams but this one she couldn't bring herself to mention before now.

'What you dream?'

'I dream that Aunty May came to me and told me that James was my partner and that we would marry.' She said all of this in one breath and was glad it was finally out. She never liked to keep anything from her mother. She exhaled with an audible sigh of relief.

'Well the dream just tell you what *will* happen. It doesn't tell you that it's right to do.' Rose retired to bed now and didn't bid

56

her daughter goodnight. Josephine locked the front door and put out the light. She crawled into bed next to Eunice who rolled over and yawned. Eventually Josephine began to drift into sleep but she was aware that Rose would not be sleeping for a while. As Josephine's eyes became too heavy to stay open she thought, I love him, so it must be right to marry him.

One Sunday afternoon, after Josephine and her family had returned from church, Josephine was changing into a simple blue dress and white sandals before leaving to have a meal with James and his parents. James always spoke about Josephine when he popped in to see them. His mother, who knew Rose and her children very well, was not so sure that this was the right girl for her son. She thought Josephine was too stuck up and that her mother, Rose, was far too proud. She thought Josephine might look down her nose at them and didn't feel comfortable about her coming for dinner. For this reason she had made sure her house was spotless. She had been cleaning since Friday and her husband just shook his head from side to side whenever his wife found some new corner or crevice that she hadn't already polished until it shone. The best tablecloth was out, the curtains neatly tied back, the cushions upright, no longer daring to collapse lest they fall victim to a dramatic pummelling back into shape. Her husband Wilfred's only job was to sweep the yard and stay out of the way. He had swept the yard three times before it met her approval.

Mrs Dennis was cooking a lavish lunch of curried chicken, which she would serve with a plateful of root vegetables from their garden. She made a large pitcher of lemonade and baked a fruitcake, to be served with a pot of tea after the meal. It was normal for them to eat fish in a nice broth or gravy. Curries were usually saved for special occasions, so she hoped Josephine would appreciate the effort she'd gone to.

Josephine did have high standards but she would never look down her nose at James' family, even though she thought his sisters never dressed well enough for church. Fortunately his sisters would not be there. They had the same opinion about Josephine as their mother. They were both married and busy with young children but still found time to let their brother know what they thought of her: she was too full of herself and he would do better with one of the girls from town, who at least had something to be hoity-toity about.

James walked Josephine into his parents' house and they stood to greet her.

'Well Josephine, what a pretty dress. You make it yourself?' Mrs Dennis asked with a very convincing smile.

'Yes I did.'

'You think you could make me something so lovely one day?'

'Yes of course, you just say when.' Josephine was just as polite.

'Just remember to buy a lot of material for it.' Mr Dennis remarked as he surveyed his wife's figure. 'Yes, a hell of a lot.'

James and his father laughed, but not for very long as Mrs Dennis shot them both a cross look.

'Let us sit,' she said.

Mrs Dennis hadn't wanted her sons to move out. They were not getting married so she hadn't seen the need. But now that she and her husband were on their own, they were able to set up a dining table in the middle of the room and still have space for a sofa and two chairs, a coffee table and two side cabinets with glass front doors.

The meal was very tasty and the conversation began to flow, especially after Mr Dennis brought out his special reserve of rum. It wasn't long before Mrs Dennis realised that Josephine was a lot better company than she had imagined. She hadn't found her to be as stuck up as she'd thought. Mr Dennis, on the other hand, never had a problem with the girl.

'So Josephine, you think you might marry this son of mine one of these days?' he asked as he raised the tumbler of rum to his mouth.

'Wilfred,' his wife exclaimed, 'give them a chance! They are just children.'

'We were married with Janet and Olivia by their age, Aggie. Besides, everyone is talking about these two, saying they must be the next pair to get married. So what you say Josephine?' This time he lifted the glass in Josephine's direction, as though toasting a bride and groom.

'I say, if James ask me I will not say no straight away, I will certainly think about it.' Mrs Dennis looked at Josephine as if to say, 'Well, you couldn't do much better than my son'. But Josephine never noticed this look, she and James had locked eyes and very shortly James was saying that it was time he walked Josephine home.

'Already?' Protested Mrs Dennis. 'Here, I will wrap up some cake and you will take it for your mother, alright?'

'Yes of course, and thank you for a wonderful meal. I hope you can come and eat with us some time.'

Josephine and James walked off into the late afternoon sun. Mr and Mrs Dennis' little dog, Moss, followed them a short way before running back to trouble the chickens in their yard.

The Dennis' house stood on a small flat plain just a few seconds walk from the main pathway and about a ten minute walk from the mountain road which rose high and away from the quiet hamlet. Travellers could look down onto the multi-coloured houses scattered about the hillside paths and slopes. James' house was on the opposite side of the main path and up a grassy slope. His was a secluded wooden house, painted in light blue. The wood surrounding the house made it barely visible from the main path.

James led Josephine up the little slope, saying that if she were to consider marrying him she would need to know where she would be living for the rest of her life. Josephine was intrigued. James had talked about his house in great detail. About how much work he'd put into it but hardly had any money to buy furniture.

'Don't expect too much,' he said, 'I've never taken on such a big task as this. And I'm doing it on my own now.'

59

The house was small but had a certain charm that Josephine sensed as soon as she stepped inside. She felt proud that James had done such a good job. Many of the houses in the neighbouring villages had fallen into disrepair, especially with the economy as it was. There was neither the money nor the inspiration to do much about it. She thought it would be nice to move into a house that was as good as new and how lucky it would be to start married life that way. There was a nice fresh smell inside, a smell of new wood and there was a new rug on the floor of the main room. In this room there was a chair and a coffee table that James had made himself. He had been crafting a side cabinet but it wasn't quite finished.

He led her to the bedroom to reveal a double bed and a wooden chair with a lamp on it. There were no curtains anywhere, Josephine noticed. The small wood that surrounded the house formed a natural curtain that obscured the view of neighbouring houses and any chance of being spied on. From the bedroom window she saw the small kitchen next door to the toilet, a little too close for her liking, but she could live with that. There was not much of a yard around the house but the outhouses were surrounded by orange lantana and a little way off she could see the red and yellow of heliconias, standing tall and swaying in the late afternoon breeze. Josephine stepped backwards to watch as a tiny green lizard toured the window frame, looking this way and that, not able to decide which direction to scurry to next.

'It's very nice,' she said and turned around, startled, to find James standing close behind her. 'You made me jump. What are you doing?' James had his arms around her waist and bent to kiss her. She responded, quite warmly, but tried to pull away when she thought the kiss had lasted for long enough. It would soon be dark, and she shouldn't get back too late. Mama would want to hear all about the meal.

James took the wrapped up piece of cake out of Josephine's hand and threw it, quite accurately, onto the chair. He began unbuttoning her dress while he kissed her. He touched her face, moving his hand, softly, down her neck, her chest and inside her petticoat. Her dress was around her ankles as he lifted her onto the bed and started then, to remove his shirt. James had undressed them both, their kisses more intense as he caressed and stroked her body. She held him tightly as James pushed between her legs, wondering for the briefest of moments if perhaps she should try to resist but her excitement was far too great and they moved in perfect rhythm. He began to moan and call her name, moving faster, his body stiffening with one final sigh until he lay motionless on top of her. Josephine lay still. James was smiling at her now and began slowly to get up.

'Why are you looking so worried? I thought you were enjoying it,' he said.

'I did, I was, but I have to get home. It's getting late and Mama will be worried. Where are my things?' She hurried to get dressed. This was not something she would want to admit to in the confessional but part of her thought that maybe she should. Had she become just like those girls she always scoffed at? Surely it was different if you loved someone.

They walked back to her house in silence. All the time she was wondering if maybe James would have nothing to do with her now, the way he was with all the other girls. When the two reached Josephine's yard, James broke the silence.

'Josephine, will you marry me?'

Before she had time to stop and consider she answered yes. They both smiled and then laughed out loud. Rose opened the door.

'Josephine, is late. You disturbing the neighbours with all that fuss you making. James you should get yourself off now. Give my regards to your mother.' Rose disappeared back inside.

Josephine and James climbed the steps at the front of the house. They held hands, she trying to get indoors before Mama came out again and he trying to steal one last kiss before parting.

They never got an opportunity to be alone in James' house

again. Josephine always made sure she had an excuse. It would be so easy to be seduced by James again and she thought it wise to resist, at least until their wedding night. Now that they had announced their intention to get married, she wanted everything to be perfect. Wedding plans had already begun. Their plan was to marry in January when they were out of the stormy season and that would give them enough time to sort out the banns, for Josephine to make the dresses for the bridesmaids – there would be four – her mother's outfit and of course, her own wedding dress. James didn't want to wait so long but had no choice.

As the tranquillity of May drifted away, the rainy season came along with an almighty crash of thunder. A heavy rain always left a fresh, clear feeling in the air and this corresponded well with Josephine's frame of mind. She was alert and happy. She was still working for Ma David but only part-time now as workloads continued to lessen. Still, she thought, I can work on my wedding dress designs. She kept herself busy and Rose, who had come to accept her daughter's intention to marry James, was enjoying Josephine's excitement. Eunice, on the other hand, was short tempered and complained all the time. She complained when it rained.

'But Eunice,' Rose said one day, 'it will only rain for a short while.' Eunice was agitated by her mother.

'Yes but it will be so wet. My shoes will be ruined.'

'Eunice, why don't you come and help me?' Josephine asked. 'I've got lots of finishing work to do on the wedding dress and the bridesmaid dresses.'

'What work? What you want me to do?' She folded her arms.

'Well, there's hems, buttons, trimmings.'

'And how you expect me to concentrate on all that when those boys are making so much noise? Mama, can't you send them to go and do something useful?'

'Eunice, you are the one who need to find something useful to do.' Her mother sighed and headed outside to the kitchen.

'Well, Eunice, come and try on your dress so I know where to make the hem.' Josephine tried again to distract Eunice from her increasingly bad mood.

'I hate that dress. Why you choose such a colour? You never think about me when you buy this material. Look. This is a colour for Dora – not for me.' She grabbed her dress from Josephine and stormed off to put it on in the bedroom.

'Look,' she said when she returned to the living room. 'What people going to say when they see me? I look so damn fat.'

'Eunice, mind your tongue!' her mother yelled from outside.

Josephine said nothing. She knew better than to try and reason with her sister. She tried only to focus on the important things and not let Eunice's outbursts worry her.

A few days later, Josephine was doing a dress fitting for Dora.

'I don't know what happen with me,' she remarked to her friend. 'With all this running around, my period is about ten days late now.'

'Well Josephine, you have to bring the wedding date forward.' Dora said, looking down at the skirt of her dress as Josephine placed straight pins along the waistband.

'Why?'

'Because you pregnant.'

'What?' Josephine stood up quickly.

'Ouch, Josephine, take care of that pin. You just stick it in my waist, girl.'

'What make you think I pregnant?'

'I know Mr Dennis.' Dora raised her eyebrows. 'With those looks and that sweet talk, don't tell me you have been able to resist him all this time. No woman can. Not even you. Of course you pregnant.'

'But Dora, it was only once.'

'That's all it takes my dear.' Dora kissed her teeth.

Josephine was afraid to tell Mama. Rose was bound to be disappointed in her. She hated to let her mother down.

The day Josephine broke the news to Rose, the women were both in the kitchen, Rose gutting fish and Josephine hovering around aimlessly, trying to find the right words. Eventually she spoke.

'Mam I have something I must tell you.'

'It wouldn't take a dream or an education to know what it is you have to tell me Josephine.' Rose just kept her head down and got on with her work. 'It's a small house, I see what goes on with all my children. I don't need the gossipers to tell me that Benjamin spends too much money at Bardouille's. That Caleb keeps company with a married woman over at Belleville Plain and that Eunice was kissing a boy at the dance last Saturday. I see how close you and James are, it was only a matter of time. I'm sorry you couldn't wait until you were married but at least he is marrying you. What he say anyway?'

'He don't know yet.'

'Soon everyone will know, so you better tell him quick and you better go and see the priest too.' Rose's tone was matter of fact. She was trying to hide her disappointment, Josephine was sure. But the fact still remained, she was pregnant. Bringing the wedding forward was the only way.

Josephine found James in his yard, busy fixing some old wooden chairs for an old, local couple. They said they had had the chairs since they were married but the chairs were so rickety now they were afraid they might fall through them. Their son was coming over from America with his new wife and they didn't want her to think they had no class. They didn't have much money to pay James with but he was grateful for the work. He had too much time on his hands and not enough work to fill his time or his wallet. He gave Josephine a big smile as she approached.

'I've got a big job coming up soon,' he told her as she tried out one of the chairs he had finished.

'Oh good,' she said, 'the money will come in handy.'

'But I won't be around for a while though. I'm going and meet Rudy – he got me the job.' He sounded excited.

'You mean you going away?'

'Yes, I have to. I will be able to live with Rudy and save a hell

64

of a lot of money and that will help us when we get married.'

'But when you going?'

'Next week.'

'Next week!' Josephine was heartbroken.

'Yes the job starts in six days and Rudy already send me the ticket. Why you look so upset? I thought you would be happy I was making some money.' James was taken aback. 'I will only be gone four or five months. I'll be back well before the wedding so you don't have to worry about that.'

'That's not my worry.' She looked down, her eyes became glassy. 'I'm going to have a baby.' James stopped what he was doing. He couldn't believe his bad luck.

'No,' he said. 'But, just that one time?'

'I know. I was coming here to tell you and to say we must get married sooner and now you say you're going away.' She couldn't stop the tears. 'I just can't believe this is happening to me,' she said.

'What about me? I never expected to be a father so soon.' He threw down the small hammer he held. 'You look at me as though it's only my fault Josephine. Don't forget you were there when it happened.' He picked the hammer up again and tried to carry on working. 'Look, Josephine, I will stay as short a time as possible and we'll get married when I get back. Everything will be fine, maybe not the way you wanted but the result will be just the same.' He put his arm round her and although thoroughly deflated she looked at him with a half smile.

'We will have to go and see the priest.'

7

I was expecting a baby. Me. After breaking up with Jules, I kept my focus on moving on, forgetting about men altogether and finally opening our café. But a baby!

Just twenty minutes and I'm bored with the film. I can't believe there's nothing interesting on. I could kick myself for not remembering to bring a book or to stop at a newsagent in the airport to buy a magazine or two.

'Changed your mind about that one have you? I've seen it. Can't say I was overly impressed. Thought it was overrated.' Has he been looking over my shoulder? He doesn't stop there.

'What sort of thing do you normally go in for then? Chick Flicks?' I turn and look at him for a second. I hold my breath and take the plunge. Even a conversation with him might be more entertainment than they've got on offer here. And God knows this guy isn't about to let me get some sleep. Finally, I smile. And it isn't a fake one.

'Well, actually, I like the old style Chick Flicks better than the current ones. Sarah Jessica Parker and Jennifer Aniston are just Carrie and Rachel in every film they're in.' We're really doing this.

'So what's "old style"?' he asks.

'*Barefoot In The Park*, *Sabrina*, *The Way We Were*.'

'Ah, but they're the classics. Not what I was thinking.'

'Well they're still what I would call a Chick Flick. They just didn't have a label for them back then. That's what I think, anyway.' He looks glad that I've managed more than one sentence at a time. He's smiling. I smile to myself because I'm remembering those old movies and the number of them Jasmin and I sat and wept over in our little flat.

'There is something to be said about old films, though. All those morals. Great storylines too.' His voice is drifting into the background somewhere. Another voice is drawing me away from this conversation.

'Well I must say, we've all been worried.' Mum said, looking at Dad, who sat quietly on the sofa. I had gone round to my parents to break the news about the baby.

'You're getting close to thirty.' I sat quietly too as Mum continued. 'No sign of marrying. But a child? I thought you girls were modern, with your pills and your condoms.' It was strange to hear Mum using that word. Mum never talked to me about sex. All she ever did was imply that I should avoid it whilst I was single. I suspect she never banked on me being single at twenty-eight.

'Mum, it's not such a big deal these days. And probably not in your day either. Women have been having babies out of wedlock for ages.'

'Yes, some people don't get married but you're having this poor child all on your own. No-one there to support you. Your father and me leaving the country for good. Who will look after you?'

'Women can look after themselves you know,' I said. 'I can change a fuse, put up shelves. I can even drive a car.'

'Don't try and be funny. You think because you go to school you know better than me. Well let me tell you something ... '

'Yes, I know. You're not an educated woman but you can tell me a story about what an idiot I am for getting caught. I didn't plan this. I could have gotten rid of it if I wanted to and you would never have known. So what if I'm the only one of your daughters who doesn't know how to find a good man and hang onto him? I'm not as smart as you and Del and Maddy. I'm Angelica. Leaving her perfectly good job and now getting herself knocked up like some over-sexed teenager.'

67

'Don't raise your voice on me. You think in my day I could talk to my mother like that? Show some respect.'

'Well you show *me* some respect. I've done the best with my life that I can. I'm not you, Mum. And I don't want to be you.'

'And what's wrong with me?'

'Your religion is your prison. You don't have your independence. You don't understand the world I grew up in because you live in the past. So how the hell are you supposed to understand *me*?'

That had to be the only time I spoke to Mum like that. The only time I'd ever known her to be lost for words. I could see hurt in her eyes. She looked at me as though I'd done the unforgivable, disrespected her. I meant those things, but in a roundabout way. I never should have said it like that. It was harsh and cruel. Yes, we were different, and whilst any sensible person would celebrate diversity, I used it as a weapon. Once I'd wounded her I could not take it back. We never brought that conversation up again but it couldn't ever be forgotten. Mum never told another of her stories after that day – I'd have to do my best to get by without them. I'd certainly done a good job of convincing her that I didn't need her help anymore.

'I haven't seen a grown up film in a long time. If we go to the cinema, it's just for Phoebe.' My travel buddy brings me back to the here and now.

'Well it's like that when they're little,' I say. 'The world revolves around them. Actually, that doesn't change. You'll find that out when Phoebe gets older.'

'I've got a few pictures on the laptop, if you'd like to see them.' Oh no.

My family couldn't believe I'd finally done it. Opened our café. When Jasmin and I walked in to the newly opened Angel's, on the High Street, I was three months pregnant.

Jules did not know he was going to become a father. I had

dragged my heels about telling him and he had not been in touch before he left. I called the number I had for him once, after the first scan, but he had gone. I couldn't even remember the name of the village he was from and wasn't sure how to trace French chefs without hiring a private detective. I convinced myself that this was the way it had to be and just got on with decorating our new café.

From Angel's, we sold our sandwiches, home-made cakes, breakfast and lunch. The kitchen was the kitchen of my dreams and we continued our outside catering business. It wasn't huge, just big enough. I couldn't stop smiling when I walked into it each morning. At least our flat wouldn't smell of food all day long. We had a new van with Angel Catering painted on the sides and two part time members of staff, who called me 'Chef.'

'Ah, this is her fifth birthday.' The laptop is on. 'Spaceman theme. All her idea. She was into space and rockets, I have no idea why. She liked to surprise us. Her mum took her to do all the girly things but she preferred to get muddy in the garden. Oh well. That's our Phoebe I suppose. Not boring you am I?'

'No, she's really cute. You must be proud parents. They're adorable at that age. A bit rebellious too. But then you remember the cute little baby girl she was and your heart just melts.'

'Of course. You have a girl too.' He smiles.

'Yes. Her name's Eva.'

'That's a lovely name. Is it after anyone?' The nurse from the Special Care Baby Unit handed my fragile baby girl to me. I was afraid to touch her, she was tiny, only two pounds when she was born, ten weeks early. I'd had an emergency Caesarean section after spending two months in a hospital bed when my blood pressure went sky high.

'No, I just looked at her and that's the name that seemed to fit. I hope she likes it.'

Jasmin had been left to cope at Angel's with the help of

temporary chefs from an agency. I felt guilty. This early maternity leave wasn't anticipated but Jasmin was happy to hold the fort. And like everyone else in my family, she fell in love with Eva. Mum came to see me and couldn't hold the tears back.

'Dad and I have our ticket for home, the house is ready and we going back very soon Angelica. I know you will be alright, but I asked the girls to watch over you as much as they can. When we go, you promise my granddaughter won't be a stranger to me? I want to know her.'

'Of course Mum. That goes without saying. As often as I can afford it, I'll bring her out there. It's a promise.'

'Dad and I are very proud of you. I know you will make a success of the business. You have more than I ever had so make the most of it. Okay?'

'I will Mum. Thank you.' It would be another two years before I saw them again.

He's dwelling on that birthday party picture a long time. Maybe it's his favourite one of her or maybe I'm supposed to comment or something.

'How long ago was that taken?' I ask.

'Oh, five years ago.'

'So she's ten now.'

'That would be right.'

I remembered, quite out of the blue one day, that there was a way I could contact Jules. He had introduced me to a friend of his, an actor. I had a telephone number for him somewhere. I dug it out and a few weeks after Eva was born I was able to call Jules in France.

'A baby girl! I can't believe it. Why didn't you tell me before I left? I would have stayed longer in London.'

'I'm sorry I left it until now Jules. In the back of my mind I worried you might think it was some sort of trap. But you had the right to know.'

'I could never think anything bad of you Angelique. And anyway, she should know her father, no?'

'Of course. But you know I don't want anything from you.'

'Angelique, I have another responsibility now. Please, I am not like that. Things are going well. I have my restaurant but I'm going to drop everything to come over there. I must see her.'

After two months there had been no sign of Jules except another call expressing how sorry he was. The business was doing badly and he'd found lots of structural faults to the property and when everything was settled he would fly back to London.

He didn't show up, and I made no other attempt to contact him.

My new flying companion has stopped being so talkative. Maybe he's tired now, needs a rest. I'd started to enjoy the company, I must admit. It helps the time go by. Just five hours until we land. That's not so bad. I'll listen to some music and hopefully drift off for a while.

April 1991. Eva was six months old. On the Wednesday just after Easter, I had collected her from the childminder, Cassie, and pushed her home in her buggy as she sat gurgling away. It made me smile. It was a sunny day, a little on the windy side. I was all excited about the changes we'd made to Angel's. We'd extended the business so that we could offer an eat-in service. The new tables and chairs had arrived that day, along with the high stools for the window bar we'd had installed the week before the Easter break. There was just enough room in the café for four tables and we'd had fun setting them up, arranging and re-arranging their position so as not to take up too much room in the small shop front.

I'd turned into our street and there, outside our flat, stood a familiar figure. Unshaven and slightly dishevelled, was Jules. He was still as good looking but he looked a lot older somehow. He came towards us and looked into the buggy. His eyes welled up as

71

he looked at me and smiled.

'She is beautiful. Like you,' he said. I smiled my thanks for the compliment, although in my opinion, I always thought that Eva was the spitting image of her father. He kissed each of my cheeks and attempted to hug me. I stiffened a little and didn't quite know how to react. I very briefly placed my arm around him and patted his back, keeping one hand on the buggy.

'I'm sorry it is so unexpected but can I come in?'

'Yes, of course Jules.' I held Eva while I folded the buggy, which he offered to carry inside. We talked for a good few hours. Just polite, small talk at first until he started going into more detail about his failed business. I had made him a coffee but never asked if he wanted a second. I felt indifferent to Jules, and found his hard luck stories about his restaurant and him being in debt to countless people a bore. I wanted him to leave soon and certainly before Jasmin came home. She was likely to lay in to him and the last thing I wanted was a scene.

'I will be going back to France soon,' he said. 'When I can see you and Eva again?'

'That's up to you Jules. You know where we are. You can call me and we'll arrange something for next time.' I honestly had no problem with him seeing Eva and being part of her life. He walked off down the street and I watched from the living room window as he turned the corner.

He visited us one last time before returning to France. He bought Eva a big cuddly penguin that made a weird quacking sound when you squeezed it. He was going to stay at his mother's apartment in Provence but didn't leave me any contact details. He said he would call me when he was settled in his own place. That was the last Eva and I saw or heard of him.

8

'But Josephine, I can't understand why you are making such a fuss.'

'Because it's not right, Father. Those bells are supposed to sound for innocent girls getting married. You heard what I said about my condition, I'm no longer one of those girls.'

'Josephine, I've known you since you were born. I baptised you, I was there for your First Holy Communion and your Confirmation too. I know your mother very well – and your father, God rest his soul. They raised you up to be a good, Catholic girl. If I met anyone more innocent than you out of all of the girls on this island, I would be very surprised. I know you slipped up once, but your young man is going to marry you before you have your baby, so I believe you should have the bells ringing for your wedding. Just like everyone else. You deserve it and I won't hear another word.'

Despite what the priest said, Josephine couldn't help but feel embarrassed. People whispered behind her back, they stared whenever she walked by. She had overheard, and not by accident, a couple of women discussing her situation when she entered the local shop.

'Not so hoity-toity now is she?'

'She's just like anyone else around here, that Mother Superior.'

'I just dare her to look down her nose at me now, that's all I can say.'

Rose had told her daughter to hold her head high and not to worry about the wagging tongues. But her mother's words did little to put her mind at ease.

'Josephine, you've done a marvellous job here.'

Josephine sat in the living room with her future in-laws. She had made a dress for Mrs Dennis who paraded around the room in it, smoothing down the skirt and feeling pleased with the results.

'What is wrong Josephine?' Wilfred Dennis could see concern in her eyes. 'You should be happy that you can work such wonders on my wife's figure.'

'Wilfred! Can't you see the girl is upset?' Aggie Dennis sat next to Josephine and put a hand on her lap. 'What is it dear? You missing James?'

'Yes I miss him. But I hate to be reminded by everyone I meet that I am in trouble.'

'Nonsense child. You are not in any trouble. My son is going to marry you. He will make you honest in the eyes of the Lord. All you need to do is relax, go about your business and look after that baby.' She patted Josephine's stomach. 'You'll see. Next week those trouble makers will be talking about something new and they won't even remember what they said the week before.'

It was approximately four months and three weeks after his departure that James returned. It was a wet, windy morning when he arrived, carrying a large suitcase and wearing a very tasteful suit. That morning, Josephine stood with Rose and Eunice in the kitchen. The girls were cleaning up after breakfast and Rose was cooking lunch to take to a sick neighbour later that day.

'Well, well, well.' Eunice, who had spotted James from the window, left her chores and rushed into the yard. Josephine looked out of the window and saw him. James stood, smiling. He carried a small bunch of his mother's bougainvillea. Josephine stepped out slowly into the yard. She couldn't believe he was there. He wasn't expected for another three weeks but there he was, as large as life, pushing Eunice aside as he rushed to hug Josephine.

'You come back early James.' Josephine was overcome with relief and happiness. She didn't know whether to laugh or cry.

'I know. The job finish quick and I wanted to surprise you. I miss you so much Josephine. I couldn't wait to come back home.' He put his hand on Josephine's stomach and smiled. He handed her the flowers. 'I have so many things to tell you.'

'Eunice – come back to your work. These two need to talk.' Rose gave her daughter a stern look and Eunice reluctantly returned to the kitchen with her mother, but not without a parting comment.

'James I thought you had abandoned my sister. I was going to come and fetch you back.'

'I hope you didn't worry, Josephine.' James was more serious now.

'No. I trusted you. I knew you would never let me down.'

The day of the wedding was drizzly and overcast. Josephine had had to let her dress out and, in fact, add extra material, much to Eunice's delight. Rose said it was good luck to have rain on your wedding day and not to worry about getting a little wet on the way to church. Everyone from the neighbouring villages had gathered along the road leading to the church to see the procession. The bells rang loud and clear. Josephine shed a tear during the service when the priest pronounced them husband and wife and she felt a strong kick from the baby inside her. She was now a married woman and soon to become a mother. She felt a deep joy.

The weeks went by. Josephine sat at her new sewing machine as her stomach grew bigger and bigger. James, who had managed to find a labouring job, came home every evening, kissed his wife and asked about the baby.

'Your son is fine.' Josephine said

'My son? How you know is a boy? You dream it?' James was excited.

'No just a feeling me and Eunice have.'

'Eunice? Why you have that troublesome girl in here filling your head all day?'

'She is good company for me when you not here. She chats and makes the work seem easier.'

'Well she should be working herself, and not wasting her time all day. Even your mother fed up with her hanging around. Nothing good will come of that girl.'

'James, don't say that. Eunice is my sister. Is me who have to watch out for her.'

'No Josephine, you need to watch her.'

'James, Eunice is not as bad as everyone think. I know she like to argue with Mama and Mama fed up with her but she is good at heart.'

'Don't pay any attention to that girl,' James said. 'She's always here there and everywhere and never wants to settle down. I'm not sure I want her around here anyway. She's noisy and silly all the time. You should be taking it easy.'

'How can I take it easy when there is so much to do? I still have some sewing work to finish before the baby come and Eunice helps me around the house, even if she is silly and noisy. She'll be here again tomorrow when I go and deliver some dresses to Catherine.'

'She should come here or you should send Eunice to take the dresses.'

'No, Catherine can't leave her father, he's too sick and I might have to do a last fitting, so Eunice can't go. I can manage, I'm not sick, I just get a bit tired at times.'

The next day, Josephine had taken the road to Catherine's house and left Eunice making a good job of cleaning the yard. Josephine had been gone all morning. Catherine was a great talker and insisted that Josephine stay for lunch.

'A woman in your condition must eat well and you need to take a good rest before you climb back up that hill home.' Catherine's sick father reiterated this command and Josephine, knowing this was her last sewing job for a while, decided to accept the invitation.

As the afternoon wore on, Catherine's chatter filled the small living room with enough joy and excitement to make Josephine forget the time. She thought that Eunice would be wondering where she was and ought to be getting back soon. Her feet were quite swollen and she was exhausted.

As she made her way back up the road she saw that the children were already on their way home from school. She had been gone far longer than planned and she might well meet Eunice heading home.

The children on the road laughed and joked, a couple of the boys were kicking a ball from one to the other. They hadn't noticed Josephine. The taller of the boys kicked the ball so hard it blasted full force into Josephine's stomach. She stumbled backwards and let out a cry as she held her middle with both hands. Two of the school girls rushed to Josephine's aid and made her sit on a low branch of a tree until she got her breath back. An old woman called Frances Petrie called from her front garden.

'Be careful, or your baby will come too early.'

'It's okay. I feeling better now.' Josephine was still a little out of breath. The children had formed a semi-circle around her.

'Mrs Dennis, you want me to go fetch your mother?' One of the girls asked.

'No, no. I'll be fine. I'll get up just now. You children better get home.' They walked away slowly and very slowly Josephine got up to leave. Frances Petrie watched as she took the road home again.

Josephine approached her little house and as she did she found Eunice leaving the yard and rushing to meet her. If her eyes weren't playing tricks on her, Josephine could swear she saw someone hovering in the backyard near the small kitchen and toilet outhouses. The figure stumbled through the thicket behind the toilet, she thought, but couldn't be sure because Eunice stood, blocking her view, her hands on Josephine's shoulders. As Eunice was about to kiss her sister on the cheek, Josephine felt convinced she hadn't imagined what she'd seen.

'Eunice, who was that man?'

'Which man?' She appeared indifferent but looked Josephine straight in the eye.

'The man I just saw running away up there.' Josephine looked at her sister with dismay. 'Oh Eunice, don't tell me you bringing your boyfriend here when I'm not home.'

'I don't have no boyfriend and if I did he would be a rich man with his own house and I would go and visit him there, not bring him to your little shack.' She slowly lowered her arms from her sister's shoulders saying, 'I'm going home. You leave me here all day working by myself, you don't ask how I am, you just stand there accusing me of seeing men.'

'If you have a boyfriend, Eunice, you can tell me.'

'I don't,' she shouted very loudly in Josephine's face, then stormed off home. Josephine watched her leaving with arms folded over her chest, much as she had done as a young girl, after a tantrum. Josephine wanted to call after her but thought better of it. Eunice would only shout again. Josephine couldn't understand why her sister always felt the need to lie to her.

Rose came the next day to see Josephine. She had heard about the blow she'd gotten to her stomach and was worried.

'You feeling any pain?' she asked her daughter.

'No Mam, I'm fine. I've been resting all day today so nothing to worry about.' Josephine was more worried about Eunice and wondered if she should tell Rose what she'd seen the day before. But if Rose confronted Eunice, she thought, another of their heated rows would start up. Josephine ran the risk of losing any trust Eunice had in her and she would probably never speak to Josephine again, so she said nothing.

In the early hours of a Sunday morning that saw the end of the storms for that year, and before the sun had time to rise, Josephine pulled hard at her husband's arm and with a tightness in her voice, whispered, 'Go and call the nurse and get Mama. The baby is coming.' Without a second thought, and without even stopping to ask his wife if she was all right, James jumped out of bed, pulled on his clothes and dashed out of the house. He ran to call Nurse Celia and then to fetch his mother-in-law.

Hours had gone by as James paced around the yard hearing

the heavy sighs and moans of pain from the bedroom. Surely it couldn't be long now? By early evening, James and Josephine had the son they'd both been praying for. He was a beautiful little baby, still and calm, waking only with a soft cry whenever he needed to feed.

On the second night of his little life the calm was about to leave the small house. Josephine put her baby boy into the cot beside her bed after a feed. He slept soundly and breathed easily. As she got into bed, Josephine felt a sharp pain in her back, between her shoulder blades and tried to wriggle into a comfortable position. No matter what she tried, she could not settle. Without warning or reason, she felt emotional and tearful, as though something very wrong was about to happen, but she couldn't tell what and couldn't explain her feeling of doom. Minutes had gone by and, although she was very tired, she could not get to sleep.

It was ridiculous. Instead of tossing and turning and probably disturbing James, who had to be up very early, Josephine got up. She placed a wooden chair next to the baby's cot and thought she would just sit and watch him for a while. A sudden jolt like an electric shock seized her back and shoulders and she convulsed uncontrollably, falling and smashing her hip against the dresser. She gave a loud, impulsive wail. Her bottles and jars fell from the dresser on to the floor with a crash and the baby woke up crying.

James woke suddenly from a dream. In a state of confusion he saw his wife, having what looked like a fit, on the floor. He peered very quickly into the cot, saw his son was not in danger, then tried to pick Josephine up. Her eyes rolled backward and it was quite clear that she could not respond or be aware of anything going on around her. James' cries of 'Josephine, please stop, what's happened, what shall I do?' were lost to her. Another peek into the cot and James ran from the house. He ran straight to his mother's house and shook her awake.

'Josephine, it's Josephine, Mam, help me! I don't know what to do.'

'What, where is she?' His mother was disoriented and was being pulled from her bed by James who was rambling about Josephine without making any sense. She could feel his terror and feared the worst.

'What about the baby, the baby all right?' His father was getting up now, too.

'Yes, he's fine. But hurry, I need to get the nurse here.'

The three ran out into the darkness: three very different silhouettes trailing, one after the other, along the path to James' house. They made no sound, their feet hardly touching the cold ground, neither knowing what to expect as they opened the door to the wooden house.

There lay Josephine, breathing heavily and seeming not to recognise any of them. The baby had stopped crying now but started again with a sudden piercing sob as his mother flung herself onto the floor in another fit. Ma Dennis reached for the baby and the two men tried to grab hold of Josephine who seemed to be stronger than both of them as she battled against their grip.

'Go call the nurse,' Ma Dennis called, 'I have seen this before. She will be alright.' But before James could rush away to fetch the nurse, Josephine's fit subsided. Calm was restored as easily as it had left.

Their baby dozed. Ma Dennis, who had rocked him back to sleep, placed him softly in his cot. Josephine lay on the bed, James sat close by and looked on as she closed her eyes and drifted off to sleep. Josephine and her baby appeared to be enjoying the same dream. She looked serene. Her son seemed to have a slight smile on his face.

9

The screen on his laptop has gone black. He's fallen asleep. I'm sure he's got a thousand pictures he could show me of Phoebe. His wife is an attractive woman. I wonder what she does? He dotes on his family. I think that's adorable but I can't help feeling that there is more to this man than meets the eye.

My immediate family at one time was Eva and Jasmin. I hardly saw much of my brothers and sisters in the early days of Angel's opening. Of course we all move on with our lives. I did, I couldn't expect them not to. Maddy and her partner Derek had bought a big house in Surrey. They both made a lot of money and it was only a question of time before they upgraded: a walk-in wardrobe for her, cars and photography for him, any new gadget on the market. My youngest brother, James, was making a success as a writer and had moved out of London as well.

I bought my first flat after Jasmin announced that she was engaged to her rich, managing director boyfriend, Steven. The flat was a little run down but it was all I could afford on my own. It would take time to do up but I had time. The business was doing well and everything was running smoothly. That is until the day Jasmin burst into the office with a big announcement.

'I can't do it,' she said. I had just answered a call to a woman who wanted to throw a dinner party to celebrate her divorce.

'Can't do what?' I asked.

'I can't marry Steven. I know you're going to think I'm crazy but I just don't see how things are going to work out with him.'

'What has he done? I don't get it, Jas, everything is arranged. You're just getting cold feet, that's all.'

'No, it's not that. It's just all wrong.'

'Jasmin, come and sit down, we'll talk about it.'

'I can't.' And with that, she left without another word.

That night Steven called me about fifty times. Jasmin hadn't come home. She wasn't with me so there was only one other place she could be. I arranged a sitter for Eva and rushed round to Angel's.

Jasmin sat in the dark at one of the tables. I lit a candle. I could see she'd been crying.

'Steven has been calling. I didn't know what to say to him.'

'I thought he might. Sorry Ange.'

I said nothing but sat and waited. I was the only person Jasmin had to confide in.

'It's all over between us Ange, I can't marry Steven.'

'But what has he done? I just don't get it. I thought everything was perfect between you two.'

'The only thing that has ever made sense in my life so far has been you and me Ange. This business just gets better and better and that's mostly because we know how to get on. We know each other so well. I've never been able to find that in any other relationship I've had with anyone.'

'Up until now. Steven is the *one*, you know he is.'

'He's more than I deserve.' She got up and stood looking out onto the quiet street. 'Steven got all secretive a few weeks back. Hanging up the phone suddenly when I walked in. He was away overnight and said it was for work. I knew that was a lie.'

'So what did he say when you confronted him?'

'That's just it. I didn't. Didn't even say anything to you. Like a fool I thought I'd do something to show him I wasn't sitting around, waiting to get hurt or dumped.' When she came back to the table there were tears in her eyes.

'I slept with someone.' She lowered her head.

'What? But who?' I sat back in disbelief.

'It doesn't matter *who*.'

'But how? What possessed you? What, were you drunk or

something?' I still couldn't believe what I was hearing.

'Well, a bit tipsy I suppose. But I knew what I was doing.' Jasmin took a deep breath. 'It was Gabriel. Yes, delivery boy Gabriel. We were his last delivery and you had gone home early. I think it was the day Eva had a temperature. Anyway, we started laughing and joking around like we always do. He didn't have to get back anywhere and popped next door for some wine. Before I knew it, we were on the second bottle. I was nervous about the wedding and just freaking out about the whole situation. I was doubting Steven like you wouldn't believe. I was sure he was up to something. I didn't know with who and I didn't want to know either. I just had it in my head that I wanted to be the one who bailed out first. I convinced myself I was right. Then, stupidly, I got all flirty with Gabriel. I thought I could play Steven at his own game. Of course, Gabriel couldn't resist this tipsy woman throwing herself at him. And then it happened.'

'In here?'

'Yes. It lasted about twenty seconds. We were in the corridor, me against the shelves and him like a schoolboy on speed.'

'Jasmin. I really don't know what to say.' I was genuinely struggling.

'And you think *I* do? And it gets worse Ange. See, that was the night Steven came home and explained why he was being so secretive. He'd gone off to Paris with a personal shopper and bought me a load of designer clothes to take on this amazing honeymoon he wanted to surprise me with. He was all happy and wanting to hug me and I was so ashamed of myself I didn't even want him to touch me. We haven't had sex in ages. I've been really distant since this – *thing*. And the poor guy thinks it's because I don't like my present. What have I done Ange?'

'Please don't say you're pregnant Jas.'

'No, thank goodness. That would finish him off completely, as though this wasn't enough. When he finds out … .'

'A twenty second shag is not enough to ruin something that has the potential to be a lifetime of happiness.'

'Did Confucius say that?' We both started laughing, forgetting for a moment that the problem had not gone away just because Jasmin was finally able to tell me what she'd been hiding.

'So you think I should lie to Steven?'

I must admit, that was my first thought. Jasmin could just brush it under the carpet, say she was in a panic about the wedding and that everything was fine now. She'd taken a time out and had come to her senses. But my heart couldn't lie.

'Honestly Jas, if I'd done what you'd done to someone who loves me the way Steven loves you – I think I might have to tell him and live with the consequences.'

I thought about how I'd been lied to in the past. Lies were the reason my heart had been broken on more than one occasion, but after every episode of heartbreak and bewilderment, I was always glad that I got to the truth. But I couldn't escape the fact that Steven would be devastated.

'Ange, I'm going crazy here. I don't know what I'm going to do.' I got up to hug my friend.

'What would you expect from Steven?' I asked her, quietly.

'Well, that he kept his trousers on around other women for a start. I don't expect him to forgive me for this. And I couldn't blame him. But I know I would hate to be lied to. I don't have any choice do I? I have to tell him.' She dried her tears with a napkin.

Jasmin and Steven disappeared for several days. I was managing the business alone. My childminder, Cassie, was kind enough to have Eva earlier in the morning and I needed a part timer for the mornings and lunch session. Jasmin and Steven never answered their telephone and I was receiving calls from the florist and the caterer and the hall for the reception. They needed to confirm arrangements, not to mention final payments. I made up a story about there being a family crisis and the couple had to be away and would be in touch as soon as they could. I said that the wedding was still going ahead.

They finally showed up five days later at my flat, with champagne. I couldn't hide my relief or the joy I had as I watched them at the wedding reception, dancing as if no one else was in the room.

'Don't they look great together?' Jasmin's sister sat down next to me with an empty champagne glass in one hand and a half full bottle of champagne in the other. She filled both of our glasses. 'What will you do without your partner in crime?'

'She only got married, she's not moving to another continent.' I sipped a little champagne, any more and the room would start to spin.

'I know, but it won't be the same will it?'

'No, it won't be the same. But just look at how happy Jasmin is.'

'Yes I know. And that'll be you one day, Ange. Trust me'

10

Josephine's son was now a year old. She busied herself with her sewing orders and making her home more comfortable. Even when the orders were few, she didn't complain, she made do the best she could. Eunice continued to help with the cooking and cleaning, watching the baby while Josephine worked.

There was a new talking point in the little village. Josephine tried not to concern herself with the gossips, who would form small huddles about the market place, analysing in great detail the demise of one of their neighbours, the person who got drunk the day before, the child who had turned bad or the woman who had worn the same dress to church for the last fifteen years.

This latest topic of discussion, however, was a lot less widespread than usual. It could not be overheard at market or outside the church as the congregation spilled out after the two-hour-long service. It spread, quite discreetly, from one person to the next, each time with the solemn oath that the news should not pass the lips of the recipient.

Quite by chance Josephine was to overhear this latest scandal as she stood, one morning, waiting for the bus to the capital. The capital, or 'Town,' as the locals called it, was the only place on the island that Josephine could buy the special trimmings she needed for her best clients. She never ventured into the capital often. It was very different from her town, where she always knew what to expect. She knew every face, the family the face was attached to, every member of that family, including age, occupation and number of grandchildren. The capital, on the other hand, had a habit of changing each time she went there. Some of the larger stores stayed the same but ownership of the smaller shops would change quite frequently. The smaller retailers who found it difficult to compete might find themselves back in the small village or countryside from where they'd ventured in the hope of making a name for themselves in Town.

Several people had told Josephine that given the quality of her clothes, she could do well for herself if she bought a shop in Town. She was never tempted; she preferred the familiarity of her surroundings and being close to her mother.

Josephine stood at the bus stop to Town, on the corner of the road and next to a big old silk cotton tree. She leant against one side of the tree, fanning herself. Two women arrived at the other side of the tree. They stood and waited for the bus and didn't notice Josephine. One leant against the thick bark, the other stood facing the road, holding an empty basket.

'They say it was only a matter of time before she get catch. She been running around chasing men since she was out of socks.'

One of the women was talking in a stage whisper and breathing heavily between sentences. Josephine recognised their voices but didn't say a word. She didn't want to be included in the conversation and was put out by the fact that these women had interrupted her tranquillity. Very soon a man approached. He nodded to Josephine but positioned himself nearer to the two women, who ignored him and continued with the ins and outs of this tale.

'Her mother must be ashamed to think that her own daughter could go and get rid of a child like that. Just destroy it like it was nothing. Only God have the power to take life and people should count themselves blessed if He grant them a child.' The first woman continued, apparently taking pleasure in relaying this story. 'I know if it was me, I would beat my daughter and I wouldn't let her out of the house for the same thing to happen again.'

'But how you know is true?' The second woman responded. 'You know how people like to chat and chat your business and add so much extra to it you can end up in jail for something you

87

never do.' The man nodded in agreement, his eyes darting from the women and back to Josephine who was evidently not following the discussion.

'I know is true because Laney work in the Medical Centre and she sure the problem the girl have come from trying to destroy a child. She bleed and bleed so much they had to call a doctor to make sure she wouldn't die.' Here the first woman took a deep sigh. 'I tell you, her mother is a saint. Is not many people know about this so you just keep it to yourself.'

The arrival of the bus ended the conversation. For the first time the women had been made aware of a fourth pair of ears being privy to their conversation. Josephine nodded out of politeness to the two women and let them onto the bus first.

'Oh, Josephine. You going to Town? How is the family?' To Josephine's amusement, one of the women spluttered these niceties. Surely she wasn't embarrassed about being caught gossiping?

'Oh, they all fine, and you?' Josephine replied.

'Yes, yes, I'm fine.'

Josephine took a seat on the opposite side of the bus from the women, a little further back. The gossipers did not utter a single word on the journey.

Josephine clung to the metal headrest in front of her for dear life immediately the doors were closed. The bus driver always rushed the bus to the capital as though there was an important deadline to meet or a record he had to break. He sped straight past a little woman in a straw hat, who held her hat down with one hand. She raised an angry little fist at the driver who had not spotted her waiting by the bridge at St Michel, just before the bus terminal.

The capital was a haphazard, loud and busy place by day. It was one of the few places in the island where colonial influence had left its mark. Large houses in the French style were scattered around the central market square. They were weatherbeaten and run down. Most of them were used commercially, with a shop space at ground level and living quarters above. In some parts of the capital, where the streets formed the more orderly rows planned and constructed under British rule, there were smaller shops and houses with no order as to the occupancy of each building: here a rum shop, there a bakery, next a house and then a person who made and sold straw bags. The capital was a mixture of small-scale buildings made of Victorian wood alongside stone town houses with large verandas. On several of the verandas it would not be unusual to find an old man or woman just watching and waiting to see what else would be crammed into the area.

Josephine completed her shopping quickly and made her way back to the bus terminal. The new buses were a far cry from the large trucks that Josephine had been used to as a young girl, when she had had to stand for the whole journey. The new buses, which were all second-hand from abroad, were a godsend for all the islanders. She took her seat, happy with her purchase and feeling excited. She got off the bus before reaching her village so that she could stop at her mother's house for a quick chat before heading home. She wanted her mother to be the first to hear that she was pregnant again.

'*True*?' Rose said to her daughter with the broadest of grins. 'And what James say?'

'Well you are the first to know, I'll tell him tonight and I'll tell Eunice when I get home.' Josephine could see her mother was happy with the news. So happy, in fact, she began to cry.

'Oh Mam, why are you crying? You not happy for me?'

'Yes I'm happy. I was just thinking about Eunice.'

'Why?'

'I just wish she could be more like you.' With that Rose held her daughter in a rare embrace. As strong as the love was between them, it was seldom shown physically and Josephine relished the moment.

This second baby, which Josephine suspected was a girl, was very lively and wanted to make her presence felt. She kicked and rolled about and was in a hurry to escape the all too small confines of Josephine's womb. She entered the world on the afternoon of a blustery, rainy day at her grandmother's house a good week earlier than expected.

Josephine had refused lunch that day, saying she felt sick and would only stay long enough to plait her mother's hair before heading home for a rest. As she stood to leave, Josephine sipped the last drops of a glass of cold tea. Her waters broke. The glass fell to the floor and smashed into three pieces.

'Josephine, it don't look like you going home yet. Change into something comfortable.'

Neither Rose nor her daughter panicked. Josephine, who was gripped by a pain in her lower back, sank to the floor in agony.

'Come, let us walk around.' Rose helped Josephine stand and, with her hand on her back, led her daughter up and down the room. She moved about in this way for a long time, stopping only to pant and hold her mother's hand when the pain was unbearable.

'Sis! What you have?' Josephine's younger brother arrived home with Eunice.

'What she have? What you think she have? She making her baby,' Eunice exclaimed with her fists on her hips. 'Go away, this is women's work. You go and find James if you want something to do.' She ushered her brother away and closed the door.

A few hours later, Josephine knelt on all fours next to Rose's couch and pushed out the impatient baby, who left no time for her mother to make her way to Rose's bedroom. Josephine had her little girl. Eunice opened the front door to address James and the small crowd who had gathered in the yard.

'James you have a girl.' The crowd congratulated him.

Josephine kissed her daughter's tiny forehead saying, 'I want the next one to be a boy.'

'Don't be in such a rush.' Rose was beaming at her beautiful new granddaughter.

In what seemed like no time at all, Josephine was pregnant for a third time. And, just as she wished, she had her little boy. The older two children played at Grandma Dennis' house on the afternoon that their new brother was born. This new child was also impatient to arrive. By Josephine's calculations he should not have been born for another three weeks. His delivery was more of a problem for Josephine than the previous one. Rose sent James to get the midwife to help her as she had an uncomfortable feeling, but said nothing to her daughter. Eunice looked on and held her sister's hand, leaving her side only to wet a cloth to place on Josephine's head.

Finally the baby arrived, one last push, a slap by the midwife but not a sound from this tiny little boy. He had a thick patch of jet-black hair on the very top of his head. He hadn't opened his eyes and his breath was very shallow.

'Mama?' Josephine looked up at her mother as she held his tiny form close to her breast. 'Why he doesn't feed? And why he doesn't cry? You think he will be alright?'

At first Rose said nothing. She leant in close to her grandson and daughter. His eyes seemed to flutter under the closed lids. His skin was thin and fair and he was just too small for her liking.

'It's alright Josephine. My first was just the same. Just quiet like that. No fuss, no crying for a good few days and just like that, he pick up. You see how big and how loud your brother became?'

'Just keep him warm, Josephine.' The midwife was smiling encouragingly. 'Keep trying to feed him. I'll be back in a couple days. And congratulations darling, he's beautiful.'

Josephine sighed, hugged her new baby boy and fell asleep with him still in her arms.

The next morning Josephine had a few callers to see the new addition to the family but didn't keep him on display for long, asking as politely as she could that they let her and the baby have some rest. When the last visitors left, she placed him in his crib and watched over him a while. He slept so soundly. Josephine leant toward him to give him another kiss and draw his cover a little closer. She suddenly dropped to her knees and placed a hand to her mouth. Her chest rose and fell as she drew long, strained breaths for air. With a pained expression on her face, she turned to look at her husband. James rose from the creaky chair in the bedroom. Their other two children sat playing, quite peacefully, just outside the bedroom door. James pushed the bedroom door to and slowly walked back toward the small crib. As he got close, Josephine wrapped her arms around his legs.

'My God in heaven, our baby is dead!' The only words she was able to utter for the next hour. She released James and sank closer to the floor.

James pulled back the little white cover and saw no movement from his baby's chest. He leaned forward, turned his head to one side and placed it very close the baby's nose. The two little ones sensed that something was wrong and the oldest pushed the bedroom door open. The children saw their mother lying as still as a statue at the foot of the bed. James tried to shake her, as though back to consciousness, but she was completely limp. He stumbled around the room before grabbing the children and carrying them both to his mother's house.

Ma Dennis took one look at her son's face as he put the children on their grandfather's lap.

'Josephine or the baby?' She asked.

'The baby. Mind them, I have to fetch the doctor.'

In no time at all, the little wooden house was filled with people again. Crying and offering their condolences. Rose and Eunice ushered everyone away when they arrived.

'Come on all you. Move from here!' Eunice bellowed. 'The doctor is on the road. Get out. Make space. I say move from here.'

James led the doctor to the bedroom where a wailing Josephine covered the crib with her body and refused to move. Rose held firmly to her daughter's arms and led her to the front room.

'Come darling. Come and sit with me and Eunice.'

The three women waited silently in the living room of the

tiny house until the doctor came out of the bedroom with James, who closed the door behind him. Before the doctor spoke, Josephine looked at James.

'We did not give him a name.'

11

'Ah this one is of our last holiday together. Cyprus.' His wife is bronzed and happy. They are a nice looking family. And there's Phoebe. About four years old I would imagine.

'It's been a long time since your last holiday together then?' I have to ask.

'Yes, I suppose it has.'

'It's a shame they couldn't come with you this time. But then the start of the school year wasn't so long ago. I know Eva's school was always strict about holidays in term time. I guess it would be hard for you to swing that, wouldn't it?'

'Extremely.'

I'm smiling. Not at what he's just said. It's just that I'm remembering Eva's first day at school.

I was in a panic that morning, worried senseless and so sure that she was too young. A two-and-a-half hour morning session in Nursery Class – that was all. But all the same, I'd made a big deal of it in my head. But Eva had been looking forward to it. We held hands. She fidgeted and jumped about and I scoured the playground for bullies. I wasn't sure the climbing frame looked stable enough.

'Good morning children!' An official sounding voice shook me from my reverie. Before I knew it, the teacher and her assistant had whisked the children into their new class and had them sitting on a rug in a circle. We lost parents hovered for a few moments before dispersing off to wherever lost parents go for two and a half hours.

'I think your wife is very attractive.' Another picture of his wife and Phoebe. 'What does she do?'

'She was a lawyer. Gave it all up when Phoebe was born. I was surprised. She's the real ambitious type, my wife. She didn't want children to begin with. Mind you, she never even wanted *me*. Went to great lengths to try and get her to come on a date. She worked in the same building, one of the Law firms two floors up. I made sure I was in the lift with her every morning, which meant a lot of hanging around, talking to Security until eight twenty-five. That's when she arrived. Always. On the dot. I think she just felt sorry for me in the end. I'd ride up to her floor and then take the stairs back down to mine. Sad eh?'

'No, I don't think it's sad. We do what we have to do for love.'

'You're a romantic like me then. I see by your ring finger you're married. What does your husband do?'

'Luke? Luke is a chef. I was sort of his boss really.'

Luke was the chef we hired just before Eva started school. I'd decided to reduce my hours so that I could be the one who picked her up and dropped her off. I wanted to be more involved. It wasn't right that I was getting all the news about Eva second hand from her childminder.

The day Luke arrived for his interview, Jasmin pinched my leg under the table. I tried to keep a straight face. He was a good looking man. His hair was dark, collar length, his skin olive-coloured, his eyes green. Of course that's not why we hired him. He was the best person for the job. Luke turned out to be a kind and intelligent man. I came to regard him as a friend and he was certainly a brilliant asset to Angel's.

I had taken a vow of celibacy after yet another relationship had failed, and would never have considered any romantic possibilities with Luke. But after I'd worked with him for a year I realised I knew very little about his private life. I wondered if I brought up the subject of relationships, he might tell me if he was dating or not. He never mentioned a partner. On one particular

95

day I decided to dig a little deeper.

'I was on the phone to yet another girlfriend who's had her heart broken by some loser.' I said. 'You know the type. So much emotional baggage, he'd need a warehouse to store it all in. Stringing her along, no chance of any real commitment. I hate that. Don't you?' We were in the kitchen. I looked up from a recipe book to see his reaction. He was chopping vegetables so didn't look at me.

'It's not good,' he said. 'But we're not all like that you know. Some of us are good guys. Anyway, I thought you women didn't go for good guys.'

'That's not true. Not for the ones with any sense, that is. So, have you been hurt by someone because she wasn't into "good guys" ?'

'You could say that. Yeah.' He scraped the vegetables into a casserole dish and looked up. 'More times than I'd like to admit. That's why I'm giving dating a wide berth.'

'So, not in the business of looking for a Miss Right?'

'Think I'd settle for a Miss Right Now.' He covered the dish and went to wash up.

'Know the feeling.' I ventured. 'I'm through with relationships for good. Safer to stay single. That way we won't get our hearts broken, eh Luke?'

Luke's Miss Right Now came in the form of Rebecca. Rebecca was our website designer. After setting up the site, she came back a few times to train me and Jasmin. Once we were up and running she would come in every now and again, claiming she was in the area. Her routine included waltzing into the café, standing at the counter to greet Jas or me and then peering through the hatch to see if Luke was in. She'd make her way to the office for some reason or other and always found an excuse to go into the kitchen. It didn't take long to hook Luke. Her tactics involved having a great figure, a good sense of humour, good teeth and long blonde hair. I hated her for every second of the three-week fling they had.

The plane seems to dip and I'm aware of the engines humming again.

'I couldn't imagine working with my wife. Especially if she was my boss.' My companion is shaking his head.

'Really? Have you on your toes the whole time would she?'

'Something like that. But it works for some people.'

Luke and I made a great team in the kitchen and out at events. If I'd missed anything, he'd thought of it and had it covered. We had grown closer during the time Jasmin had her first baby and took maternity leave. Jasmin said we were like an old married couple. And even while Luke was with Rebecca, I couldn't help wishing that there might be that possibility one day. Maybe it was because he was going out with Rebecca that I started seeing Luke in a different light. And, if I wasn't fooling myself, it often felt as if Luke was feeling the same way about me.

Weeks after their fling, Luke and I played games: having leading conversations that tended to lead nowhere, touching each other by accident for longer than was necessary, gazing at the other but turning away after being discovered.

'For God's sake Angelica!' Jasmin was in the office, her new baby asleep in his basket.

'What?'

'You and Luke. Will you please just get in that kitchen and tell that man how you feel.' She gestured with her hands to show her frustration.

'You *know*?' I was surprised.

'Do I *know*? The staff know. The customers know. You both *know*, so just get on with it.'

I marched back to the kitchen. It wasn't awkward, I didn't have to be brave. I tapped Luke on the shoulder to get his attention. His response was to wrap a floury hug around me and return my kiss. We stopped when we heard applause coming from the other side of the hatch. Jasmin and our waitress beamed at us on the afternoon that changed everything.

It feels like time to get up and stretch my legs again. We've had the 'Wedding' folder, the 'Holidays 2002' folder, the 'Christmas 2000' folder and folders whose names I can't even remember. Surely there is a limit to this man's hard drive? Somehow I get the feeling he won't stop showing me photos unless I say something.

'Not bored yet?'

Is he reading my mind?

'Perhaps a little break for now.' I smile and he takes it well.

'I'll just look for one more folder of Phoebe for later and I promise to leave it at that.'

He dotes on that little girl. I won't spoil the surprise of the teenage years. He's got all that to come.

It all started with a present. Eva was given an acoustic guitar by her Uncle James when she was about eleven years old. James had bought it on a whim and never learned how to play. Eva was the only musical one in the family so he thought she'd appreciate it. Eva had had ballet classes, piano classes and was attending a drama club on Saturdays. After getting that guitar, though, Eva convinced herself and us that one day she was going to be famous. She spent hours playing scales, devouring the lessons in her guitar book and was eventually writing her own songs. But her school work suffered. Our house became a battlefield, and Luke the negotiator.

'Ange, you shouldn't let yourself get so worked up about Eva. She likes to wind you up to get a reaction,' he said one day.

'She's driving me crazy. I would never have spoken to my mum the way Eva speaks to me.'

'I know. It's like she's thirteen going on thirty. But still – don't get so stressed. Lighten up on her a bit and she might stop snapping so much. I don't know. Ask how her day has been, don't talk about the homework as soon as you come home.'

'Luke, what am I supposed to do when I've got teachers calling me every two minutes asking why Eva hasn't read this or written about that? I have to show her I mean business.

Homework is important.'

'Eva is a smart girl. She could demolish her homework in no time. You know that.'

'So what's her problem?'

'Well from where I'm sitting, I'd say she just wants you to pay more attention to her music. I know the school stuff is important. I know how you feel about her education. Trust me, I feel the same. But music is a big part of her. It's been a while since we all just sat and listened to her.'

'You mean, *I* haven't sat and listened in while.' Luke's point was filtering through.

'Ange, your job is stressful enough as it is and you don't need all that teenage angst when you come home every night. Maybe we should try another approach with her.'

'You think so?'

'I know so. Eva's just after your attention. If you get more involved with the things she loves, she'll be happy. We tell her that she can only get to do the things she loves when homework and chores are out of the way.'

'That's brilliant. No grey areas.'

'And we make time to listen to her music more.'

'You mean, I do.' Luke just smiled. 'Okay, it's a plan. How did you get be so sensible Luke?'

'How come you never noticed?' He hugged me.

'Too busy noticing the wrong things. But that all changes, starting now. We're going to Joey's for ice cream and not once will I bring up healthy options or spots.'

I look up and see they're serving our last meal – a light snack before landing. I think he's found that 'Phoebe' folder and can't wait to show me. He is a nice man. A family man. Like Luke.

In another three hours we part company. In another six, I'll be there.

12

Nothing inside Josephine's house moved. Her business was at a standstill. Her hair was never combed. She never changed out of her house clothes. She never cooked. Rose came every day to cook and clean and Eunice looked after the children and the yard. James left for work each day as normal.

In the yard Eunice would sweep and clear weeds to the sound of birdsong, her bare arms caressed by the balmy warmth. Above her was a deep blue sky, tinged only by the occasional hint of white clouds that floated by carelessly in the gentle breeze. She would hear the idle chatter of passers-by and smell the fragrance of the brightly coloured flowers from the roadside. But each time she set foot inside the house, she would shiver from the coolness within. The house wore a shroud. The curtains on the little windows were open but somehow the sunlight could not penetrate the gloom and despair.

Things continued like this for a whole month until one evening the sound of crickets grew louder for a brief moment as the front door opened and James arrived home announcing that he was going to England. Josephine sat at the table in the main room. To the back of the main room and separated by the long curtain that was now drawn, were her two children. They were fast asleep. Rose and Eunice were already on their feet, ready to leave for home. Eunice was the first to speak.

'What you mean, you going to England? You have a house there, you have a job, or a wife in England?'

'Eunice, be quiet, this is between a husband and his wife.' Rose was pulling on her shawl and picking up the laundry bundle she had gathered earlier. She hurried Eunice out of the house. The sound of crickets rose and fell as they left.

Josephine got up and walked to the bedroom.

'If you want to go, go,' she said. 'If that's what you saying – then fine. But I will not be going with you. I'm staying here to raise my children.' She was about to go into the bedroom when James rushed over and grabbed her wrist.

'No Josephine, you are not staying here by yourself. And the children are mine too. I'll find myself a job, I will find somewhere for us to live and I will send for all three of you as soon as I have the money.'

'Money doesn't grow on trees. I'm telling you now, if you leave this place and set foot in England you will never turn back for any of us. I know you won't.'

'Is that something you dream?' James was becoming increasingly agitated by her mood. 'If that is what you dream, why you never dream our son would die and do something about it. Instead, you carry on working, taking orders and parading around as though you are some high and mighty business woman?' The tears streamed down both of their faces. Josephine didn't move. James released his grip from her wrist.

'So you think that of me? That I parade around as though I were high and mighty?'

'Yes, that's exactly what you do. You are not the man of the house, I am. *I* should bring in the money and if you were resting here instead of working, the baby would have been stronger. He would have lived.'

'Well pardon me, Mr Dennis, but I didn't know that when you qualify as a carpenter they give you a doctor certificate too. My mother was by the river, bending and washing clothes, in the garden side-by-side with my father, growing food and carrying it home on her head when she was carrying each and every one of her children. We will never know why our little boy die, James. Only God knows why He take him. And if He take him it's for a good reason, so don't you dare point your finger on me.' She turned on her heel and slid effortlessly through the bedroom

101

door, closing it quickly and silently behind her, leaving a weeping James on the other side. He rested his head on the door.

'I miss my baby too. But I am the man of the house and I must find a way to give us a better life. I will have no work here soon and there is work in England. I have nearly enough to book my passage on a ship and someone to help me find a place to stay.' He straightened up and sniffed, wiping his nose on the back of his hand. 'Please, Josephine. Look after the children and the house while I do this. You'll see. I'm not running away. I'm running to something better. A better life for you, for me, for all of us.'

After a few minutes the door opened. Josephine looked tired.

'If you believe this is the right thing for us, I'll trust you,' she said. 'If you send for us I will come, but I will carry on working to feed my children in case you never send me any money.' Warm tears spilled onto her face while she spoke.

James stepped up to his wife and held her. His embrace was filled with the warmth and love that had been missing from their lives during that painful month. She fell against him, head against his chest, relieved to feel his arms around her again. They stood like this for a long time.

'You'll see, Josephine, everything will be fine.'

13

I've got that nervous, butterflies in the stomach feeling right now. It's putting me off my snack. Now that we're eating, he's saying less. I've got too much time to think and that lonely place I was in is waiting to suck me in again. It's not as though I was ever free of it but it's a relief when I don't have to think.

I'm just sliding food around my plate like a little child who doesn't want to eat their vegetables. He'll notice and he'll ask whether I'm enjoying it. I'll have to fix a grin on my face to answer. Think of something nice. A time when I got something right with Eva. There must be one memory that I can call on.

I could hear laughter coming from upstairs when I got in that day. It was Luke's afternoon off. I wanted to share the joke. I had always given them their space. Luke and Eva shared the same interest in films and sport so I was happy to opt out of cinema trips or watching television with them at times. I know I couldn't have joined them in a conversation about Chelsea's away match with Manchester United.

They were in Eva's bedroom. It was looking pretty neat for a thirteen year old. Luke was at her computer, Eva sat on the bed.

'What are you two up to?' I smiled at them both.

'Don't get mad Mum, you have to have an open mind about this.' Eva looked at Luke so that he could do the talking for them.

'It's not a biggie,' he said. 'Well perhaps not. Depends on how you see things I suppose.'

'Luke, don't talk in riddles. I'm tired.'

'Sorry babes. Eva and I were looking up some stuff on line.'

'Yes?'

'Well she'd heard about this stage school that takes kids from Year Nine onwards.'

'Are you fed up with your old stage school then Evie?' I was relieved that that was all it was. I thought there was some major catastrophe about to unleash itself.

'Well it's not that Mum. This one is full time. Not just Saturday mornings. I'd have to leave school if I wanted to start in September. That's if I got a place of course. You have to audition and everything.' She was sounding excited.

'I'm sure you'll get in Evie.' Luke said cheerfully.

'Hang on,' I said. 'So this is about you wanting to leave school? But you've got your options coming up and you're doing really well. Won't that mess things up?'

'But I want to be a singer-songwriter when I leave school, Mum. You always knew that.' Eva had the broadest grin on her face and Luke seemed to be encouraging her.

'Wait, wait. I need to take this in.' I said. Eva immediately frowned and crossed her arms over her chest.

'I *told* you she wouldn't let me go!' she blasted at Luke.

'Evie, stop.' Luke remained calm. 'We have to talk these things through. This is the first Mum has heard about it so we need to discuss it a bit more, have time to think. Okay? Mum hasn't said you can't go. So don't you start getting all grumpy and acting like a little kid.' Eva sat back and started twiddling her long black curls, tossed them backwards and stared at me for a response.

'So where is this school Eva?' I asked with as much calm as I could muster.

'Surrey.'

'*Surrey*?' I caught Luke's expression and composed myself. 'Surrey may be a little far to get to everyday, don't you think?'

'I was worried about that,' Luke said. 'The school is actually in Cheam. Not *that* far really. We did work out how Eva could get there but it's a very early start and she'd be coming home a lot later too. She'd have to be good about getting homework done because there's less time in the evening. So that would mean less television, less time on line and less chatting to friends on the phone.'

'So you guys have really thought it through. Guess that just leaves me.' I put my hands on my hips and paced, slowly, back to the door. I had to sum up how I felt about this idea right there and then. And make sure I got the answer right. I could feel their eyes boring into my back. It only took a short time but my mind was made up.

'I know you know what you want Eva and I believe in you. Let me look at the website for this school. Let's see what they have to offer and you can tell me what you're doing for your audition.'

Eva's eyes lit up. She couldn't believe I was going along with the idea. She leapt from the bed and threw her arms around my neck and we both almost fell backwards. I took in the scent of lavender conditioner from her hair. When did Eva get to be my height?

'Well, you stay with Aunty Del on some of the weekends we work. Maybe Aunty Maddy might help out too. She's very near Cheam. Maybe you could go there some Fridays, after school. Just a thought. I'll have to speak to her first. And of course there's your Uncle Derek to consider.' Eva rushed over to her computer and clicked *Enter*.

When she comes round with the tea and coffee, the flight attendant is smiling at me. A sort of 'that's better' smile. Thinking about Eva must have brightened the look on my face. I've managed to give the flight attendant one less thing to worry about. I wish it was as easy to sort myself out. I'm going to try and focus my thoughts on whether to go for tea or coffee with my biscuits. Nothing else.

'Once we've landed we can say goodbye to the good old British cup of tea. It'll be all rum punches and Caribbean beers. Love those.' He gives me a friendly wink.

'I thought you were on a business trip.' Maybe he's in hospitality. I never did ask.

'Oh I'll have time to relax once in a while. Don't worry, I'm not going to go mad.'

'I never found out what you do. You know what line of business I'm in, and I know your wife is an ex-lawyer. So?' I am genuinely interested.

'Nothing as glamorous as either of your jobs. I'm in sales.'

'And what do you sell?'

'Insurance.'

'*Insurance*?'

'Yes, I told you it wasn't glamorous.'

'I just wondered how selling insurance can have you on a business trip to the Caribbean.'

'You'd be surprised,' he says and then starts to reach for his case. I'm hoping it's not because he wants to sell me a policy. No, he gets out a book. He's reading. He's shutting me out. Just when I thought I could stay out of my head for a while.

When Eva is happy so am I. She had been at her new stage school for almost three years and it had been the making of her. The academic side was thriving, her musicality was blossoming and my relationship with her was the best it had been in ages. Eva stayed with her Aunty Maddy and Uncle Derek on occasional weekends when Luke and I both needed to go on catering jobs, especially events outside London. Maddy had a room specially decorated for her. She'd bought her new clothes and God knows what else. The amount she spent was way over the top and I had to put a stop to it.

One morning I watched Eva eating toast, with her head in a book. Thankfully I had the morning off after a particular late night. There had been a party. The host got drunk and a huge fight broke out. The police were called and none us from Angel's were allowed to leave until we gave statements, which took forever. I made myself a cup of peppermint tea and was going to crawl straight back into bed but decided, instead, to sit with Eva for a while. I noticed that she was twiddling a little pearl pendant that hung from a fine gold chain round her neck. I'd never seen it before.

'Where did you get that?' I asked her.

'What?' She was distracted. She was reading something for school.

'Your chain.'

'Oh, Derek gave it to me.' She let the pendant drop. I put my cup down.

'Why did Uncle Derek buy you that? It's not your birthday. I've already told Aunty Maddy that they've got to stop buying you all this stuff.'

'Well it was ages ago now. Actually when I think about it, it was Aunty Maddy who bought it. And that was way before you put the curfew on gifts for Eva. I don't know why. They're rolling in cash. No kids. Who else are they gonna spend all that money on?'

'Well there are Aunty Del and Uncle Marcus' children. What if they found out about it? They could be jealous.'

'Mum are you sure it's not you who's jealous?' Eva was trying to make light of it so that I wouldn't go on complaining.

'I'm going to have to talk to Maddy again.' I said.

'There's no need Mum. Like I say, this present is ages old. They must have bought it a good while ago and I've had nothing since then – as per your orders.' She made a salute and went back to her book. I grabbed an apple from the fruit bowl on the counter before going back up to bed. I looked at Eva, who kept her head down. It was a pretty necklace, the sort Maddy would wear.

He's still engrossed in his book. I put my headphones back on and look for some music to listen to. An old favourite of mine is playing. My eyes are closing. I'd like to sleep but I don't think my mind can.

I turn to see what he's doing now. His book is closed. He's restless too.

14

Days had gone by, then weeks. The weeks had turned into months. Almost too soon, Josephine was counting the length of time she'd been apart from her husband in years. It had been two very long years since James left for England. Josephine was convinced that the children would not remember their father's face because they had been so young when he left. The oldest was just four years old. Every time they asked Josephine, 'Where is Daddy,' she had to remind them that Daddy was working very hard in England.

Josephine remembered the day James left. He was wearing a brown suit. The overcoat he'd carried over his arm had belonged to someone who had taken the long journey to England, a year earlier, only to return shortly afterwards. He never said exactly why. Secretly, Josephine thought that if the overcoat had brought this first man home so soon, then perhaps it could do the same for James. For as much as she loved her husband, respected his decision and fully understood his reasons for leaving, she still wished he had not gone. She would have been happy to carry on living in their little wooden house, building on extra space when they needed to. She so wanted another baby.

Josephine was coping with the loss of her third child but she felt as though the family was not complete. There should be a father and there should be more children. That was what she hoped for. Even though she managed without James, this way of life was not right for her. Unless she was widowed, then her place was with her husband.

The number of letters from James had become fewer and in the past year she had only received two or three. She occasionally read some of his earlier letters because they were more descriptive than the few scribbled lines he had written more recently.

17ᵗʰ February 1957, London

Dear Josephine,
Well I reach England fine. A lot of fellows on the ship were sick and we were so happy to be on land after so long. I never pray so much. The sea was so wide and it was so cold. I thought the sea might swallow me up and I wouldn't see you again. Anyway, I meet with Rufus. He share a house with several others in a place call Paddington. The man who own the house is a very big man who drive an old blue car. Lots of dents and scratches on this car but he act as though he own the world and he really believe he own all of us. He calls us boys as though he is our father. I don't like him. I keep out of his way and Rufus mainly deal with him. The only time we see this man is when the rent is due. When rent is due he drive here fast fast fast. He never come quick like that when we have a problem like the toilet don't flush or the electric fire broken.

I have another fellow in my room and his name is Philip. Comes from home like me and Rufus but all the others are Jamaican. One day I will find a bigger place that has room for us but I need to save plenty as houses are expensive to rent. Philip say how hard it is for us to find somewhere. I won't spend any money unless it is necessary. As you know. Tomorrow morning Rufus will take me to a place where have jobs building and he told the man there that I am a carpenter.

I have to borrow some warm clothes until I can buy my own. England is not like home. It is like another world. If I try to say good morning to anyone they turn their eyes away. I prefer if I am walking with Rufus and Philip and I don't like Paddington late at night. I hope I can get used to this cold.

Please kiss my children and tell my parents I write and
I will write again soon.

Your loving husband
James

When James landed on English soil it was cold, damp and almost dark. He'd left the island several days earlier on a sunny January morning. He could feel the distance between the two islands, just by the difference in the sky. He was a long way from home. He shivered.

Throughout the long journey, he had to keep reminding himself why he was on that ship. *A better life for me and my family, a better life for me and my family.* Like a mantra, he repeated those words. The words kept him sane. They confirmed his decision to go. Some of his fellow passengers tried to draw him in to conversation but he mainly kept to himself. He had a plan, it was to meet up with his cousin, Rufus, who would show him to his new home and help him find work. The next part was simple, he would save all his money and send for his family and prove that he was capable of providing for them. They would have clothes, food and good schooling and Josephine would not have to go out to work.

He pulled the collar of his brown overcoat tighter around his neck as he stood at the dock, altering the grip he had on the handle of his small suitcase. He thought that any movement he made with his hands could help keep them from freezing. In the dim light he could just make out the outline of his cousin, Rufus. Rufus' figure was unmistakable. He stood no more than five foot two, almost as round as he was tall. He wore a trilby hat and a dark overcoat, much thicker than that of James', and smoked a cigarette. His grin was wide, his eyes sparkling above his puffy cheeks. It was the warmest sight James had encountered since he boarded the ship. The two men shook hands. Rufus pulled James closer and patted him energetically on the back. James smiled at his cousin and allowed him to grab his case.

'And now to show you to the palace you will be living in, cuz.'

They took a train. It was night by the time they stood in front of a tall, grey house with pillars on each side of the front door – Number 115. They climbed the four stone steps and Rufus reached into his pocket for the key.

A light went on in the hallway as the two men entered. A white man with steely blue eyes and very red cheeks stood there. He looked straight at them without greeting them, turned his back and went up the first flight of stairs. He turned on the light to a small room that James would later discover was the only bathroom in a house of six grown men.

'Don't worry about Irish. He live here amongst us blacks but he don't speak to us very much.' Rufus said, smiling.

'He own this place? Is he the landlord?' James asked, assuming that only someone who owned such a big house could afford to be so rude.

'Oh no, he is foreigner like us. Came here from Ireland. The landlord doesn't live here. He just comes to collect the rent every week. Follow me, I'll show you where you can sleep.'

They mounted the stairs. James could hear the sound of a transistor radio. On the landing just above the bathroom there was laughter coming from one of the rooms. The door was slightly ajar and James saw two black men, one seated, the other standing and gesticulating as he recounted the story of his day at work. Rufus called in to them, as he carried on up to the next flight.

'Evening. All you alright?'

'Rufus!' They called back and one of the men came to the door.

'Rufus, call the landlord and tell him we got no heat in here, man. You have your brother wit' you?'

'Yes, yes, he finally reach. I'll speak to Mr Bellamy when he come Friday.'

'We cold. This room cold. England cold!' The man called up

to Rufus as the second joined him at the door.

'They rely on me for everything in here.' Rufus turned to look at James, who continued to follow behind but had turned back to see the two Jamaicans carrying on in the same animated way as before.

'I was one of the first in this house so I seem to be in charge.' Rufus said. 'This is my room and this is yours, opposite me. You'll be sharing with a boy called Philip, same island as us. He still at work. He work for London Transport, driving trains in tunnels at all different times of the day and night. Sometimes you might have the room for yourself. When he's here, is usually to sleep. He just come, sleep, eat and go out again. Such a miserable job. Just sit and drive the train up and down up and down. The same lines all the time all the time. But at least it's a job. And we need to find one for you.'

'I can't drive a train, cuz.'

'I know that. I'm sure we can get you something though. On a building site. You can use your hands can't you? That's all they really want us for here. Not for our brains.'

Rufus handed James his suitcase and opened the door to a cramped and dusty room with two single beds. The foot of one greeted him as he opened the door. He squeezed past the bed with his suitcase held up above his head. The other bed was under the window. Over the window hung a torn green curtain and through it James could just make out a small yard that housed, amongst other derelict objects, a pushchair, a bicycle frame and a football. Grass and weeds worked their way up and around the broken items that must have lain in the yard for years. No one had attempted to cut the grass or pull up the weeds in a long time. James thought that had Josephine been here she would have cleared that yard and tried to grow flowers in it, small as it was.

'That's your bed by the window. Put down your case, James. Make yourself at home man.'

There were two chairs in the room, one right in the middle with a pair of old trousers draped over the back. The other sat under a small sink, which had four pairs of socks soaking in it. The water was dark and cold. James wondered where he would keep his clothes. He saw a short wardrobe on the wall opposite the window. On opening it he found, hanging inside, a formal looking jacket, probably to match the trousers on the chair, two white shirts and one blue. There were two spare hangers and James thought they would do for him. On the shelf above the clothes rail he saw a flannel, a few items of underwear and a bible. He picked it up and flicked through the pages.

'Philip's bible. He stopped reading that a year ago.'

James was not a regular churchgoer but he suddenly felt he would need something to believe in if this room and this house were representative of life in England. He knew there were castles in England, large areas of greenery, farms and idyllic country roads. He'd read about them and seen pictures. Perhaps he might be able to see those places once in a while. Somewhere to escape to.

Already the small room was closing in on him.

26th May 1958, London

Dear Josephine,

I manage to find a new place to stay. The room is small but I have it for myself. I have been working on a building site but I never get to use any carpentry skills. Just banging nails, cementing and carrying but the money is not too bad. My landlady is an Irish woman who marry an English man. Me and one other fellow the only blacks here. Mrs Langley like to chat and chat and she never stop talking if I am in the kitchen. I can use the stove between seven and eight at night and I'm glad that is all it is because if that woman have more time to talk I don't think I will get any sleep.

Because Mrs Langley know I am a carpenter she always find me work to do in the house. She say her husband is useless and cannot bang a nail in straight without it bend or he bang his finger. She always shake her head when she talk about him. She say My Charlie not good for anything except work and buy me things but even then he still have no taste. I call them Mr and Mrs even though she wants me to call them by their Christian name. Her name is Delores by the way. They don't have any children. She say My Charlie tools don't operate too good in her factory. She laugh so loudly at her own jokes. Mr Langley come in the kitchen to find out what is all the noise one time. It was just her, laughing as though she have no sense. But I used to their ways now.

A kiss to you and the children from your loving husband.

James

Most mornings James found it hard to get out of his bed. He had never been a lazy man. He'd had more strenuous jobs to do than his current labouring job. What ate away at him was how insignificant he felt himself to be in this country. Like so many before him, he was convinced that there was a pot of gold just there for the taking in England and all you needed was to be able to work hard to achieve it. He'd worked hard all his life so that wasn't his challenge. He missed his home. Back home he could leave his house each morning and before he'd gotten to the main road he would have been greeted with a fond, 'Good Morning James', by at least three people. Although the people from his island continued to struggle with the failing economy, there was never a sense of disaster amongst them. Back home, people never walked around with sullen, grey faces, never looking up from the ground, never smiling. He wondered how long it would be before he could feel welcome in this place.

He had known his time at the house in Paddington was limited from the day he got there. He needed to be in a place where he could at least come home and have his spirits lifted after

114

a hard day of working on the building site.

Philip, his room-mate, had not exaggerated about how hard it was to find somewhere to live. He couldn't count the number of times he would see a notice in a newsagent's window or in the local newspaper saying, 'room to let', only to arrive and have the door slammed shut in his face. Or to see the curtains twitch and not have the door answered at all. Or worse, to see a prominent notice informing him that, because of his skin, he was not welcome. So it was with surprise and relief that he rang the doorbell at his last stop for the day and was greeted by a beaming smile and a mess of auburn hair.

'Have you come about the room?'

'Yes I need a new place, I ... '

'Well, come in. It's draughty standing here in just my housecoat. Come and see if it suits and we'll see how we go.'

James stepped inside. This house was like a palace. All the carpets matched, the walls were papered with bright colours, not peeling off or waiting to be decorated. There was no smell of damp, just cooking and hair spray. The room for rent was not wallpapered but painted blue, like a child's bedroom would be. The bed looked comfortable and the bedspreads looked clean and fresh, rather than moth eaten and thin.

Her name was Delores Langley and she talked non-stop for the whole time he was there. She said he could move in right away but needed a week's rent in advance and that rent must be paid prompt by nine pm on a Friday or he'd be out.

On days when he was being snubbed by some of the work mates on the site, James knew he would have a warm welcome home from Delores, as she insisted he call her, when he came home. He wasn't able to talk with her much because there were not sufficient gaps or breaths between her sentences to allow a two-way conversation. She was the same with her husband but with him, she asked a question and answered it too. James was convinced her husband was mute for the first couple of weeks of being there until one morning Charlie Langley nodded to him and said, 'Good Morning.'

Charlie worked as a supervisor in a department store in the West End. He had fought in the Second World War but James was sure he could never have seen action or ever have killed a man. He was far too meek. Charlie tried to avoid having much contact with his two black lodgers. Delores on the other hand couldn't get enough of James.

After three weeks of James moving in to the Langley household, Delores made it perfectly clear that the attention she gave him was more than just friendly. She talked a lot less and left enough time for James to speak about his home. Delores knew he was married and asked him if he missed sleeping with his wife.

'Well of course,' James said. He was eating some left over rabbit stew that Delores had left for him. 'That goes without saying.'

'Yes a man and woman should sleep together. My Charlie isn't like most men. He doesn't hug his wife or tell her how lovely she looks, even when she buys something new to attract his attention.'

'I find that very hard to believe.' James was sitting back in his chair now and smiling at Delores. 'Well, I think you are very attractive even without something new.'

'You do, do you?' Dolores rested her elbow on the table and her chin in her hand and stared at James. James just smiled and got up to take his plate to the sink. He began to wash up. Delores followed him. He went to place the clean plate on the draining board when she reached for his wet hand and held it as she unbuttoned the front of her housecoat.

'As a matter of fact I do have something new to show him but he won't care. My new nightdress. I bought it from the High Road. What do you think?' She had not let go of his hand. She placed it on her breast, where James' hand remained as she looked up at him. Very quickly he slipped her housecoat off her shoulders and took hold of the shoulder straps of her nightdress, pulling them down to her elbows. She stepped in closer and kissed him.

116

Just then there was the sound of a key in the front door. Delores was out of the kitchen before Charlie could close the front door behind him. She was closing the door to their downstairs bedroom when Charlie walked into the kitchen, saw James washing his fork and glass and said a quiet, 'Good Evening' before disappearing.

James could hear them talking as he went upstairs to his room. That night he didn't go upstairs to start calculating how much money he had saved and how long it would be before he could afford to bring his family over. That night he thought only about Delores. Her naked torso, how smooth her skin felt, how she smelt of perfume and longed for the next time they could be alone.

There were several more opportunities for the two to be alone in the house. They had made love in the kitchen, his room and in Delores' and Charlie's bed.

Dolores discovered she was pregnant just a few months after the affair began. She told her husband she was going to visit her mother in Ireland and went to Liverpool where a friend helped her arrange the abortion. On her return she kept away from James and made it clear that they must stop. James, on the other hand, did not know why she had changed so much. She had not told him about the pregnancy. He thought, perhaps, she had confessed everything to her mother in Ireland and that her mother had compelled her to stop. For him, she had become as distant as everyone else in London and he felt hurt.

Charlie came out of his shell whilst his wife was away and invited James to the pub for a drink one night. James had accepted the invitation. He started drinking more than he usually did after that. It helped him to stop missing Delores.

14th July, 1958

Dear Josephine,

117

I still cannot believe how it stays so light at eight o'clock at night here. I think the people are starting to get used to having us here. More of the chaps I work with talk to me better, they see I have a brain in my head. My foreman can see I am not lazy and I work very hard. When it is time for tea break, they have stopped sending me to buy their pies from the shop. They send the young boy instead.

But the other night I meet with a group of young white men they calling Teddy Boys. I don't know why they have this name and I don't want to know either. When I try to walk past them they stand in my way. One of them raise his hand and give me one blow on my face. Another two start to kick me hard on my leg and I fall. Before I know I feeling blows and kicks everywhere and try to hold my face. I hear shouting and it was a policeman who tell them to move on and don't be so noisy. He take one look at me and say I must watch where I go and not to annoy the people around here. Blood was pouring from my nose. Maybe the policeman wanted me to keep my nose and stomach out of the way of the Teddy Boys' fist and foot. But don't worry, it was not so bad. I didn't have to go to the hospital thank God. So please don't be afraid to come here. I know you are strong enough for people like them.

I have to wake up early in the morning to go to work so I will say goodnight now and I look forward to hearing the news from home.

A kiss for everyone and I have more money saved.
Your loving husband
James

One summer evening, James was restless. Thinking he could walk off his supper he decided to go and visit his cousin, Rufus, and try to persuade him to take a drink. Rufus asked if he could bring his girlfriend, Maisie Baker, and the three of them went to the local pub.

They had no problems being served at the Red Lion. They sat and drank in peace, sharing stories about their work. Maisie talked about the hospital where she worked, Rufus his new job as a bus conductor on the number 18 and James told them his job was coming to a close and that the foreman had offered him another contract. He would also try for a refurbishment job one of his co-workers had mentioned.

It was a warm and balmy evening, the pub was not full but the front doors were wedged open. The pub stood on the corner of Castle Road and on the corner opposite was a small café. The café was closed for the evening, but there was a low wall surrounding it that was occupied by at least five Teddy Boys. All night long they yelled conversations at each other, jeered when anyone walked by and caused the punters from the Red Lion to stare out at them only to have two fingers waved at them from across the road. Eventually they were moved on by a policeman.

At around ten-thirty James and his companions decided it was time to leave the pub. All of them had very early starts. They set off in the direction of Maisie's one bedroom flat. Rufus would stay the night there and James hoped to catch the bus at the end of her street. The couple waved him off and James walked quite briskly toward the bus stop, head down and whistling to himself.

'What 'ave we got 'ere then chaps? Another one o' them jungle bunnies, lost their way again?'

James looked up and saw the Teddy Boys from earlier. They stood blocking his way. James looked at their faces. They were all much younger than him. He could see nothing but hate in their eyes, though each of them grinned and stood like a wall of suits and greased back hair, moving closer and closer to him, their shoulders hunched. James found himself slowly backing up.

'Well, are you gonna move out the way or what?' A boy with ginger hair had his face up close to James'. James cringed at the foul stench of his breath. As James shuffled to his right, the boy moved to block him, his head almost touching James' forehead as he stared, unblinking into James' eyes. James moved to the left and the boy blocked him again.

'You're not supposed to get in our way, you're supposed to move when a white man passes you in the street you ignorant nigger.' They were no more than seventeen and eighteen years old, hardly men, James thought.

'Well maybe I'm not the ignorant one because how can I move out of your way when you won't move out of mine?' James had had a few whiskies and perhaps would not have spoken up for himself in such an aggressive manner if he'd been sober. There was no time to take it back. James felt the blow of a fist, hard on his left cheek. It sent him sideways onto a second of the thugs, who reacted quickly with a punch to his ribcage. He fell to the ground, breathless, crouching in a ball to protect any part of his body he could. The gang continued to deliver kick after kick as they jeered and called him names and told him that he should go back to the jungle with the other monkeys. All James could think of were his wife and children. These boys would make sure he never saw them again. He looked up to see one of the boys poised to smash his face with an empty milk bottle. Closing his eyes he heard the loud shout of a man from across the street. The boy lost momentum and he failed to strike James with the force he'd intended. The bottle cut into James' face, just above his eye. The boys ran off quickly when they realised that the shout had come from a policeman.

'Drop that bottle and move on lads!'

The constable bent down and hovered over him. Blood trickled from James's brow, his nose and out of his mouth. His clothes were dishevelled and dirty and every part of him ached. The constable straightened up.

'You want to be a bit more careful around here son, you're lucky I came along when I did else they would 'ave done for you. Live 'round 'ere do you?'

'No, I need to catch the bus.' James lifted himself to kneeling and slowly to standing, as the constable looked on with his hands in his pockets. James dusted himself off the best he could. He looked up and down the street, half expecting to be ambushed again.

'I'll see you get on that bus of yours, they'll leave you alone now I'd imagine. Get off home and get those cuts seen to. Got a wife indoors?'

'No, she back home – in my country.' James wiped blood from his nose on to his shirtsleeve and coughed.

'Well maybe it's time you joined her, son.' He accompanied James for the next fifty yards to the bus stop. When his bus arrived, James boarded and could feel each passenger, staring, as he shuffled along the lower deck to take a window seat at the front. The black bus conductor did not take his fare. James would remember that night for two reasons. One of them being the silence on the bus,

3rd October 1959, London

Dear Josephine,

I am so cold today my hands are shaking whilst I write you this letter. I have taken a basement flat off the Portobello Road. This is our new home and now I have the money for the children too. The place is going to be perfect for when you come. I won't even recognize my children by now and maybe you won't even recognize me.

I will write to you when I have booked your passage. I think that will be very soon so start to make preparations and warn Mama that she will have to say her goodbyes.

James

The basement flat in 239 Shirley Road had two large rooms. The room at the back contained a double bed, a sink, an antiquated wardrobe but no hangers. In the front room there was one single bed, a green PVC sofa and a small dining table with two rickety chairs. James had had to clear out a bunch of old newspapers that he'd found in the bottom drawer of the wardrobe, but aside from this, the flat had been left quite neat and tidy by the previous occupants. All of the carpets had been swept. Even the little mat that lay just inside the front door held no nasty surprises underneath. There were no signs of damp or rot. This was going to be perfect for Josephine. The bathroom was along the narrow corridor and was positioned to the rear of the flat. It contained a bath, a toilet and a sink, a little stained with age but clean all the same. In the bathroom stood an empty olive-coloured paraffin heater. It was the only source of heating in the place.

The occupiers of the basement flat had to share a kitchen with the people on the ground floor. James gained access to the kitchen from the stairs leading up from the basement. Anybody from the house could walk down to his flat. Although no one ever did, he kept the doors to both of the rooms locked when he was out.

On the ground floor, James discovered, were two Jamaican women: a girl of nineteen and her mother, twenty years her senior. Both of them were nurses. The mother was a midwife and the girl had just started training after leaving secretarial college without a certificate and not knowing what to do. Her mother had decided to take charge of her career and encouraged her to start training at the same hospital.

A radio played loudly from their rooms as long as they were home and as they often worked different shifts, the radio seemed to be playing constantly. It was something James had to get used to pretty quickly as he could hear the radio clearly from his basement.

Both women were flamboyant, alike in looks, the mother being slightly on the larger side and supporting a generous bust that James couldn't fail to notice. They were very friendly and after a while they were both offering to cook for him and take his shirts and dirty work clothes for washing. It seemed to James to be somewhat of a competition between them to see who could be the most hospitable. James did not complain, he imagined that if they were as generous as this at the hospital, patients would be queuing up to be ill.

One night Marcia, the mother, came halfway down the stairs from the kitchen and called out to him. He came out of the bathroom, where he had just been brushing his teeth and getting ready for bed.

'Yes?' he called back to her and looked up to see Marcia leaning over the banister wearing nothing but a see-through negligee.

'I'm sorry to disturb you James, but I wondered if you knew anything about radiograms. Mine seems to have stopped working.' She smiled. It was eleven-thirty at night and she wore fresh bright red lipstick.

'Well, I don't know anything about them, I'm sorry Marcia. Anyway I'm just about to go to bed.'

Marcia had come down the stairs and was looking around the flat, peeking her head around the doors of each of the rooms.

'It looks nice and cosy in here. Which one do you sleep in? Oh I think I know, the one with the unmade bed, so typical of a man not to tidy up after himself.' She had a high-pitched, shrill laugh that James had often heard coming from the ground floor flat. She laughed as she pulled him by his open shirt collar and dragged him without effort to his bed where she fell backwards, pulling him with her.

It was the start of a relationship that she insisted should remain a secret. Her daughter must never find out under any circumstances. She said her daughter, Margaret, missed her father, who had died of lung cancer when she was twelve and was still mourning his passing. James thought Margaret's way of mourning a little different to most. Only ten days ago she'd placed her hands quite firmly around James' neck when he was in the kitchen, preparing an evening meal, kissed him and said if they were quick her mother would never find out. After which she had led him down to the bedroom. In a week where Marcia was on nights, James had sex with her daughter on every one of her shifts.

15

I don't want our conversation to be over yet. Not when there's all this time to pass. I thought he said he likes to talk. Being this still and quiet isn't helping me at all. I've sat on this plane and gone through so many emotions, thoughts and memories. I need to talk, walk around, do something. I feel like I'll burst if I don't let it all out. I don't know how much I can tell this man, though. I don't want to be judged. It's always Jasmin I turn to when I need to talk but even she has gone. I miss my friend. I miss Luke. I miss Eva.

It was the start of spring term 2006. Eva was talking non-stop about her latest assignment at school. She had to work on a scene from a musical to perform at the end of year school performance. I remember how frustrated she was when she wanted to do a scene from *Chicago* and the rest of her group wanted to do *Grease*. She moaned and moaned to me and when that wasn't enough she'd call her friend, Saffron, and moan to her. Eva could get pretty miserable when she didn't get her way.

'How about this, Eva? You'll be sixteen this year. What if we have a real girlie celebration? Go out shopping, have lunch and in the evening I take you out to see a show.'

'A West End show? That would be brilliant Mum.'

'Not West End. Broadway. What if we go to New York for a weekend? We could see a couple of shows.'

It was all Eva talked about from that day on. By the summer we had planned the whole thing. That was the year I let Eva down.

The air conditioning had packed up. It was lunchtime and the café was deserted. Luke was prepping for a party in the kitchen with Eva helping him. Jasmin had popped in to do wages. I stood at the door to the café. I'd wedged it open and stood and watched as one or two people passed by. I knew that most of the smaller shops were empty. It was always the same in summer. My old friend from the hardware shop was sweeping up outside. He wore a flat cap regardless of the weather and always touched its tip when he saw me. When he touched it this time, I felt Jasmin tapping me on the shoulder, saying that my mobile had been ringing in the office. She answered it when she saw it was Maddy calling.

'Hey Mads. What's up?' Maddy was always bright and loud on the phone. I could feel a chill when she took a few seconds before she spoke. And then she told me that my little brother had died. It hit me harder than Dad's death. His passing wasn't unexpected. Dad had had two strokes. He was ill and frail. But my brother, James, was young, bright and talented, his career mapped out in front of him. All lost in an instant because of a road accident that wasn't his fault. I felt lost. Numb. I was in a constant fog for months. Then Eva's sixteenth birthday came around.

'So who has an important birthday coming up then?' Luke was grinning at Eva who was munching away on some toast at breakfast. It was the week before half term and our trip was planned for the coming weekend.

'Well I guess that would be me wouldn't it?' She smiled sweetly and then turned to look at me. 'And only days before we go off on my birthday trip to New York.'

'Eva!' I dropped my piece of toast onto the plate.

'Mum, what is it? What's wrong?'

'I've completely messed up.'

'What do you mean?' She asked and took another bite of toast but slowly this time and chewed tentatively. I looked at Luke. I think he had already guessed what I was about to say.

'It's not that I forgot your birthday or anything like that but ... '

Eva stood up abruptly and pushed her chair back with the

125

backs of her legs.

'Mum. Don't tell me. You haven't booked the flight have you?'

'I can easily fix that Eva, I'll sort it all out today. I promise.'

'And what about the Broadway show you promised me? It's going to be too late to book anything now!' She stormed out of the kitchen and marched up the stairs. Luke and I heard the bedroom door slam. It was far too early in the morning for slamming doors. I suppose Eva thought she had the right to wake up the neighbours so rudely. Luke looked at me and said nothing.

'Oh Luke, not you as well?' I held my head in my hand, closed my eyes.

'Well what do you expect me to say? You guys have been planning this for nearly a year. How could you forget?'

'Hello? A little thing called a death in the family. It hasn't been easy for me to keep on the ball all the time.'

'Well Ange, we've all noticed that. But Eva? How could you forget?'

'I know. I can't believe it myself. I'm sure I can book a show. They have eight performances a day. I'll go on-line and book *Wicked*. That was the one I was going to surprise her with.'

'I think you've surprised her already.' Luke got up and started clearing the table.

'That's not fair, Luke. You sound like Eva. Isn't a mother allowed to mess up once in a while?' I pushed my plate away. I wasn't hungry anymore. I was upset. I looked up to see Luke coming back to the table with a sorry look on his face.

'What happened to James was – well, you know. I still can't get my head around it,' I said as Luke sat beside me and pulled a chair in closer. 'He was the baby of the family. He had so much ahead of him. He was writing and … .' I had started crying again. Luke put his arms around me.

'I wasn't being fair,' he said. 'I shouldn't have said what I said. I guess I could just sense Eva's disappointment. Ange, I'm so sorry. I don't expect you to have gotten over James. That's going to take forever. But the rest of us are still here and we've lost a huge chunk of you. I'd do anything to bring that back.' Luke was drying my eyes with kitchen roll.

'I'll go up and speak to her,' I sniffed. 'Hopefully she'll let me in. Give me a chance to make things right.'

I'm twiddling my headphones around; he's tapping on his book. Here goes.

'You know I never introduced myself or even asked your name.' I finally turn to him.

'Oh, I'm Martin. Martin Staples.'

'I'm Angelica. Ford. Nice to meet you.' We shake hands.

'Angelica, you asked earlier about my family not coming on this trip. Why isn't yours with you?'

'Well, this is a trip I had to make on my own. Anyway my daughter is in New York now, so … .' I shrugged my shoulders,

'On her own?' Martin looked surprised.

'Yes.'

'That's terribly brave. She just upped and went?'

'Well she's been out there before. She knows people. I'd taken her there before, for her sixteenth birthday. We spent a long weekend there. Bit of a last minute rush job, but we made it. She was stroppy with me. Teenagers are. But I think she had an alright time. Second time she went was because she'd won a singing contest. The prize was a recording session with a top producer. She failed to tell me when she entered the contest that she'd have to leave the country to claim the prize. She made a real impression on them, though. The stuff she recorded was great. She said they were quite impressed by her own material too. My husband and I were so proud of her. He went with her that trip. She had a better time going with him, I could tell that.'

I think I've managed to cover that without giving too much away. I haven't left him with the impression that I was a lousy Mum who forgot her own daughter's birthday.

'I don't know anyone in New York.' Whatever was bugging him earlier seems to have gone. He's as cheery as when he first came and sat here.

'Funny, I didn't before, but now I know two people there.'

Just before summer, Jasmin had been acting strangely for weeks. I couldn't understand it. I thought at first she might be pregnant. But after her twin girls were born, she'd vowed 'never again'. She wanted her waistline back. She had trained for three years solid with a personal trainer and looked better than she had at nineteen. Then I wondered if the problem might be between her and Steven. But Jasmin told me everything in the end anyway, so it was really just a waiting game, as unbearable as it seemed.

One particular morning after sitting in the office with her, and long after the morning trade had passed through the café, Jasmin hadn't uttered a word. So I decided to break the ice. I talked about Eva, one of her favourite topics.

'So, anyway, Eva has been writing a lot of new songs and she's going to do one of these singer-songwriter nights sometime soon.' Nothing. 'I think she and Saffron might go away together for a week or so this summer. They're so glad to have their exams out of the way.' Still nothing. 'Can you believe she's finished her 'A' levels? University coming up. Even I can't believe I've got a grown up daughter. But you couldn't tell could you? I still only look twenty-five myself.' But Jasmin wasn't taking the bait and my patience ran out.

'Jasmin!'

'Eh? What?' She looked up from the computer screen, frowning.

'What's gotten into you these past few weeks? You're not sick or something are you? Something serious I mean.'

'No. Don't talk crazy. I'm as fit as anything these days. Have you seen my personal trainer bills?' She shrugged off my concern.

'Well I guess if there was something you wanted me to know, you'd say. Right?' She didn't answer straight away. She got up and walked to the door. She changed her mind, came back and sat down again.

'Jasmin. Now you've really got me worried. Please tell me what's wrong. *Is* something wrong?'

'Well yes and no. We've had some really good news, me and Steven, and I want to share it with you but I'm worried about what you'll say when you hear it.'

'Monday morning is not a time to be cryptic, girl. Just tell me, Jas.'

'Okay. But promise you won't say anything until I get to the end.'

'Promise.'

'You know Steven?' she began.

'Er, hello? I think so.'

'Sorry, yes. Well it's his work. Or rather what his work could be if he relocated. That is, he's been offered a job. He was head hunted.'

'Sounds good. Big pay rise I'm guessing.'

'Massive. I mean Steven wouldn't even have considered it otherwise. He's really happy where he is at the moment.'

'So this lot have made him an offer he can't refuse. Is that it?'

'That's right.'

'And he can't decide.'

'Well he's decided now. We both have, in fact.'

'So are you telling me you'll be moving?'

'Yeah. That's right.'

'Far?'

'Very.'

'So this company is located somewhere in London and I have to guess where.'

'It's not in London, Ange.'

'So … ?'

'The job is in New York. He'll be going out there in one month. I'd be following him out once I've come to some sort of arrangement about Angel's with you.'

My heart sank. I was silent for what seemed like ages as I ran the conversation around in my head a few times.

'Jas, you're really going to leave? You're going to live in New York?'

'It kinda looks that way Ange. I'm so sorry to break it to you like this but I just couldn't find the words. Steven kept asking me, 'Have you told Angelica, have you told Angelica?' but I kept on chickening out because I knew you'd be heartbroken – the way I am, and have been for weeks.'

'Jasmin. God.' I could feel a pricking sensation in my eyes and I blinked several times. 'You're right. I am heartbroken. We've been together forever. I can't believe I won't see you anymore. What will I do without my best friend?'

'I'll always be your best friend Ange. We'll see each other as often as we can. It's not like I'm deserting you. You know I'm always going to love you no matter where we end up.'

We sat in silence for a while, probably thinking the same thing. What would happen with Angel's? Hanging over our heads were a multitude of issues that we needed to sort out. But neither of us had the heart. We left it there for the time being. It was the only way to make it through the day without breaking down.

16

Josephine noticed that James never signed 'loving husband' on his letters anymore. She wondered if by now he had stopped loving her. They had been apart for so long. Surely he must still love her if he was finally, after nearly three years, sending for her and the children? But for all she knew, as Eunice kept reminding her, he might have been married and divorced in that time and now needed someone to cook and clean for him.

'Well he is *my* husband, and I am the one who has to worry about what he does or does not do. So please stop trying to interfere.' Josephine resented Eunice's continual criticism of their marriage.

'Mam, you think after all this time, James still love me and the children? He is so far away now.' Eunice's words had stayed with Josephine and she needed to hear what her mother thought. They had spent the day going through Josephine's things: clothes, crockery, furniture, looking for what Josephine could sell, take or give away. She had sold the house to James' cousins.

'My dear, in the eyes of God once you are married you are married for good. The distance is nothing. James has worked hard and you will be together soon. Maybe more children? That would be a wonderful thing. I know you miss him.'

'I miss him and I still love him. But what if nothing is the same as before? It's been a long, long time, Mam.'

'If there is a problem you sort it out together. That is what marriage is. There is always a way for a couple to sort out any problem they might have between them. Nothing is ever too big.' Rose continued to sort through old clothes. The children were growing and would have to have new clothes for England.

Josephine was reassured by her mother's words. They served to confirm her own beliefs about marriage. She continued her preparations to wind down her work and said goodbye to her clients, family and friends. She promised everyone that she would write to them as often as she could and hoped, one day, to be back to visit them.

Eunice helped Josephine pack. In doing so she became more excited and anxious than her sister, as she herself had the prospect of moving to England.

About a year after James left for England, Eunice met and married a man from a district called Four Lakes, at the northernmost point of the island. He was a very fair-skinned black man, what the islanders called 'high colour'. A very tall and quiet man. She met him while visiting a distant cousin on her father's side who was sick. The cousin normally cared for her old, frail mother, so they both needed someone about the house to cook, clean and look after them. Rose had received a letter from a worried neighbour, who, perhaps not wanting to take on the job herself, had searched her memory for anyone she thought would be willing to help. Eunice had complained about the arrangement and kept asking Rose why she wanted to get rid of her.

'This is family,' her mother had said. 'I can go by Josephine's to help if she needs me. Right now it would do you good to help someone out of the goodness of your heart. God sees everything and it would help you a great deal if you showed a bit more kindness every now and again.'

'So you saying I'm not kind?' Eunice was all ready to flare up with rage. Her mother shot her a look and her anger quelled.

So off she had gone on a long and bumpy ride to Four Lakes. Once she arrived, Eunice spent no time at all fitting in with a new community of people. Most of them knew nothing about Eunice. Some knew she had a sister who was well liked and respected. Most knew that she was the youngest daughter of a very strong matriarch who had single-handedly raised a very large and poor family following the unexpected death of her husband. Eunice was quick to tell them that she was the one who helped her older sister in troubled times, that she'd nursed her back from a virtual nervous breakdown after the death of her third child and was there to give comfort when her husband had taken off to seek his fortune in England. She even implied that she had stepped in to meet the dressmaking orders and that clients preferred her sewing to that of her sister's.

She attended church in the little village of Four Lakes on a Sunday and that was where she met her future husband. His name was Nestor. He came from a small family and Eunice knew very little about him apart from the fact that he was very handsome and always had his eyes on her whenever they passed each other. On the third week of Eunice's stay, Nestor, waiting outside the church, offered, quite loudly, to walk her home. She laughed inwardly at his shyness. She was only half his height and she grinned up at him constantly, not believing how lucky she was to have met someone so handsome. They chatted to each other with ease and it was quite clear to onlookers that a close bond was forming.

Eunice went to draw water one day and a young girl stood behind her, watching as Eunice opened the tap at the side of the road and waited as water slowly filled a large pail. Eunice lifted it onto her head.

'You know a lot of girls are interested in that Nestor,' the young girl said. 'He looks very handsome but he have a very hot temper.'

'Well,' said Eunice, as she began to saunter off toward her aunt's house, 'he will never get angry with me because I know how to keep a man happy.'

On returning from Four Lakes, Eunice proudly declared to her mother that she was getting married.

'You are what?' Her mother was open-mouthed.

'Doing a good turn for my poor old aunty and cousin was a good thing after all. Seems you were right, Mam. Let me tell you all about Nestor. You will love him even more than James.'

Eunice proceeded to fill her mother's living room with talk of how she first encountered Nestor, how good-looking and tall he was and what good manners he had. Also, how much money he had saved over the years. She told Rose about Nestor's family: his mother was a kind woman and her future father-in-law was a fisherman, just like Nestor. But Nestor hated the smell of fish and desperately wanted to go and work in England after hearing the radio announcements that said they needed good workers there.

'Maybe we could make a lot of money there and come back here as millionaires,' said Eunice.

'Millionaires!' Rose kissed her teeth. 'What is here that is worth a million?'

Six months later Eunice was married: a small wedding in her home village. Rose frowned throughout the ceremony. Nestor's parents looked on and smiled, proud of their son. The priest read through the service while over the rim of his glasses his eyes were fixed firmly on the groom he knew next to nothing about. Nestor was hot and nervous and stammered through his lines. Eunice beamed as brightly as the bouquet her sister had made for her and smiled continuously. As for Josephine, she looked at her mother and then at her sister. Their faces couldn't have been more expressive, but for different reasons. Josephine wanted to be happy for her sister and tried not to show on her face how concerned she was. She wondered why her sister agreed to marriage so quickly, as they knew so little about the family Eunice was marrying into.

Outside the church, Eunice grabbed her sister by the shoulders and grinned. She gave her a big hug and whispered into her ear, 'Look sis, we are both married women now, both equal.' She rushed back over to Nestor and clasped his hand.

Eunice went to live in Four Lakes alongside her new family and returned every other week for a weekend visit to her mother or to Josephine saying how much she hated the smell of fish and she couldn't wait until she was in England.

The day couldn't come soon enough for either of the young

women. Nestor went ahead of Eunice to settle the rooms he'd arranged for them, which meant Eunice was back living with Rose for the time being.

Josephine had spent a tearful afternoon at her mother's house saying her goodbyes. Eunice, on the other hand, spent the day rushing from house to house saying fond farewells and asking everyone what they thought about the outfit she'd chosen to travel in. Several of the neighbours dropped in from time to time to see Josephine, some with letters for loved ones in England. Mrs Lambert had a letter for her son in Liverpool and asked Josephine to pass it on to him when she saw him even though Josephine insisted that she wasn't sure if Liverpool was anywhere near London.

'Josephine, I can't believe this day has come.' Her mother was distraught. 'I know a wife has to be with her husband but I wish it wasn't so far away. I don't know when, or if I will ever see you again.'

'Of course you will see me again. I will always come back and see you. You never have to worry about that.' Josephine had to stop herself crying for her mother's sake. She felt as if her heart was breaking and took deep gulps to try to stop another outburst.

'Josephine, my Josephine.' Gently, Rose placed the palm of her hand on Josephine's face. 'Losing you is like losing my right hand.'

Josephine, Eunice and the children arrived at the English port on a very cold and foggy morning in December 1960. They had never known cold like it. It wasn't like sinking into the cool of the river when they went to bathe on a warm morning back home, this cold crept around their necks, down past the collars of their coats, slinked its way around their bodies and seeped into their skin to settle, like icicles, on their bones.

The children stood shivering at the top of the gangplank.

'Mammy, this is England?'

'Yes darling we finally reach.'

All four of them scoured the grey dock as they tried to find their respective husband or father.

'Look, there's Nestor.' Eunice waved her hand and slowly put it to her mouth whispering, 'He's standing beside James.'

'I don't see James,' Josephine was squinting now.

'Look, he's waving too,' said Eunice and began walking toward the men. Josephine stood her ground until she realised that the man standing next to Nestor was, in fact, her husband. He had changed. This was not the slim, handsome man she remembered leaving the small house all those years ago in a second-hand suit. Instead she saw a very tired-looking man with a large stomach and the beginnings of bald patches on the top of his head. He was smiling and walking toward her with a laboured waddle. He'd lost his confident swagger. Although still only in his mid-thirties, he looked closer to middle age than he should.

'Josephine, at last. My goodness, look at my children. Come and hug your daddy.' He bent to grab the two bewildered children and kissed them both. Even his voice had changed. What had happened to his accent? He gave his wife a brief kiss on the cheek.

'You haven't said anything to me. You find I've changed that much?' he asked Josephine.

'But James, what have you been doing here all this time? Seems you've had more time to eat than to write us letters.' Josephine looked her husband up and down.

'It's probably too many pies and Guinness. But you are here to cook for me now and I won't have to go to the pie shop.'

'James, I think you have a woman here that is cooking for you like that,' Eunice chimed in.

'Eunice.' James bowed a quick hello to his sister-in-law.

'James.' She beamed. 'Let me introduce you to my husband, Nestor Didier. Nestor, this is Josephine's husband, James Dennis. He has changed a lot since we last saw him.'

'Nice to meet you Nestor. Where are you two living?' He shook Nestor's hand.

'Oh we have a place in East London,' replied Nestor.

'Well we won't be neighbours. Our house is in West London,' said James.

'Oh, and which is the best?' Asked Eunice, 'East or West?'

'There's no difference,' said Nestor.

After a train ride into London, Nestor took Eunice on the tube and James and his family caught a taxi for home. There were brief goodbyes and exchange of addresses before the sisters parted, ready to start their new lives.

17

This guy has a really good sense of humour. He's got me laughing out loud. It's been a long time since I could crack anything more than a fake smile. My whole existence up until now had been one of getting by, getting on with things but not getting anywhere. I throw my head back and I laugh.

This is the last folder of photographs he wanted to show me and he's left the best until last. This time he's telling the story surrounding the photos of his beloved Phoebe. She's quite a character. I'm warming to her as though I were her aunt.

I think the little girl in front of us thinks we're crazy, all that laughing. She's standing and looking over the back of her seat. She must be about three years old. Martin looks at me and then back at her, and smiles. The same thought is going through both our minds.

'Sit down Georgia,' her mother says, but she could be Phoebe or Eva when she was younger.

Laughter abates and the laptop has taken its final curtain. That only leaves conversation. One hour until we land.

'So, if you're here, your business partner is your partner no more, daughter is in New York – that leaves poor old hubby holding the fort, right?'

Sunday morning after a long, deep sleep. For what seemed like the first time in absolute ages, there hadn't been a job on the Saturday night. Eva had stayed over at her best friend Saffron's house. Luke and I had just chilled in front of the television. When I woke up, the sun was in my eyes, a narrow beam of light trickled through a tiny crack in the curtains. When I could focus, I saw

Luke leaning on one elbow and smiling down at me.

'Good sleep?' he asked.

'Not bad. Just glad we don't have to get up early. What time is it anyway?'

'Doesn't matter. We can spend the whole day in bed if we want to.'

A bright, yellow haze of colour filtered into the bedroom. The next few hours were spent wrapped around each other. Arms, legs, warm kisses all over my body. Sleeping, waking, talking and not having to be anywhere by any time. Passion and peace. It was bliss.

I snap myself back into the present. 'Everything is on hold for a time. Lots to sort out and I have to decide on which direction I'll be taking the business.'

'I see.'

'You do?'

'More than you know. I know a couple in trouble. I know the signs. Ana and I have had our fair share of problems. If there's the slightest hope that you can come through this, you must try.' Martin is looking serious now.

'I want to.'

'If you don't mind me saying. Looks a bit like you're running away. It's not the way to go. Believe me.'

'Don't tell me – you've been there, bought the t-shirt, right?'

He goes quiet.

'I'm sorry. I've spoilt things. I'm doing an Eva. Says something rude when she can't face the truth.'

'It's okay. I understand. Sorry, I'm speaking out of turn.'

'Not at all. It's me.'

'Talk to me about Eva. That will cheer you up. Tell me how she ended up in New York. That absolutely fascinates me.'

'Are you trying to get tips off me about teenage girls?'

'You got me that time.'

'It's a long story.'

I'm taking him back to the summer. Even though it's autumn now, I remember everything as though it were yesterday.

Eva knew exactly where she was headed. Subject to her exam results she had been offered a place at The Guildhall School of Music, for which she'd already passed her audition. She'd decided that she would move out and live in halls. I couldn't really see the point as the school was in London.

'Mum, every musician I admire had to struggle to survive. They faced adversity to come through shining and making the kind of music that will never be forgotten.'

'Really? You sound like a documentary. Did any of these musicians have mobile phones or trainers that cost one hundred pounds?'

'*Mum.*'

'*Eva.*' I hugged her. I felt blessed to have such a beautiful, talented and intelligent daughter.

'So now I have the summer to sit chewing my finger nails, hoping I'll get a place at Guildhall.'

'Oh, I've no doubts about that.'

'Saffron and I have decided to spend our week away in Cornwall. Maybe camping or a hostel or something cheap and cheerful.'

'You could have gone away to see Grandma in the Caribbean this summer. I would have paid for you.'

'I know, but I prefer this.'

'But your aunties and your cousins are all there. Grandma would have loved it if you had gone.'

'Yeah, well, maybe next year. I feel restless and I didn't want to be around all that lot anyway. Wanted to stay here with you and Dad and Saff.'

I turn to my flying companion.

'One thing I would advise you and your wife to do.' I say. 'Talk to Phoebe. All the time. Especially when she's older. They have so many secrets and when you think everything is alright, they could be crying out for help. For guidance. Don't ignore anything.'

'Sounds serious now.'

I'm not sure I can tell him this next thing. What I'd discovered. I wasn't snooping, just trying to be helpful.

Eva had a lot of her stuff at Maddy's still. She and Luke had driven over there one Sunday afternoon to pick up some books, clothes and CDs. Eva was so self-assured, a lot more mature than I ever was at that age. I hadn't even decided what I wanted to do with my life until I was in my mid-twenties. And here was my little girl about to set the world on fire. I wondered how she'd cope in halls, looking after herself and cooking. She did less around the house than I ever did at her age so I hoped she knew enough.

I had told Eva, I don't know how many times, to sort out her washing and there I was again, traipsing upstairs with an armful of her folded t-shirts and jeans from the utility room.

I walked into her room and saw, as usual, piles of clothes on the floor but resisted the urge to pick them up. Instead I dumped her clean clothes on the bed. Just as I did so, I heard her mobile go off. It made me jump. I was used to the ring tone but didn't expect to hear it. It was impulse that made me grab it and press the little green telephone symbol. Before I could say 'hello Eva's phone' I heard Saffron's voice.

'Bitch, what do mean you've been having sex with someone in your family? You can't send me emails like that and not expect me to call you right away. Who *is* it?' I pressed the red telephone symbol straight away and threw Eva's phone on the bed. I stood there staring at it. A few seconds later it rang again. I picked it up but this time I was ready. I saw the 'Saffron calling' sign as I gathered my thoughts.

'Hello,' I said.

'Who's that?' Saffron sounded worried.

'Oh Saffron. Did you just call? I picked up Eva's phone but I couldn't hear anyone so I hung up.'

'Mrs Ford. You've got Eva's phone?'

'Yes, she must have forgotten it when she went off to Surrey with Luke. Shall I tell her you called?'

'Er, yes please. So you didn't hear me talking when you picked up?'

'No. I don't know what happened there. That's technology for you.' I laughed. A fake laugh. I hoped Saffron wouldn't see through it. 'Any message?'

'Oh no, that's okay Mrs Ford. I'll just try her again this evening. Will she be back then?'

'Yes, she should be. Bye then Saffron.'

'Bye.'

I sat heavily on the bed. The pile of clothes I'd just put there slipped garment by garment onto the floor in slow motion until the last few t-shirts flopped quietly onto the jeans in real time. I got up quickly. I still had Eva's phone in my hand. Why did I answer that call? No. I had to answer that call. The biggest secret that Eva could ever have kept from me, I had discovered by answering that call. But was Saffron serious? Why would she say it if it wasn't true? My head was spinning. If it were true then who the hell could this family member be?

I walked around and around the house, stopping to sit at the kitchen table to think, getting up again, walking around, stopping to sit on the sofa in the living room, the breakfast bar in the kitchen, the bench in the garden. Eventually I walked back upstairs and lay on my bed. I reached my arm out to Luke's side of the bed and then I heard his car pull into the driveway. I got up and looked out of the window. They were standing at the open boot. I could only see their legs as they lifted out bags and boxes. They walked together to the door. Side by side. Standing extremely close to each other. Their arms touching. Eva looking up at Luke. Luke looking down at Eva and they were smiling. Looking straight into each other's eyes. Smiling.

I ran to the bathroom before they came into the house. I started running a bath. I locked the bathroom door. I never locked the bathroom door normally, but I didn't want to see either of them.

It was nine-thirty at night. I took off all my clothes and I got into the bath while it was still running. They both called out to me as they passed the bathroom but I didn't answer them. I was seething. My chest hurt from the constant deep intakes of breath. My eyes were dry, I couldn't cry. I couldn't go running to them, asking if it was true, because if the words came out of their mouths that they were sleeping together I would have died right there and then. I kept praying for the possibility that it couldn't be true. I had no problem with finding out like that, that Eva was having sex but it was the 'with who' part that made my head spin and my heart race. Any member of the family would have been unacceptable – but *this*.

My life flashed before my eyes as though it were on the verge of ending. I was piecing together the evidence and realising it had all been there, right before me and I'd never worked it out. How could I? I leaned forward to turn off the taps. I was numb as I leant back and then sunk my head under the water.

When I came up, gasping for air, Luke was knocking on the door asking if I wanted something to eat and wanting to know why the door was locked.

'Nothing for me.' I called back, lightly. 'I'm tired and I'm going straight to bed.'

Neither of them bothered me for the rest of the night. They must have had something to eat and stayed up watching a film. They very often did that. I always went to bed before they did.

I was still awake when Luke came to bed but I pretended I was asleep. I didn't sleep all night.

The next morning, I asked Luke to go in and open up without me. I told him I had a bad headache. He came to hug me when he was leaving but I pulled away.

'What's up babes?' He asked.

'Nothing. It's just my head. It's making me cranky. You better go or you'll be late.'

'Yes, boss.' Luke had on one of his very wide grins. It made my stomach turn. I could hear Eva's music start up.

'Should I tell her to turn it off before I go?'

'No. You don't have to go to her room. I'll do it.'

Eva would be getting the train to Cornwall with Saffron the next morning. How was I going to survive the day? I wanted her gone.

18

Josephine never believed that a time would come when she could call the new place home. From the moment she took that first tentative step onto English soil she did so with a heavy heart. She had travelled for days with barely any sleep. Each waking hour she saw the only life she knew, slipping further and further away as though it were nothing but a distant memory. She remembered her mother's parting words and whenever she got the chance to be alone she cried for the pain and guilt she felt for deserting her. It was a wife's duty to be with her husband but Josephine had not felt like the doting bride for a long time. She knew she still loved James but the sadness she endured during that long journey made her want to go against her beliefs and leave her husband. But she was not the only person to consider. She had to put the children first.

All around her was the vastness of a cold country, an enormous canvas painted in more shades of grey than she could ever have imagined. She had stepped onto stony ground, as cold as the air around her. This new island, in complete contrast to the one she'd left behind, neither enticed her nor warranted more than a moment of her imagination. In fact she tried not to let her gaze settle on anything for too long in case it should suck her in and drain from her any of the life or colour she'd managed to bring with her from home.

The streets that surrounded their basement flat seemed endless. Her house number was over 100 and still the street continued. She could walk up and down these streets all day and never once be greeted by a neighbour, as the people here stayed firmly within their four walls, the only evidence of their existence being the twitching of net curtains as she walked by with her children. If she passed anyone on the street she would lower her eyes and hurry by. No-one wanted to make eye contact with her and she felt like an intruder.

'I thought the houses would be grand, like palaces,' she said one rainy morning as James got ready for work, 'Yes, they are big and tall, but they look so tatty and miserable.'

'Don't forget there was a war, Josephine. A lot of places suffered and the country needs time to get back on its feet.' James was searching for clean socks.

'Yes but that war was ages ago. Why does it have to take so long?' She handed James a clean pair of socks from the draw he'd just been looking in.

'We are not living in the most expensive part of London you know. I am not a rich man, not yet anyway.' He was pushing his feet into his work boots and reaching for his thick coat.

'Yes but what about trees, what about flowers and how far away from the sea are we?'

James kissed his two children. He stopped to take Josephine by her arms, looked deep into her eyes. 'It takes about an hour to get to the sea. We can go to Brighton one of these days. And when the weather is bright I will take you to the English countryside. I've been a few times and you'll love it. London is not the countryside. We are city people now, so that's what you have to get used to.' He promised that as long as he had the train fare he would take them in the summer. Summer seemed a long way off to Josephine. Maybe the sun would make the people smile.

Sharing her bed with James again had been quite an adjustment. James had waited before attempting to touch her or suggesting they make love until he saw a sign that she might reciprocate. This took a whole month. In the first week, after she had settled the two children on the old single bed in the front room, with each child sleeping at opposite ends, Josephine had changed in the bathroom even though it had been freezing cold. She'd come to bed, said a quick prayer, bade her husband goodnight and had faced away from him before falling asleep. By the second week, Josephine would kiss her husband on the cheek, bid him goodnight and then close her eyes to say her prayers. On the third week, now undressing in the bedroom, she would send a warm smile in her husband's direction as he watched her from the bed. On the fourth week they happened to be undressing at the same time and Josephine lay on the bed before putting on her nightdress. They made love for the first time in over three years. The act was systematic, played out without words and devoid of emotion on either part. Like making a cake for the first time, following the instructions to the letter and after tasting, deciding what to add or subtract for the next time for a better result.

James was gentle and Josephine submissive. There was no longer the passion of their earlier days and, although their lovemaking grew to become more pleasurable for them both, there would never be that same spark of desire they knew back home.

James had made a point of coming home from work early in the first week of his family's arrival to make sure they were settled and happy in their new home. He'd shown Josephine where the nearest shops were, shown her the library and the bus stop from where he caught the number 7 bus in the morning. He had taken them all to register at the local doctor's surgery and showed her how to get to the hospital in case there was ever an emergency with the children. He told her that the women upstairs were both nurses and they would be able to help her if she ever needed it. Once she'd gotten to know them, though, Josephine had vowed never to ask them for anything. She never complained to her husband about them but Josephine did the best she could to avoid them as far as possible.

The early days dragged by. She made her way to the shops now and again with the children and made visits to the local Council Offices to enquire about schools for her boy and girl. James had told her which bus to take but she preferred to walk so that she could be away from the flat longer. She was nervous about boarding a bus without James to help her with the change he left for fares.

Each of the tatty houses along her street was now etched in her memory. Number seventeen – a tabby cat sat on the windowsill. Number fifty-three – a chipped window on the first floor. Number seventy-eight – only the seven on the front door and a few nails where the eight should be. Every window of the long row of houses in her street was decorated with net curtains. She imagined as she walked along that those unfriendly people were behind them, sneering at her. She very often stood in her basement flat looking out of the window onto the street from behind her own net curtains, where she would see the occasional pair of legs walking by, always hurriedly. No one had time for anything in this country. Just like James. He seemed to walk faster than he did back home. She imagined that some day she would become like everybody else here, the way James had. They rushed around so much, they were rushing themselves into an early grave.

At home, Josephine was making every effort to come to terms with the aloofness of the women upstairs. If either or both were home, they would head straight to the kitchen whenever it was Josephine's turn.

'So, in the Caribbean, they still wearing such flat shoes?' The older of the women bellowed at the top of her voice, her question more of a proclamation to the whole house.

'Well, these are all I have.' Josephine answered, but both of the women had started laughing so loudly she could not be heard above the din.

Josephine tried to get on and cook and ignore them. She struggled with the stove, forgetting how to get the ring to ignite if it didn't work first time. It was a knack that Josephine had not quite mastered, but neither woman came to her assistance.

'Why you don't just go and buy some chips on the corner? James likes them,' one of the women said as the laughter died down.

148

'He like sausage too,' said the other.

'And he like cod fish. He love the cod and chips.'

They seemed to have started a conversation of their own about James' likes and dislikes and had completely forgotten about Josephine, who gave up on the stove and went downstairs to make sure the little ones were happy and not getting too close to their new electric heater. Josephine found the two playing happily together. She sat on the old sofa and lowered her head toward her lap and then hugged her knees and began to rock gently

'Mummy? You sad?' her son asked her. 'Don't be sad. Daddy will come home soon and he will tell you how to start the stove.' He placed his small arm around Josephine's shoulder. She didn't raise her head because she didn't want him to see the tears that had already started welling up. She reached to hug him close to her saying, 'If we get too hungry we can always buy some chips. Daddy left us some money.'

'What are chips?' Her daughter had joined the hugging and Josephine smiled as the tears spilled onto her cheek. She laughed out loud. She didn't know what chips were either.

By February, Josephine had finally found a school for the children. It was the local Catholic school, which was a ten minute walk from their house. Josephine sat in the Headmaster's office with her two children as he peered at them over thick-rimmed, reading glasses. His gaze hovered about two inches above their heads.

'Well it looks as though we have no choice but to take your children. Everywhere else is full and we do have some places. It says here that you and your family are baptised Catholics. I will need to see your baptism certificates of course, and I will expect to see you all at church. Now then, because of where your children have come from I need to find the right classroom for them so that they don't feel out of place and will be able to cope with everything they are going to be taught.' Josephine shifted uncomfortably in her seat for a moment but had no time to speak before the Headmaster continued in a loud voice.

'As you know our children are familiar with writing and reading in English. They are able to apply themselves to mathematics and are used to following instructions and doing as they are told. No rudeness, no laziness. Being punctual and wearing clean clothes are a must.'

The headmaster's gaze sank down to the papers on his desk and without pausing for breath he continued. 'As the situation stands, I shall put them both in Sister Camilla's class. She has a way with these children and she will get them reading and writing their name in no time at all. I'll just go and call Mrs Sanders to take you around there and they can start to settle in.' He got up and opened the door leading to the school secretary's office.

'This way.'

Josephine did not leave her seat and the children remained still and silent. All six eyes stared at the back of the Headmaster's head. He swung round and said in an even louder voice, 'You must come with me now to get the children settled in. You can't stay here. I have work to do. This way to the classroom.'

Josephine stood. The children stayed seated.

'There is no need to shout,' she said. 'I understand what you are saying perfectly well. I think you are the one who does not understand. My children are two different ages. How can you put them in the same class? What kind of system do you have here? You think that because we come from a small island we don't know how to read and write. My daughter is almost six years old. She can write her full name and address. She knows her date of birth. She can recite the Lord's Prayer and the Hail Mary. She can do her multiplication tables up to number four. My son is eight years old. He can read any book you put in front of him. He can talk to you about the Kings and Queens of England and the history of the First World War. He know his multiplication tables up to number 10 and he got the Golden Standard in his class back home as the most promising student. If your school is so backward that it put children anywhere it takes a fancy, then your school is not for me and I will go back to the Council Offices to tell them so.'

With that, she looked at her children, who promptly got up and started to follow their mother to the door.

'Oh, Mrs Dennis.' The Headmaster smiled. His face turned red as he placed a hand on Josephine's shoulder to stop her leaving. Mrs Sanders was out of her seat and watching with interest from the school office.

'Please remove your hand.' Josephine locked eyes with the Headmaster. 'I think we have wasted enough time here.' Josephine started again to exit the room and stopped when the Headmaster, even more sanguine than before, stepped in front of her.

'I think there has been a misunderstanding. Of course they both need appropriate classes. I shall arrange that. Mrs Sanders, the young lady is for Mrs Reed and the young man is for Sister Hilda. Make sure their names are correctly spelt on the register.'

Josephine and her children, now standing in the school office, turned to see the Headmaster's door close rapidly and a very puzzled school secretary stood waiting to take them to class.

Each morning, after dropping her two children at school, Josephine would walk slowly back to the house and often saw the white woman who lived on the first floor. Josephine had seen her taking her own son to school in the morning. They had often smiled at each other but neither made a move to start a conversation. Josephine wished that the woman would say something or maybe invite her upstairs for a cup of tea. She also wished that she had the courage to do the same. But each morning when she returned, Josephine would simply take the stairs down to her basement flat, unlock the door and spend a long and boring day drifting from room to room, trying to keep occupied.

Back home she would have had a list of things to do. She had already cleaned the flat so that it practically shone and if she brushed the already threadbare carpets anymore, the floorboards would show through. Each day she would sit and read the

151

newspaper from the day before that James had left on the table after work. After that she took out her bible and read psalms. She attended church with her children on Sunday mornings, despite the looks from the congregation. James never went to church. He preferred to lie in on a Sunday morning, the only day of the week he had that luxury. Josephine was surprised and disappointed that James had never set foot in a church to pray since he'd been in England. He'd attended Rufus' wedding and that was the only time he'd received Holy Communion. Josephine usually spent most of the hour-long service praying for James' soul.

One Sunday afternoon when James was at the pub with Rufus and the children were busy with a puzzle, Josephine thought she could hear crying from the flat above. At first she assumed it was the radio. But as she started to make her way upstairs to the small kitchen, she was rooted to the spot when she heard Marcia and Margaret's raised voices.

'But I don't want to move away. I like it here. What about work? You think we can find work in Birmingham so easy like here in London? Why do I have to go? It's not fair.'

'Life isn't fair. Sometimes we have to do things we don't like. Life isn't always sunny, you're a fool if you think it is.'

'I'm old enough to take care of myself and I have friends here who can help me and maybe I can stay with them until things are sorted out.'

'No, it's not possible. I made a promise to your father on his deathbed that I would take care of you and make sure you grow up to be a girl he could be proud of. What kind of mother would I be if I went away and left you here to fend for yourself? He would turn in his grave.'

'What kind of mother are you to drag me to a new place where I don't know nobody and to live in I don't know where?'

'We will manage.'

'I don't want to manage. I want to stay here. It's not fair.'

'Why do we have to keep saying the same thing over and over? We have to go and that's that.'

'But why?'

'Because there is no room for a baby, that's why!'

Josephine froze. In all the time she was there she had never spotted a male caller for either of them. Josephine broke the news to James over their meal later that day. She was very surprised at his reaction.

'Pregnant? The girl?' He almost choked on a mouthful of food.

'Well I can't be sure but I think it's the older one. You ever know any of them to have a man here? I've never seen one. And if she wants to move away then maybe he doesn't want to marry her.'

'Maybe he can't.' James kept his eyes down.

'What you mean? If he make her pregnant then he must marry her. That is the only thing to do.' Josephine was cutting up her daughter's food. James ate slowly and in silence.

'Ever been to Birmingham?' Josephine asked after a while.

'What?'

'Not what, where? Birmingham. Have you ever been?'

'No. Why?'

'That's where they going. The mother said there's no room for a baby here so I think Birmingham have bigger houses than London. Should we move there?'

'I thought you didn't like those two.' James had had enough of this conversation.

'Well I don't but I was just thinking that … .'

'Well don't. Let them move where they want. Maybe it's better that way.' James left the table and walked toward the bathroom, stopped, then came back and picked up his coat.

'Where you going?' Josephine asked

'I'm going for a walk.'

'But you just come from outside. And you haven't finish your dinner yet, that's not like you. You sick or something?'

'Maybe.'

The door closed firmly behind James and Josephine could see

through the net curtains that James stood for a few moments before slowly climbing the twelve steps leading to the street. He hesitated before he chose a direction to walk in and when he did, it was with eyes raised to the sky, letting his feet take him wherever they wanted to go. Josephine could not understand what was wrong. It was cold outside and he hadn't done up his buttons.

19

Mum would not be happy with me if she knew what I was doing. Telling someone I'd just met all about my personal life. She always taught us to be proud, to keep our private life private and be careful who we trusted.

He's looking at me in disbelief. I've told him something so private. It came out before I could stop myself. But it's all just there, you see, a fresh wound.

'I've shocked you, right?'

'Well I think I see now why you were so cross with me about what I said. I was trying to be helpful. I had no idea why you and your husband spilt up. I shouldn't have assumed ... .'

'It's not your fault. You expected the usual married couple squabble, not an episode of *Jerry Springer.*'

'I don't know how you can laugh about it.'

'Martin, if I don't laugh, I'll cry. And you wouldn't want to see that. To be honest, I don't think I *can* cry anymore.'

On Tuesday evening Luke was really worried about me. Once again, I hadn't gone into work and was still complaining of the same headache. It was all fake of course. He came into the bedroom with a cup of one of my herbal teas and put it on my bedside table, then sat next to me.

'Angelica, I think there's something up. Something more than this headache you've had. Is it something to do with Angel's and Jasmin going? I know we talked about future plans, but I was probably too pushy about us starting a new restaurant somewhere else. Look, if you don't want to start a restaurant with me I can understand. I know you want to keep Angel's going. It's still a big part of you even though Jasmin is leaving. She's moving on but you're not ready to let go of your baby. Am I right?' He leaned forward to place his hands on mine. They felt warm but I moved my hands and put them under the duvet.

'You know, you've been pulling away from me every time I've tried to touch you the last couple of days. Have I done something? Said something wrong?' I looked at Luke for a long time. My throat was dry. I had built up a list of things I wanted to say over the last forty-eight hours but if I opened my mouth they would all come tumbling out at the same time. I turned my head away.

'Angelica. This isn't fair. Don't shut me out like this. You have to talk to me. Everything was alright until the Jasmin thing so I'm guessing that's what this is all about.'

'It's about everything. Everything we've ever done. Everything we've ever been and everything that's going to happen next.' Luke remained silent. 'I found something out about Eva.' I looked into his eyes as I sat up. 'She's been sleeping with someone.'

'She told you?'

'Not exactly, but the truth always comes out in the end.'

'So how do you know?'

'It doesn't matter how I know. What matters is *who* she's sleeping with.' He was quiet again and just looked at me. 'Luke, I know it's someone in the family.'

'So? Hold on a second. If you didn't get this from Eva, how did you find out?'

'Saffron let it slip.'

'Angelica. This is crazy. Someone in the family?' He waited for a response. I held his gaze without blinking.

'Jesus Christ.' He said finally. 'You think it's *me*.'

I got out of bed and nearly knocked him over as I rushed to get out of the room. I was suffocating. He grabbed me by the arm and swung me round. I pulled away from his grip and stared straight into his eyes.

'What is wrong with you?' he shouted. 'You can't walk out at a time like this.' It was the first time he ever raised his voice at me.

'Luke, don't start. I've seen the way you two are with each other. Always laughing and whispering. Secret jokes, always going places together.'

'Angelica. This, this is crazy. Look, I love you and I love Eva.' He choked and tried to catch his breath. 'You're serious. You really believe that I ... ?' He shook his head and looked down. Was that the best he could do?

'Angelica. You. Look, I – I can't do this.' He walked past me in a hurry to get somewhere, making sure he avoided any physical contact. He hesitated for a second at the door, but didn't turn around. I could hear his footsteps on the stairs. Very quickly he was at the front door. I heard his keys coming off the hook and the front door open and close. Seconds later, I heard him drive away.

I sat back on the bed and picked up the phone. I called Jasmin

'Hey gorgeous – what's up?' she said.

'Jasmin, I won't be in again tomorrow and I don't think Luke will. It's up to you what you do. You can put a sign up to say we've had to close temporarily or get a chef in. I won't be back for a while.' I held the phone in my hand, and I could hear Jasmin's voice in the background.

'Ange, Ange, what's happened?' I hung up, rolled over onto my side and closed my eyes. Tears soaked my pillow. I did nothing to try to stop them.

20

'What was all that whispering about?' Josephine stood at the foot of the stairs that led down from the kitchen to their basement flat. Her arms were crossed and there was a vexed expression on her face. She followed James into the bedroom, where he sat on the bed with his back against the headboard, arms crossed behind his head. He was still wearing outdoor shoes. His eyes were closed and a slight furrow creased his brow. Josephine had no idea what was wrong. She stood patiently by the bedroom door waiting for a reply to her question. The children were asleep in the other room.

James had come home late and eaten his dinner up in the kitchen while Josephine took a bath. She'd expected him to have finished eating by the time she came out of the bath and be getting ready for bed himself. But he was still in the kitchen. She could hear him talking to one or other of the women from upstairs in a rushed whisper. She had put on her nightdress and lingered in the corridor to hear as much of the conversation as she could, but she could hardly make out what was being said and could get no closer without revealing her presence. She was sure she heard something about money and the place name, Birmingham.

Losing her patience, she pulled James' shoes off and threw them toward the door. She pulled hard on the bed covers as she climbed into bed and sat up next to James.

'Don't pretend you didn't hear me ask. What whispering about? Was that the mother or the daughter you were asking money from?' She didn't look at him but faced straight ahead trying to control her breathing, her chest rising and falling, with her arms crossed.

'I didn't ask for money. I was offering it.'

'What?' Josephine now turned to face her husband. 'We have no money of our own and you want to give it away?'

'It was the mother, Marcia. You know they're going away. She was just a little short that's all. She will pay it back.'

'But how? And when?'

'It was next to nothing. I thought you were a Christian. We have to help our neighbours.'

'Your church is The Princess Alice. Why didn't you just offer her a drink?' She paused for a moment. 'You will never see that money again. Your children need it. We need it. What happened to you James? You act as though those women own you. I'm here now and *I'm* your wife.' Josephine stopped as James got up. He left the bedroom and went upstairs to the kitchen. She could hear water running from the tap and the sound of a glass filling. She slid under the blankets and listened as he came back to the room. Facing away from him she felt the bed yield to his weight as he sat unbuttoning his shirt. She didn't turn to watch as he left the room again, this time for the bathroom. The water ran for a long time as he brushed his teeth. Josephine closed her eyes. James came back into the bedroom and turned out the light. He crawled silently into bed without a word as she lay in angry silence. Eventually, they both drifted off to sleep.

James was up and out of the house very quickly the next morning with very little time for them to exchange more than a few words. Josephine knew her husband. She knew she could never get the truth from him as well as she knew she could never get satisfaction from an argument with him. He had few words but an astounding ability to wear his wife out with the strength of his silence. She never raised her concerns about the money he'd given to Marcia again. But she never forgot.

There were changes happening at the house. Two weeks after the women left, someone new moved in. A single man. His name was

Anthony Magyar and from what Josephine and the rest of the household could make of him, Anthony Magyar was a drunk. He kept himself to himself. James had spoken to him on Josephine's behalf about the sharing of the kitchen. She was glad to be able to establish rules about the kitchen afresh, rules that would suit her needs. She needn't have worried about privacy because Anthony Magyar was a reluctant cook. He had one bottle of milk in the fridge that usually went off before it was used, a small loaf of bread and some cold meat or cheese. In fact, Josephine hardly heard him in the kitchen for more than five or ten minutes at a time. She occasionally saw him going up to the front door or saw his legs heading away from the house toward the Princess Alice. James said he was in the pub on a Sunday afternoon but usually looked as though he'd been there all night. Of course, there was evidence to prove he had returned home from the pub on a Saturday night because, as religiously as Josephine took herself and the two children to church on a Sunday morning, Magyar would be throwing up in the bathroom on the first floor.

There had been complaints from the people who lived on the first and second floors, as Josephine found out after her first conversation with Hannah, the white woman on the first floor. After several weeks of smiling to each other in passing, Josephine and Hannah finally spoke. It started with a 'Hello'. This became a 'Hello, how are you?' And the answer, 'Fine', seemed no longer to suffice. Soon both women were sharing ten and fifteen minute conversations on the street outside their house. One day Hannah invited Josephine in for some tea.

'I've got some biscuits in. Would you like some?' As Hannah removed her coat, Josephine could quite clearly see that she was pregnant.

'Oh, when is your due date?' Josephine asked.

'I'm expecting at the end of September.'

'I am expecting too.' Josephine smiled. 'But not until November.'

'Then the two of them can be friends. Sit down, love, and I'll make us some tea. My husband wasn't very happy that we're having another one. He says the expense will kill us. I just think he should get himself a better job.'

'What he do?' Josephine had placed her coat over the back of a chair and sat at the dining table.

'He works as a caretaker in a hospital.'

'Oh, in a hospital.'

'More like a glorified cleaner if you ask me. Not a job for a man. What does your husband do?'

'Well he works as a builder but he is a trained carpenter.'

'Oh – just like Jesus.'

'He's not like Jesus. He don't believe in church anymore.'

'Your kids go to the Catholic school don't they? They've got the uniform. I've seen you out of the window on a Sunday morning going to church. Here … .' Hannah put down a tea pot with a knitted blue and green tea cosy. She fetched two teacups from a wall cupboard and then produced a bowl of sugar from the sideboard that had the final few sprinklings of white, granulated sugar in it. She placed a side plate on the table and emptied half the contents of a packet of shortbread biscuits onto it. She sat down and began to pour.

Her rooms were quite gloomy. This one faced onto the street. It was a large room with patterned wallpaper with large, dark red flowers on a background that was once the colour of fresh yellow sand, but now resembled fallen leaves in autumn. In one corner of the room there was a hotplate, a small fridge and a sink. The dining table was positioned by the windows, which were draped with thick, deep red curtains. There was a sofa and two easy chairs in the room. A pillow and neatly folded blanket on the floor next to the sofa told Josephine that Hannah's young son must have to sleep there. A double door adjoined this room to the bedroom which looked out onto the garden. The garden, to which all four sets of occupants had access to via the ground floor kitchen, was only ever used to hang out washing. Three washing lines hung in a triangular pattern on six metal poles. The patchy

161

grass was cut once in a while by the landlord's brother.

'I love my tea,' Hannah said. 'Here, help yourself to a biscuit, don't be shy. We are eating for two aren't we?' Hannah had a happy smile, Josephine noticed. Her thin, brown hair was always neatly tucked into a bun. She was slight and on the short side, like Josephine.

'So, your husband, … happy to be a father again?' Hannah asked as she reached for a biscuit.

'Yes, I believe so. That's what he said anyway. I think everyone should have a big family. I don't know why your husband only want to stick with one.'

'Well he's had more than one. He was married before. His wife died when the last was born. He's seven now, Little Joe is. That's who I take to school every morning. He's got three grown up kids, my husband, and Joe was a surprise. He's quite a bit older than me and he didn't want to go down that road again – having babies. But I don't see why I should miss out. Do you?'

'Well having a child is a blessing and I think all women deserve them.'

'I say to him – you don't have to do anything. I'll do the nappy changing and all that. You just bring home the bacon. Am I right?'

'Yes, you are.'

The two women saw each other most days. Hannah was Josephine's window to the world. Well, to West London at least. She showed her the best places to shop for food and they looked after each other's children once in a while. Josephine had found a good friend in Hannah. Up until then the only other adult Josephine could converse with had been James. Conversations were limited most days with him to good mornings, good evenings and goodnights. Other than that, there was Eunice. Being clear across the other side of London, Josephine had not seen her sister since they parted at the train station on the day they arrived in England almost three months ago. Their only form of communication so far had been by letter and neither had exchanged more than two or three.

Eunice wrote to Josephine to say that she and Nestor had moved to a place with a telephone. She had given her new address and telephone number, and Josephine had replied, giving the number of the payphone on the ground floor of her house.

Josephine called Eunice one morning after dropping the children at school and the regular pot of tea with her neighbour.

'I can't believe I'm hearing your voice so clear.' Josephine was excited to finally speak to her younger sister. 'Tell me, how are you and how you finding it here? You think you will like London, Sis?'

'Well, it is certainly different. Different to what I was expecting. I have a job now.'

'What you doing?' Josephine was pleased for Eunice.

'Just packing things in boxes.' Eunice sounded indifferent. 'I could do it in my sleep. But the rent here is more expensive, and Nestor say I had to find a job. So you must be big belly by now, Sis?'

'No, not yet. I'm sure I'll get a lot bigger. I usually do. What about you? You going to make a baby anytime?'

'We'll see.'

'What? Nestor don't want children?'

'I don't know what Nestor want these days. I don't know if he even know himself what he want. Always bad temper, bad moods. He make me sick sometimes.'

'He is your husband. You must talk to him and ask him what's wrong. Maybe it's nothing.'

'Maybe it's everything.'

'What you mean by that?'

'Never mind. How are the others? James, the children?'

'Yes, all fine. One of these days we must come to see you.'

'Maybe.'

'When is a good day? Saturday?'

'I said maybe.'

'Eunice, what's wrong. You ashamed of your place or

163

something? I don't live in Buckingham Palace you know. I won't mind what your place look like.'

'I don't think Nestor like to have visitors. He made me move because I was making friends with people in the house before. Here nobody talk to you when they see you. I wouldn't be surprise if Nestor don't tell them not to speak to me.'

'Eunice, don't exaggerate. Why would Nestor not want you to have friends?' There was a long pause on the other end of the line.

'Eunice?'

'Look Sis. Don't put your nose in places that don't concern you. It's best when Nestor and I don't have a problem so don't come unless I say it's okay.'

'Alright. But if you and Nestor are in any kind of trouble you would tell me wouldn't you?'

'You tell me everything that happen between you and James?' Eunice sounded annoyed.

'That's not what I mean. I just don't want you to feel alone over there.'

'I'm not alone. I have my work and so you don't have to worry. I have to go. Nestor have a half day and maybe he might come soon.'

'You telling me he don't want you to speak to your own sister?'

'Look Josephine, I have to go. I'll call you another day. Remember me to the children.' She put down the receiver before Josephine could say goodbye.

'Problems?' Hannah put her head over the banister.

'I hope not.'

After six weeks of telephoning her sister at different times of the day and either getting no reply or having Nestor come to the phone to answer in her place, saying she was out, Josephine became increasingly worried about Eunice.

'I want to go there,' she said to James one night just as he was about to turn off the light. He hovered by the light switch.

'It doesn't seem as though your sister really want to see you,

Josephine. Why you think she never come to the phone?' He switched off the light and made his way to the bed. 'Besides, it's a long way to go without an invitation. What if they are not home? We would have had a wasted journey.'

'I mean to go by myself. You watch those two tomorrow. Tomorrow is Saturday, you don't have work and she should be home. I just need you to tell me what bus to take.'

'You have to go on the tube. It's far. It's a long way to go on your own and in your condition. What if something happen?'

'Nothing can happen. I'll pay my passage like everyone else and go about my business. I'll go early and come back as soon as I know my sister is alright. You know you would do the same if it was your little sister.'

'Eunice is not little anymore. I think you are wasting your time going there. Just call her again tomorrow, she might answer this time.'

'No, something tell me I should go.' It hadn't been because of a dream. Josephine just sensed that something was wrong. She was not about to give up on trying to see her sister. If Eunice no longer wanted her involved in her life, then she must tell her to her face.

Josephine sat on the train. It was the first time she had travelled by tube. James had given her instructions and she had written them down. She knew she needed the Metropolitan Line from Ladbroke Grove and to change at Liverpool Street for the Central Line to Bethnal Green and then catch a bus on Cambridge Heath Road. The bus number was also scribbled on the piece of paper she continually felt for in her pocket throughout the journey. She was to ask the bus conductor which stop she needed for the hospital and then ask for directions to Robinson Road.

The journey by tube was long and noisy. She recognized Portobello Road as the train pulled away from Ladbroke Grove tube station. She spotted the direction for the school, the Halfpenny Steps and Great Western Road as she gazed out of the window. Very shortly she was underground.

Few words were exchanged in her carriage, Josephine noticed. Most read a newspaper or kept their eyes fixed to one spot, never looking up at anybody else. When she finally got to East London, Josephine stood in a wide and busy road, waiting for her bus. There were two other women at the bus stop, one holding the hand of a little boy. They talked non-stop until the bus came. At one point one of the women smiled at Josephine but turned back to her conversation before Josephine could even say good morning.

'The hospital please,' she said to the conductor. He was a tall, skinny black man with golden tones to his skin and brown freckles on his nose. His conductor's hat was tipped back on his head, revealing neatly cut brown hair. He smiled at Josephine.

'You going the wrong way, Sweetie. Get off next stop, cross the road and go in the opposite direction. You visiting someone Sweetie?' Josephine only smiled but didn't answer.

When she finally got to the hospital she found it difficult to ask anyone for directions. People walked straight by her even though she smiled and politely said, 'Excuse me.' It was a young, black couple that eventually stopped to help her find her way.

She hesitated before walking up to the front door and knocking. This house had no basement flat. She had no idea what floor Eunice lived on or who would answer the door. After knocking twice she heard a door inside opening and a cat meowing in the corridor. As the door opened, the cat rushed past Josephine's feet and out onto the pavement. An old white woman, short and stocky, stood in front of her.

'You want the top floor,' she said before Josephine had a chance to speak and ambled back to her room. Josephine closed the door quietly and walked slowly up the stairs. At the very top of the stairs were two doors facing each other and Josephine had no idea which to knock on. Just then one door opened and a very dark skinned black man came out holding hands with a tall, slim white woman whose blond hair was piled on top of her head and tied with a big white bow. They smiled at Josephine, said nothing, and walked past her. Josephine stood for several minutes outside what she knew now to be Eunice's flat. She listened for any sound but heard nothing. Perhaps James was right and she'd come all this way and they were out.

'Well, ain't you gonna knock then?' The voice came from behind her and made her jump. It was the old lady from downstairs. She stood on the bottom step and gazed up at Josephine.

'I'm not sure anyone home.'

'Oh someone's home alright. I know that for a fact. Making enough noise last night and this morning to wake the dead. But only one of 'em's gone out. Go on – give it a try. Family are ya?'

'Yes. Thank you.'

Josephine gave a timid knock. There was no answer straight away and the old woman held her position on the stairs below. Josephine knocked a little louder and after a long pause the door opened about three inches. Seeing her sister standing there, Eunice sighed and leaned her head against the door so that only part of her face was showing. She appeared to have no intention of opening the door any further.

'Josephine. I told you not to come.' She closed her eyes then stepped away, pulling the door open to let her sister in. Josephine went inside and glanced quickly around the room. She turned and smiled at her.

'My God in heaven. Eunice. What happened?'

'I told you not to come.'

The side of her face that had been hidden when Eunice answered the door was swollen to twice normal size. One eye was almost closed and completely bloodshot. The swelling around her eye was reddish in colour. The blow that caused it must have been fairly recent. Josephine went to embrace her sister who pulled away and went to sit on an old, battered easy chair.

'Why don't you ever listen to me?' Eunice said without looking up at Josephine. 'You're worse than our mother. I told you and I told you not to come.' With each 'I told you', Eunice beat the palm of her hand with her fist.

'I had to come, I felt something was wrong.'

'You still think you are some kind of witch then?'

'No that's what *you* think of *me*. Remember! But never mind that now. Eunice, did Nestor do this to you?'

'Yes.'

'But why? What happened?' Josephine was kneeling on the floor next to Eunice, holding her sister's hands as they trembled on her lap.

'He never used to be like this,' Eunice said with a whimper. 'Not at home. He has a bad temper, but so do I. But, … but I never seen him like this. He's always angry. Angry for what I don't know. And I can never do or say anything before he raises up in anger.'

'He done this before?' Eunice did not answer. 'Eunice! How many times he hit you?'

'Maybe a few. This was the worst one. He lost his job a while ago and can't find anything yet. Only me who work and the money not enough. We owe the old lady a few weeks in rent and she say she will put us out.'

'The lady downstairs?'

'Yes.'

'She won't put you out. I will talk to her.'

'Oh Josephine.' Eunice got up abruptly and went to the window, where she stood looking out with her arms folded tightly around her body. 'You think life is all sunshine and roses. You always see the good in people and you can't see what's right in front of your eyes.'

'What do you mean by that?'

'That woman won't care about me. All she want is her rent. Just like Nestor don't care about me. He can't stand the sound of my voice. I talk to him nicely, I try to make him happy but nothing I can say can stop him acting like a madman. He have a woman, you know?'

'What? Nestor have another woman?'

'Yes – a woman. Don't sound so surprised, Josephine. He's a man isn't he?'

'Eunice, I'm sorry.' Josephine stood by her sister and placed a hand on each shoulder.

'She pregnant.' Eunice said and gently pulled away from her sister. 'I can't give him a child so he think I'm worthless.'

'Eunice, you are not worthless. Not all women fall pregnant straight away. You must be patient.'

'I've had a year of patient. Nestor lost his patience with me a long time ago.'

'So he beat you because you can't have a child?'

'He beat me because someone make him angry at work. He beat me if he don't like what I cook. He beat me if I give him a wrong answer. He beat me because he have no job. He just beat me, he just … .' Her voice trailed off as she broke down in tears. Josephine held her trembling sister whose bony frame she could feel through the old housecoat she was wearing.

'Oh Eunice. My Eunice. You must come back with me. Come back with me now and I will look after you. I can't leave you here with this man. We never knew anything about him or his family before you marry him and now we know exactly who he is. Come I'll pack you a grip.'

Josephine looked about the room. Walking into the adjoining room she saw an unmade bed. Looking about her she recognised the old suitcase Eunice had brought from home and took it down from the rickety wardrobe. She opened the wardrobe and started looking for Eunice's clothes. Eunice had stopped crying.

'What will James say?' she asked as she stood between the doorway of the living room and bedroom.

'You're my sister and I must look after you. No matter what, James has reason and he won't stand by to see a woman being beaten like this.'

Josephine continued to pack as Eunice began getting dressed. With the suitcase packed, Eunice looked around the living room for her shoes. Just then the door opened. It was Nestor. Both women froze. The suitcase was at Josephine's feet.

'Josephine. It's been a long time. How are you?' He grinned at Josephine as though there was nothing wrong. He never looked down at the suitcase but straight at his sister-in-law, ignoring Eunice for now.

'I'm fine but my sister is not.' She was deciding whether or not to pick up the suitcase. Eunice's eyes had glazed over as she looked down at her feet.

'Just a little misunderstanding.' He smiled sweetly.

'*Little*? You take me for a fool Nestor?' Josephine was finding her courage.

'No Josephine, of course I don't.' He moved closer to her, hands open and his voice softening even more. 'I know what the problem is here. I lose my job. I was upset and I took it out on Eunice. She kept on bragging that she was the only one bringing money in. How is a man supposed to feel?'

Josephine looked at Eunice whose eyes never rose from the floor.

'But, look, I have a job now.' Nestor continued. 'I just been to see a fellow in Forest Gate and I can start on Monday. You see Eunice – everything will be alright.' He placed a large hand on his wife's shoulder. She shrank at his touch. She gave no verbal response but looked to her sister, still with that glazed look about her eyes.

'Eunice? You coming with me?' Josephine had desperation in her voice.

'I'll stay and talk this over with Nestor.' Eunice's voice was a monotone.

'You see? It's not as bad as you think Josephine,' Nestor said. 'Oh, Josephine, you're pregnant! You never told me that, Eunice. Congratulations to you and James. Sit down and I'll fix you a cup of coffee or something. That's a long way to come in your condition.'

'I don't need coffee, I don't need to sit down. I should be

getting back. What about if Eunice come with me for a few days? Let her feel better after this, this misunderstanding. What you say Nestor?'

'Well it's up to Eunice. What you think Eunice?' He turned to her but kept his hand on her shoulder.

'Josephine,' Eunice said stiffly, 'I've got work on Monday and bills to pay.'

'So, I should go then Eunice? Is that what you're saying?' Josephine struggled to keep an even tone in her voice. A lump had come to her throat.

'Yes. But it was so nice to see you. So nice.' Eunice pulled away from her husband's hold and hugged her sister tightly, so tight Josephine almost lost her balance. Josephine squeezed her sister to her and stroked her messy hair. Nestor did not move.

'When I call you, Eunice, please come to the phone. I need to hear your voice more often,' Josephine pleaded, still holding her sister, her eyes on Nestor.

'I promise,' Eunice said.

'Oh I'll make sure she behaves,' Nestor cut in.

Josephine backed slowly to the door. The couple made no attempt to see her to the front door. Eunice and Josephine's eyes were locked. Josephine retreated as if in slow motion. Nestor stood next to his wife with his large hand on her shoulder. Josephine turned, left their flat and closed the door. She slowly made her way downstairs and was startled to find the old woman on that bottom step.

'Alright love? Look like you've seen a ghost. Need a drop of water?' the woman asked.

'Er, no thank you. But could I trouble you to use your bathroom?'

' 'course you can dear. In the family way aren't you? 'spect you gotta go all the time. It's through here, dear.'

When Josephine came out of the bathroom and made her way to the front door, the woman was at her side.

'Come back for 'er, won't you love? Gotta come back.'

'I will.' Josephine put her head down and walked to the gate. She looked up at the upstairs window before closing the gate softly behind her and heading home.

21

It was Saturday and I hadn't answered the door or the phone to Jasmin. She came over every day. I eventually replied to one of her texts and told her I was still alive but that Luke and I were finished. She sent a text saying: 'Please let me in, I'm coming over now.' She was knocking on the door just over an hour later and I felt I had to give her an explanation. I'd left her completely in the dark and we still hadn't sorted out a way forward for the business as yet. Everything was happening at once and I just didn't know how to deal with it.

Jasmin ran me a bath and poured me a big glass of red wine. She sat on the lid of the toilet while we drank, not asking any questions until she thought I was ready to talk. I had been crying for most of the time she'd been there. She kept handing me pieces of toilet paper to blow my nose and holding my glass while I did so.

'So, Eva will be back in a couple of days. Does she know you guys have split up?'

'No.'

'She's not going to take it well. She absolutely adores that man. So does everybody else. Isn't there a way you two can sort this out? I take it you argued about something. One of you has to say sorry. Can't you do it? Whether it was your fault or not? You can't be without Luke. Look at what it's doing to you.'

'I really can't be with Luke, Jas. He's not the person we thought he was. Not at all. If he ever was. He's changed. Something or someone has changed him.'

'You mean an affair?' She asked and her lips stayed parted. I looked down at my glass. 'No, Angie, not Luke. He's the last

173

person … .'

'Remember, Jasmin, it's always the one you least suspect. And no-one ever thinks it's going to happen to them.'

'So this is it? He's gone?'

'Yes.'

'With her?'

'No, not with her.'

'So it's over between them?'

'I really don't know. And I don't want to think about it.' I put my wine glass to my lips, tilted my head and drained the contents.'

'More?'

'Yes please. One thing I haven't done yet is get drunk.'

'Well you needed your old wine drinking buddy for that.' She poured me another. 'I'm going to miss this.' She said. Then she caught the expression on my face. 'Sorry Ange. But one of these days we'll have to talk about me going.'

'Yes, I know. About that. We'll have to dissolve the partnership and sort out all the assets with the lawyer.'

'Is that what you want us to do?'

'It's all we *can* do really. Unless you change your mind and say you'll stay.'

'Oh Ange. I'm so sorry. This is Steven's chance of a lifetime. It's ours. I can't.'

'I know, babes. I wasn't being serious.'

'What will you do?'

'Well without Luke to consider now, I've decided to carry on the outside catering.'

'And the premises?'

'Not sure. I need somewhere to operate from. We've built up a good reputation. I'm sure I can keep going as long as I can use the name.'

'Of course you can. It's your name.'

'Well you came up with the idea. I don't know, I just thought maybe … .'

'Angie – don't give it another thought. This is all about how to make things easiest for you. My life is taken care of. I'll be living in a swanky apartment in New York, shopping for clothes all day and having a housekeeper and a nanny look after my fat, spoilt kids who'll end up with American accents.'

'They're not fat or spoilt.'

'It's just a question of time, my friend.' She lifted her glass as if to toast the fate of her children. She smiled. I struggled to do the same.

Jasmin left in the early hours of the morning. I'd had about a bottle and a half of wine and she tucked me into bed before she left. I woke late on Sunday morning and felt as though a herd of elephants had just trampled across my head and were coming back for an encore. I fell asleep again until three. The phone rang. It was Eva.

'Mum, you'll never guess what?'

'Eva stop shouting.' I had the phone under the covers. I wasn't able to sit up.

'Sorry Mum, you sound like I woke you.'

'You did.'

'But listen. I just got a call from Benny. You remember the producer from the States from last year when I did that recording? Well he's been having a lot of interest from the songs and one of them got released on a compilation CD. They want to organise a tour of the college campuses with a handful of the artists on that album and guess who's going to be one of them.'

'Well, you of course.' I was trying to sound positive but the only thing that was going through my mind was what Eva had done.

Then it occurred to me that Eva sounded as though nothing had changed. Luke had obviously not been in touch with her to tell her that I knew. I couldn't understand why. Maybe he was too ashamed and was hiding out somewhere. I knew I couldn't confront her about what I'd found out. I wasn't ready to face up to it. It would destroy me completely to hear it from my own child's mouth. Her disappearing for a while seemed like an answer to a prayer.

'So what about Guildhall?' I asked, trying to sound as normal as possible.

'Well I know they don't allow deferrals. I'd just have to apply again if I ever wanted to go.'

'Well, sounds like you're doing this.'

'Mum – you're so cool. I thought you'd go crazy and want me to stay here and study.'

'Well this is an education too. It could be a real chance for you.'

'Where's Dad? Why hasn't he been answering his phone?'

'You've been ringing him?'

'Well a couple of times, yeah, when Saff and I got stuck for something to do.'

'Why didn't you call me?'

'I called the house but no-one answered. And I wanted to speak to Dad 'cause he's been to Cornwall and you haven't.'

'Oh, right.'

'Tell him I called and I'll see you guys in a couple of days. I'll be off to the States in about a week. They're paying for my flight. I just need to try and rush through a visa. I've got enough money saved for this I think. Isn't it great?'

'Fantastic, Eva.' I hung up.

I sank back beneath the covers. I had not heard from Luke. I had no idea how he'd react to her going to America and I was equally unsure of how to handle things when Eva came home and asked where her dad was.

'You must have been going through hell.' Martin seems genuinely concerned about me. 'I understand now why you sounded unsure when I was asking about the business earlier.'

'The thing is, this is just not like me. Telling you all of this. It's not my way. But nothing is the way it should be right now.'

His face is grey. It's as though he's hearing this story being told by a close friend. We'll never see each other again after this. Maybe that's why I can't stop myself.

Of course I could not put off the inevitable. Eva bounced into the house on the Wednesday afternoon, rucksack on her back, hair all frizzy and wild, not her usual tamed curls. She was on the phone to someone as she walked up the path and I could hear her laughing. It was like watching a TV commercial about some happy young girl about to embark on a wonderful journey with the aid of some fabulous new toothpaste. I felt cold inside. I couldn't bear to have her in the house but at the same time I wanted to run to her and hold her close to me and let her know that she would always be mine no matter what.

'Hey Mum!' she called, after dumping her rucksack by the door.

'I'm in here.' The living room door was slightly ajar.

'Dad at work? His car isn't here.' She flopped on to the sofa next to me and gave me a big hug. Her hair got into my eyes and I gently pushed her away, saying that I was going to suffocate under all that hair.

'I didn't bring any leave-in conditioner and Saffron went crazy with the blow dryer. Do I look bad?'

'A bit like Phil Lynott meets Wizard.'

'Who?' She sprang up from the sofa. 'Mum. I've got masses to do. I'll catch up with you for a chat in a bit. I need to get my computer on and get organised.' She was brimming with joy. It was obvious that Luke had not been in touch.

By the evening Eva had calmed down. She was in the kitchen, singing. She'd made me some pasta.

'I didn't do any for Dad. I assume he'll have eaten by now. It's late.'

'Eva, I don't know how much you know, but Dad isn't at work.'

'No?'

'He's not here anymore. He left.'

177

Eva dropped her fork. 'What do you mean, left?'

'As in we broke up. He walked out and I haven't seen him for a week now.' I had my head down.

'But I don't get it. Is this some sort of argument you guys have had? What's it about?' I stopped and looked at her. A long hard look to be sure I was reading her right. Eva was being genuine. She had no idea.

'It's something I can't ever see us getting over Eva. Do you understand?'

'No I don't understand. You and Dad love each other. He's always saying how much he loves you.'

'When did you talk about that?'

'All the time, Mum. I wish I could meet someone who loves me as much as he loves you. It's not making sense. You have to tell me what it's about. I'm ringing him.' Her mobile was at her ear before I could stop her.

'No answer again. Where's he gone?'

'No idea.' I was relieved that he hadn't replied.

'Mum, this is freaking me out. Whatever it is you're not telling me, you better sort it out before I go. It's going to be awful to leave you like this.'

'Leave it to me to sort out, Eva. You just concentrate on getting yourself to New York.'

'Before I go, I've got some goodbyes. I need to see one or two people.'

'Like who?'

'Just people.' She had started eating again.

'Well Maddy and Del and the girls are still in the Caribbean with Grandma, remember? They won't be back for about another ten days so you probably won't get to see them. Only your uncles are still around. You'll have to write to the girls.'

'I will.' She got up from the table and went upstairs. She was back on her phone.

Five days later, Eva was gone. She had managed to get in touch with Luke who came to see her off at the airport. She hugged us both. She held my hand with her right hand and Luke's with her left.

'Please you two, make up while I'm away. Come out and see me – together. Please.' She kissed us on the cheek and was gone a second after putting our hands together. We held hands for the ten seconds it took for her to disappear through the crowd, rucksack on her back, heading off to her departure gate. Then we let go and went our separate ways.

22

Josephine's mother had always told her that it was wrong to interfere in a couple's marriage. Had her mother seen Eunice's face that day, even she would not have stood for the way Nestor had treated his wife. When she broke the news to James his face changed. He looked worried. His next reaction was that of anger.

'He can't get away with this. Give me the address, I'll go and show him he can't treat women like that.

'I think we would make it worse for her if we went in there and started a fight with Nestor,' Josephine said. 'Behind their own four walls, a couple can do or say anything to each other. So once we'd left, who knows what could happen? It was so hard to turn and walk away from my sister like that. The best thing we can do is take Eunice out of there.'

'But where would we put her?'

'Here. With us. With her family.' The look on James' face told her that this was not acceptable.

'We are too crowded as it is,' he said. 'There is nowhere for Eunice to sleep. It would make more sense for her to find a room near where she's working. At least she has a job, she can look out for herself and she won't have to listen to any of Nestor's rubbish anymore.'

'I suppose you're right. Next time I speak to her I'll tell her what you said. Maybe she will find something. Maybe she should save some money first.'

'Yes, that's the best thing.'

It was Thursday. Josephine had tried calling her sister every day since her surprise visit but Eunice had not once come to the phone. The phone, as in Josephine's house, was in the hallway.

Twice, the woman who had opened the door for Josephine answered.

'They're both at work dear. I heard them come in last night but they seem to be mostly out of the house. I think she has a friend from work. I seen someone come for her once. A woman. I ain't heard no more rowing from up there but it's like that sometimes. Quiet for ages and then it flares up. Polite as anything 'e is to me. Both are really. Seems a shame they can't get on, eh?'

'A big shame. I wonder if you could ask my sister to call me when she get home? I been worried about her.'

'I will dear. Soon as I see her.'

Josephine wondered whether Nestor having a new job might have calmed the situation between him and Eunice. But, considering what Eunice had said about his temper, she held very little hope of it staying that way. Josephine had had her ups and downs with James but she knew that he would never strike her.

Not a second passed during the days that followed without Josephine wondering about Eunice. She remembered the forceful young girl who had walked along the road from her little house in the country, hips swaying from side to side, head held high. Now she pictured the shrunken shell she had become. No fire left inside her and that strong will of hers broken. Josephine hoped that separating herself from Nestor would be enough to restore the vibrancy that Eunice once had. She was determined to save her sister and continued to call the house in East London each day that week until finally she spoke to Eunice.

'Oh, Josephine. You really are a worrier. I'm perfectly fine. I'm more than that. I've got some friends from work now and they are going to take me to bingo with them next Friday. I can't wait. I have a brand new lipstick. Bright red. Just like a movie star. Nestor say he will take me to the pictures when he get his wages. You see. Everything is fine between us now. I just wish I could fall pregnant and then I will have everything. Patsy from work, she came by my house and she say how handsome she find Nestor. She tell all the women at work and they jealous, jealous, jealous.'

Eunice hardly paused for breath. Josephine didn't get a chance to speak to or advise her sister before Eunice declared she was tired and wanted to have a bath before bed.

'I have to hurry, the other lady lodging here always use up all the hot water. I have to get in before her.' She barely said goodbye before she hung up. Josephine had been worrying about her sister for a week, now she had been brushed off in the way only Eunice could. Josephine had felt sure she'd lost her sister at Nestor's hands, but it would appear that Eunice had not gone far.

Five minutes after saying goodbye to the children at the school gate that morning and making them promise solemnly to pay attention in class and not chatter, Josephine felt her first contraction. She was ready to ignore the pain as she had been having small contractions during the previous month. But about two hours later, the warning signs that her baby was on the way could not be ignored. She doubled over as she felt a gripping pain in her lower abdomen and knew it was her time. Once the pain subsided, she went upstairs to ask Hannah if she would pick up the children from school and keep hold of them until later. Hannah would probably have to feed them and quite possibly put them up for the night. There was no one else for Josephine to ask.

At about six-thirty in the evening, James came home and saw his wife crouching by the old sofa.

'Josephine! What's happened?'

'The baby is coming. The children are upstairs by Hannah. Go and call an ambulance. I haven't got long to go.'

James took the stairs two at a time. Josephine, meanwhile, put on her old coat which no longer fastened in the front, and sat at the table waiting for James. He rushed downstairs and said that an ambulance was on its way.

'Where is your case?' He looked desperately around the room but could see nothing. 'Have you packed it?'

'Yes, of course. My grip is just inside the bedroom door. You can get it now but we still have to wait for the ambulance.'

The ambulance arrived some fifteen minutes later. The flashing lights caused twitches from several curtains at nearby windows. At least three people came outside to see what the emergency was. Two male paramedics jumped out of the ambulance, but before they had time to go up to the front door, James was outside signalling them down to the basement. From inside the flat they heard a long, low groan from his wife. The medics rushed in and found Josephine straightening up from a stooped position and asking where her grip was.

'I've got it,' said James who rushed to pick it up as the two men led Josephine to the door.

'I need it,' she said. 'Pass it to me, James.'

'I'm sure your husband can manage that. You've got enough to worry about.' The two men watched in amazement as Josephine took the case from James and placed it on her head before walking up the stairs to the street and climbing aboard the ambulance. One of the paramedics, the driver, looked on in disbelief but went speedily about his duty of getting his patient to the delivery room at the Princess Louise Hospital. The other looked from Josephine and back to James as Josephine sat with the suitcase still on her head.

'It's alright. I know what I'm doing. I don't want to have my baby in an ambulance. So like this, I know I won't deliver until I'm on the hospital bed.'

'Oh. I see,' he said. But obviously he didn't. He had actually never come across anything of this kind in his twelve years of working for the ambulance service. James was deeply embarrassed and kept his head bowed until they got to the hospital. The hospital was a twenty-minute drive away. Josephine did not have another contraction until she handed James the grip as she crossed the threshold of the hospital.

November had been a particularly cold month. At the beginning of the week, the weathermen had forecast snow but Josephine knew that there would be no snow until the day she came out of

183

the hospital. After a year of living in London, Josephine had not had a premonition in any of her dreams. Except one two nights ago. Her dream told her that there would be snow on the day she came from the hospital after having a girl baby. There would be no complications. In the dream she had been getting ready to leave the hospital after having the baby and asked the nurse if it was snowing and the nurse had told her that it had snowed overnight.

Only one midwife was in attendance in the delivery room with Josephine.

'Hang on, Love. Don't push until I get back, I just need to get a few things for in here. Someone's only gone and swiped some of me equipment.' Josephine watched the midwife disappear out of the room and ignored her instruction to not push. She knew that with this next contraction she would finally see her long-awaited child. As she felt the urge to push she did so with all her might and her baby's head emerged.

'You daft cow.' The midwife had returned. 'I told you not to push.' She slapped Josephine on her leg as though she were a disobedient child.

'Okay, let's get the rest of this one out then.'

It was a few minutes before the little girl had been delivered and whisked away from her mother to be cleaned up and wrapped in a tiny sheet. When the midwife placed the infant in Josephine's arms, Josephine cried. She had almost forgotten how rewarding the feeling of giving birth could be. She looked at the little girl, who slept soundly. She looked like an angel.

'Bloody 'ell.' The midwife remarked. 'She looks a bit light-skinned. You sure you ain't been messing around with the milkman or something. It's not the first time it's 'appened, don't look so shocked.'

Josephine could barely look at this woman who came over and started trying to flatten the baby's nose.

'Looks a bit too pointed. If your 'usband thinks she's not 'is there'll be a row and I can't be doing with all that excitement you people 'ave sometimes. I'll call 'im in shall I?'

'If you don't mind.' Josephine was so angry by what this absurd woman had inferred, she had to fight back the hot tears that pricked her eyes. The very idea that she could be unfaithful to her husband appalled and saddened her at the same time.

Two days later, Josephine was getting ready to leave the hospital. She folded her belongings into her grip and handed it to James. He was busy pulling faces at his little girl, who lay quietly in the portable hospital crib. Josephine picked her up and wrapped her in the warm knitted shawl that Hannah had given her as a present.

'Got everything with you, Mrs Dennis?' one of the nurses asked.

'Yes, I believe so.'

It was a dark morning and the lights were still on in the ward. The nurse started pulling open the curtains. Josephine could see the greyish clouds in the sky.

'Has it been snowing?' she asked.

'Yes,' said the nurse. 'It snowed overnight.'

23

'Good afternoon ladies and gentleman. This is Captain Howell, speaking to you from the flight deck. Just been informed by VC Bird International Air Traffic Control that there seems to be a bit of a weather problem on the ground. So we're just going to be in a holding pattern for a while. Landing time will be delayed but only while we give the unfavourable weather some time to pass. Just sit tight. We'll keep you informed as soon as we hear more.'

'Wonder what the unfavourable weather is. Hope we don't have to make a crash landing or anything.' Martin is looking anxious.

The *Please Fasten Your Seatbelts* sign flashes on. There is a general buzz on the plane. Concern, agitation. Lots of lights are flashing for assistance. They can't tell us anymore than they know.

'Relax Martin. This is nothing new. If we choose to fly to this part of the world in hurricane season, we have to expect unfavourable weather. Just take it easy. Listen to music to take your mind off it.' I try my best to reassure him.

'Don't you think you should buckle up?'

'Yes I should. But I'm not worried. I'm sure we won't be making a crash landing. This is exactly what happened last time I came. Similar time of year. I'm only worried about making my connection in time. Don't fancy having to try and find a hotel for the night again.'

'If it's any help, the hotel I'm staying in is quite good. It's where my wife and I stayed on our honeymoon.'

'You came here for your honeymoon? Then she really should have tried to come.'

Once again, Jasmin was there for me. Dealing with the lawyer while the business partnership got dissolved. Helping me when she had a million and one things to organise for their move. Any enquiries for bookings I received from Angel's, I was putting off if they fell within the next three months. I couldn't cope with the pressure of any catering jobs. Jasmin put a big notice on the window saying that the café was being refurbished and not expected to open until after Christmas.

'Just make sure you keep checking your in-box for anything crucial,' she told me over the phone one day. 'We have to make an appointment with the lawyer to sign some papers. Shall I just sort something and let you know when it is? Don't answer. That's what I'll do. I've cancelled as many events as possible without leaving anyone in the lurch. That just leaves two but I can get a chef in and do them with staff. Don't worry about anything to do with work, Ange.'

There were so many times before this trip that I thought about calling Mum. Asking her advice. But at the time of all of this, Del and Maddy were still there with the girls and I couldn't face questions from Mum as well as both my sisters. But one day I gave in and called Mum's. I think I needed to hear another voice in the house, instead of listening to my own voice going over and over all of this chaos in my head.

'Ange! How are you?' Maddy was as bright as ever.

'Well I was calling to see how all of you were, actually. Mum?'

'Oh she's fine. At the moment anyway. She's being charmed by Del and her two. She's sorry you and Eva couldn't come. Do you want a chat with her?'

'No, it's okay. I'll give her a call in few days. I'm a little pushed. Just checking in.' Mum would detect something in my voice and I wasn't able to talk about it to anyone else quite yet. Maddy hadn't noticed a thing.

'Well I might come back a bit earlier.' Maddy said. 'I should be there really. The work is just piling up and besides I miss that big ugly bloke of mine. Three weeks of sun and sand is enough for me.' She laughed and hung up.

I was missing Luke. It had been two weeks and neither of us had tried to call the other. There was the house to sort out. I couldn't put it off forever.

Maddy called me two days after she got back from the Caribbean. 'I need your help,' was all she had to say. It had to be serious or she would never ask. I rushed over. She sounded cold on the phone, but there was an urgency in her voice.

'I've kicked him out,' was the first thing she said to me when she answered the door. There was bitterness in her voice. I didn't understand. I just stared at her. She was wearing a short, floral summer dress. She looked amazing – except for the expression on her face. Her eyes stared off into the distance. Her lips were a thin, straight line, missing that familial slanting smile. I followed quietly behind as she walked toward the living room, placed the backs of her legs against an armchair, bent her knees and flopped into it. The armchair seemed to swallow her up. Before my eyes I saw her shrink, become weak and lifeless.

I waited for a moment before saying anything myself. I assumed that when she said 'kicked him out', she meant she kicked Derek out. Again I thought of Luke. Maddy didn't speak until I was sat in the armchair opposite her. I cleared my throat, ready to listen whenever she was ready to continue.

'I was right all along Ange. About Derek. I didn't want to be – but I was.' She looked at me with a strange expression. It didn't look as though she wanted to cry. She didn't particularly look sad. Just resigned and numb.

'Right? You mean, you think he's been … .'

'Having an affair, yes.'

'Did he admit it to you?' I asked.

'No, he messed up. He got caught out because he brought her here.'

'What? In your bed you mean?'

188

'No. At least he had the decency to use a guest room. Nadia comes on a Friday and usually dusts all the rooms even if I don't have guests. She said she thought only Derek would be here while I was away and didn't know anyone else was staying over. I asked her what she meant. She said, 'Well you had a couple sleeping here.' She made it very clear from her expression that whoever stayed had done more than sleep if you get me. She got all worried when she saw my face. She realised I knew nothing about any couple staying here. The first thing I thought was that Derek was up to something. I didn't even check with him to see whether he had invited guests or not.' I lowered my eyes and gulped. Maddy just continued in a low tone.

'Nadia said that they'd tried to tidy up after themselves but the bed was not very neat. She said she pulled the sheets off to wash them and found this' Maddy held up a gold chain with a little pearl pendant, which she'd had clenched in her fist the whole time. I recognised it straight away as the one I saw Eva wearing a while back.

'But Maddy, doesn't that belong to you?' I stuttered.

'No. Derek has never bought me a pearl. He knows I don't like them. He bought it for her – the bitch he's been shagging in *my* house.' Her face changed. Her teeth were clenched. Her eyes were filled with rage. She stood up and walked across the room. She looked at the pendant again then turned and threw it. It landed at my feet. There was no doubt. It was Eva's. I couldn't mistake it. So delicate, so pretty.

My head was spinning out of control again. It was already full of images of the nightmare I thought existed within my own walls. Now my head and my heart were in a battle to decide how I was feeling. Again, those pictures in my mind of Eva in the arms of an older man. But not Luke's arms. Again I'm sick to the stomach. This time I had to fight every urge I had to scream the truth right then and there. I had to protect my daughter, my sister, our entire family.

I sat looking at Maddy who now stood at the window. Her

sobs were jagged and low. Like a long, interrupted sigh. My sobs were loud. Inside my head. They deafened me. I should have gone up and comforted her but I was frozen to my seat. I felt cold.

What kind of mother had I been to let this happen? What kind of wife was I to accuse the only man who ever loved me the way I wanted to be loved, of sleeping with his own daughter?

I rose, very slowly, and walked toward Maddy, my legs felt like lead weights. I touched her shoulder and she turned to face me, the whites of her eyes were a tearful, pink. Maddy leant toward me to rest her head on my shoulder while she cried. I put my arms around her slender waist.

'It's all over,' she kept muttering. 'It's all over. I've lost everything.' She would never know just how much was lost.

24

'James, it is time we find ourselves somewhere new.' Josephine had just finished feeding the baby and was putting her down. James hadn't long returned from work. He was tired. His back ached, his hands were still cold and had been since he left for work that morning.

'Josephine. What are you talking about? I'm going and get my dinner. I'm starving.'

'I know you starving Jamon. But you have to be honest. This place is too small for all of us. Especially now since the baby.' James looked into the cot. His baby's eyes were just about to close. She looked peaceful, warm and just as Josephine had described her, an angel.

'To me this baby look perfectly happy. She so small. Why we have to worry about space.' James made his way to the kitchen. He needed to eat. Josephine followed behind him.

'But James. Babies grow. Where will we put another bed? Supposing God grant us another child?'

James was not listening. He was mumbling to himself as he took the stairs two at a time. 'It's cold. I'm hungry. I just walk in the door. All I'm hearing is space this, space that.' Josephine was hurrying behind him, not taking in what her husband was saying, she had issues to resolve. She nearly walked into James who picked up his plate of food, still covered, and turned around abruptly.

'Josephine. Enough. Why can't I come home and have some peace for once? Just one night to come home and not hear about you wanting to move house.' He searched for a fork and stood with his back against the sink and started to eat, loud and fast.

'James. It's not just because I *want* to move. It's because we *need* to. Why can't you see that?' Josephine turned and went back to the children.

The year their baby girl was born, the weather forecasters said it had been one of the coldest winters on record. When he left for work that morning, James thought it was darker than usual and that the days were drawing in faster than he'd known them to. But James' mind was not on the weather when he arrived at work. It was not on the fact that the contract he was working on was the refurbishment of a large draughty house with no heating, neither was his mind on his nagging wife or the baby that woke too early every morning for his liking. James' mind was on the women who used to live on the ground floor when he first moved to Shirley Road.

It wasn't that he missed them. It was because he knew that in some other part of England, he had another child. He didn't know if it was a boy or a girl and had had no contact with the mother, Marcia, in all this time. He had given her some money, not a loan as he'd told Josephine, but something to help her on her way. It was reasonable to assume by both of them that James would not be able to supplement two families. He supposed that that was why she had never contacted him. If he couldn't support his child then James was useless to her. Not knowing exactly where she'd moved to, he could never find out about his son or daughter who must be about eighteen months old.

It was not surprising then that quite absently he managed to hammer the forefinger of his left hand that day. The hammer came down hard and he felt an intense pain seconds after it happened. One of his co-workers rushed over to him.

'What on earth have you done? That's not like you.'

'No, I'm okay,' said James. But he wasn't okay at all. His finger was swelling and hurt so badly all he could do was hold his left hand up by the wrist and squint at it through partially closed eyes. The foreman came over and told him to get it under some cold water. A blood red swelling to his finger was causing enormous pain and James didn't know what to do with himself. He felt the need to yell out in pain, but his anger and frustration would have come out with the cry. He refused to go home because that would mean losing money. He decided, instead, to wrap his finger with his handkerchief and just carry on working. When he got home that evening, Josephine hadn't even noticed.

He stood in the kitchen and continued to eat vigorously, his sense of taste numbed by his anger with Josephine. He thought about his wife, comparing her to his relationships with other women. It was a well-known fact that he had been a womaniser as a young man. As he got older his desire for sex hadn't changed and neither had his attitude to the number of women he wanted. He thought about past conquests and how willing a woman could be. Josephine, he felt, was never as willing as some women. When they were married, it became clear to him that his wife viewed sex as simply a means for procreation. Just like the bible said, he thought. Since being in England he had slept with several women. He had curbed his affairs since Josephine's arrival – but James knew himself. It was just a question of time before he would be seeking comfort from someone who did not demand his attention for the mundane rituals of married life. James loved his wife. He loved his children. He wanted to be a good father. But something purely physical was what he craved right now.

The following evening, James expected much the same as the night before and suspected his evenings would never be peaceful until Josephine got what she wanted.

'Our biggest problem is money.' James had just walked in through the door. His boy and girl rushed to give him a hug. He welcomed them, warmly. He joked and played with the children as his wife continued.

'Well I was upstairs talking to Hannah yesterday and she gave me a wonderful idea.'

'What idea is that?' Asked James, wearily. The children had gone back to their game. They were in their pyjamas and would say good night to their parents after James had eaten. He sat at the little dining table in the front room where they both slept.

'Well, Hannah has a sister who works in a factory building quite close to here and she asked Hannah if she wanted a job packing with her. Two women have left and so they need someone. Well they need two people but I'm only thinking about one of the jobs they have.' James was confused. Josephine was excitable and started to lose patience with James, who appeared not to be listening to her.

'Listen, James. Hannah has told me about a job in a factory and I think I should take it. It would just be part time but it would help us a lot.'

'*I* work for this family.' James sat back in the chair. Josephine had not taken the hint that he was waiting for her to bring his dinner to him.

'James, you work very hard for this family but the money you are making is just not enough to rent a bigger place. You have to admit that.' Josephine ran up to the kitchen to fetch her husband's plate of food which was covered with a saucepan lid and sitting on the stove. Anthony Magyar was in the kitchen making a cup of tea. He nodded to Josephine who smiled and carried James' dinner downstairs. She placed it in front of him.

'It's just a few hours in the morning. I will walk the children part way to school and get to the factory for nine. I finish at one o'clock. Plenty of time to collect the children from school.' She was a little out of breath from rushing up and down the stairs.

'And the baby?'

'Hannah will mind her for me. I will only need to give her a little something for her time. As she say, she have to stay and look after her own baby anyway.'

'How little is the something you giving her?'

'Very. Hannah is my friend. As long as I can provide milk and nappies she'll be happy.'

'You sound like you have the job already, Josephine.'

'I have. I found out today. I start Monday.' Josephine looked down at her hands. The baby had started to stir in the other room but wasn't crying.

'Well I suppose that settles that then.' James said.

'I suppose it does.'

'Could I have a fork?'

'Yes of course.' Josephine went back up to the kitchen.

25

'Angelica, if you don't mind my asking. Is that where you're going now? To find Luke, talk to him? Tell him you know the truth?'

'Actually, no. When I get my connection, I'm going to see my mother.'

'Your mother? But – I would have thought … .'

'Don't you think I've already tried talking to Luke? God knows I've tried. Mum is the one I need now. She'll know what to do.'

When I got home, I called Luke. His phone was, of course, still off. I sent him a text. I knew he would read it.

Luke, please forgive me. I know the truth. I really need to see you. Apologise to you properly. Can we meet? Just to talk. I'm going to be right by the phone, not moving until you call. A x.

About two minutes later the phone rang. I'd never been happier to hear someone's voice.

'Luke. Thanks so much for calling.'

'I had to call. How did you find out? Did you finally speak to Eva?'

'No, Eva's completely oblivious to all of this. She's the next person I need to speak to. She's been ringing but I haven't been able to talk to her yet. I couldn't face it.'

'I'm confused though. If Eva didn't tell you then what and how did you find out?'

'Maddy called to tell me that Derek was having an affair and …'

'*Derek*? That fucking arsehole.'

'Yes I know. I couldn't believe it either.'

'But it was so easy to believe it was me.'

'Luke. I know you hate me. It was my jealousy getting in the way. The way you two were together. So close. So secretive all the time. To the point of shutting me out.'

'Never Ange, I could never shut you out.'

'That's how I felt sometimes. I know it was stupid. You two are the loves of my life.' I heard nothing from the other end of the line.

'Luke?'

'Angelica – have I ever done anything that could make you doubt me?'

'Never Luke. But I've been hurt before.'

'Not by me. I'm not one of those idiots you've gone out with in the past.'

'I know that. For the life of me I can't understand why I could ever think like that.'

'It's obvious why.'

'What do you mean?'

'There's no trust between us.'

'That's not true.'

'If there had been, do you think we would be here right now? Me holed up in a mate's flat and you alone in our house.'

'But Luke we can change all that now. Can we just get together and talk? Can you come over or can I meet you somewhere?'

'I can't handle it right now. I've never been this angry or this hurt before. It's because it's you, Ange. I can't believe that you could think *that* of me. Can you get how I feel right now?' His voice sounded weak, not angry anymore. I felt guilty. Ashamed. I wished I could find a way of making it right but I just had nothing to offer.

197

'Could we give it a while?' I asked. 'Meet some time when you don't hate me so much.'

'I don't hate you. I couldn't. I love you. Probably too much. That's the problem.'

'How can that be a problem?'

'Because you don't feel the way I do.' And then he hung up.

I had to speak to Eva. Instead of letting her call go to voicemail, I picked up the next time she rang which was early on Saturday morning, straight after her first gig. She had been in rehearsal for the previous three days.

'Hey Mum. It was brilliant. I only got to do four numbers but it was awesome. The band was great and the college crowd loved us. They're all back from summer holidays over here and ready to party, which is great for us. I know it's the first one but I'm already dreading the last show. I don't want it to end. Mum?'

'Yes, I'm here. Just tired still. It's just coming up for six in the morning for me.'

'Oh sorry. I just couldn't wait. Is Dad with you?'

'No.'

'*No*? What's up with you guys?'

'Eva I have to be honest. We fell out over you.' I swallowed hard to get rid of the enormous lump in my throat. I didn't want to ruin Eva's buzz but she had to know what was going on here.

'What did I do? I'm all the way over here.' She laughed and I could hear her talking to someone who had passed by saying, 'Great voice you've got there.'

'Eva. I know about. I found out that. I'm angry because. Luke and I fell out because of what I found out about *you*.'

'Mum – what are you talking about?' Her voice was serious and the background noise faded as though she had distanced herself from the mayhem around her.

'Eva, I know about you and Derek.' At last, it was out.

'Mum, I … but how?'

'Things happened and I pieced it together. I haven't spoken to Derek. I haven't seen him. Aunty Maddy kicked him out.'

'Is she going to come after me?'

'She doesn't know it was you. And she won't hear it from me. I couldn't do that to my sister.'

'Mum, I'm sorry, I … .'

'Eva, I thought I could but I can't do this with you right now. You're out there having the time of your life and the last thing I would ever want is to spoil it for you. But I hope you are woman enough to know what kind of mess you've left behind, just as you were woman enough to start sleeping with another woman's man.' I sounded like my mother. 'Words can't explain how this has hurt me Eva. I accused Luke of being your lover.'

'What! *Why*?'

'I can't even begin to tell you, Eva. We have a lot to talk about when you get back.'

'Is Dad angry with me too?'

'I don't know how he feels. I only know he loves you. I only know he can't forgive me, and I can't blame him.' Between her very loud sobs I heard Eva tell me she was sorry and that she loved me.

'Please say you forgive me Mum. I'm coming home right now.'

'Eva, you have an obligation. Be an adult about it. I'll see you in two weeks okay? I'll call you tomorrow or you call me when it fits in with your schedule.'

'I will. Bye Mum. I love you.'

'Bye Eva.' I whispered.

26

Josephine was very nervous on her first day of work. It was a small biscuit and cake factory which did a reasonable business and supplied to several outlets nationwide She had no idea what to wear or how she should act. Hannah had told her to make sure she wore comfortable shoes because she would be standing a lot of the time and that her sister complained of a bad back every time she saw her.

'So, Josephine, this is your workstation. You work with Betty. Follow her and you won't go wrong. Very simple. The stackers load you up with packets of biscuits. You're a packer – you pack the biscuits neatly into boxes. Different types of biscuit and they all have to go into boxes in a special order. Betty will show you, won't you Betty?'

'Yes Mr Carsdale.' Betty made a saluting action and then winked at Josephine.

'When you pack a box you shout "ready" and someone takes the box off you and sets it aside to be taped up and loaded on the van. Got that?' Josephine nodded.

'You get fifteen minutes for a tea break. Victoria is the supervisor,' he waved to a tall thin woman with glasses propped on the end of her nose, the frames of which formed sharp points at the outer edges and curved upwards. She nodded and looked at Josephine over the top of her glasses but didn't utter a word to her.

'She'll tell you when your break is and I'll leave it to her to show you the toilets and things like that. All yours Victoria.' Mr Carsdale sauntered off nodding and smiling at the women in the packing department.

Victoria continued her conversation with a couple of the women across the room and motioned to Josephine to stay put. She would come to her in her own time. Josephine felt uncomfortable and shifted from one foot to the other. She turned and saw Betty smiling at her.

'Alright love? Ever worked in a place like this before?'

'No,' said Josephine. 'It's my first job in this country.'

'How long you been 'ere then love? You speak the language really well. Not like Kaveeta Kaur. Can't understand half of what comes out of her mouth. She's Indian. Her husband wears a turban.'

'Well we speak English where I come from. I'm from the West Indies. I'm West Indian.'

'Of course. I live next door to a coloured woman. She's West Indian. Jamaica her lot are from. You Jamaican love?' Before Josephine could answer Victoria had walked quickly across the packing room floor and cleared her throat loudly.

'So, new girl. Come with me and I'll show you where to put your coat and bag.'

Josephine followed Victoria, who walked at quite a pace, out of the packing room, down a long corridor along which the smell of cakes and biscuit mixture was overwhelming. Josephine looked about her and saw, just in time, Victoria disappearing into a room on the left. She quickened her pace and found the supervisor standing in a square shaped room. On three of the walls were rows of tall lockers. Victoria stood in the middle of the room with her arms folded tightly across her chest. She looked over the top of her glasses at Josephine. Her eyes darted around the room before she spoke again.

'Listen. I don't want any trouble out of you. The last coloured that worked here got fired. My husband says you people can't be trusted. You're lazy and you're only over here for a free ride. So let's get this straight. You work hard and pull your weight and you won't get a problem from me. You turn up late, take too long a break, get sloppy or try and walk out of here with free biscuits –

you're out. You understand me girl?' Victoria pushed her glasses up her thin crooked nose and frowned at Josephine as she waited for a response.

'I'll be on time, I'm not sloppy and I'm not a thief. I'm here to do a job and that's all,' Josephine stared back at Victoria without blinking. Victoria's glasses had slipped back down her nose. She uncrossed her arms and pointed to a locker in the corner.

'You can take locker 15. That belonged to the last coloured girl. The toilets are just out this door and to your left. Don't take ages when you go.' From her overall pocket, Victoria took out a chain with six keys of various sizes attached. She opened a cupboard.

'Here.' Victoria tossed an overall in Josephine's direction. Josephine retrieved it from the locker room floor after quickly putting her coat and bag into locker 15.

'You got to take this home with you each night. It's up to you to wash it and keep it clean. Right?' Josephine nodded and put it on. Victoria held a hair net between her fingers. 'Keep your hair in this and then tie it with a headscarf. You need to bring your own headscarf, we're not supplying that for you.' Josephine took the hairnet. It was well used and had lost its elasticity. It went on easily over the hair that Josephine had taken great pains to style nicely to make a good impression on her first day. She followed Victoria who had left the locker room without speaking.

'How did you get to hear about this job then?' Victoria barely turned her head to address Josephine.

'My friend sister tell me about it.'

'Who's that then?'

'Caroline.'

'Oh – Madam Caroline. Off sick more times than she turns up for work. She'll be next for the chop if she doesn't watch out.' They were back in the packing room.

'She's all yours Betty. Take her with you when you go on your tea break. You're on eleven-fifteen this morning. Got that?'

'Yes Vic,' Betty smiled. Victoria didn't. 'I mean Victoria. Sorry,

202

forgot for a minute.' Their supervisor sped away. Like a spider, she seemed to scurry from one spot to another, appearing very quickly beside a person, when at first glance she was several feet away.

'So, Miss Jamaica. I'll show you what to do. You just follow old Betty.'

Betty was all of four foot eight. She stood, proudly, in an overall with a very snug fit. So snug the seams appeared to be splitting to accommodate an overwhelming stomach and breasts. She had chubby cheeks, thick ankles and stumpy hands that were too small for her stature. Much to Josephine's relief, Betty was by nature the complete opposite to Victoria. She called Josephine 'Miss Jamaica' all morning despite Josephine insisting that she wasn't from Jamaica and to please call her Josephine. Betty relented after their tea break but had shortened her name to 'Josie', by the time the lunchtime whistle blew at one. Josephine went to collect her coat and bag, then set off for home.

For a first day at work, it hadn't been too bad. Josephine reckoned that if she just did her job and stayed away from Victoria she would be fine. She went up to tell Hannah all about it and to collect her baby girl.

'This little one's been perfect all day, bless her. Hardly knew she was here half the time.'

Josephine lifted her daughter from the new pram Hannah bought for her baby, who slept soundly in his cot. She tried not to wake her as she took her downstairs and gently put her down again in her own cot. Josephine yawned and sat on the edge of her bed. She rubbed her lower back with both hands and within minutes, had fallen asleep on her side only to be awakened at two-thirty by her baby crying. With only an hour before she had to be at school to collect the older two, Josephine couldn't believe how one morning at work could be so tiring.

It took a few weeks before Josephine was able to take the job in her stride. She had noticed, in those early days, that Victoria continually peered over the top of her glasses at her. But

Josephine was a hard worker, regardless of the watchful Victoria, who could find no fault in her work. Although she chatted to Caroline and Betty at times, Josephine had not come there to make friends. She was there to make sure that she and James could move to a new flat with more space and she set her mind on that happening.

She had not opened a bank account but, instead, kept all her money in a tin that she hid in the bottom of the wardrobe, making sure the rooms were locked whenever she was out of the house. She had not spent a penny of her wages but had paid Hannah the few pennies to look after the baby that they had arranged between them on a weekly basis. James had managed to get a bank account the year before at the only bank in the high street willing to allow a black man to open an account. He had insisted that Josephine pay her money into his account but she had refused. James had given up arguing with her and wished that she would listen to his advice more often instead of taking matters into her own hands.

It was springtime, and Josephine had saved quite a bit of money. She stopped at the shops on the way back from work one afternoon to buy a few items for her household and for her friend Hannah. She let herself into the basement flat, took off her coat and overall and took her shopping bag up to the kitchen. She was about to start sorting the shopping when Anthony Magyar walked into the kitchen and startled her. She never usually saw him in the daytime. He worked at the Princess Alice public house in the evenings and on a few afternoons if they were short staffed.

'Your baby cry too much.' He gave Josephine a serious look. His irises were jet black, his pale skin had an olive tinge and his lank, black hair hung, uncombed, about his long face. For work he would grease his hair flat to his head. He looked as though he hadn't slept in days and Josephine noticed how gaunt he was compared to the last time she saw him. His clothes were loose and he had not tucked his shirt into his trousers. Josephine thought he drank too much and cared too little about his appearance.

'My baby doesn't cry. She sleeps all through the night. Maybe something else is keeping you awake.' Josephine tried to go about her business and just ignore Magyar.

'Not night time. Cry all morning, all daytime. Cry too much.' He stood very still and held Josephine's stare. She was incredulous. Hannah always insisted that the baby was as good as gold, was an absolute angel, and she never got a peep out of her. Maybe there was another baby in the next house or maybe it was Hannah's own baby doing all the crying.

'I don't understand. I'll speak to Hannah and see what she have to say.' Josephine sorted the shopping while Magyar just stood there. She walked past him to go up to the first floor flat. He followed her out of the kitchen.

'You ask nobody, you just listen for yourself and tell me if I'm wrong.'

Josephine watched as he disappeared into his rooms. She walked slowly up the stairs to Hannah's. She decided not to mention this conversation with Magyar to Hannah, or to James come to that. If James suspected that anything was wrong with the way Hannah looked after his daughter he would go up there all guns blazing. If there was one thing Josephine was certain of, it was that James would do anything for his children. He might not be very affectionate towards her but he took his responsibility as provider very seriously indeed. He seemed to be particularly taken with the new little girl and cuddled and played with her more than he had the older ones.

A couple of days later, Josephine was taken ill at work.

'You know you've not been here long enough to get sick pay.' Victoria had informed her. 'So if you go now your wages will be docked.'

'It's okay, I know, and I wouldn't go unless I was really bad. I've had a very bad headache all morning and a sore throat so before I make everyone sick I better go. I think it's a cold I'm getting or something.' Josephine said. Victoria had already stopped listening to what Josephine was saying and had rushed upstairs to Mr Carsdale's office to tell him that the coloured girl was going off sick.

It was just coming up to eleven, and as Josephine approached the house she could hear her baby crying. She knew the sound well enough and knew that it was unusual for her to be crying so forcefully. This baby, unlike the older two, only cried when she was hungry or needed to be changed, otherwise she was quite happy to lie in her cot peacefully. Immediately Josephine remembered what Magyar had said. She let herself into the basement flat as silently as she could, all the time her heart pounding as she heard her baby's cry sounding more and more strained. Her poor little throat would be as sore as anything.

Quietly she took the stairs to Hannah's flat. The crying persisted and became louder as she got to the first floor. Josephine did not knock on the door. She tried instead to open it and walk in on Hannah and catch her doing whatever it was that was making her baby cry so much. She could not open the door fully – something was blocking it. She called Hannah by name and could hear Magyar's door open. She pushed harder on the door as she heard Hannah call, 'Coming!' The door was open just wide enough for Josephine to put her head through the gap. When she looked down to see what had jammed the door, she saw Hannah's old red coat spread out on the floor and Hannah picking up the crying baby who had quite clearly been lying on the coat. Hannah stood holding Josephine's baby with her mouth open.

The two women stared at each other a long time before either of them could find words. Hannah turned her eyes from Josephine's glassy gaze, a quiet storm brewed in Josephine's veins. She grabbed her daughter from Hannah's arms.

'I wasn't expecting you back so early.' Hannah stuttered in a quiet voice.

'I can see that. Hannah. What is going on here? How could you stay and let a baby cry like that? Where is your baby?'

'He's lying in his cot.'

206

'And why mine is on the floor on top of an old coat? I thought you said if when she was sleepy you would put her in your son's pram.'

'I did but I don't think she liked it in there. She keeps on crying.'

'Rubbish. She never cry unless she hungry or need to be changed. When last you change her?' Josephine held the infant to her nose and sniffed.

'Oh, if she needs changing, Josephine, I'll do it now – before you go.' But Josephine was not listening.

'Why Hannah, why you do this?'

'It's not easy with two little 'uns in tow. Both wanting things at the same time. I get tired and I have to take a rest so if they cry they both have to wait till I get to them.'

'Hannah, don't tell me anymore. Give me my baby's nappies and her milk and I will be on my way.' The baby had stopped crying now.

Hannah looked about the flat and began turning around, looking here and there as if she didn't know where anything was kept. She reached for the tin of dried baby milk from the shelf and placed it on the table and then went into the bedroom. Josephine picked up the tin in one hand holding her baby against her with the other. She shook the tin. It was practically empty. It wasn't possible for her baby to have gotten through so much on her own. She could see through the door that divided the two rooms that Hannah was not having much success getting the nappies together. Josephine walked into the bedroom and saw about six nappies drying on a clothes rack in front of an old electric heater.

'They're not quite dry yet. I could pop them down later.' Hannah said this with her eyes on Josephine's feet.

'Don't trouble yourself. Keep them for your baby.' Josephine left without taking the milk and without another word. Hannah never looked up.

Josephine got down the stairs but slowed down when she saw

Magyar standing in his doorway. Concern and anger filled his eyes. Josephine acknowledged him with a look of gratitude but hurried down to her flat before she began to cry.

A few hours later, after she had collected the older two from school, Josephine was back home with all three of her children. They had been fed and bathed and were ready for bed. Her son was reading to his sister as they sat on the sofa in their pyjamas.

'Who is that, Mummy?' The curtains were drawn. It was late and James was not home yet. All three had heard someone opening the gate to the basement flat, coming down the steps and then tapping gently on the window.

'Just ignore it,' Josephine said. 'Finish the page and then both of you, into bed.' Josephine was not interested in an apology from Hannah, but the tapping persisted. Josephine got up and stood by the window.

'Go away Hannah, I don't want to see you.'

'It's not Hannah – it's Eunice.'

27

'Don't look so worried, Martin. I'm sure not all parents with teenage girls are this stressed out.'

'No of course. They're all different.'

'Before Phoebe gets to be a teenager, you and your wife need to stay on top of what she's about. Eva was always very opinionated, knew what she wanted and went out to get it. I know when I was her age I wouldn't say boo to a goose. I had to learn to become more demanding – in business and in my personal life. It paid off, though. I've done well. But I wonder if along the way I spent too much time thinking about me, and not enough time with Eva: keeping an eye on what she was up to, being around more. But having said that, she's very independent and that's not a bad thing is it?'

'Not at all. It doesn't do to spoil them. It doesn't sound like you did anything wrong. I'm sure you're a great mum. Eva's doing well and you have to take credit for that.'

'I'd like to. But if I can take credit then I should accept some blame.'

'I don't know, Angelica. I just think that you making a success of your business will benefit her in the end. And, you know, when our children leave us, we do have to move on with our lives.'

Move on. That wouldn't be enough to solve *my* problems. I'd cried myself to sleep for three consecutive nights and even on waking, the lump in my throat was still there. Jasmin had seen Steven off at the airport about a week before and she was due to fly out to join him in New York with the kids in about a month. She asked if I needed her to stay around longer. She had called round earlier that day and was concerned that I'd lost a lot of weight.

'Angelica, I can't leave you like this,' she said. 'If you've got no jobs on, then why don't you just drop everything and come with us? It would be great to have you. The children would love it and I could look after you,' Jasmin was pacing the living room floor whilst I sat slouched on the sofa.

'But Eva will be coming home and then there's Luke.'

'I thought you didn't want to have anything to do with him after what he'd done. Come on Ange, a bit of distance would do you good. Eva can look after herself. It's what she's doing now isn't it?'

'Jasmin – I have to tell you. About Luke. I got it all wrong.'

'Got it wrong?'

'Luke is innocent. He never cheated on me. I just didn't trust him enough to believe him.' I lowered my head.

'But I thought you must have had proof before you kicked him out.' She flopped down next to me and put an arm around my shoulder.

'Well I didn't get rid of him. He walked out after I accused him and now he'll never come back.'

'This isn't making much sense to me Ange, you'll have to explain.'

I did explain. I sat and told Jasmin everything. The way I always did. I could always rely on Jasmin coming up with a solution, just the way I always did for her. This time, though, Jasmin was at a complete loss.

She didn't speak at first and when she did it was to say, 'My God Ange, no wonder you've been like this.'

There was no answer to the mess. The damage had been done and there was no getting out of it.

'The best thing to do, Jas, is just get on with your arrangements – really. There are only four catering jobs in the next two weeks. And then Eva comes back. The two of us haven't talked about this properly yet. I was too upset with her. I sounded like *my* mum when I talked to her on the phone and she's probably too afraid to come back.' I looked up at Jasmin, I saw the pain I was feeling in her face.

'No matter what, I want to be there for Eva,' I said.

'Of course babes.' She held my hand.

'Somehow I've got to get my head around everything that's happened. Be her mother, not her judge. That's what she needs right now. The way I left things on the phone – well, I've got to show her how much I love her. She's missed the chance to go to Guildhall this year, so we'll have to plan something – the two of us, together.'

Sunday morning. It was warm and breezy and when I looked out of my bedroom window I saw at least three joggers pass. One was a woman of about my age and she looked spectacular. She ran, with a spring in her step, in the direction of the park. The other two joggers had headed that way too. That's where they escaped to each Sunday morning, I imagined. I wished that I could join them but I had been in the same clothes for days. I hadn't showered, I hadn't brushed my teeth, combed my hair or anything. I felt awful. Just then someone else jogged by, this time coming back from the park, he was smiling. I peeled off my clothes and reached into the bottom drawer of the tall chest in my room. Buried under some jumpers I'd find some of my exercise gear.

I got ready to go for a run. It had been a long time, I wasn't even sure I could make it as far as the park but I was certainly going to try.

My trainers felt heavy on my feet but I wasn't going to let that stop me. I was either going to run so fast my problems couldn't keep up or I was going to chase them away and never have to deal with them. Either way – I was going to come back looking as pleased with myself as those Sunday morning joggers.

I didn't come back smiling. Running hadn't chased away my demons, but it made me determined to make some changes. I was hot and tired when I got back home and finally found my way to the bathroom. Once I'd emerged from the warm, rose petal bubbles I had made a decision. The only way to bring sanity and peace to my life was to take positive action. I was going to call Luke and ask him to meet me. I was going to make him change the way he was feeling about me. There was no doubt in my mind about what I felt for him, despite what he had said, and I intended to show him.

'Ladies and gentlemen, this is your Captain again. Sorry about the delay but we now have clearance to land. We will be starting our descent shortly. We're due to land local time fifteen twenty-seven. Apologies once again and on behalf of myself and the crew, we thank you for your patience.'

The good news has gone down well. I can sense the sigh of relief in the cabin, not least by my jumpy companion. Martin has been very attentive and supportive the whole time but I get the feeling that flying is not for him. He's still tense.

The flight attendants are doing the rounds, checking our trays are in place, seats in an upright position, collecting any leftover rubbish we want to get rid of. Some people are standing, getting jumpers out of their hand luggage, some are putting jumpers into it.

But not me, and not Martin either. We sit quietly for a while. My story isn't quite told.

'You must have had an awful week of confrontations before you got on this plane.' Martin says. 'I mean Eva comes back, you planned to see Luke.'

'And there was Jasmin. She came round with the children to say their goodbyes. They only had a week to go before they were off. It'll sound like I'm wallowing in self pity, but, how many times can you have your heart broken in one lifetime? You know, I keep stopping and telling myself "there's always someone worse off than you." But, you know what Martin, I seriously pity the poor soul who is.'

28

When Josephine opened the front door she couldn't believe what she saw. Eunice had come all the way from the other side of London with a swollen jaw and lip. Around her mouth there was bruising and scabs were forming. Her right eye had disappeared behind an enormous swelling.

'Eunice.' Josephine's voice was no more than a whisper. Eunice did not speak.

Josephine held her sister's thin frame and guided her to her bedroom. She sat her on the bed. The baby was fast asleep now. She quickly went into the front room and told the children to stay put until she came back in five minutes to tuck them in.

'Yes, Mummy,' they said in unison.

Josephine returned to her room to see her sister shivering as she sat on the bed. Although it was spring, it hadn't been a very warm day. In fact, the sun had not shown itself once. Josephine sat close to her sister and stroked her hair.

'Take off your coat and lie down. I will go and make you a warm drink.' Josephine watched as Eunice removed her thin mackintosh. All she had on underneath was a bra and knickers. On her feet was an old worn-out pair of shoes. She had still not said a word but got into bed and pulled the blankets up over her head. Josephine slipped out of the room and scurried up the stairs to put on the kettle. Anthony Magyar was in the kitchen.

'Visitor?'

'Yes,' said Josephine. 'My sister has come to stay.'

Josephine came back down stairs to put the two children to bed.

'Children, tonight all you must both sleep on the sofa. Here, one each end, like before.' She held up the blanket for them to get under.

'Mummy, we're too big to share now,' her son protested. 'Why do we have to share?'

'Shh, is just for now. Come on, get in.' The children did as they were told. 'Your Aunty Eunice is paying us a visit. She's going to sleep with me and Daddy will be in here with you. Okay? Now be good, close your eyes and sleep.' She turned off the light and went back upstairs to make a strong tea with two heaped sugars for Eunice. James' dinner was keeping warm on the stove but it couldn't feed two so she made a jam sandwich for her sister.

Josephine sat on the side of the bed and waited until Eunice sat up and took the cup and plate from her. She got her dressing gown and placed it over her sister's shoulders, as Eunice sat silently contemplating her food. Eunice had no bag and Josephine wondered how her sister had managed to get to her. She said nothing and watched as Eunice finally picked up half of the sandwich and ate it hurriedly without looking up or even thanking her sister. She ate the second half of the sandwich and handed the empty plate to Josephine who placed it on the bedside table and waited. Eunice held her cup of tea with both hands.

Finally she said, 'I'm sorry', without looking up.

'You have nothing to be sorry for. I'm glad you came to me. I would hate to think you could end up this way and not have anyone in the world to turn to.'

'You're always there for me aren't you sis?' Eunice's head was still down.

'Of course. You never have to question that.'

'So where were you when this was happening? Why haven't you been back for me? Why didn't you look after me?' Tears dripped into her teacup and Josephine took it and placed it onto the bedside table.

'Eunice, I've been calling you.' Josephine cupped Eunice's face with her hands and gently tilted it up. 'Every time I manage to speak to you, you say you're fine. Did you want me to accuse you of lying to me? That would have started bad feeling between us – you know that. You always say how bossy I am.'

'You sounding bossy now.' Eunice pulled her face away and turned to face the wall. 'I'm tired and I don't want an argument. I've had enough of them. I can't go back home. I need to sleep.'

'I know.' Josephine tried to smile. She looked at her sister's beaten face.

'I will have to phone my job tomorrow and tell them I'm sick or they'll sack me.' Eunice frowned. 'But I don't have money to call.' She looked at her sister.

'Oh Eunice, don't worry about that.' Josephine paused for a moment. 'Are you going to tell me what happened?'

'Not tonight.'

'But how did you get here with no money?'

'The woman from downstairs. I run out of my flat with nothing. She give me a whole pound. She even try to give me her old hat too. Silly woman.' Eunice paused a while. 'I must look like a monster. Don't let the children in here. I haven't seen them in so long I don't want them to see me like this.'

'Don't worry.' Josephine pulled the dressing gown tighter round her sister's shoulders. Eunice looked at the cot at the end of the bed.

'I haven't even seen your baby, Josephine. How is she?'

'Oh, she's wonderful.' Josephine got up and looked into the cot at the baby, who was sleeping soundly.

'Eunice, this is Angelica. Angelica, meet your Aunty Eunice.'

Just at that moment, James put his key into the front door. Josephine hurriedly gave Eunice her tea back and rushed out of the room and into the corridor so that she could stop James coming straight into the bedroom.

'Everyone asleep?' he asked. 'I need to get to bed straight away. But I'm starving too.'

'James can you come upstairs with me? Have your dinner up in the kitchen tonight? There's something I need to tell you.'

'Josephine, if this is about finding somewhere to live...'

215

'No James, it's not that.' They were up in the kitchen now. 'Look, your dinner – you want me to warm it up for you?'

'No, I can't wait.' He began rushing his food down.

'Eunice is here.'

James stopped chewing for a second, then continued as he spoke.

'A bit late for a visit isn't it?'

'Nestor beat her again, James. You should see what he do this time.'

James put his plate down and dropped his fork. Metal clattered against Formica. Too loud for that time of night. He placed both hands on the counter and stood with hunched shoulders, head down as Josephine continued.

'She's in such a bad way. She doesn't want anyone to see her so I've kept her away from the children. Perhaps her face will look better in the morning. It looks like the eye was done the day before, and the lip earlier today. I hate that Nestor.'

'Why don't you want me to go there and sort him out?' He swung around. 'I could take Rufus with me and let him feel a beating for himself.'

'I've told you already. That's not the way to do it. The only way is if she leave him.'

'And I've told *you* that there isn't room for her here. You've told me every day for five months that we need space. She can't stay here forever. I don't want to be driven out of my own bed.' He took a breath. 'Besides a man and his wife should sleep in the same bed.'

'If this is about my duties as a wife then I have to remind you that I have a duty to my sister too. My mother told me to look after her and even if I hadn't promised Mama, I would look after Eunice anyhow.'

The couple spoke in lowered voices. When they had gone around in circles with their argument, and it was clear to Josephine that James was winding down for the night, she gave up and they went back downstairs. James, to the front room to sleep

216

on the single bed and Josephine, to their bedroom.

Josephine could not settle all night. She drifted into a light sleep and then woke to find that the clock on the bedside table had only moved its luminous hands by ten minutes. For most of the night she lay facing her sister. The misshapen face of a stranger was all she could make out. Eunice shifted about in her sleep and spoke several times. Nothing she whispered made any sense.

Eunice kept out of the way while James and the children got ready to leave the next morning. It was Thursday and Josephine should have been getting ready for work herself. Instead she crept up the stairs and made a call to Mr Carsdale, the site manager, and said that she was still unwell and couldn't come in.

After walking the children part way to school, Josephine braced herself for what was to come. She was about to learn how Eunice came to be tapping at her window at nine o'clock the night before.

'Did you call your work?' Josephine asked as she came in. Eunice was sitting at the table in the front room, drinking some tea.

'Yes. Thank you for the change you left. I will pay you back.'

'Oh Eunice, that's the last thing on my mind right now.'

'They all know, you know.'

'Who knows what?'

'The people at work. I can't hide the bruises from them. He always hits me on the face. That's why I never get the sack for having time off. My boss feels sorry for me.'

'Oh Eunice.' Josephine sat at the table with her sister.

'He even came to work one time. Shouting and swearing like a mad fool. Just because I didn't iron a shirt for his night shift. My boss had to chase him away. He said he would call the police if Nestor didn't go.'

'So this all happened because you didn't iron for him?'

'No, that happened the other week – I think. This was something else. I was stupid. I let one of the girls, Michelle, come

217

in for a cup of tea after work. We were talking about Nestor. She told me I should run away from him. She said she would be happy for me to stay with her until I could find a place of my own. But all the time we were sitting, chatting in the living room, he was there. He hadn't gone to work. He was in the bedroom lying still, still, still, like a statue. I chat and I chat with Michelle. I tell her how I hate him and the worse thing I ever do was to marry such an ignorant fool. All the things I would have said to you if he hadn't been listening on the stairs every time you call.'

'So that's why you always tell me everything okay?'

'Yes. But you knew everything wasn't okay. Why you didn't know that?'

'How could I know when you yourself told me you were fine? I thought you were telling me the truth.'

'Like I always do you mean?' Eunice drew a long deep breath that wavered, slowly, as she exhaled.

Josephine stopped for a moment. How could she have been so blind? Since they were children, Eunice hardly went a day without making up some story or telling a fib. Eunice had sounded so convincing on the other end of the telephone that Josephine had no reason to doubt her. But to discover that beneath the charade Eunice had been crying out for help broke Josephine's heart. She should have known her sister better than that.

'So you blame me then?' Josephine asked. Eunice was silent. 'You don't have to say anything. I blame myself. I'm sorry Eunice.'

'Josephine. Please don't apologise. You looked after me all my life. And you forgave me everything. Every time I was unkind to you, every time I did or said something bad. I took your things, I broke them, I never showed you any respect. I stole from you.' Eunice bowed her head.

'You stole from me? What did you steal?'

'It doesn't matter now. But only know I'm the one who's sorry. I don't blame you for anything. This is my punishment for all the bad I have done.'

218

'Nothing you have done can make you deserve this. A man should not even beat his animals like this.' The women sat for a moment in silence. Just then Angelica started to stir.

'Can I give her the bottle?' Eunice asked.

'Of course you can.' Josephine returned to the room shortly with a bottle and a crying baby. 'She's all yours.'

'I wish she was,' said Eunice as she sat on the sofa to feed Angelica. 'Looks like I can never have one of my own. Imagine if I have a boy for Nestor – he could turn out to be another monster like him.

'Anyway, after Michelle left I turn around and there he was. Still in his pyjamas saying, "so you think I'm ignorant? I'll show you what is ignorant." And then he started hitting me. I didn't think he was going to stop until he finish kill me. The woman from downstairs and the lady from opposite were banging on the door saying they will call the police. That's when he stop. I thought that day was going to be the last day of my life. Even when I went to sleep that night I never think I will wake up. But the next day, when I was getting ready for work, I put on my underwear but I start to feel dizzy. Really bad. I couldn't go in. So I put on my dressing gown and I go downstairs to call work.

He came home early again. I see now he changed his shifts and didn't tell me. That's why he been there when Michelle came. He start asking why I never went to work and how I expect for us to pay the rent if I don't go.'

Angelica had stopped feeding and Josephine tried to wind her while Eunice continued.

'I said to him. How can I work when I can't even see? He said I can still do what I do best and that is to run my mouth. Telling me how dare I tell people about our business and don't bring any white women in his house again. I just started laughing at him. He really is an ignorant fool and I was just as foolish to still be with him. All I could do was laugh. I laugh and laugh, like a mad woman, until I almost cry. He stand there telling me shut up or he will shut me up. Before I know he was on me and I feel one big

219

thump in my mouth. He wouldn't let me go in the bathroom. He make me sit there for a long time, just watching me. Then he eat something and then he go in the bedroom and slam the door. Never say anything to me. I just sit in silence, telling myself I have to get out, I have to leave. But all my clothes was in the bedroom, so I just pick up that old coat, grab my shoes and go out the door. I didn't close the door behind me. So he would think I was still there. The old woman was standing in the corridor downstairs. Listening. The way she always do. I tell her I need money and she take my hand and lead me in her bedroom. She give me a whole pound and tell me run to you. And here I am.'

'Let me put her down again, Eunice.' Josephine put Angelica back in her cot and returned to the living room.

'But all that happened in the morning. What did you do the whole day?' she asked her sister as she placed her hand on Eunice's lap. Eunice took a deep breath.

'That was the longest day of my life. With that pound I go and buy myself a cup of tea in a café. I needed change for the bus. People were staring at me so I fold my arms on the table, put my head down and I must have fall asleep. The man in the café was closing. It was two o'clock and lunchtime finish he said. I get up and I go. I stand outside thinking to myself, I don't even know the way to Josephine from here. I knock the café door again. The man didn't want to open but I beg him to tell me how to get to Notting Hill Gate. He tell me go and ask a policeman.

'I go all the way to the police station where they make me wait for hours to see someone. Then they ask if I want to press charges and I better not waste their time for a domestic. Finally one of them take pity on me and really listen to what I have to say. It's lucky I know your address by heart. I been praying and praying for the day I could come here. Just run away from him. Anyway the policeman tell me exactly how to get here. I would have come earlier but my head was paining me and I fall asleep on the train and miss where to get off. Nobody want to help me, I suppose for how I look. I stop asking people and I find my own way. I couldn't believe it when I see the name of your street marked on the sign. I nearly run the rest of the way.'

Josephine could no longer resist the urge to hug Eunice. She wanted to protect her and right now Eunice was more fragile than the baby lying in the other room.

'Eunice, I'll run you a bath. Then I'll get you something to eat and some clean clothes. And after that we have to find you somewhere to live.' Eunice smiled a tear-filled smile.

James only had to give up his bed for a few days. Eunice was able to contact her friend, Michelle, and stay with her until she eventually found a room off the Romford Road. James and Rufus borrowed a car and went with Eunice to collect her things from her flat. There wasn't much to collect. Nestor cussed and stormed around the whole time Eunice was packing but did not lay a finger on her when he saw the two men at the doorway. As she walked downstairs, he rushed out of the flat after her and stood at the top of the stairs, where James and Rufus waited and watched like guards.

'Go on go, you old prostitute. Go and live on the streets where you belong. A person with no class. You not good enough for me. I don't need you. You worthless. You less than that.' Eunice slammed the door before he'd finished his rant. The old lady had come out in to the hallway and looked up.

James delivered the first punch. Rufus followed this with a hard dig from his elbow into Nestor's ribcage. It was the kick to the back of his knees that sent Nestor tumbling down the stairs.

He landed in a crumpled heap in front of his landlady.

'Right, that's it – you've got one week's notice to leave this place then I'll want me key back.'

29

The day after my run in the park I went to the hairdressers and had my hair cut short, just like a boy. Making changes, that was what I was doing. It seemed like a good enough place to start. All I was doing was putting off what I should be doing: calling Luke. I came home and stared at the phone for ages. I wanted to be sure I could get the words right.

Suddenly the phone rang. It was Eva.

'Don't freak out Mum, but I've decided to extend my stay. Indefinitely.'

'You're doing *what*?'

'I know, crazy right? But you don't have to worry I'll let you know where I'll be.'

'Eva, crazy isn't the word. How will you live?' I asked her. No matter what she'd done, she was still my daughter and I loved her.

'I'll do what all my idols have done before me. Play music and grab every opportunity that comes my way.'

'Eva, this isn't right. When the tour is over, I thought we could sort your next move. This sounds like you're running away from home.'

'Is that what it is? I'm not seeing it like that anymore. You were pretty upset with me when we last spoke and you never called me back. I don't feel as though you want me there.'

'Eva, I'm sorry I was like that. I was upset and it all came out wrong. We need to talk, about this, the future. Us. I need to know you're safe.'

'I'll be safe. I want to do this, Mum. And I'm going to.'

I knew I couldn't convince her to come home. Neither did I want to. Somewhere, deep down, Eva's decision meant I could put aside one of my fears. What would happen if Maddy ever found out the truth? This was something I could never tell my sister, no matter how I tried. And I didn't want Eva to either.

'I'll be fine Mum. I've already got a place sorted and I have some work lined up after this tour. I'll sort everything out and I'll keep myself safe, don't worry.'

'Eva, I'm just sorry it has to be like this. You're so far away. I wish I could be there but there is so much I need to fix.'

'You mean with Dad?'

'Yes.'

'I spoke to him. He was so disappointed in me. And I know you are. I suppose I *am* running away from you. I can't handle any of this right now. I don't know how. I'm too ashamed and not as big or grown up as I thought I was.'

There was a pause.

'Eva, why Derek?' There was no way I could hold that question in.

'Why Derek. Good question. You'll think it's stupid, but I fell in love with him. It wasn't like a schoolgirl crush or anything. We used to talk a lot. He was great with me after Uncle James died. You weren't yourself and I felt left out by you. Now that sounds selfish. I was selfish back then, a brat sometimes. But he was the one who helped me see that. He took me out. We went walking and started holding hands and things. I just felt this connection with him. Like electricity every time we touched. My stomach used to dance around when I thought about him being near me and I could feel he was being more than just a shoulder to cry on. He was looking at me differently. Not like he used to, but like he thought I was grown up I suppose. We didn't plan it.'

'How old were you when you first slept together?'

'I was seventeen. He was so kind.'

'I don't want all the detail.'

'You say that but you'll just go off on one and imagine the worst. I started it you know. I made him touch *me*. I kissed *him*, not the other way around. He was so ashamed afterwards.'

223

'Oh poor Derek.' I closed my eyes and shook my head as though that could shake away the images.

'Mum, he and Aunty Maddy wouldn't have lasted. He told me as much.'

'And he promised to leave her for you did he?'

'No, he would never have done that to her. That's what was so hopeless about it. The last time I saw him it was to say goodbye. And he was getting prepared to say goodbye to her. He had fallen out of love with her ages ago. If it hadn't been me it would have been someone else. Believe me. He was crying when he told me he was afraid of hurting her.'

'And once again. Poor Derek. I'm more concerned about my sister than that needy wimp.'

'He's not needy and he's not a wimp. He's quiet but he's kind, patient, smart and so deserves to find someone.'

'So why not you? Since he was found out why didn't he just come clean and you two could be together now. Or does it turn out he has other plans?'

'Like I said Mum. He couldn't do that to Maddy. He loved her too much for her to ever know about us. It would have killed her. I was torn apart. I wanted to be with him but I couldn't. I knew what it would do to all of us as well as he did, and I didn't know who to talk to.'

'So you chose Saffron instead of coming to me.'

'Mum, think about it. How would you have reacted towards me? I thought you would kick me out and never want to see me again. We all had something big to lose. I could never build up the nerve to tell you and that's why I sat and poured my heart out to Saff. Not even face-to-face but in an email of all things. I almost put it all in a letter to you but I chickened out.'

'But Eva, what was it about me that stopped you telling me? Was I that bad as a mother?'

'It's not about you, Mum. You're the best. I love you. Always have. But, I've been moving on. This tour couldn't have come at a better time. But now it's out – it's just like I thought. I can't look you in the face. I've been feeling awful about everything but never think any of this was down to you. I hope you can forgive me one day.'

'So that's it. I've lost you as well as Luke.'

'You haven't lost me and you will never lose Dad. He'll come around.'

'Is that what he said?'

'Not when we spoke last. He didn't have to. I know. We just talked about me really. He was telling me how concerned he was. Talking like I'd been raped or seduced by Derek. But it just wasn't like that. I knew what I was doing. I hope Dad can understand. I hope he doesn't think I'm some kind of slut now.'

'Never. Not Luke. Look Eva, Jasmin will be in New York soon. I'll send her number. She'll be the closest you'll have to family out there. If you need anything, she'll be there straight away. It doesn't have to be an emergency. Just call her.'

'Okay, I will. I don't know how long it'll be before we see each other again, Mum.'

'I don't know either. But take good care of yourself until then. I'll be worrying the whole time. Your terrible eating habits, dressing inappropriately, not to mention that tattoo.'

'Who told you about the tattoo?'

'What? I was only joking.'

'So was I Mum.' Eva laughed out loud then was quiet.

I felt the urge to scream 'Eva, come home.' Then, *sotto voce*, I heard, 'I love you Mum. Speak to Dad and I'll see you both soon. Okay?'

I found my courage. Straight after I spoke to Eva I called Luke. He agreed to come over to talk.

'What happened to your hair?' The first words past his lips when I opened the door. But he was smiling.

'I just needed a change.'

'It actually quite suits you. Makes you look younger.'

We were standing at the front door and I felt embarrassed because he hadn't made a move to come in. It was almost as though he was waiting for an invitation. Like a guest. Like he wasn't my husband anymore. It hurt, but I didn't let it show. I smiled and walked to the kitchen and he followed me. I had laid the dining table in the kitchen rather than going for the formality of the dining room. I wanted him to feel at home. To feel like coming home.

'Something smells nice.' He said.

'I hope so.' I turned to look at him. 'I've made all your favourite things.'

'Well you can't have made *all* my favourite things or this would turn out to be the longest dinner ever eaten in the history of man.' I had taken his hand and led him to the table.

'I didn't bring anything,' he said. 'Like wine or anything. I wasn't expecting you to cook. I thought we would just talk.'

'You don't mind, do you?'

'Of course not. I haven't had a decent meal in ages. Andy is a lousy cook and I can't be bothered these days.'

'So you've been in Streatham all this time?'

'Yes.' He stood by the table and started playing with a piece of cutlery. The phone rang. I should have turned it off.

'Sorry, Luke. I'll just get rid of this.'

'Not a problem.'

'Hello. Oh hi, Mads. You okay? He was what? Did he say how it happened? When? I can't tonight Mads. I'm so sorry, just sit tight and I'll definitely call you first thing tomorrow. Yes, I will. Bye darling. See you tomorrow. Okay.' I hung up the phone and looked at Luke in astonishment.

'Derek got mugged,' I said.

'He didn't get mugged.'

'What do you mean? How do you know?'

'I was there. I beat him up. I didn't mug him.'

'You did what?'

'I beat him up. I couldn't help myself. I waited for him after work and followed him to where he was staying. Some swanky flat in Fulham. I just wanted to talk to him. Face to face. Find out what the hell he thought he was up to with my daughter. Then when he told me he was in love with her I lost it and started hitting him. He didn't even defend himself. I thought it would make me feel better.'

'And did it?'

'Yes and no. It still didn't take all this away. The way everything has changed. All this time we've been apart. The fact that Eva is gone now and Maddy is probably a wreck. Nothing will ever be the same between us.'

'But, Luke, why? Couples get over things together. They rebuild. They start again. Carry on where they left off before everything started to go wrong.'

'Truth is – I don't even know when that was. When things started to go wrong that is. I thought everything was perfect. What you said to me that day just hit me like a bolt out of the blue. I've been round and round it in my mind and I'm just … .'

'Just what?'

'I'm just finding it so hard to forgive you.' He looked away from me.

'You can. You will.' I stepped in close to him and he had to face me.

'You'll learn to. Just come back and let me prove how much I love you. How much I know this can work. Stay. Luke. Please'

We hadn't stood this close together in a long time. I didn't want him to walk out of the house without knowing if there might be some small chance that he might come back to me.

He placed his hands on my face. They were warm and rested there with ease, like they were meant to be there. He stared deep into my eyes the way he always used to.

'I've missed you so much.' His words were like fresh air on my face. We went up to our bedroom and forgot everything. All our worries, our problems, everything that happened in those last few, terrible weeks.

It was dark when I rolled over to touch Luke, but he was not in the bed. I got up, picked up a t-shirt from the chair and put it on while hurrying along the landing, looking for signs of him. None of the lights were on downstairs. I went to the living room window and looked out. His car was gone.

I sank to my knees and covered my face with my hands. Sinking further, my back against the radiator, my eyes clenched together, with the stark realisation – Luke could never forgive me. An involuntary moan left my throat. Lying on the floor, curled up like a child, I cried hopelessly.

30

Josephine's family life was restored. Eunice was settled and Mr Carsdale said his sister would gladly babysit Angelica so Josephine could go back to work at the factory.

James' trips to the pub on a Sunday afternoon became less frequent. He was either working or he would be put off going by Josephine's disapproving looks. Either way, Josephine always found herself busy in the kitchen on a Sunday, preparing a big lunch after church.

'Good afternoon, missis.' Magyar bowed his head and gave Josephine what she thought could be a smile.

'Good afternoon,' Josephine replied with hardly a glance in his direction. She had been, and would eternally be, grateful to him for telling her the truth about baby Angelica and Hannah. But she tried not to become too involved with him. He was, after all, a drinker and it worried Josephine that she had three small children and she was left alone with them for most of the day while her husband was out.

'I go very soon back to my country,' he said. He stood at the kitchen door but did not enter. He generally kept to the agreement about allocated times for using the kitchen but this was an exception.

'You going on holiday?' Josephine asked.

'No, this is my holiday. Now I go back to my country for good and never come back.'

'This is a holiday for you? This cold miserable place?' Josephine stopped stirring her gravy and turned to look at him.

'Well it was better for me to be here than over there for a while and now I go back.' An almost-smile again.

'So the rooms will be empty?'

'Until you have new neighbour.' But Josephine had already formed the idea in her head that perhaps she and James could start to rent his rooms. She smiled.

'You happy to see me go?' he asked.

'No, no. Well yes and no. We need more space, so I was just thinking … .'

'That is good idea. Maybe you have another baby.'

'Maybe.' Josephine put down her spoon and turned to shake his hand. He seemed taken aback.

'So, goodbye,' he said. This time Josephine could not mistake the fact that he was smiling.

About a month after Magyar first told Josephine he was going back to his country, and after having arranged with the landlord to start renting his rooms, Josephine and James moved in. The bedroom was a familiar place to James and he watched as Josephine pulled up the bedding to take to the launderette, his mind fixed momentarily on the times he'd spent in that bed with one or other of its previous occupants, Margaret and Marcia.

Anthony Magyar was not the neatest of men and had left quite a lot of cleaning to do. But this did not bother Josephine in the least. She was cleaning her new rooms. She had the space she craved for so long and that made her happy. Josephine stood back and proudly looked around after she and James had done the best job they could, moving and cleaning the shabby furniture and worn carpets. At last she could look out onto the street and see more than the feet of passers-by.

She stood at the bay windows overlooking Shirley Road and rubbed the small bump on her stomach. Her baby was not due until the following spring but she had already started to show.

'Maybe this one will be a big baby,' she said as she turned to look at James who was fixing a framed photograph of the children to the wall.

'Have your dreams told you if it's a boy or a girl?' he asked as he stood back to check the angle of the photograph.

'No. Since I been here I don't seem to dream much. But I would like if it's a boy to call him James.'

'Good choice. And Josephine if it's a girl?'

'No. I like my Aunty's name for a girl: Madeleine, Madeleine Rose.'

'Whatever you decide – I don't mind.' He came over to where Josephine stood and as she continued to look out of the window, he hugged her from behind placing his large hands on her stomach.

Lately James had been content with his life. His earning potential had improved. The increase in construction of high-rise flats and council houses in London kept the large building company he worked for inundated. He could also go moonlighting whenever he needed it. Josephine was still earning a small, helpful sum at the factory but she would have to give up the job when the baby came.

Josephine had got on well with her boss' sister, Florence, who, like her brother, was a kind and friendly person. Florence didn't need the pittance she received from Josephine each week. Had Josephine been privy to the conversation Mr Carsdale had had with his sister regarding looking after Angelica while she continued working at Crowley Foods, she would have realised that it was more of an act of charity than need that Florence had agreed to take on the job.

Every time Josephine went to collect Angelica, Florence would have a 'little something' for Josephine's children: a packet of biscuits or a loaf of bread, a bottle of squash, some chocolate, even pairs of socks on a couple of occasions. Josephine did all she could to resist her acts of generosity but Florence looked extremely dejected when Josephine said the gifts were too much, so in the end she simply accepted them with thanks.

Josephine had gone to collect Angelica one afternoon after work. Florence, opening the door to her, smiled, crooked her index finger and beckoned Josephine up the stairs.

'I've got a little something for you. Well it's actually a big

231

something but I think you might appreciate it.' She led Josephine to the attic, lowered the hatch door and set up a small stepladder. She stepped up onto the first few rungs and the ladder creaked under her weight. Josephine held the ladder with both hands and could now only see Florence's floral, print skirt and stockinged legs. An old sheet covered the window in the attic. Florence pulled a little string on the wall and a dim light came on.

'There it is,' Josephine heard her say from above. 'I'll swap places with you so you can see.' She stepped back down and stood aside while Josephine climbed up to peer into the dusty room.

'Right in the corner to the right is an old sewing machine.' Florence called up to her. 'Well I say it's old. It's never been used. Just been here a long time. My old man bought it for me in the wartime. Said we'd hit on hard times and I'd have to make my own clothes. I think he must have gotten me mixed up with someone else. I wouldn't know what to do with a sewing machine if one bit me on the behind.'

Josephine saw a sewing machine not unlike the one she used to own when she was back home. She smiled to herself as she stepped down, remembering those busy times, sewing for so many people. That memory could have dated back a million years as far as Josephine was concerned, her life was so changed.

'But I can't take it Mrs Bailey. That really is too much.'

'Nonsense. You'd be doing me a favour. I need a clear out in here. Didn't you tell me you used to sew for a living?'

'Well yes but … .'

'No buts about it. Tell your hubby to come and pick it up at the weekend. It'll go in the rubbish if you don't and my poor old fella would have wasted his money. We can't have that.' She shut the hatch and was going back downstairs before Josephine could protest again. Florence Bailey had made up her mind. Florence knew how proud a woman Josephine was and she had planned her speech well so that there would never be any question as to whether or not Josephine could refuse *this* little something.

The first thing that Josephine was commissioned to sew was a new dress for Florence. Josephine had let it slip to Betty about her new sewing machine. Betty, in turn, was curious to know how Josephine managed to afford a sewing machine on her wages. Josephine had said it was a gift but Betty needed to know from whom, and wouldn't stop questioning her friend until the truth was out.

'Mr Carsdale's sister?' she exclaimed. 'Lucky you. How about making me a nice blouse. I'll pay you. Can never find my size in these silly little shops. What d'you think?'

'Well yes, if you would like.' Josephine smiled but she was all the time aware that Victoria had been listening in on this conversation during their tea break and that her ears had pricked up when Betty revealed her secret benefactor. Victoria was up and out of her chair in one fast movement. She stood at the door, glanced back briefly at Josephine and Betty over the top of her glasses and was gone.

'Tea break ends in two minutes,' they heard her call over the sound of her heels clicking loudly and swiftly down the wooden corridor floor.

It was eleven o'clock on Saturday morning when James set out to fetch the sewing machine from Florence Bailey's attic. He said goodbye to Josephine and the children and left the house. It was four thirty in the afternoon when Josephine looked at the clock on the wall and realised that James had been gone all day.

At about eleven-thirty that morning James met Rosie Carter for coffee and spent most of the day with her. Rosie was a woman that James had met at the Princess Alice. Older than him, at forty-nine she still retained the figure she'd had in her twenties. But at forty-nine she was dressing as though she were still in her twenties. She wore a fake fur coat, five-inch heels and her lipstick was the brightest red that James had ever seen. She always looked right at James if ever she saw him at the pub.

The first time he had the nerve to speak to her, James had been having a drink with Rufus. Rufus had downed the last of his Guinness and said he had better get back to Maisie. Rufus had not noticed how Rosie had stared at James from across the smoky bar or how his friend had reciprocated. She was wearing a tight, light blue, polyester cardigan. Her pencil skirt hugged her smooth hips and her blond hair, worn far too long for a woman of her years, fell over her right eye. Her blue eyes were framed by false eyelashes that fluttered quickly as she saw James approach her table. Up close James could see that she was much older than he had thought but his attraction to her did not wane. In fact, their secret meetings had increased in number and showed no signs of diminishing.

'Look at the time,' James said as he came back from the bathroom, buttoning his shirt and tucking it into his trousers. 'I have an errand to run. I can't leave it too late.' He sat on the edge of the bed, put on his socks and pushed his feet into his shoes. As he leaned over to tie his shoelaces, Rosie, naked beneath the bedclothes, sat up and reached her arms around his shoulders. He stopped for a moment. He could feel her breasts against his back and knew he should leave before it got too late to call on Mrs Bailey. It would be rude if he were knocking at her door at dinnertime. Besides, how would he explain his delay to Josephine? Any later and he would have no believable excuse to offer. But Rosie had pulled James to face her. She started kissing him. He responded by allowing her to pull him on top of her, back onto the bed. She took his hand and placed it on her lower abdomen, held it there for a brief moment and started moving it further down.

Josephine was already thinking about dinner. She heard the key in the front door and came out into the hall, ready to question James about the time he'd taken to run this errand for her.

It was Hannah. The two women had not spoken since Josephine stormed out of Hannah's flat with her baby. A few days following that incident, Josephine had discovered a small basket of neatly folded nappies on the doorstep of her basement flat. Hannah gave a faint smile.

234

'I see you're expecting another,' she said to Josephine, who stood silent and motionless next to the banister.

'Well, congratulations.' She hesitated, apparently expecting a response from her neighbour. Nothing came.

'Looks like it's going to be a cold winter.' Hannah tried again but to no avail.

Just then the front door opened and James appeared. Hannah put her hand up as a goodbye gesture and took her leave, all the time looking at Josephine who did not acknowledge her.

'Where you been since this morning?' Josephine walked along the corridor towards James.

'Oh I bump into Rufus. He was glad to see me because he needed help moving an old wardrobe out of his room.'

'An old wardrobe?'

'Yes Maisie wanted a new one so he had to make space.' All this time James was holding the sewing machine in his arms and its foot pedal and accessories in a bag over his shoulder.

'Put that in a place James.' She followed him into the front room where he put the machine down just in front of the radiogram.

'You mean to tell me that since this morning you were with Rufus?'

'You know how Rufus like to talk? And eat. He make me stay, have lunch and after that we move the wardrobe. The bus took a long time to come before I get to Mrs Bailey house. But anyway. Here is your new sewing machine.' He stepped back and opened his arms as though he had just presented the sewing machine as part of a magic trick. Josephine bent to see it close up. She was very excited.

By February, Josephine was enormous and found it hard to stand all morning at work. Mr Carsdale had seen her distress and had found her another job to do that didn't involve standing the whole morning. He had her in the office alongside his secretary, Mavis. She helped Mavis open the post, do some filing and entering numbers into a large ledger. Josephine was also responsible for making tea for Mr Carsdale and Mavis. They both had two cups of tea in the morning. The first cup without biscuits and the second with. After the second cup Josephine had to go back to the packing room and sit at the large table helping to tape the boxes that were then ready for distribution. Betty insisted on calling over to Josephine every now and again regardless of Victoria's continued complaints that shouting across a room was 'neither ladylike nor satisfactory' for the packing room floor.

A few weeks after Josephine's redeployment, Victoria called Mr Carsdale into the locker room.

'I think when you've seen this you may want to call that coloured girl in here,' she said to the puzzled factory manager.

'You mean Josephine? What's this about Victoria?'

'I overheard some talk in the toilets and did a little bit of investigating on your behalf.' She had a smug grin on her face and pushed her glasses up her nose, waiting for some sort of thanks from Mr Carsdale but he remained silent.

'Look!' she said and darted across to locker 15. She opened the locker and pulled out Josephine's bag. She held it under Mr Carsdale's nose pulling it open so aggressively, the clasp almost broke. She could see that Mr Carsdale was losing his patience with her.

'See? Stamps.' She said. 'Stamps from the office. How did they get into Josephine's bag?'

'Well perhaps you could tell me?' He raised his eyebrows.

'Isn't it obvious? She's stealing office supplies. She can't be trusted to be up there.'

'What gives you the right to open another person's handbag Victoria? I must admit I am a little surprised.'

'It's like I said. My suspicions were aroused when I overheard something. I thought you'd be pleased that I'd caught her, not looking at me as if I'm being accused of something myself. Well – aren't you going to question her or anything?'

'I'll have to speak to you both in my office.'

Victoria pushed the bag into his hands and rushed to

summon Josephine from the factory floor before he could finish the sentence. She left no doubt in the mind of any of the other women that Josephine was in some sort of trouble as Josephine followed her up the stairs.

It was almost one. Nearly time for Josephine to leave to collect Angelica. Her unborn child pressed against her bladder and she wondered what nonsense Victoria had dragged her into. Josephine noticed her bag on Mr Carsdale's desk. Also on the desk were the letters and forms she had opened earlier on without the supervision of Mavis who had a hospital appointment that morning and wasn't due back until the afternoon.

'What are you doing with my bag in here? I thought the locker was private and no-one is allowed to look in them.' Josephine glared at Victoria.

'That's quite right Josephine but Victoria thought yours might be worth looking in because of what she's found inside.' Mr Carsdale coughed slightly and loosened his tie. 'There are stamps in your bag Josephine. Could you explain how they got there? Could you have picked them up by mistake?'

'There hasn't been a mistake. I didn't take any stamps. I am not a thief.' Josephine remained composed.

'Well how do you explain this, Madam?' Victoria pointed a spindly finger at the bag.

'I don't have any explanation. I don't know what the stamps are doing in my bag and I don't like people to go through my things.' Josephine went over and grabbed her bag, pulled the stamps out and threw them onto Mr Carsdale's desk.

'Now,' she said. 'You happy? I don't have the stamps anymore.' She directed this to Victoria.

'Just a minute, young lady.' Victoria was looking angry. 'This is a police matter. This is theft and those stamps are evidence.' Josephine could not believe what she was hearing.

'Now hold on, Victoria.' Mr Carsdale intervened. 'Let's not get carried away. Josephine is a trusted member of staff. There must be an explanation.'

237

'I heard what I heard.' Victoria left Josephine no time to speak up in her defence. 'I was in one of the toilet cubicles and I could hear her telling one of the other girls how she could easily take things when no-one was about.'

'That is a lie!' Josephine was furious

'I don't think Mr Carsdale will take your word over mine. Will you Mr Carsdale?' Both women looked at the boss. He was at a loss for words.

'Tell her this is a sackable offence Mr Carsdale.' Victoria placed her hands on her hips.

'I would have to sack you Josephine if … ' he stuttered. But before he could get the rest of his words out, Josephine had closed her bag and marched to the door.

'You don't have to sack me – I'm leaving.'

'Josephine. Wait. Come back. Let's talk about this.' Mr Carsdale went to follow Josephine but Victoria stepped in front of him.

'Oh just let her go. We can find someone else. Someone who is a lot fitter and doesn't have to work sitting down all the time.'

Josephine rushed down the stairs. Her cheeks were hot and her eyes glassy. Betty, who hovered around at the foot of the stairs instead of going to have her lunch in the staff canteen, tried to catch her friend's arm to ask her if she was alright but Josephine was too fast for her as she headed for the locker room to fetch her coat.

'Josie, what's up? What's all the fuss about?' Betty was panting as she rushed to follow Josephine along the long corridor to the locker room.

'They just tell me I been stealing stamps.' She was putting on her coat.

'*Stamps*?'

'Yes. From the office. Victoria said she find them in my bag and take my bag to show Mr Carsdale.'

'That skinny bitch. She's behind all this I'm sure. Anyone who knows you knows you're as honest as the day is long. Whereas her on the other hand. Well she's a different kettle of fish.' Betty looked over her shoulder.

'Well Mr Carsdale has to believe her over me.' Josephine said.

'So he sacked you?'

'No, I leave the job. It's near my time anyway so it's for the best. I just could have done with the money – you know?'

'Of course love. I know. Well I'll still be wanting those dresses I ordered from you finishing – don't forget. And I think you will have more orders from some of the other girls now they've seen your handywork. That blouse you made me was the best fit I've ever had. You could open a shop with your skill you know. I'll pass your number on wherever I can. Promise me you'll stay in touch.' She placed her chubby hands on Josephine's shoulders and pulled her closer for a long hug.

'Thank you Betty. You been really kind to me.' Josephine was close to tears. Tears of anger and sadness

'Oh Josie, it was my pleasure. And between you and me, I don't suppose Mr Carsdale suspects you for one moment.'

Just then, Victoria slid into the locker room. She made no attempt to look in the direction of the other two women. Instead, she pulled from her locker, her coat, handbag, an old pair of shoes and some magazines. The shoes and magazines she put in the bin. She took off her overall and threw it onto an old chair, then started to put her coat on.

'Half day Victoria?' Betty asked. Victoria didn't answer. Betty and Josephine looked at each other and when they turned back to look at Victoria, both she and her handbag had disappeared. Mr Carsdale walked in next.

'Ah, Josephine. I wonder if I can have a word.' He looked at Betty who winked at Josephine and left.

'Victoria has resigned. She had holiday owed to her so doesn't need to work her notice. I got the full measure of her antics and she could not deny that she was the one who put the stamps in your bag. Said she wanted to make a point about security. Ridiculous. So I would ask you, please, to reconsider your resignation and stay on with us.' Josephine smiled but stuck by her decision to leave.

'It's best if I go. Maybe other people don't like me to be in the office.'

'I'm not bothered about other people, I'll see you tomorrow.'

'Yes, but I do give you notice all the same. I'm too heavy and uncomfortable to stay any longer. It is time for me to leave.'

'Josephine you know whenever you need a job – if I've got one going – it's all yours. You're a real asset to this place and don't you forget that. And there's Florence. I know she'll miss you.'

'That's good to know. Thank you Mr Carsdale. And I will see you tomorrow and work out the rest of the week.'

'You go home and take it easy. That couldn't have been very pleasant for you, I'm sure.'

When Josephine walked out onto the street she could hold her head up and be proud of her first job in London. For the first time since she arrived, she felt a sense of belonging.

31

'Thank you very much.'

'Thank you, enjoy your stay.'

The cabin crew will be saying that over and over again. I wonder how many times it is said in, say, a week. Hundreds, I would imagine. I look over my shoulder. Martin is following close behind carrying his laptop and a small holdall. He's not looking as though he's into the idea of business meetings. Can't say I blame him. A Caribbean island – who wants to work? I smile at him. He tries to smile back. I turn to the flight attendant at the door.

'Thank you very much.'

'Thank you, enjoy your stay.'

The heat is overwhelming as I walk down the steps. I don't exactly know how I'm feeling. If anything, I'm quite drained. I'm sure I must have done the same to Martin. Drained him that is. I should never have told him all of that. He's walking slowly as though he wants to avoid me. I should have kept my mouth shut instead of depressing the hell out of him.

Before I get my connection I feel I should apologise.

'Martin.' I stop just outside the arrivals hall, in the blazing heat. 'Just wanted to say goodbye and apologise really, for pouring my heart out like that.'

I don't expect this reaction from him. He's quiet. His smiling mouth is turned downwards. He has tears in his eyes.

'Oh my God Martin. I'm so sorry. I should never have gotten you involved in my problems.' I wait. He could at least say goodbye to me if nothing else.

'Angelica. I'm not. This is stupid. Let's just step inside before we get sunstroke. I need to take my jacket off.' He quickly wipes his eyes with the back of his hand.

Just inside the door there are officials pointing us in the direction we should be walking. We ignore them and stand to one side. Martin and I need to speak. I put my bag down. Martin does the same and takes off his jacket. The officials are watching us, suspiciously. I forgot how authoritarian they can be here. The security guard is staring at me and looking at Martin. Any second now she will come over and ask what we're doing I'm sure.

I pull Martin in front of me so that his back is to her and I watch over his shoulder as she gives me a sullen look.

'You've got me worried Martin. Don't tell me you're some kind of smuggler and you've lost your nerve.' Making light of the situation isn't a good move. He blinks and a tear trails down his face. I'm uncomfortable because Martin is practically a stranger to me.

I touch my hand to his arm. He is hot and sweaty.

'This isn't a business trip.' He finally says.

'I beg your pardon?'

'The reason I'm here. It's not a business trip. I don't even have a job. Not anymore. I used all the last of my savings to come here.'

'Martin, have you left your wife? Is that what this is?'

'If anything it's the other way round. She left me – ages ago.'

'You mean the two of them upped and left?'

'Something like that.'

'Something *like* that, but not quite? I don't understand you. What are you saying?'

She's looking at me again. The security guard. Coming over.

'You can't stay here Madam – Sir. You must go through. This way.' She holds up a large hand and points in the direction our fellow travellers are heading. There are still one or two more coming through, so she doesn't have to hassle us quite yet.

'I'm sorry. But I need to help a friend. It won't take very long, if you don't mind.'

She cuts her eyes at me and walks off, back to her fellow security guard.

242

'We're looking suspicious Martin. Shall we take this through to arrivals? At least get out of this section, away from those guys. Is that okay?'

'Yes, yes. But Angelica you have a plane to catch. You'll miss it.' I look at my watch. One hour and a half before takeoff.

'I've got time Martin. You just sat and listened to me for the past few hours, surely I can spare you one.'

We walk through to the arrivals room and are met by a sign. Arrows pointing in the directions that will separate us. 'Arrivals' 'Connecting Flights.' I spot a place at the foot of some stairs where we can stand, hopefully uninterrupted, next to a door marked 'Private'. This is the best we're going to get.

I wait for Martin to speak.

'You see,' he eventually says. 'Phoebe. She's not actually ten.'

'She's not.'

'No. She would have been.'

Now I understand.

'Martin I'm sorry. Why didn't you say something before? I kept going on about her, saying how old she must be now and … I'm sorry.'

'She was five when it happened. That birthday picture I showed you was one of the last we took. I love that picture.'

'And your wife. You said she left you. Does that mean?'

'No, no. Ana hasn't died. She literally has left me. Lost all feelings for me after the accident. Without Phoebe our bond just … just disappeared. I tried to help Ana out of her grief and she mistook it for thinking I didn't care about what happened to Phoebe. She still blames me, even now.'

'But why? If I can ask that. You don't have to say if it's painful.' But I can tell that now, he does want say it all. Telling the truth might unburden him of his misery. I'm hoping it will help. His eyes don't meet mine as he speaks.

'Phoebe was on a play date one Saturday afternoon and I was supposed to go and collect her at three. The mum called and asked if it was alright for Phoebe to stay a little longer to wait for their cakes to come out of the oven. She said she would drive Phoebe back home. I didn't even think to check it out with Ana, I never thought she had a problem with that sort of thing.

'Ana came back from the shops just before four and asked where Phoebe was. When I told her she went mad. "I don't know what car that woman drives, does she have a child seat? You must be crazy! Why do you have to be so lazy?"

'She went on and on, so I said, "Okay, fine, I'll go and get Phoebe when the cakes are ready." But when I rang back, the husband said they'd already left. We waited … and waited.'

He bows to put his head in his hands and stands there like this for a good while.

'I suppose this means you're running away?' I ask.

'No, I didn't run away. This is the place we came on our honeymoon right? Well I've been trying to get Ana to come back to me for five years. This was my last-ditch attempt. Blew everything. But she already met someone else. Didn't stop me trying.' He sniffs and shakes his head, eyes half shut.

We stand in silence. I offer all I've got by way of sympathy. We exchange a few words of small talk. It's not what he needs. It's time for him to move on. He knows that. I just hope he knows how.

I watch as he puts on his jacket, straps his laptop case over his shoulder and picks up his bag.

'Good bye Angelica. It was a real pleasure meeting you. You're the first person I've really opened up to in all this time.'

'Oh Martin. You were there for me, too. Look, I wish you all the best, okay?' We exchange a brief hug. 'Goodbye.'

I watch as he walks toward customs, then turn to make my connection. Just before I go through the door, I hear my name.

'Angelica.' I turn around. Martin is standing with one hand up and waves to me. 'I hope you find what you're looking for.' He gives a faint smile and then he is gone.

I look at my watch. It is time to make my connection. My journey is far from over.

32

Josephine's fourth child was born a few weeks earlier than anticipated. Rather than trying again for a job at the food factory, Josephine began making the odd sales here and there through her dressmaking. Betty had been championing Josephine's skills as a seamstress, especially at lunchtime in the staff canteen at Crowley Foods. Her sales patter was such that it had encouraged several of the women to seek the services of a dressmaker and eventually Josephine's popularity grew. She was by no means inundated with orders but there were enough to help toward food bills and a little something to keep for a rainy day.

'At this rate, you will not have to go out to work ever again,' James remarked. Josephine sensed the bitterness in this comment. James was old fashioned. He didn't want his wife to work at all. Josephine was as religious as he was old fashioned, but could find no psalm in the bible that forbade her to work.

'James, I will do what I have to do for the family. You know that. I don't want to create a problem between us but, this is London, life is not easy and we need all the help we can get. You are the educated one. You should see that for yourself.' James said nothing. He shook out the newspaper he had been reading and pulled it closer to his face as if to establish a partition between him and his wife. Somehow he had to find a way to make this woman appreciate that the man of the house needed more respect.

About two weeks after this incident an almighty argument broke out between them. It was late one evening. James was in their downstairs bedroom, where the new baby slept soundly as James read the sports pages of his newspaper.

It was nearly ten-thirty and Josephine noticed, after clearing away the last of the washing up, and just as she was about to put off the hall light, that there was a person standing at the front door. The frosted glass on the top half of the wooden door obscured the identity of the person but as Josephine slowly made her way along the corridor she could make out the outline of a woman standing with her back to the door. She could have been mistaken for a guard on duty had it not been for her long fair hair. She had not attempted to knock on the door as far as Josephine was aware, she just stood waiting, quite patiently, for someone or something. Josephine wondered, at first, if she might be hiding from somebody searching up and down the street for her. Perhaps she was visiting Hannah or the people on the top floor. Josephine had no idea why this woman simply stood there without alerting anyone, and if in fact someone from 239 Shirley Road was expecting her.

Josephine left the hall light on and went downstairs to tell James about the mysterious woman.

'James,' she whispered, 'there is a woman standing on the front stairs.'

'Which woman is that?'

'I don't know. I never seen her before. She have long blonde hair. She just stand up there.'

'I'll go and see. Maybe she here for someone. Let me see.' James got up and Josephine went to follow.

'No, you just wait there,' he said and held up his right hand. 'Just in case is something wrong.'

The baby started to stir and cried for a short time. Josephine did not pick her up but leaned very close and shushed her gently. In a sleepy, singsong voice she called, 'Madeleine,' then softly sang a lullaby. This seemed to settle the baby who yawned, shut her eyes and quietened down.

Josephine could hear voices coming from the front steps. She crept into the hallway but could not hear anything clearly enough. She was curious about this woman and wondered if James would be sensitive enough to handle the situation should she be in distress.

Josephine slowly climbed the stairs to the kitchen and waited there quietly to hear what was going on. She was sure she could hear James say 'You should not have come here', also something that sounded like 'You're making trouble for me.' Her curiosity got the better of her, and she went to the front door.

'What is it? What's going on James?' she asked, looking from one to the other.

'Josephine, just go back inside – I'm dealing with this.' James said nothing more and the pair stood staring at Josephine as though *she* were the intruder. But Josephine was not about to disappear. She glared at her husband. As he offered no immediate explanation, she looked to the blonde woman. She had on a flimsy coat: black, imitation satin. Not suitable for this weather. Around her eyes and above her top lip there was a network of fine lines. Josephine would have placed her in her fifties, although her attire would suit someone of half her age. She held a cigarette in her left hand. Josephine noticed the false eyelashes that fluttered against the long shock of blonde hair that hung down and shielded part of her face. She raised her hand to her lips and sucked hard on her cigarette. She wore fake gems on gold rings on two of her fingers, but no wedding ring. As she lowered her hand Josephine noticed her very high, pointed shoes. Dark brown with velvet bows on the toes.

'Josephine, you better go in, you're letting in a draught and you know how much it costs to heat this place.' The woman laughed and turned her face away before drawing on her cigarette again. She exhaled a long mist of greyish-white smoke with an audible hiss, like air being let out of a tyre. Not wanting to lose her temper, or to create a scene outside, Josephine did as her husband told her. Pushing the front door to an almost closed position, Josephine made her way back along the corridor but stopped in the doorway of the front room where she stood in the darkness. James reached his hand through the crack in the front

247

door and turned off the light. With only a sliver of light coming from the kitchen at the end of the corridor and the sound of muffled voices coming from behind the front door, Josephine waited.

'So that's the little lady is it? Pretty. Good figure for someone who's had four kiddies. Nice big bosom. But you like 'em like that don't you Jimmy?'

'You know what I like.' Josephine heard James stifle a laugh and she grimaced. 'But coming here is a big mistake. What will I tell her?'

'Not my problem.' She exhaled loudly and blew smoke in James' face. 'I thought I was expecting you tonight. Got me toenails painted all special.' Her voice softened. 'Cooked and everything.'

'I couldn't come. I finish work late and she start talking to me and I couldn't get out. I will try tomorrow. Okay?'

There was silence for a few moments, then there was movement on the top step. Josephine took a deep breath and was as still and quiet as possible. She shut her eyes very tightly and saw only the image of James standing at her front door, kissing a white woman. She thought not of herself but of her children. How would they view their father if they could see him now?

Then the front door closed with a faint brushing against the doormat. James walked past the front room, not noticing Josephine who followed directly behind him toward the kitchen.

'So, of all the women you could choose as a mistress, this is who you find?' James nearly jumped out of his skin.

'How long you been standing there?' he demanded.

'Long enough. My God in heaven. James? How could you *do* that to me? To your family?'

'What you talking about? I'm not doing anything.' He puffed out his chest.

'You mean apart from bringing shame to my house!'

'Lower your voice. You want the whole house to hear?'

'I don't care who hear. What I care is who *see*?
248

'What you mean by that?'

'God. God will see you and He will punish you. Don't you have any shame to stand there and tell me you don't do anything? You. Don't. Do. Anything?' With every one of those words Josephine pushed James in the chest with both of her small fists, causing him to take a step backward.

'Josephine. She is not important to me. This is my family. Family is what is important to me. You know that. It's been so long since I seen her. I didn't even know she knew where I live. I only seen her once or twice at the Princess Alice to talk to. You ask Rufus. She like to follow me – I have to tell her to leave me alone.'

'Why you have to talk to her in the first place? You are a married man. You have children. What is wrong with you?' Josephine thought she heard Marcus stir and lowered her voice. 'You know, you are not so special.'

'What?'

'I said you are not so special. This woman taking you for a fool. You spending your time and your money on her. She only using you. Spending money on a woman who look like a prostitute when you have children at home to feed. You know you wasted your time getting an education. How could you be so *foolish*?'

James advanced on Josephine, his right hand clenched in a fist.

'Oh, so now I see? Well just go ahead.' She tilted her head upward. Still angry but coming to his senses, James unclenched his fist and lowered his hand. Just behind Josephine, their young son, Marcus, stood rubbing his eyes and yawning

'You get back to bed boy. It's late. Get some sleep.' James said.

'Good night Mummy.' Marcus said, all the time looking at his father as he went back into his bedroom.

'Good night, darling.' She didn't look at Marcus.

Angry tears spilled from Josephine's eyes and onto her cheeks. She brushed passed her husband and went downstairs and straight to bed. Very soon the baby would wake again for a feed and Josephine should have been in bed ages ago.

She heard James when he came into the bedroom. He did not put on the light. He undressed in the dark and got into bed.

'I won't see her anymore. I am your husband and a father. I did wrong. Forgive me Josephine.' His eyes closed tightly as though he were a small child saying his prayers. 'Please forgive me,' he whispered.

The couple lay in the bed with their backs to each other. Their baby slept soundly in the cot at the foot of the bed. Neither uttered a single word more. Josephine rolled onto her back and sighed heavily. She had forgotten to close the curtains in the bedroom. She could see the outline of her Singer sewing machine by the window being lit by the street lamp outside. James held his breath for a moment and waited for her to say something. Anything. From the street, Josephine heard the footsteps of a couple walking past the window. The woman was wearing high-heeled shoes.

33

For days Josephine was cold and silent around her husband. James tried desperately to prove his love. Even going as far as to use the words, words that were late coming. He stopped drinking at the Princess Alice for a while. He had gone to see Rosie about a week after she'd dropped in on him saying they must stop seeing each other. She started drinking at the Westbourne Hotel and Public House, some ten minutes further from her flat. James drank on his own at the Princess Alice but went to Rosie's another five times to say goodbye. Each time they made love. On the sixth occasion, Rosie did not open the front door. She was tired of his goodbyes.

In time, Josephine developed resilience to her pain. Her church said that marriage was for life. James had sinned but sins could be forgiven. He had never struck her nor said a bad thing against her.

He provided for his family and she was convinced that he would repent. Eventually Josephine began to respond to his attempts to re-establish a physical relationship. Late at night he might run his hand along her inner thigh, raising her nightdress above her waist and she would not stop him.

Their fifth child was born a year and a half later. A little boy called James. Her children were flourishing at school and so was her dressmaking business. Just like the days on her small island, she was making quite a name for herself in West London. She had made several sales, which included at least five orders for wedding and bridesmaids' dresses. She had taken a suitcase of her home-made lingerie to local factories and had a growing request for half-slips, petticoats, nightdresses and negligees.

One Saturday, Josephine came home from shopping with the two oldest of her children, Marcus and Delphina. She was brimming with an idea, the seed of which had been planted in her mind by her old friend, Betty.

'I have this idea.' She was beaming at James who was watching over the younger three, all the time getting ready in his mind to beat Rufus and his mates in a dominoes tournament.

'What's your idea this time?' He sighed.

'Don't say it like that. It's a good idea.' Josephine was packing away the shopping. 'Well, what do you think of me opening a stall in Portobello Road?'

'Ridiculous.' James turned his back and retired to the front room. Josephine stopped what she was doing and followed him.

'What do you mean 'ridiculous'?'

'No wife of mine is going to stand on a street corner selling her wares.' He held the newspaper he had picked up from the sofa in front of his face. He was not reading it.

'It is a market. People sell things. We had them at home. My mother sold food in the market. Why is it I can't do the same? I'm capable of opening my own stall.'

'We don't need the extra money Josephine.' He placed the newspaper beside him. 'What will people think if they see my wife standing in the cold on Saturday morning shouting from a stall "come and buy my knickers!"?'

Josephine burst out laughing. She thought it was his idea of a joke, at first. But then she realised that he was neither laughing nor smiling. If anything he looked hurt that she was not taking him seriously.

'James. What's the matter with you? Why you have to be like this?'

'Josephine. For once, would you let me be a man in my own home and let me make a decision that you don't have to argue with?' He scrunched the edges of the newspaper in his fist and shook it in her direction as he spoke.

'So you're the only one who can make decisions here, James?'

She kissed her teeth. 'So what – you telling me I cannot open a stall in the market?'

'I don't want you to. It's enough what you're doing already. The children need to have their mother around.'

Josephine turned on her heel and went back to the kitchen. She held her tongue. The children would be hungry for lunch and she had sheets that needed to go to the launderette.

In the years that followed, several changes to the household of 239 Shirley Road occurred. Hannah moved out, as did the people on the top floor. The owner had intended to sell the house but could find no buyers for a place as old and rickety as this was, and in a street where half the inhabitants had mice.

James and Josephine bought the house at a reduced rate and moved Rufus, Maisie and their daughter into the top floor and another of his cousins in to one of Hannah's old rooms and charged them rent. But with her sewing jobs becoming fewer and farther between, Josephine was obliged to go out to work to cover some of the bills.

She started working part time cleaning offices at the BBC in Shepherds Bush. She worked on Tuesday and Friday mornings from five-thirty. Her oldest children, Marcus and Delphina, watched over and gave the younger three breakfast until Josephine returned at around eight-thirty and saw the first four off to school. She would then stay at home with little James. On a Wednesday and Friday night she was back at the BBC, cleaning a different suite of the offices from five-thirty until eight-thirty.

Her supervisor at the BBC was friendly enough and so were the other women on her cleaning teams. She had little to do with any other members of staff.

The first week on the job had gone by without any problems for Josephine at all. She arrived at her allocated offices, appropriately armed with her vacuum cleaner and a bucket containing a large bin liner and materials for dusting. On the Friday evening she noticed someone still at work. The offices all had glass doors and she could see him sitting, very still, reading some papers. She wondered, first of all, if he had fallen asleep and forgotten to go home. His office was number twenty-three and Josephine knocked very timidly on his door. He called for her to come in without raising his eyes.

'I'm very sorry but I have to clean your office.' Josephine smiled. He looked up at her and stared for a brief moment.

'Ah, yes. Go ahead and dust. I'll just nip out to get myself some tea. Only bother to vacuum if you think it needs it.'

He worked late every Friday, it seemed, but left his office before Josephine got to it so that she didn't have to ask permission each time. After a few weeks Josephine discovered his name. Peter Spencer. She called him Mr Spencer, regardless of him insisting each time that she call him by his first name.

For six weeks office twenty-three was her last stop on a Friday. On the sixth week she was stopped by Peter Spencer, who handed her a small bar of chocolate.

'Oh, thank you,' she said and smiled at the kind gesture. 'I'll give this to the children.' She was about to put it into her overall pocket.

'No, no, no. That's a present for you, for doing such a good job. You're so quiet and polite and you don't stop to chatter like the last woman used to and put me off my work.'

'Well I think you have an important job here why you work so late in the night.' She couldn't help thinking what a nice man he was and that his family must be proud to have a father who is such a hard worker.

Peter Spencer bought her little bars of chocolate each Friday. Sometimes he would hand it to her when he was leaving, other times he would walk past the office she happened to be cleaning and would call to her above the sound of the vacuum cleaner.

'Oh Josephine, I've left a little present for you on my desk.'

'Mr Spencer, I will become very fat indeed.' She would call back.

One Friday night, Josephine had office twenty-three as her

last port of call as usual. Spencer didn't have his coat on ready to go. He had his feet up on the desk and was reading a report. His tie was loosened and his jacket hung over the back of his chair. A cold cup of tea sat on his desk as he looked up and saw Josephine hovering by the door.

'Oh, Josephine, I don't suppose you could get me a fresh cup of tea?' He smiled and took off his reading glasses. He pulled his legs down off the table and held the cup in his hand. She looked at the cup in his outstretched hand before putting down her bucket.

'You not going home yet?' she asked as she took the cup in her hand.

'No, I've still got a bit to do. I tell you what, don't bother with my office. It's not that grubby. Just be a sweetheart and do me a tea and then you can pop off home.'

Josephine hesitated. It was part of her job description to clean *all* of the offices and not miss a spot, her supervisor had said.

'Oh don't worry so much, Josephine,' Mr Spencer could sense how uneasy she was with his request. 'I won't tell if you won't tell. Two sugars please and make yourself one.'

'No thank you.'

Josephine went to the kitchen and spilled the contents of the cup into the sink. She put the kettle on and waited for the water to boil. She poured the steaming water onto the teabag in Mr Spencer's cup. As she did so she felt a hand on her shoulder. She let the kettle slip from her grasp on to the table as she spun around to see Peter Spencer standing behind her. He was holding a small bar of chocolate.

'I said to make yourself one so that you could have this.' He held the chocolate out to her but she did not take it. She felt uncomfortable. There was something about his manner that seemed different from before. It wasn't relaxed and easy. His voice had a strict tone somehow and he looked straight into her eyes but not in the casual, friendly way he normally did.

'I told you, I didn't want a drink.' Josephine tried to turn back to see to the tea.

'And so you don't want this chocolate then?' He held it in front of her face between his fingers.

'Well no, I suppose … .'

'No? But you've never refused before. What's so different about tonight?'

'Mr Spencer, I think you should finish your own tea. I have to go.' As Josephine tried to leave the kitchen he swung her by the shoulder to face him, dropping the chocolate on the floor. He advanced on her, forcing her to make three very quick steps backwards, until her back was up against the wall.

'Josephine, you're not being friendly today. Why aren't you being friendly?' He had clasped her thin arms with his hands and was so close to her, she could feel his breath on her forehead as she struggled to get away from him. He was not that much taller than her but a lot stronger.

He pushed his body up against hers as he leaned closer to try to kiss her. On impulse, she spat in his face. He released his grip to wipe it. Josephine rushed toward the door as he tried to grab her. As she ran into the corridor, she felt both of his arms around her waist, pulling her past two offices while she kicked her legs frantically. Spinning her, face forward, to his open office door, he threw her onto the floor and was on top of her before she could lift herself up.

She beat him with her fists and cursed him as she shifted from side to side to avoid his kisses and attempts to touch her body. With his forearm wedged into her throat, pressing down hard he reached for the bottom edge of her dress.

'Mr Spencer. You must stop!' Josephine managed to splutter. He looked into her face. All he could see was hate and anger. She took long, deep, jagged breaths and stared, unblinking into his eyes. He lowered his eyes and abruptly got off her. He sat next to her as she lay on the ground for a few seconds, not sure if her ordeal was over.

Josephine got to her feet and fixed her dress and overall. She left the office without turning back and headed for the stairs. Her instincts told her that she should run but she had a responsibility to get her equipment back to its cupboard. As she came back out onto the corridor, Peter Spencer stood, staring at her. She froze for a moment.

'Josephine. You ... I, I'm very sorry. I don't understand. I thought you liked me a little bit.' His face was red and he could not meet her gaze.

'Is that the way you show a person you like them? I have a husband. I have children. I don't need any other man in that way. I liked you because you been friendly to me.'

'I'll never do that again. Please don't say anything to anyone. I just got it wrong.'

'I never do anything to tell you I wanted you like that.'

'It's my mistake. I'm not good at understanding people. Can I trust that you won't say anything?'

'Yes, I will promise. But can you promise to go home on a Friday before I have to clean your office. It's best if we don't speak again and if you stop buying me anything.' Josephine gathered up her equipment and bolted for the stairs.

'I'm sorry Josephine,' he called. She did not respond.

When Josephine arrived for work on Tuesday morning she got a message that Miranda, the cleaning supervisor, needed to see her urgently before she started work. Josephine knocked on the glass door of the supervisor's office.

'Come in,' Miranda called. 'Ah, Josephine, take a seat dear. I don't know what you think you were up to last Friday but I've had a complaint from upstairs. Apparently you never cleaned office twenty-three and the man in there complains that you very often leave it untouched. Is that right?'

'No, that was only the first time.' Josephine tried to defend herself.

'Josephine, there's no cutting corners in this job. I told you that in the beginning. If the job was too big for you, you should have said so.'

'It's not that the job was too big it's just … .'

'What? You couldn't be bothered? I told you there's no slacking around here. Everyone must work hard. I'm putting you on a warning. If I get any more complaints you'll have to go, I'm sorry.' Miranda looked from Josephine to the door and then back at the rota she was drawing up. Josephine got up and went back to work.

It happened that Miranda got another complaint from upstairs. A cigarette lighter was missing from the desk in office number twenty-three. Josephine was given one week's notice.

34

The beach was quiet. The sky was completely blue with not a cloud in sight. The sun beat down so heavily that the young girl had to walk to the edge of the sea to at least cool her feet. But the water was warm, still, with not one wave, not even a ripple. She looked out to the vast horizon and there was no land in sight. Just a line where the sky met the sea. No sign of a ship. That was unusual, she thought. Along the beach, in either direction, there was no one, not a single soul. The girl looked down at her feet. The sea had begun to ripple and rise above her ankles. The ripples turned into waves and the girl felt afraid and alone for the first time. The waves rolled quickly in and out and splashed her legs. Before she could turn and make her way home, an enormous wave reared up to her waist and dragged her a little way into the water. She splashed and scrambled to the beach as the wave rolled into the shore and then back again. Unable to stand, the girl rolled onto her back to watch for another wave. The sea was still restless. She edged her way away from the shoreline on her elbows and looked up to find that there were clouds in the sky. They raced along but, at first, she could not feel the wind that blew them. Suddenly, the wind closed tightly around her body and spun her up, high above the sand and lifted her over a row of trees, then higher. The wind swept fast and thoughtlessly toward the mountainside with the girl still in its grasp. In seconds she would be thrown against the mountain and smashed to death. She tightened all the muscles in her face and awaited the inevitable. Nothing. Releasing the tension in her face, her eyelids opened slightly and bright light overwhelmed her as she hovered only millimetres from the rocks lining the mountain. The light became more powerful and

259

she no longer saw the rocks. Instead, the light appeared to be shining around a person she thought she knew. A very tall man, only inches away from her. She couldn't make out his face but heard his voice very clearly. 'Don't worry. I will put your mother in a safe place. I can't save them all but you will see your mother again.' The unnatural light faded, replaced almost immediately by sunlight. The girl found herself lying on her back on the beach once more. She leant up on her elbows, looking out to sea. The sand was warm, a gentle breeze blew, and from the distance a ship was sailing at speed straight toward her stretch of beach.

Josephine woke with a start.

Since she'd been living in London, Josephine had had fewer and fewer dreams of any significance. The dream seemed to have no meaning to her. It was as though her gift was only with her in part in London and she was never sure which of her dreams were premonitions.

Almost four years before, the family had moved to their new house in the suburbs. This had been the first dream of this kind since the move. She recognized the girl in the dream. It was her, at about sixteen. A young and innocent girl, without a care in the world. A trainee seamstress, living at home with her mother.

Her mother. She thought about her now. They had exchanged numerous letters over the nineteen years since Josephine said goodbye, with promises of seeing her again. The years had sped by before she had time to count them. Until now, she had never found herself in a position to go back. But on this August morning in 1979 she turned onto her back, took a brief look at her husband sleeping beside her, raised her eyes up to the ceiling and thought, why not now?

James had set up his own business as a building contractor and was making a reasonable living. Nineteen years. It was time.

Later that day Josephine's phone rang. It was Eunice.

'Sis, *sis!* Did you hear the news?' Eunice sounded shaken.

'No. What news?'

'The hurricane! So many people back home have been killed.

None of us have been able to call because all the power lines down. Didn't you see the news?'

'No. What about Mama? How will we find out if she's alright – if everyone alright?'

'I see the news in my coffee break and my boss gone and call the Embassy for me. He say to just sit tight while he find out what he can. I will call you straight back as soon as I hear anything.'

Josephine called Delphina at work and asked her to contact a travel agent and book her a flight home straight away. When she came off the phone to her daughter, she sat on the sofa and remembered her dream. She knew she would see her mother again. Her heartbeat calmed, she was able to relax.

When Josephine landed on the island, she didn't know what to expect. The blues and greens of her home had always been vivid in her mind. The church, the market square, the little wooden house she moved to when she got married. Imagining that all of these could be gone, swept away by the devastation the hurricane left behind, filled her with dread. Those terrible scenes from the news were heartbreaking. She had prayed non-stop since hearing the news and for the entirety of her flight. What would the house she grew up in look like now?

After an hour-long journey by bus from the airport, Josephine tentatively climbed out as it stopped just a few feet from her old home. She was wearing a light blue fitted seersucker blouse that had a belt of the same material, fastened at her waist. She wore loose fitting, beige, cotton trousers that hung just long enough to cover most of the tops of her brown wedged heeled sandals. Over her left shoulder she carried a brown leather handbag and in her right hand she carried a red canvas suitcase. It bulged at the seams and was extremely heavy for someone with a frame as small as hers. Behind her was Felix, her young cousin who had met her at the airport and accompanied her home to her mother's village, who was carrying her other suitcase. People from England had sent bundles of clothes and various supplies to their loved ones and every time they discovered that someone would be flying out to the island they would beg them to find space in their suitcase to send more.

Just before entering the front yard, Josephine hesitated when she saw an old woman standing at the door of her mother's wooden house. The woman, once so tall and elegant, was now hunched over slightly, looking frail. Her hair, what could be seen beneath a red, checked headscarf, showed flashes of grey. The blue dress she wore, which Josephine recognised as her dress for church, hung off her shoulders as though it belonged to someone much taller and broader. The slanted smile she knew so well was minus at least two teeth on the side. But there she stood, proud and happy. Her mother, Rose.

Josephine dropped her suitcase and rushed towards the house. A member of the crowd, which had gathered on the little road to greet her, picked up the case and followed her, the rest of the welcoming party close behind. Josephine took the steps two at a time and nearly sent her mother tumbling backwards as she rushed to embrace her. The women hugged each other for a full minute. They laughed and cried at the same time whilst the crowd in the small yard clapped.

'Josephine, my Josephine. I can't believe you are here after all this time.'

'I would always come back. You know I would always come back.'

'I'm only glad I see you again before I died.'

'Oh Mama, don't say that. England is not an easy place. We never had enough money to pay my passage until now.'

'That's okay. The important thing is that you come. Let me look at you. Even though I can hardly see these days.'

'What you mean you can hardly see?'

'When you left I was an old woman, now I am even older.'

'Maybe all you need is some glasses.'

'Like yours?' Josephine had on gold-rimmed glasses, decorated by a twirling design in each corner of the frame.

'Well, if I need glasses at my age,' Josephine replied, 'then so must you.' The women laughed and hugged again.

Rose was not living on her own at her house. Her youngest son, Little Raphael, who actually grew to be the tallest of all her sons, was back living with her. As were his wife, their eight month old baby boy and his wife's six-year-old daughter from a previous relationship. Raphael was glad to see his sister. His wife, Julianna, however, looked at Josephine from the side of her eyes and asked if she wanted tea before she left.

'I'm not going anywhere.' Josephine replied. 'I came to see my mother and this is where I'm staying.'

'And very welcome you are, Sis,' her brother said, staring at his wife who went out to the kitchen to boil water.

The days Josephine spent back on her island went by too quickly. Her four-week stay was near its end and she found herself finally alone with her mother and they could have a good long talk. The house was usually full of family and friends. They came to see Josephine to hear about England, commenting that Josephine now sounded like a 'Londonier', even though most of them had never heard a Londoner speak before. Julianna was always watching everything Josephine did in the kitchen or around the house. She would look at Josephine from head to toe every time she stepped out of Rose's bedroom to see what Josephine was wearing. And every time Julianna would say, 'In London you buy this?' and Josephine would answer, 'Yes Julianna, that is where I buy all my clothes now.' Then Julianna would walk out of the room saying, 'In London they have more clothes than they have people to wear them.'

As for Rose, she would look at Josephine's clothes and exclaim, 'But Josephine, this is too good to wear in the house, you must save that for church.' Josephine had brought a new dress and some nightdresses for her mother. Rose refused to wear them, claiming that the nightdresses would do for when she was sick and had to go the hospital and the dress would be the one she would be buried in. Josephine smiled. It was what she expected her to say. Josephine only wished she could have had time to make a dress for her mother before she'd left London.

When the islanders saw how Josephine dressed they all assumed she was a millionaire. They had no idea how much work it had taken for her and James to be in their current situation. Not rich at all, but comfortable. Of course the islanders would either not have known or cared to acknowledge what a struggle Josephine and James had had. They talked about Josephine as though she owned the plane she arrived in and many of them thought she should be handing money out to them. She heard people say as she was passing, 'You know her house have five bedrooms? I expect she even have servants.' Josephine had not told anybody how many bedrooms she had, except for her mother and so suspected that an eavesdropping Julianna had been able to fill the gossips in.

'How many days you have left with us Josephine?' her mother asked.

'Just three.' Josephine was helping her mother into her nightdress and was going to plait her hair before bed.

'You sure you already been here four weeks? It seems too quick.'

The two were silent for a long time. Josephine rubbed her mother's feet with oils. After this she combed her hair. She parted it carefully and began weaving a tiny network of thin cornrows from her hairline up to the very top of her head. She wound the ends of the plaits into a bun, which she secured with two straight hairpins and then tied it firmly with a headscarf before pulling back the bedclothes for her mother to get into bed.

'I'm going to brush my teeth and get my nightie on so I can join you.' Josephine said. 'I tired after my trips to say goodbye to people. I forgot how hot it gets here. I get out of breath.'

'You are a real Londoner now. You like the cold.'

'No, I don't like the cold. I never will, but I suppose I get used to it. Well both Eunice and I have.' As Josephine mentioned her sister's name, she noticed how her mother's shoulders sank and how her smile closed into a thin line.

'You missing her?' Josephine asked.

'Who Eunice? Yes of course – I miss both of you.' Rose hadn't looked up at her daughter who stood by the open bedroom door.

'Is that why you look so sad Mum? You wish Eunice was here too?' Rose said nothing for a long time. It wasn't sadness Josephine saw in her mother's eyes, but something else. Closing the bedroom door, she walked over to the bed and sat on the edge.

'Can you tell me what you're thinking?' Josephine asked.

'I wish I didn't have to say what I have to say to you, but I don't want to take it to my grave. It's something between two sisters that only one of them know about.'

'Something I know and Eunice don't?' Josephine felt a little afraid. She looked into Rose's eyes. 'Mama, are you sure you want to tell me?'

'I just know that if you ever knew the truth one day, and you found out that I already knew, you would ask yourself why I, as your mother, never tell you.'

'Well, if I never knew about it all this time, then maybe I don't need to know.' Josephine tried to smile.

Rose folded her hands on her lap. She sat, barely moving, unable to look her daughter in the eye. At last she looked up at a patient Josephine.

'Eunice once lost a baby.' Rose spoke quickly. Afraid if she didn't start speaking she would say nothing at all.

'A baby?' Josephine was confused. 'But since she been married she could never fall pregnant. How she could lose a baby?'

'It was before she marry. While she was still here. A young girl. Some people already know – they used to talk about it.' Rose paused. Took a breath. 'I think is because you always see the good in people, Josephine, why you never find out yourself.'

'Well I'm not surprised Eunice had a man before she marry. She was always a wild girl.' Josephine stopped suddenly before

265

finishing her sentence, instead she had a question.

'Who was this man?' Again Rose sat motionless, she hardly dared breathe. Josephine did not need her mother to tell her. A feeling overwhelmed her. She knew.

'James? Mama, you telling me that James was the father of Eunice baby?' Rose hesitated before answering. Swallowed hard.

'Yes Josephine. I'm so sorry but you should know your own sister. You don't know her as well as the rest of us do. I worried when she was going to England with you. I worried she would try to take James the way she always wanted to.'

'What are you saying?' Josephine sat up with a straight back.

'She always love James. Even before she leave school. If she could have take him then, before you marry him, she would.'

'So you think James loved her too?'

'No. You know James. He can't resist the women. His father was just the same. That's why I never marry him when he ask me and that's why I was scared when you say you want to marry the son. But then you fall pregnant and so it was his duty to marry you.'

'I married him because I loved him. I slept with him because I loved him. You never tried to stop me seeing him.'

'No but I tried to warn you about him. But, as you say – you love him, so you couldn't hear me.' Rose shook her head from side to side.

'When?' Josephine asked her.

'When what?'

'When did Eunice lose this baby? Before, we even marry?' Rose put her head down. 'You mean she sleep with James *after* I marry him?' Josephine raised her voice but Rose lowered hers when she answered.

'You were carrying your first child.'

Josephine rose from the bed and paced the floor, both hands rested in the small of her back as she began to think back. What had she noticed about the pair of them? She never saw them together. In fact, James went out of his way to keep Josephine from having her sister around. Always saying she was too noisy and silly. Was that because he couldn't resist her or was it because he was afraid that Eunice would reveal their secret? Josephine continued to pace around the small bedroom. She stopped suddenly and looked at her mother when she realised that she could not have heard the whole story.

'So if Eunice hadn't lose the baby, then she would have been walking around here with James' child – all the time I was married to him. What would people have said?'

'Eunice couldn't live with that burden.'

'So, what, she was going to leave?'

'No, she went to a woman. She ask this woman to take the baby out before it have time grow.'

'My God in heaven.' Josephine began to shake. 'So, she didn't lose the child – she throw it away.' She sank onto the bed again next to her mother, who by now had tears falling from her eyes. Rose shook her head from side to side again and started to utter a prayer under her breath.

'So who knew?'

'Some people. But just a few. You see Eunice had to see a doctor after going by that bad woman place. She bleed so much. People were bound to find out. But who knew never spread it far because of the respect people have for me and for you. I thought then that she would never have another child. And I was right.' She dried her eyes.

'But Josephine. You know you must forgive your sister. She was young and foolish. And look at her life. She already been punished.'

'I can't forgive her. And I can't forgive James. If I stay with him it will only be for my children sake.'

'Josephine you cannot break up your marriage because of a foolish young girl's mistake. Men are weak – they don't know how to control themselves. James has done a lot for you and his family.'

'Did Papa ever go with another woman after he marry you?'

'As far as I know he never did. But some men are like that

267

Josephine. You know that. You're a grown woman. You can't leave your husband. You made your bed.'

'And what an ugly bed it is.'

When Josephine flew back to London, it was not with the excited anticipation that she felt on the outward journey. She wished that the plane could go anywhere but home. She could easily start again in some anonymous place. She would have no family to worry about, no cares in the world if the plane could just land somewhere else, and give her another chance to find happiness.

The plane landed at Heathrow. James and their daughter Angelica had come to meet her. As James put her suitcases into the boot of his Ford Granada, her daughter gave Josephine another hug.

'You don't look glad to be back, Mum. You missing Grandma already? Anyway, guess what? I've got a job. I start on Monday.'

Josephine smiled.

gn of life was a fat cat, which, ignoring the couple, disappeared
etween two parked cars. Finally, Garry placed his hands gently
n Eunice's arms. She shivered in the cold and he smiled and
lled her closer. She trembled as he placed a kiss on her lips. Her
es were half shut when she suggested he came inside. Here was
man, she felt, she could let down her guard for, if only a little.

'Unless you have someone waiting for you at home,' she said.
was a question she needed to have answered.

'No, I wouldn't be here if that were the case. My wife passed
ay three years ago and I live with my son. He's eighteen now
d probably out somewhere with his mates.'

'I thought you looked like a family man. You can come in for
ttle while.'

Eunice felt in her handbag for her keys. She unlocked the red
r and Garry followed her up the narrow staircase to her room.
as cold. Eunice put on the electric heater. In the corner of the
m, head next to the window, was a single bed covered by a
p red candlewick blanket. At the foot of the bed stood an old
chair with a new red and yellow cushion, a sunken seat and
ral pairs of tights hanging over the arm rest. There was a
ll wardrobe and a full-length mirror on the wall. Under the
dow was a wooden table with a lamp on it. Along the wall
g the window was a counter, which housed a hot plate and
e and various cooking items. Above it was a cupboard for
ce's food and utensils.

It's small, but it's home, and it's all mine. Well for as long as I
he rent anyway.' Eunice laughed, Garry had hold of her face
was kissing her before she could offer him a drink. She
med his kisses. They threw off their coats, shoes, and
es in their haste to get into bed.

ater, they lay beneath the covers, tired but laughing and
ng. They talked about the party, about work, their interests.
wanted to know more about Eunice. He was surprised that
ould be single at forty-two, childless and living alone. She
im very little about her past, only to explain that she was

35

'I'm sorry, what did you say your name is?'

'Eunice.' Eunice had to raise her voice above the music. The DJ was looking very pleased with himself. He had stacked up all the latest pop chart hits and some trusted oldies to get the party started. This was a done deal. Works crowds were always easy to get going. Just one round of drinks and most of them would be up and dancing and it wouldn't take long before the others joined them.

During the rest of the year, the factory and office workers of Hollings Pharmaceuticals would be content to turn up for work on time, exchange a few pleasantries, take part in the usual gossip and leave for home without a glance back at their work stations in the evening. Apart from the day they received their payslips, there was only one other day that the employees of Hollings Pharmaceuticals looked forward to with even a modicum of excitement. That was the day of the works Christmas Party. On that day, there was always a noticeable buzz of anticipation. On the night of the party, which was always on a Friday, everyone would let down their guard, speak to someone from another department and totally lose their inhibitions. Between seven-thirty and eleven on that Friday night, the workers stopped talking shop, everyone applauded the person brave enough to start the dancing and everyone drank far too much. Everything that happened on that Friday night would all be forgotten by the following Monday morning. At eight-thirty on Monday the different sections and departments would be as divided as they ever had been. But for this particular year, Monday morning after the party would be an exception.

For several months, Garry Roberts had noticed Eunice at work. He hadn't been around in the days when she arrived with black eyes and bruises and knew very little about this attractive, spirited black woman. When he'd walked past the factory floor, he'd heard someone singing, put this head around the door and noticed that several of the factory workers had stopped to listen as she sang along to the radio. She hadn't noticed the new man from accounting as she threw back her head to harmonise with the last chorus. Applauded by her work mates, she revelled in the attention. Everyone commented on her wonderful singing voice.

In the little room Eunice had found after leaving her husband she had been happy enough. She had decorated it brightly in reds and yellows, played her transistor radio loudly and danced to and from the bathroom on the lower floor with abandon. But sometimes, and more frequently than she liked to admit, she found herself craving companionship. Since her husband, Nestor, had returned to the Caribbean several years before, she'd had two relationships. Suspicious of men, unintentionally she'd chase them off.

Garry Roberts had joined the company six months before the Christmas party and that's where he first encountered Eunice in person. He didn't know her name until the evening of the party and was too embarrassed to ask anybody because he was afraid to let anyone know he was attracted to her. It may have started with physical attraction, but Garry longed to get to know the person he saw chatting and laughing in the canteen, amusing colleagues and acting as though she hadn't a care in the world. He watched her from his office window some mornings and sometimes saw her on her way home. She always dressed in bright, bold, colours, which fascinated him. She walked with a confident swing in her hips, but never seemed to be partnered with any of the men on-site.

Once, in the queue in the canteen, he happened to notice that she didn't wear a wedding ring. On that day she noticed him too. She saw a man of about six feet in height, broad shouldered with

reddish-brown hair. When she looked at him his f bright red. She smiled to herself. From that day, notice each other from time to time but neither dared divide was quite clear to them both. They worked departments and came from very different backgrou they could overcome the barrier between sections at debatable whether they could break down the one between their races.

On the night of the Christmas party, neither ca about barriers. Attraction surpassed prejudice and t the whole evening.

'I like that name,' he said. 'Very old fashioned.'

Eunice smiled.

'Are you an old-fashioned girl?'

'Not really, well maybe in some things but not i

'I'd like to get to know you more,' Garry said. 'I meet for a drink one night. Somewhere not so no full of people we know.'

'Everyone is staring at us.' Eunice took a sip of

'I wonder what they would do if we started da

'Well I suppose there's only one way to fin placing her glass on the table.

The song being played was quite slow and t close to each other. The DJ had switched on fla flickered in rhythm with the music. As the cou were aware that all eyes were on them. Half a couple left, arm-in-arm.

It was a short bus ride to Eunice's flat and see her home as it was late. The red door leading the shops sat between a café and a chemist. He first floor, above the chemist, and looked out street which in the daytime was filled by the traffic and lively passers-by was deserted now.

They stood outside the red door, eyes n Eunice looked one way while Garry looked t

once married but the marriage had ended because of her abusive partner. She insisted that they never speak about it.

'This is a part of my life I regret ever happen. I spend all this time trying to forget, trying to be happy again.' Eunice grew quiet, pulled the blanket up around her chest, and yawned.

'You're tired.' He smiled at her and rolled a little closer to her. 'This bed is a little small for two. Should I leave you to get some sleep?'

'I suppose,' she said. 'But could I make you that tea before you go, so you can warm yourself up a bit. It's very cold out there.'

'Yes, that would be really good of you.' Garry got up and started to dress. He sat on the bed and watched while Eunice, still naked, made them both a cup of tea. With the long, red curtains closed since morning and blocking out the street lights, Garry admired her body by the light of the lamp.

'Can I see you tomorrow, Eunice?'

'Oh.' Eunice hesitated a moment. 'Well, yes. That would be nice.'

'I can come here at midday and we could have a coffee in one of those coffee shops along here. What do you think?'

'I like your idea very much Garry.'

'I like the way you say my name. It sounds a nice name, the way you say it.'

'You find I sound funny when I talk?'

'Not at all. You sound beautiful. Especially when you sing.'

'I have to go to the kitchen to get the milk. I better put something on.'

'Don't.'

He took her hand and led her back to the bed. They fell asleep after making love again. It was midday when they got out of bed and had coffee at the café next door.

On Monday morning Garry made a special effort to come to the factory floor to wish Eunice a good morning. All the other workers, including her boss, looked on in amazement. They were positively speechless when Eunice and Garry sat and ate lunch

273

together that day and every day that followed.

James and the children could not understand what was wrong since Josephine's return – why she often sat quietly and never sang about the house.

On the night of her return, James touched his wife's arm and kissed her good night on the cheek. She lay as still as the tiny ornaments that lined the mantelpiece in her living room – no response, no movement, no sound. He said nothing but rolled over to sleep. He had missed his wife. She was the glue that held the family together. He only coped without her because the youngest was fourteen and now needed little management. Before he fell asleep, he reflected on how much Josephine meant to him. He had loved her since he was a young man and now, in middle age, there were an abundance of reasons for him to love her more. Just before he started to dream he wished that he could have been more worthy of her.

Josephine did not sleep. Even after a long flight, her eyes did not blink with fatigue, she did not yawn, she did not assume a position conducive to sleep. She was wondering. Wondering if God would give her the strength to survive her burden. To her knowledge, James had been unfaithful once before. A woman that she would never see again or that her family would ever have any contact with. That she could cope with and put behind her. But that her husband had sex with her younger sister shortly after they got married would be impossible to forget. She put her trust in God that He would provide an answer. She could not trust herself to make a decision.

During the weeks that followed a controlled storm brewed within her. It threw itself with gusto against her heart and made it beat fast and out of time most days, causing her to stop and press her hand to her chest so that she could breathe again. It pounded at her brain and made her forget things, lose concentration. It beat at the window to her emotions and made her cry when she least expected to and turn sullen at the drop of a hat. Her family put her new self down to her time of life. But Josephine knew that if she let the storm have full reign it would crash out of her with such force it would tear a hole into her family that no amount of time and care could repair. It was no ordinary hurricane.

For several months, Eunice had been finding a new peace, a new calm that, no matter how hard she tried, she could not stop it showing on the outside. She was making everyone around her happy. Her work mates had said how lucky she was to be going out with a man with money. He bought her presents: jewellery, clothes, shoes, handbags. He had taken her to the cinema, restaurants, museums and even a trip to Bournemouth that summer.

Prior to Josephine's trip home after the hurricane, Eunice had not mentioned her relationship with Garry. She thought it best to keep it a secret from her sister in case nothing came of it. But nine months had passed and Garry was making no secret about his feelings.

'Eunice, you know Toby and I think the world of you, ' Garry said out of the blue one day. 'You know how much I love you and want to be with you. Well, I was wondering how you felt about us getting married.'

Eunice had been washing up in the kitchen of Garry's three-bedroom house in Ilford. He very often picked Eunice up on a Friday evening and she would stay until Sunday after dinner when he would drive her back home so that they didn't arrive at work together. Eunice insisted they didn't make a public show of their intimacy.

'Garry – marriage is a big step. You sure you want me?'

'I couldn't be more sure of anything, Eunice.' He stood next to Eunice and removed the side plate and dishcloth from her hands. He placed them on the draining board, without taking his eyes off her. She dried her hands and took his hands in hers.

'That is something I would love dearly, Garry. You know that. But I have to confess something to you. I am still married.'

'What?' Garry stood back and released his hands.

'That fool I married went back home years ago but we never signed any divorce papers.'

'But do you want to be married to him?'

'Of course I don't. You know I forgot about him a long time ago and I even let myself forget my wedding day.'

'I see. But a wedding day is a thing to be remembered. I want us to remember ours. I'll get solicitor. We'll sort this out – I promise. If you'd only promise to marry me.' He gently stroked her face.

'I promise.' She smiled up at him.

'Good.' He kissed her and felt in his pocket for a little box. Inside it was a ring. A slender gold hoop with a red gem surrounded by tiny diamonds. He placed it on Eunice's finger.

'Ah, it's a little loose,' he said. 'Take it off and I'll have it altered.'

'We can have it altered but I don't want to take it off – not just yet.' She looked down at her hand and smiled, then she threw her head back and laughed.

'We could have a little party, maybe a barbecue to celebrate our engagement.' Garry said. 'Invite some friends and family – just close ones. 'I haven't met your sister yet. We could ask a few people from work. Mum and Dad know you, but my sister hasn't met you yet.'

'You think she will like me?'

'She'll love you.'

'Well your mum and dad were funny with me at first. They still don't think I'm right for you. You know that don't you?'

'Mum and Dad are old, what do they know?'

'And what about us? Aren't we old too?' She wrapped her arms around his waist. 'Aren't we too old to be acting like teenagers in love?'

'I feel like a teenager. And when Toby goes out later I'll show you how much.'

Eunice shrieked with laughter.

It was with difficulty that Eunice called her sister to reveal not only how serious she had become about Garry, but that they were now living together. It was with even greater difficulty that Josephine accepted her sister's invitation to the engagement party and had to go accompanied by James.

James and Josephine arrived in the late afternoon. Josephine had baked a cake. Eunice looked bright and radiant as she kissed her cheek, but Josephine stood back to watch as Eunice kissed James. A tall white man with reddish-brown hair marched down the corridor to meet them.

'Hello there! You must be Josephine.' He held out a big hand, warm and welcoming, and planted a kiss on her cheek. Josephine managed to smile and say, 'Pleased to meet you.'

'This is James, her husband,' Eunice said as James stepped forward.

Josephine and James followed the couple to the garden where more introductions were made. Josephine was afraid that she came across as cold. It was not her intention. It was just that in her head she had conjured up, for the millionth time, images of James and Eunice writhing naked in her bed in their little blue house back home. It was warm for September, but Josephine felt a chill.

As the afternoon wore on, Josephine became tired of trying to be pleasant. The smiling hurt her face. Polite conversation stuck in her throat and put her off the food. Finding an opportunity to go inside, she excused herself and went to the bathroom and sat on the edge of the bath with her eyes closed. In her hand was the glass of white wine that Garry had offered her earlier, but she hadn't even taken a sip of. Just when she was about to pour the wine into the sink, there was a faint tap on the door.

'Sis, are you alright? You been a long time.' Eunice stood there smiling as Josephine opened the bathroom door.

'I'm fine Eunice. I was just starting to feel a little chilly so I thought I would warm up before I go back out.'

'Come to my room to see if I can find you a warmer cardigan.'

'No it's okay. I'll be alright. James and I will have to go home soon anyway.'

'But I haven't shown you around the house yet. Come on.'

With a great effort on her part, Josephine followed Eunice to the bedroom.

'Very nice,' said Josephine.

There was nothing special about the room. It was painted white. A double bed sat opposite the window. The curtains were floral and so was the bed cover, both of which clashed.

'I think something is wrong, Sis. You don't like Garry?' Eunice asked as she relieved her sister of the glass of wine that looked likely to spill with all the fiddling Josephine was doing with its stem, and placed it on a side table.

'Garry is very nice, Eunice. You have met a nice man. Treat him well.' With this Josephine started to walk toward the bedroom door, which was slightly ajar. Eunice grabbed her sister by the shoulder and pulled her back to face her.

'Josephine, why you have to be like that? What have I done to you?' Something within Josephine finally snapped.

'Your question should be what haven't you done.'

'Josephine you sound mad. I don't know what you mean.'

'Well I know what *you* mean now.' Josephine had raised her voice slightly. And Eunice raised hers to the same level.

'You know what *I* mean?' Eunice asked. She made a face to show she was puzzled.

'Yes. One day you told me you stole from me and I know what it is you stole.' Eunice remained as still and as quiet as stone.

'I couldn't believe what I heard from our own mother's mouth.' Josephine stopped to remove her glasses and wiped a tear from her cheek. 'Eunice, how could you steal my husband like that? He was not yours to take. How could you sleep with him in my own bed? Our bed, for our life together. How could you do that to your own sister?' And still Eunice could not speak.

Her eyes turned toward the bedroom door. It was opening, slowly. And there stood Garry, his face bright red. Josephine

278

turned around in surprise. The three stood looking at each other for seconds until Garry spoke up.

'Is this true Eunice?' he asked.

'It's not true Garry. I don't know what has gotten into my sister but she going now, anyway.' Garry looked at Josephine who looked away.

'Eunice – tell me the truth? Did you sleep with your own sister's husband? I have to know the truth.' Eunice let seconds go by before she could answer.

'Garry, it was a long time ago. I was young. I thought I loved him. He is older than me, he – he shouldn't have encouraged me.'

'Yes, he was wrong to do that Eunice,' Josephine interrupted. 'But you are my blood. I expected more from you. My only sister who I loved so much. I trusted you. I stuck up for you when Mama was angry with you, when anyone was angry with you, including James. You broke my heart more than James ever could. This is the thing I just cannot forgive. My own sister.'

'And how can *I* ever forgive you Eunice?' Garry took two large paces in Eunice's direction. Eunice ducked as though to avoid a blow.

'I'm not going to hit you, you silly woman. I was going to hold you and beg you to tell me it's not true. I don't want it to be true.' He gripped her arms and pulled her towards him but her eyes could not meet his. Instead she looked past his shoulder at Josephine.

'It is true, then?' Garry released his grip and stormed over to the other side of the room. 'I want you out.'

'What?' Both women spoke this word simultaneously.

'You heard me.' He turned to look at the astonished women. 'I want you gone, Eunice. You are not the woman I want to marry. I was married for sixteen years to someone I loved with all my heart. You were the first woman I ever looked at since she died. I thought you were worth it but I was wrong. You're nothing like the person I thought I was going to marry – nothing like her. I want you out of here just as soon as I can get everyone else to leave.' He tried to leave the room but Eunice pulled him by his arm.

'What will you tell people?'

'Don't worry. I'll just say you're sick and get rid of them. I'm sorry Josephine. Truly I am.' He went out to the garden while the two women remained there in silence.

'Eunice, I didn't mean for this to happen.' Josephine finally said.

'But you are happy though. You have your revenge. I'm alone again now. As usual, you have everything and I have nothing.' She stepped closer to Josephine. With clenched teeth, her face just an inch from Josephine's, she said, 'I have nothing.' Josephine stepped back.

'You did this, not me. I'm not taking the blame for your mess.' Josephine left the room and walked slowly down the stairs. She hovered by the front door as the guests started to make their way for home. When she saw James come through from the garden she left the house and walked toward the car. She looked up at the bedroom window and saw Eunice staring down at her with an expression that felt like a cold, hard slap against her face.

That was the last day the sisters ever saw each other.

James and Josephine drove home in silence. James, oblivious to the events before their departure, simply assumed that Josephine was worrying about Eunice's ill health. Not wanting to discuss Eunice, he remained silent. About three miles in to their journey home, James noticed that his wife was sniffing and turned to look at her. She was crying. She made no attempt to dry her eyes, instead the tears streamed down her face. She had not been able to say what was on her mind since her return from visiting her mother and she felt relief, anger, betrayal and exhaustion all at the same time. Her ordeal was not over. There was still James to confront.

Before she knew it, James had turned into a side street and stopped alongside a large park. Josephine turned her head toward the tall, green railings surrounding the park and could see a woman walking a large brown dog. She took off her glasses to dry her eyes.

'How sick is Eunice that you have to cry like that?' James asked. 'Don't you have a hanky or some tissues in your bag?' Josephine wiped her nose with her sleeve and looked down. She managed to stop crying, her voice trembled.

'Eunice told me all about you and her.'

'What do you mean she told you about me and her? There is no "me and her".' James kept his eyes fixed on the windscreen but was not looking out. He knew exactly what Josephine meant. In all of this time, James' biggest worry was that Eunice would finally tell Josephine the truth.

He remembered the day Eunice had told him she thought she might be pregnant and how he had told her to go away and leave him alone. He blamed her for their affair, saying that she hung around too much and shouldn't have called on them those Saturday afternoons when she knew Josephine was visiting her mother. Eunice could not believe her ears. She loved James. She had convinced herself that James would not have slept with her unless he had fallen out of love with Josephine. She satisfied herself that it was only a matter of time before James admitted his mistake in marrying Josephine, and she could take her place by his side. She thought that her trump card would be the baby. Eunice had stood, grief stricken when James leant close to her face and told her he would deny their relationship with his last breath. He would never speak to her again if she revealed the paternity of her child and that he had serious doubts that he was, in fact, the father. James' words were cold and menacing. In his mind he had chosen the only way out of the shame and hurt that would follow if the truth came out. He hated himself then, and made a promise to himself that he would never let any other woman into his life again.

'This is not the time to lie James,' Josephine said. 'If anything, you should fall on your knees now and ask God for forgiveness.

281

He will hear your pleas. But as for me – I am not Him and I never want you to touch me again. I am your wife only in the eyes of the law and of the church.

'I am the mother of five children and I will keep your shame from them. How would they feel knowing their father is less than he should be? I only hope that none of them ever turn out like you. And I only hope none of my children ever have to suffer the way I am suffering today.

'If Eunice still have God in her life maybe He will forgive her too. But I don't believe I can ever find it in my heart to forgive her.'

James turned as if to speak but Josephine cut him off.

'James, just take me home.'

As James started the engine, the brown dog, sniffing curiously next to the tall green railings, looked up at the car and barked loudly. His barks startled Josephine who put on her glasses and watched him running along the path in the park when they pulled away.

James drove along the length of the park, turned right at the top of the road and right again. He hesitated for several minutes before turning left to continue their journey home. He stared at his wife and not at the oncoming traffic. A car horn sounded loudly behind them. James' focus shifted to the road and he continued to drive.

36

It was a sunny afternoon, a Friday in July 1989. Josephine had just been speaking to her next-door neighbour and noticed that there were two butterflies dancing amongst the roses in her front garden. Josephine was very proud of her roses and grew them in the back garden too: pink ones, yellow, red and white. The family knew she took pride in her gardens but never got involved in her hobby. In her gardens she could lose herself and not care what time it was.

Deep in thought as she watched the butterflies dance away, Josephine looked up and thought for one second that she might be dreaming. A young man was walking towards her. It was her husband James as he had looked back home when they were young – the young James who tried to win her over with his charm, a string of eloquent love letters and constant requests to take her out.

She blinked and thought there must be some sort of joke being played on her. But this was not a dream. The man striding towards her was made of flesh and blood and held himself in the same way James had done as a young man. He was smiling – with James' smile.

'Good afternoon,' he said when they were face to face, standing on opposite sides of the front gate. His voice was different from James'. He had an accent she wasn't familiar with. She stood motionless for a while and managed, at last, to answer the polite greeting.

'Good afternoon. Can I help you?' She eyed him suspiciously now, maybe she was still not convinced that this was an actual person.

'I'm very sorry to trouble you but I'm looking for Mr James Dennis. I believe he lives here?' the young man said.

'Maybe. But who are you?'

'I'm sorry. My name is Milo James Thompson. My mother, Marcia Thompson, knew James Dennis when he lived at 239 Shirley Road. I went there a few days ago but the houses are all gone. Just a row flats there now.'

'But they knocked those houses down a long time ago. And why are you looking for James Dennis?'

'Well, if he's not here then maybe I should call later. It's a little complicated and not something I should talk about on the street.' He looked up and down the small, quiet road. It was a lazy day and no-one was about.

'Well I know who you are looking for but I need to know why, before I can help you find him. So you better explain yourself before we go any further, young man.'

'Yes, I understand. It must seem like a strange request and I don't mean to invade your privacy like this. I hope this is not a bad time.' He raised his shoulders, displaying open hands and waited for some sort of response from Josephine, who gave him none. Memories of her basement flat in Shirley Road returned as she waited for him to continue.

'I grew up in Handsworth, that's in Birmingham, with my mum and my sister. My mum died when I was fourteen. She had a stroke. My sister was the one who brought me up after that. She sacrificed a lot for me. I was a bit of a tearaway after Mum died but Margaret got me on track, she really … well, you don't want to know all that. The fact is we got talking about our fathers. Margaret knew hers and Mum never told me anything about mine. So Margaret said she'd help me look for him.'

'Your mother and sister lived in the ground floor flat of 239 Shirley Road?'

'Yes. Did you know them?'

'Yes, I believe so.'

'Then you know James Dennis?'

284

'James Dennis is my husband.'

'That's what I thought. Well I'm very pleased to meet you.' He held out his hand. Josephine shook it limply.

'You telling me my husband is your father?'

'Yes, I suppose I am. I'm sorry to give you the news like this but I really wanted to meet him – even if it was just the once. It is important to me. I didn't want to cause a problem. I know he was married when he met my mother. I know she left London when she found out she was pregnant and that he knew she was expecting his child when she left. I hoped he might want to meet me.' He bent his head. Josephine opened the gate and stood back. She waved her hand towards the open door, beckoning him inside. He gave a slight smile, and entered the house with his head still bent. He stopped in the corridor and asked if James was home.

'No, my dear. He is still working. He may not be home until late. I'm the only one home.'

'So is it just the two of you living in this big house?' he asked after looking up and down the long hall and then back at Josephine.

'The children have all moved out. Some married. I have grandchildren. You have half brothers and sisters.'

'How many?'

Josephine sat Milo James at the table in her kitchen and made him a cup of tea and cut him some cake while she told him all about his family. She felt a strange maternal feeling towards him. Even though she knew he was a result of yet more infidelity on James' part, she was not angry with the young man in her kitchen, who sat laughing freely and talking with a strange accent. He was the image of her husband but reminded her so much of her youngest son. His energy and exuberance were infectious and she was happy to be in his company.

Josephine had suspected that James was likely to have slept with one of those women from Shirley Road but would have expected him to have chosen the daughter rather than the mother. Josephine had adopted a resigned indifference to her husband's affairs. By removing all emotion attached to his infidelity the couple were able to coexist. They had shared the same bed but without any form of physical contact since she discovered the truth about his affair with her sister. They lived together more as companions or lifelong friends.

James, who had had no intention of remaining celibate despite what his wife had decided, had, on at least three occasions, the opportunity of taking a woman to bed. On all three of those occasions, he was unable to perform. Not wishing to find himself in the same predicament a fourth time, he denied himself any opportunity to be alone with a woman other than his wife. He started going to church again. He prayed at night and took to reading psalms.

Hours went by and Josephine and Milo sat talking into early evening until pangs of hunger seized them both.

'You had better stay for dinner,' Josephine said.

The front door opened and the pair could hear the laboured sound of feet wiping across the mat, a large bag being placed heavily on the floor by the door and a pair of heavy legs walking down the corridor towards them. James couldn't smell dinner being cooked as he normally did. He was hungry and the house was quiet. Where was his wife? He called to her.

'I'm in here. Come in James, there is someone to see you.'

James came into the kitchen and stared from the young man to his wife and back again. His jaw opened slightly but he said nothing.

'Hello Mr Dennis.' Milo bounced toward James with an outstretched hand and a smile that James recognised as one a child of his might give him.

'I'm Milo James Thompson. You knew my mother Marcia. I'm the child she had when she left London. I'm your son.'

All this time Milo had his hand outstretched but James had failed to take it. As Milo began to lower his hand James reached to shake the young man's hand. He looked to Josephine.

'For goodness sake James, we all know what happened. I've made acquaintance with your son and I think it's time you did too. Go in the living room. I'll make us all dinner. Go on.' The two men disappeared out of the kitchen and Josephine shook her head and smiled.

They discovered that Milo was a solicitor. He had gone on to university despite a shaky adolescence. He told the couple about the sacrifices his sister made after their mother died of a stroke. How, despite his protestations and adolescent rants, she'd gotten him to abandon the group of wayward youths he had found himself amongst shortly after his mother's death. He loved his mother and found it hard to cope at school without her influence. He realised, later, that he worked as hard as he did at school to make his mum proud, something that she had drummed into him as being the most important thing that he could ever do for her. After her death he couldn't see the point anymore. There was no-one to impress and he couldn't see anything positive about his future. The school constantly sent letters home and telephoned regularly to a very weary and unprepared Margaret. Margaret gave up her job and found two part-time jobs that afforded her the time to escort Milo to school in the morning and be at home at four so that she could supervise homework and chores. In time she made Milo see that his mother would have wanted this for him, for his future, not just to keep her happy.

'So you're not married,' said Josephine. 'But do you have a girlfriend?'

'Yes, as a matter of fact I'm engaged and we'll be getting married next year. Do you think you can both come? I've spoken to Vanessa about trying to find my father and I'm sure she would be glad to have you there.'

'Of course we will, won't we James?'

'Yes, of course. And what about your sister? She ever marry?'

'No, she was too busy with me to find someone. But she is settled down now. Has been for the past few years, with an ex-serviceman. He was married before, and has three children. I

287

think they are planning to leave Birmingham and move to the coast. Back to where he came from originally. I think they might open a bed and breakfast or something like that. Anyway, she's very happy now.'

'That's good,' said James.

When it came time for Milo to leave, he asked if he might get to know his brothers and sisters. James looked at Josephine.

'It will take a bit of explaining.' Josephine was solemn for a moment. 'I want to decide what's best before I answer. Is that okay with you?'

'Yes, of course.' Milo smiled at her. 'I understand. Here are all my contact details. Could I take your telephone number here?'

'Yes,' Josephine said. James went to find a pen and paper.

'The children see their father in a certain way.' Josephine tried to explain her reticence. 'I'm not sure how they would take the news. I hope you can understand. News you never heard before can change everything when you finally come to know.'

'Yes, I've got first-hand experience haven't I?' Milo said. 'So, I'll leave it to you. I'll put an invitation in the post. I'll be going back to Birmingham tomorrow so I suppose this is goodbye for now.'

Josephine reached up to put her arms around his neck and pulled him to her. She kissed his cheek and wished him a safe journey. James opened his arms and Milo leant toward his father for a long awaited hug. Milo had forgiven him years ago for never coming to find him. He was only glad that he'd taken the initiative and felt thankful for the welcome he received from Josephine. He hoped that one day he could be united with the rest of the family. For now, the photograph that Josephine had given him would have to do.

37

I can't believe my flight is being delayed. This airport is closing in on me. It was quaint an hour ago but now it's a pain in the neck. Three souvenir shops, all selling the same things: straw fans, hats, little dolls of Caribbean women wearing large skirts, with aprons and head scarves; pen knives with maps of the island on them and plates with maps of the island on them. A snack bar come café downstairs and a restaurant upstairs.

As it's my third tour of the shops, I feel obliged to buy something. Not that anyone cares. The shopkeepers completely ignore me. They don't seem to have time for customers, too busy talking amongst themselves.

I spot a book rack I didn't notice first time around. Mills and Boon. I don't care, I've found something to read at least. I stand at the till and the girl carries on a conversation with someone who might be a cleaner here. There's nothing wrong with my throat but I have to clear it to get her attention.

'You want something?' She has large hazel eyes that just dare me to ask for anything.

'How much?' I ask and wave the book, meekly. She points at the sticker on the back. We exchange dollars for cents and without further conversation I leave the little booth with my book.

I need to find somewhere a bit out of the way. Upstairs I pop my head around the restaurant door but there are too many people in there for my liking. Better to give strangers a wide berth from now on. Especially as one particular man looks up at me and tries desperately to make eye contact. It's the last thing I need now.

I make my way to the departure lounge next the restaurant. It's just three rows of seats. Two facing each other, two of them overlook the planes landing and taking off. Only three other people are here and two of those are deep in conversation. Perfect. I position myself on a row facing the planes and wait. My book is unopened on my lap but I open it quickly when I notice a man staring at me. The man from the restaurant has followed me into the lounge. He stands a short distance away, contemplating his next move I suspect. I don't know how many free seats there are in this place but he's coming over and sitting next to me. I shuffle about in my seat, pretending I haven't noticed. My book is now right up to my face. I screw up my eyebrows to make myself look engrossed.

'That face,' he says. I ignore him. 'I'm sure I know that face, you couldn't mistake it.' He has a local accent so I assume that's what gives him the right to sit and interrogate anyone he sees fit.

'You're probably mistaken. I very rarely visit.' Eyes still on the book.

'Well you should, it's a beautiful part of the world and you're missing it all, stuck on that little grey island of yours across the sea.'

'How do you know where I'm from?' I put the book on my knee.

'Well I can tell from your clothes, your accent and your rudeness.'

'I beg your pardon. I'm not rude. You are the one that interrupted me.' I have to keep my cool to convince him I'm not the rude one.

'I was just trying to be friendly. I'm sorry.' He gets up to leave but stops. 'I know why I know that face. I knew your father – James Dennis. That's right isn't it? Mr Dennis was your father?'

'Yes, that's right.'

'Well, we are cousins. I was at his funeral but you don't remember me do you? I don't live on the island anymore. I live here now but I'm popping back to visit my mum. I should drop by to see yours too. But if you don't want me to talk to you when I get there, I'll understand.'

'Please – forgive me. I really didn't know and I wasn't trying to be rude. I just wanted to keep myself to myself.'

'Escaping?'

'I'm sorry?'

'You have a look of someone either trying to escape or looking to find something.' He stands in front of me and pauses for a moment as I look down at my book, now closed on my lap.

'I hope you find what you are looking for.' He turns as if to leave. I get up quickly to stop him.

'Please don't go. We should get acquainted. We are family and I don't want you to think I'm some bad tempered monster. That's just my mood for now but I'm hoping I can change it soon.' I hold out my hand for him to shake.

'My name is Angelica and I'm very pleased to meet you. Really.' Thank goodness he shakes my hand.

'I'm Frederick. I'm a second cousin to your dad.'

My flight is called. Looks like I've got another flying buddy.

We board the plane and sit together. This carrier is tiny. I think about twelve passenger seats in all but no time to count. We get strapped in and the crew announce our departure without an apology for the delay.

In the short island hop I find out that my cousin Frederick is a teacher and married with three grown up children. His wife had been a journalist and has now started teacher's training herself. They are both black belts in karate and had been on a yoga retreat in Portugal last summer but had not been tempted to go to England while in Europe. He'd been to London once and hated it and vowed never to return.

I look out of the little oval window every now and then, just to watch the sea. The waves foam and rush along. The sea looks as troubled as my mind and in the end I'm trying hard to focus on what Frederick is saying. I am interested but it's been a long, hard day. I'll see him again and I hope he won't mind repeating some things.

The plane arches and begins to dip as we approach the island. It comes in fast toward the mountains, curves neatly away and glides safely onto the tarmac of the short landing strip then comes to a sudden halt.

I hope you enjoyed your flight, please take all your baggage with you. Have your landing documents ready and have a wonderful stay.

It's getting dark now. This airport is even smaller than the last. We hand over our passports, have them stamped and make our way over to two large office tables to collect our luggage. A man puts a cross on my case and pushes it to me without once making eye contact. There are very few people in the arrival lounge. It's the last flight for the day, twenty to six in the evening.

Frederick guides me by the elbow and says he's got us a taxi. The taxi is a transit van that doubles as a bus by day. There are three other passengers. We take our seats and I look out into the night sky as we speed toward Mum's house, stopping twice to let the other passengers off along the way.

Outside, all I can see is black. I crane my neck to look out of the windscreen. Where the headlights fall I see a grey road lined by trees and thick bushes. Insects flutter in front of us and weave their way into the distance. I remember how much I like the sound of night-time on the island.

An hour later and we are finally at Mum's house.

'Let me walk you to the door.' Frederick is yawning now.

'No, no. You get going and I'll catch up with you soon.' I kiss my cousin on the cheek.

From the veranda, Mum waves Frederick off as I walk slowly toward the house. Mum has changed. She's lost weight and looks older and smaller somehow. I can't begin to tell her how much I've missed her. In all this time I have never forgotten my harsh words to her the day I disrespected her and more or less told her that she was out of touch with reality, that she lived in the past and had no idea what modern women go through. I never tried to smooth those words over, it would only have made it worse. We'd always carried on as if that day never happened, and I'd hoped that time would erase some of the damage. Although it was nineteen years ago, I suspect Mum has not forgotten.

I drop my bags and we hug. She reaches up to kiss me on my cheek, then notices my small case.

'Not staying long?'

38

The house is quiet. The air conditioning is switched off. It feels warm inside. Only the lights in the hallway, living room and kitchen are on. I look up the stairs and it's dark. I'm sure Mum has burnt something in my room to ward off mosquitoes. She's made one of my favourite drinks. Sorrel. She had the flowers collected especially for it and made a large amount because she knows how much I love it.

I leave my bags at the door and follow Mum to the kitchen. She pours me a drink without a word. I remember that when we were younger we were not allowed to start a conversation with our parents or any other adult if it was the first time seeing them that day, without a formal greeting of 'Good morning,' 'Good afternoon' or 'Good evening.' It showed respect. I had done neither when I came in. There is no look of disapproval of my bad manners from Mum. She just looks happy to have me here.

'How you like the drink?' she asks.

'It's lovely Mum, as always.'

'It's been a long time since you been here. I'm surprised you even remember the taste.'

'Of course I do.' I smile. 'Does it feel like a long time?'

'A very long time Angelica. Too long. I missed you when all the others were here last month. It was a shame you never come. I haven't got long to go you know?' She smiles at me and takes a sip of her drink. 'So it would be nice to see more of you. Promise me from now you will come more often.'

'Mum, I promise. Anyway, I'm convinced you'll outlive us all. You won't be leaving that quickly.' I try and make her laugh. Mum's expression is serious.

'Angelica, you come here so sudden. You don't come with your husband, you don't come with your child, so I feel something is wrong. If it's something you have to tell me, it's okay, you know you can.' She puts a warm, work worn hand onto mine across the table.

'I do need to tell you something,' I say as I stare at the thin gold band on her ring finger. 'Lots of things. I don't even know where to begin.'

'Well, at the start is always a good place.' She claps her hands together. 'But not now. You been travelling whole day. I can see you are tired and I feel tired myself. I made you some food. Eat that. Sleep. Tomorrow we can talk. You agree?'

'I agree.'

When I wake in the morning, I feel rested. My sleep was peaceful. The first peaceful night in a while. The sun shines through the pastel coloured curtains in my room and I feel different. None of my worries have gone, my situation is still the same but I feel different.

I smell coffee and can hear Mum singing in the kitchen. She's left out a silky dressing gown. I put it on and head downstairs.

'I haven't had real coffee for weeks now. Good morning Mum.'

'Good morning, darling. You sleep well?' Mum looks up from the pan on the cooker, a spatula in one hand.

'Very well. Never woke up once during the night. I can't believe it.'

'I can. When you come yesterday, you look like you had the troubles of the world on your shoulders. Today you look like you only carrying your own. Come, let us sit outside to eat our breakfast.'

The veranda at the back looks out onto a brown and green mountain. A thick forest of trees lines most of the mountain, the rest is rocks and slopes. On the other side of that mountain a winding road leads off to a nearby village. The sky is more than one shade of blue. I feel a warm breeze on my face.

It's secluded where we sit. A lime tree is just inches away from the little table that Mum has set. Her washing line runs from the lime tree to the mango tree. There is no fruit on the mango tree, just as there is no washing on the line. It's quiet. From the front of the house I hear the occasional car and the occasional voice. Otherwise I could be posing for a picture called 'tranquillity'.

Mum has made eggs and a salad of large, red tomatoes and sweet onions. She's sliced some fresh bread that sits next to a ceramic vase filled with sorrel and pours me a cup of that wonderful smelling coffee. I feel spoiled. I shouldn't just sit here. Mum moves slowly but she puts her hand out in a stop gesture to make sure I stay seated. It's her treat.

I would hate to think that Mum has stayed angry with me all these years for those angry words of mine, even if they are not forgotten. If she is, there is absolutely no sign and there hadn't been on any of the occasions that I came to visit her with Luke and Eva. But I feel that now is the time to confess that I have been feeling guilty and to say I'm sorry.

I look at Mum as she sips her coffee and softly chews her breakfast. I don't know where to begin. Mum breaks the silence.

'Angelica, you were always such a quiet girl when you were small. You remember?' I smile and look down. 'But look how much you change. Your dad and I used to worry because all the others was so sure of themselves and you never want to speak up for yourself. You know your dad was so proud of you. To see how well you do with your business. How you raise your child.'

'I never knew that.'

'Oh yes. But he would never say. Just like you, he was quiet.'

'Well that I do remember. But I remember there was no messing around with him. Well you were both pretty strict with us when we were younger.'

'I suppose we thought that was the way to be. London was not an easy place when we reach there. The only way to keep you safe was to keep you close to us and listen to what we have to say. I hope you understand. You are a mother now yourself. You know how difficult it is to keep your children safe.'

'I do, Mum. I understand.'

'I always did what I thought was the best for my family.'

For the next two days, Mum and I sit on that veranda at the back of the house. We only leave to shower, cook or sleep. This should have been my time to tell all to Mum, to have her resolve my situation. A story, advice, a telling off, anything. But I never speak a word of my problems. I'm listening.

Mum talks about her past. She tells me all about the girl she was and the woman she became. In all of my time growing up, Mum never went into as much detail. I am sure I am the only one of her children she has ever told her story to.

My mother's life has been laid out before me. Her pains and struggles, revealed in all their colour and magnitude. Pains she has carried with her for over eighty years. Mine have not lasted more than eight weeks. I don't belittle my pain. It is real. But my mother's story has taught me how strong a woman can be.

Right before my eyes she has emerged from being the strict matriarch that governed my life with a will of steel to becoming a strong, determined woman who did all she knew to do, to maintain a marriage and a family that were her responsibility to keep together.

I may not agree with all of her choices, but I understand why she had to make them. I know now that it is not fair to ask her to make choices for me. I must find the strength to determine my own future. I feel renewed.

'Angelica.' Mum is coming back to the table with two glasses of sorrel. 'I'm sure it must be your turn?'

It's the third day of my visit. My cousin, Frederick pops his head around the front door, just after we finish breakfast.

'Come through.' Mum calls to him. He greets us and kisses us both on the cheek.

'I have hired a car. I'm going to show you your home,' he says to me.

297

'What a wonderful idea,' Mum exclaims. 'See how much you recognise from what I been telling you.'

I am relaxed. I've slept through the night every night for over a week. On an evening after Frederick took me trekking through the island, I sit on the front veranda with Mum and look out at the lights from the hotel a little way in to the distance. The hotel is by the sea. If we are quiet enough, I'm sure we'll hear the waves. It's a cool night, a little breezy. Now is the time to tell Mum why I came.

'Luke will not divorce you.' She rocks easily on the tall chair on the veranda and I turn to look at her.

'Do you know that because of a dream you had or is it just wishful thinking?'

'I don't dream anymore. I would be surprised if I had one of those dreams at my age. I only know because I've seen the way Luke looks at you. I know that look. Your father never looked at me like that. It's the way *my* father looked at my mother. I remember it well. I know what it means. There is love and there is love. Lots of different kinds. Not everyone can feel and show it in the same way. You see when my father died, my mother never married again. He love her so much she had enough left to last for the rest of her days. And she wouldn't have found another love like that – not on this small island anyway.' Mum grins at me. 'You say you destroyed the trust between the two of you but all you did was make the foundations weak, not destroyed forever. Together you will fix it.'

'But only if I can convince Luke to want to fix things. He thinks I've ruined everything. I'm sure he hates me now.'

'You have a lot of things to fix. Not only with Luke but also with your daughter. Eva is young and we make mistakes when we are young. But please, forgive her one day, Angelica. I know what it is like to have a heart that cannot forgive. I never spoke to my sister again and she died not knowing that it was because my love for her went right to my core why I couldn't look at her again. She was my blood, my family, and that's what killed me most. Not because of a man's affairs.'

'So you think Dad was less of a man than your own dad?'

'No, it's not that. You can expect more or less the same of most men, of anybody come to that. But every once in a while you find something in someone that is rare and not everyone can have. That is why my life was a happy one and my mother's life was paradise. Don't bury your paradise if you find it. Hold on to it, Angelica, because it is a gift.'

'So you put up with Dad's affairs because he was just a man?'

'I loved him, Angelica. I still feel it. He was the love of my life.'

'But not your paradise?'

'My paradise is waiting for me, and your father will be there when God decide to call on me.'

Mum makes the sign of the cross and she starts to get up from the chair. The conversation has ended and it is time for bed. I go to help her out of the chair but she stops for a moment. She has one more thing to say.

'I kept something from all of you children because I didn't want you to think badly of your father. But now you know all about my life with your dad, Angelica, there is something I can't go to my grave without you knowing.'

I sit back down and wait. Her eyes turn away from me and towards the sky, growing darker now, over the hotel rooftop.

'One of your father's affairs was with a woman who died a while ago. She had a baby for him. A boy. Well, he is a man now, married with two children. He came to find your dad when he was a man and Dad and I got to know him. We were at his wedding. None of you knew about it.' Mum is gently patting her fingertips together as she speaks and rocks slowly on her chair.

'Before you leave I want you to take down his name and address and let him know his family. I think it was wrong of me to keep it a secret. A big mistake. He wanted to get to know you all and now he'll never know your brother James. They were alike you know?' She bows her head and stops rocking. 'His name is

Milo. Promise you'll see him, speak to him. You'll do that?'

'Of course Mum. That's another chapter you can tell me about tomorrow.'

It's getting darker and chillier. Sleep is in her eyes. She gets up and walks slowly to the front door.

'Don't forget to lock everything up before you come up Angelica.'

'I won't Mum. Goodnight.'

Mum is frailer than I've ever seen her. I want to hold her and tell her how much I love her.

'Mum!'

'Yes my dear.'

'Will you ever forgive me for the way I disrespected you?' I stand up.

'I don't look at it as disrespect anymore, Angelica. You were a quiet mouse and I never expect you could raise up on me like that. I was shock. But you are your own woman. You have your right to speak. We are both different. I did things my way. Just as I was different from my mum, so you are different to me. You must do and say what you must in this life, Angelica. As long as you do right. Goodnight.'

I decide there and then that it was time to go home.

If Luke is my paradise then I must fight tooth and nail to hold on to it. A three-course meal with candlelight was a poor gesture. Even if I had to follow Luke around every day of his life, shouting declarations of my love for him while he did his weekly shop, threaten to throw myself under the train he was waiting for, run up and down his street naked in a storm, until he let me in – I would do it.

I feel sad about leaving Mum, but I'll keep my promise. I will come back. Again and again.

39

There is one more thing I have to do before I leave this part of the world. Something very important and will mean the world to my daughter, Eva. I have to let her know that I love her and I can't wait for her to come back. When we spoke on the phone, my heart was full of anger and disappointment but I know that Eva is suffering. I have to help her move on and stop her thinking that she can never come home.

It's a dark and chilly autumn evening in New York. Jasmin has told me how to get to the little club that Eva will be singing at tonight. She is one of three acts to perform. Jasmin wanted to come with me but I insisted I had to do this alone.

I arrive at the nightclub early because I don't know where on the bill she'll be. It's a lively place: wooden floor and dark wood furniture, the ceiling is quite low and there are photographs on the white walls of various musicians and singers of different eras and genres. I recognise the faces of musicians from the jazz world, a couple of soul singers, but the others remain a mystery.

My waitress is friendly. She stops for a quick chat every time she passes by my table. She's told me she wants to go to London one day and would do once she's finished studying. She is twenty years old and doing a business degree. I am tempted to ask her if she knows Eva, but I don't want Eva to know I'm here yet.

The lights dim and flicker each time an artist takes to the stage. Each appears from the other side of a little door to the side of the stage and is introduced by a short, friendly man, quite young, with a thin moustache and a New Zealand accent.

The name, Eva Ford, sounds strange when it comes from his lips. And there she is. Completely changed from the little girl who left London, all excited, a couple of months ago with a floral rucksack on her back.

Her hair looks a little longer and seems thicker too. The curls, less like the ringlets of the plump three-year-old Eva, but wilder, with streaks of gold and seasonal browns. Her eye make-up is dramatic, smoky. As she announces her name again and introduces her first song, her voice sounds darker to me. She is so relaxed and at home on stage I feel as though I'm watching a seasoned professional. Memories of Eva performing at school come rushing back.

The colours of the lights change on the stage. I know she won't be able to see me because of the lighting and I can just relax and enjoy her music. I have a bottle of mineral water on the table. I've already had a large glass of red wine but I want to stay alert and to speak to her afterwards.

I am mesmerised. I don't move an inch, not even to take a sip of water. Her performance is moving. My heart is in my throat as I listen to the words of the song she announces as her last of the evening.

I'm just a fragment of the whole you are
Scattered pieces of a shining star
And when you held me up your eyes had pride
Yours is the beauty that I feel inside
If I travel half a world away
Your words will lighten up the darkest day
You teach me all the things I fail to see
And lead me back to where I ought to be

Here I am with hope in hand
Some scribbled words you'll one day understand
The smallest hint that you could let me in
And I'd come running back from where I've been
I would come running back from where I've been … .

Eva's eyes are glassy as she sings these last words. She seems to be looking out into the crowd at someone. She looks in my direction but her gaze is directed at someone standing further back from where I'm sitting.

She gets up and takes a bow. Everyone claps and shouts for more. She just blows a kiss and disappears through the little side door as the young man from New Zealand comes out, clapping and asking how much we all enjoyed that.

I turn now to see what it is that Eva has spotted. Along the far side of the bar, and sitting on a bar stool next to the door is a face I know. He is smiling and clapping. It's Luke.

He stands up and is about to leave. For a second I wonder if it might just be wishful thinking on my part but I grab the jacket Jasmin lent me along with my bag and rush outside. There he is, just standing there, hands in his jacket pockets and looking up the road in the opposite direction from where I stand, motionless. I hear the heavy clunk of the stage door open. Eva appears. She spots me.

'Mum!' Luke spins around.

I smile so broadly at the pair of them it hurts my face. My first instinct is to rush up to them and sweep them up together in one big embrace. But we all hesitate for a moment. In a split second I remember something my cousin Frederick said to me, about how reserved the English are. They spend so much time in the cold, he'd said, wrapping their arms around themselves to keep warm, they've forgotten how important it is to hug others.

I drop my bag and my jacket and practically fly into them both and hug them with everything I have.

'Mum, this is New York, you can't just leave your bag there. Someone will take it.' Eva laughs.

'I don't care, I'm just so happy to see you both.' I look up at Luke. He's smiling. He looks happy to see me too.

'Angelica. It's strange. Somehow I knew you'd come. I came here a few days ago and I was going to come to see you at your mum's. Eva said that's where you were.' He holds my hands. 'This can't go on. Look at the three of us. This is the way we should always be. Together – a family. If you still want it.'

'Luke. How could you ask that? It's all I ever wanted. It's all I'll ever want.'

'Mum – I'm sorry.' Eva's soft hand is on my face. 'I'm the cause of all this. I know what you think of me.'

'No you don't Eva. Believe me. The only thing I think and feel now is love. You did something that I didn't think I could forgive. But you are much more important to me than the mistake you made. I'm sorry I treated you so badly over it. I'm your mother and I should have been more understanding. I should have flown out here ages ago and put things straight.'

'No Mum, if I was my daughter I would have killed me.'

'Well I never said I wasn't going to kill you – but I do forgive you. We have to put this behind us and move on.' I look at Luke. 'Can we do that? Can we move on?'

'That's what I want more than anything.'

That chilly autumn breeze catches hold of me again and I turn back to pick up my bag and my jacket. Luke helps me on with it. Eva hails a taxi.

40

It happened just like the dream:

A group of people stood on the beach beside a small hotel. A couple, in their forties, looked at each other as though they are in love for the first time. They were renewing their wedding vows, surrounded by a small gathering of people. The woman wore a long summer dress of peacock blue and green. She had flowers in her hair and was very happy.

There were two rows of chairs in a semi-circle behind the couple. In the front row were two women who held hands and had flown in from London for a second visit that year and had not expected to find themselves on that beach again so soon. One of the women was crying the other looked on with an approving smile. A young woman who held a guitar sat beside them, having arrived the day before from New York, she cried and smiled at the same time.

Beside the young girl, was an old woman who sat as upright as possible in one of the hotel chairs that were taken down to the beach especially for this occasion. In the row behind were two more young women with their father, and a husband and wife with their sons. Another family had flown in from New York two days earlier for this occasion. Joining them was a man, his wife and two girls from Birmingham.

It was late morning. Christmas Eve. The sky was practically cloudless and very blue. Waves rolled in from the vast ocean before them, formed tiny bubbles that swept across tiny crabs and stones on the sand and then rolled out again, calmly, quietly, lazily. In, and then out again.

The people gathered for this celebration on the beach were sheltered from the twenty-seven degree heat by large white umbrellas from the hotel. From the veranda of the hotel, groups of tourists sipped cool drinks and observed the colourful spectacle from the comfort of their reclining beach chairs. They did not mind in the slightest that part of the beach was out of bounds to them while the ceremony took place. They could have gone further along the beach if they wanted to but preferred to sit and watch and could just about hear the young girl who sang and played her guitar.

By late afternoon the party were still celebrating. They ate a lavish meal and were served by young waiters and waitresses dressed in pea green uniforms and yellow neckties. The newly united couple danced to a three-piece band and everyone clapped before getting up to dance themselves. Even the old woman danced for a few minutes after some coaxing.

The old woman said to the woman in the long, blue and green summer dress, as the evening drew to a close, 'This has been a wonderful day for me.' The woman in the long blue and green summer dress held a champagne glass high and replied, 'To even better days to come.'

It's seven years since the celebrations on the island. These same people are gathered together again. This time for Josephine's funeral. They make up part of an even larger number than before. Some from the island, some from abroad.

The church is small and crowded. Everyone ignores the heat as they sit in formal blacks and greys, praying, and mouthing to hymns the choir sings. At the end of the service they form a procession to the cemetery. It isn't far to walk. They take their time. Long, heavy footsteps, all the way, until they reach the plot of land where Josephine's mother and her husband, already lay at rest. The priest leads them in prayer and Josephine's coffin is lowered into the soft brown soil.

It is a beautiful day. Beautiful enough for laughter and song, but the people gathered here don't notice the sky, the cool breeze, the sun. Instead, they say their goodbyes. Some cry, some share happy stories from the past.

Conversations fade into the distance, as the gathering, finally, disperses. They walk away, slowly. Angelica stands alone by the grave. She touches a damp tissue to her eyes, overcome by the undeniable sense that, at last, Josephine has peace.

As she looks up, Angelica gradually becomes aware of her surroundings. The greens, the blues, the smell of the earth, and the faint sound of her daughter, walking back to her side.

Eva takes her mother by the hand. The two women smile at each other. They turn and follow the congregation just before it disappears from view.

Indigo Dreams Publishing
24 Forest Houses
Cookworthy Moor
Halwill
Beaworthy
EX21 5UU